three

little

truths

Eithne Shortall studied journalism at Dublin City University and has lived in London, France and America. Now based in Dublin, she is chief arts writer for the *Sunday Times Ireland*. Her debut novel, *Love in Row 27*, published in 2017, was a major Irish bestseller, and her second novel, *Grace After Henry*, was shortlisted for the Irish Book Awards and won Best Page Turner at the UK's Big Book Awards.

Also by Eithne Shortall

Love in Row 27
Grace After Henry

three little truths

eithne shortall

CORVUS

First published in trade paperback in Great Britain in 2019 by Corvus, an imprint of Atlantic Books Ltd.

This paperback edition published in 2020.

1 2 3 4 5 6 7 8 9

A CIP catalogue record for this book is available from the British Library.

Paperback ISBN: 978 1 78649 620 1
E-book ISBN: 978 1 78 649 621 8

Printed in Great Britain

Corvus
An imprint of Atlantic Books Ltd
Ormond House
26–27 Boswell Street
London
WC1N 3JZ

www.corvus-books.co.uk

For Fidelma Curran, who is my mother –
and for that, I'll forever be grateful.

'Blood is thicker than water, but neither's as thick as mortar.'

Shay Morrissey, long-time Pine Road resident

*** Pine Road Poker ***

Bernie:
Hi, all. Number 6 found a hole in their back garden this morning.
That makes *three* in one week. I hope we can all take this seriously
now? I have spoken to Island Stores and they've ordered in extra rat
poison. Remember to say 'Pine Road Discount' to get ten per cent off.
Regards, Bernie Watters-Reilly

Ellen:
So well said, Bernie – as always. We've already put down two doses.

Edie:
Will buy ours asap. Thanks for organising, Bernie! X

Ruby:
I wonder where the little buggers are coming from?

Ellen:
From Number 8, no doubt. I don't like to speak ill of the dead, but
for the lack of attention Mrs Ryan paid to her garden she should have
been taken out and shot before the pneumonia had a chance to get
her. Yes, she was 97, but how much upper body strength do you need
to pull a few weeds? I just hope the new people sort it out.

Any sign of the woman yet?

Ruby:
Saw the husband and daughters leaving again this morning. No sign
of the wife, though.

Carmel:
I've got Robin on window watch.

Fiona:
She's definitely in there, Ellen hun! I can hear the radio. XXXX

Rita Ann:
Did anyone take the Irish Times from my doorstep this morning? I need yesterday's Sudoku results. The paper of 'record' would appear to have made a mistake.

Ruby:
Are you asking if we stole your newspaper?

Rita Ann:
I'm wondering if someone took it by accident.

Ruby:
Maybe the rats took it.

Fiona:
Do you think so??

Ruby:
No.

Fiona:
Do you think the rats might affect house prices?

Ellen:
I didn't know Robin was still staying with you, Carmel. Everything okay with her at home?

Fiona:
We already have poor aspect. I wouldn't like a rodent rumour to depreciate our value any further ...

Rita Ann:
Who cares about a few mice when there's a thief in our midst??

If my paper is returned by dinnertime, all supplements intact, I'm willing, on this one occasion, to turn a blind eye.

Ruby:
Rita Ann and the Case of the Missing Broadsheet. 🕵️

Bernie:
Poison, ladies! Do not forget the poison!

ONE

· · · · · · · · · · · ·

Martha Rigby had been sitting at the kitchen table since Robert left for work. The girls, who had taken to their new school with such ease it almost seemed pointed, had set off before either parent was awake.

There were boxes everywhere, furniture still stacked in corners, gas and electricity readings jotted down on a pad in front of her waiting to be registered, a to-do list lying unticked beside it.

She knew she should stand up, make a start on things.

The radio played on and the light through the grubby windows grew brighter.

She looked around the room and felt a profound sense of detachment. The idea of doing anything was so exhausting that the only reason she could think to stand was to go back to bed. Oscar snored by the back door. She'd have to get up eventually, if only to let him out to do his business.

Her distorted reflection glinted in the oven door. The old her, the *real* her, would never have let it get to this.

Maybe she should take the tablets Dr Morten had prescribed. There was no shame in it. Most people who'd been through what she'd been through would have been knocking them back well before now. Dr Morten had made that very clear. But Martha took pride in her will-power. She'd had her wisdom teeth out last June without so much as a painkiller. In fact, the last time she took paracetamol was four years ago, and she'd only allowed herself that indulgence because it was the morning after her blow-out fortieth birthday party.

Martha didn't take drugs unless entirely necessary. If her body had something to tell her, she wanted to be able to hear it.

But then, this wasn't a toothache or a hangover she was dealing with. To put it mildly.

The radio jingle went for the eleven o'clock news. She could have sworn the ten o'clock bulletin had just ended. She'd hear the headlines, see if anything had happened beyond these walls in the past hour, and then she'd stand up.

Hospital bed shortage . . . No-deal Brexit a possibility . . . Calls for improved sex education . . . Irish accent voted sexiest in the world.

The male Irish accent, she noted. No mention of its female counterpart. Presumably this was what Sinead meant when she said the patriarchy was always at work. 'And *we're* working for it, Mum,' she'd insisted the previous evening before Robert told her pubic hair was not a suitable topic for dinner-table conversation. That just set her off again. Her father's views were 'a domestic iteration of the institutionalised subjugation of women's bodies'. Robert gave up then and went back to his microwaved lasagne.

Martha hoped this new school would be as good as the last. Both her girls had loved their old place. Sinead had been chair of the debating team and had just been made editor of the paper, despite only being in fifth year, when she was yanked out of her old life and shoved into this one. And with that, Martha's mind was off, rushing down the M7, fleeing their new life, heading back to their old one, but she caught herself just before the Limerick exit.

She redirected her attention to the radio.

Was that really news, though? About the Irish accent? An international poll conducted by some travel company you'd never heard of and verified by nobody?

Martha thought of all the terrible things that happened in the world and never made the news. She wouldn't have wanted their

5

ordeal broadcast on national airwaves – the local papers picking up on it was bad enough; though Robert hadn't minded at all – yet it was amazing how there'd never been a question of it. Nobody had considered such an event worthy of twenty seconds of radio coverage, not when matters as important as 'orgasmic accents' needed the nation's attention. What had been on the news the day it happened? She thought and thought but she couldn't remember.

Perhaps she was doing a better job of blocking it out than she realised.

She'd leave the tablets for another while so.

The bulletin ended, the weather was reported and Martha continued to stare out the kitchen window into a garden so overgrown the weeds were practically coming in to get her. The old woman who'd lived here before had gone into hospital with pneumonia and never come out. The place had smelled faintly, but persistently, of fermented cat urine when they arrived. Robert insisted he couldn't smell anything, of course. It had lessened now, or maybe she'd just gotten used to it.

Martha hated her new kitchen. She hated the whole house. She knew these red-brick homes were highly sought after, but she couldn't stand how old they were. No matter what she might do – and admittedly she hadn't done much yet – everything felt dirty. She hated how the floorboards creaked even when she wasn't standing on them and how there always seemed to be a draught coming from somewhere. She missed their home; the nice, modern country pile about 12 miles outside Limerick city, with its high energy rating and underfloor heating. She and Robert had it built right after they were married, with the plan of never moving.

Number eight Pine Road had cost almost twice as much as their forever home. It was an obscene amount of money for a place that wasn't half as cosy. But the worst bit, the bit that made her want to twist a tea towel into a ball and stuff it into her mouth to muffle her red-hot rage, was that they could only afford this money pit because

Robert had gotten a promotion – and he'd only gotten a promotion because of what had happened to them, because of what had caused them to move in the first place.

Martha knew her family blamed her for the move. She was the one who could no longer sleep in their house; it was her who'd uprooted everyone, moved the girls away from their friends, made them change schools. Robert, meanwhile, had swooped in and saved the day, yet again. He had made an alternative possible. Three months on and he was still the hero.

The thoughts boiled up and Martha wondered if she'd have to get up and grab the towel from the draining board. She couldn't even scream freely in her own, empty home. A terrace was supposed to be safer, that had been the idea, but all Martha felt was suffocated.

Anyway, no. She was fine. A few deep breaths and it passed. She stayed put.

Inane theme tunes and canned laughter reverberated faintly through the walls. It wasn't fair, she knew, but she instantly presumed her new neighbours were stupid, lazy. Martha had never been tempted to turn on her own television before dark. There'd be no coming back from that. Besides, before, she wouldn't have had the time.

There had been car-pool rosters to draw up for school runs; club meetings and soccer practices to supervise; Meals on Wheels to deliver; evening walks with Helen and Audrey; morning yoga; afternoon coffee. She'd been so busy she usually didn't have time to read the monthly book club selection and resorted to stealing opinions from GoodReads right before the meeting. The idea of sitting down to watch an afternoon rerun of some sitcom was inconceivable.

The weather report ended and the current affairs show returned, straight into a more detailed report on the hospital bed shortage. Still, Martha sat and stared out into the weeds. Still, she did not budge.

•••••••••

'Muh-ummm!'

'We're home!'

The door slammed and several kilos of books hit the barely varnished floor. Martha, who'd been carrying bathroom wares upstairs, put down the toothbrush holder and bolstered herself.

'I'm starving!'

'No you're not!'

'Yes I am!'

'Starvation is a serious state endured by millions of people worldwide every day, Orla. It's when you haven't eaten for, like, ten days. You had a Chomp on the way home.'

'Muh-ummm! Tell Sinead to shut up!'

Martha hurried down the stairs. 'Girls! Keep it down! The neighbours will think a pack of wolves has moved in.' She picked up the backpacks dumped in the hallway. Had they been this heavy at their old school? 'Don't leave these lying around.'

'There's nowhere to put them.'

'How about under the stairs?'

Orla looked at her mother like she'd been personally wounded. 'We never used to put them under the stairs.'

'She's right, Mum,' said Sinead, who only ever agreed with her sister when it enabled her to more robustly disagree with Martha. 'We used to put them below the coat stand in the hall. But this house doesn't even have a coat stand.'

Martha observed her daughters: Sinead giving her a look that said 'tell me I'm wrong, go on, I dare you', and Orla watching from behind a curtain of lank hair and massive glasses. They were so entirely fine. It was as if nothing had ever happened to them.

The sound of another key in the lock made Martha jump. She had a hundred mini heart attacks every day; this had occurred to her

8

upstairs earlier, in the bathroom, when the hot tap had unexpectedly creaked. There was a thud from the other side of the front door as it jammed in its frame. Her husband's voice floated through: 'Will you just – bloody – work!'

The girls shrugged and sauntered down towards the kitchen. When the front door finally opened and Robert appeared in the hallway, Martha let the schoolbags slump to the ground.

'Hello, darling,' said Robert, reaching around awkwardly to kiss her cheek. 'I managed to finish up early today. At least someone's here to greet me.' His daughters were disappearing down the couple of steps and through to the kitchen without so much as a backwards glance. 'I remember the days when they used to come running to greet me.' He shook his head and smiled ruefully. 'How are you?'

'Fine.' Martha moved away from him to shut the front door, which he'd left ajar. She could feel his eyes on her.

'I was going to close that.'

'We need to get it fixed,' she said, doing her best to make it lock.

'It's grand. It's just a little stiff.'

'It doesn't' – Martha pushed it again – 'close' – Robert came to help and she gave it a final, massive shove – 'properly!' The thing slammed into place just as he went to touch it and, for a moment, they both just looked at it.

Martha lifted the schoolbags again and carried them over to the storage area under the stairs. The estate agent had told them a lot of the neighbours had turned this into a downstairs bathroom. Martha found that hard to believe. It was so small. She pulled the door open and went to toss the bags in but was confronted by more boxes. So this was where the movers had put the contents of their old utility room. 'Is there no space anywhere?' she muttered, closing the door again and sliding the bags back to where the girls had originally thrown them just inside the front door. 'We need to get a coat stand.'

'We need to get a lot of things,' Robert agreed, offering his wife a sympathetic smile. Her expression didn't change so he dropped it. 'Don't worry, darling, we'll get to it.'

Martha welded her mouth shut. *She'd get to it*, he meant. He'd keep saying everything was grand and eventually she'd fix it. As soon as their old house went on the market, Robert had acted like the nitty-gritty of the move had nothing to do with him. He was just here for the grand gestures.

She hated him.

The thought was so strong, and so unexpected, that it frightened her. She felt guilty, then angry again. She wanted to grab a sleeping bag from under the stairs and scream.

'Get up to anything today?'

Martha watched as Robert shrugged off his jacket and looked around helplessly for somewhere to hang it and his briefcase.

'Nothing very interesting, no.'

'Did you get a start on the unpacking?'

'Yes, Robert, of course I did. Do you think I've been lounging around drinking cocktails all day? I mean, maybe when I find the cocktail shaker, but I haven't gotten to that box yet.'

'Of course not. I was just asking. Did you . . .' He hesitated. He was trying to annoy her now, looking at her like she was going to bite his head off.

She let out a heavy sigh. 'What?'

'Did you see about joining some classes at the community centre? Not that I mind if you don't, of course. It's just that you said you might . . .'

'Not yet.'

'Okay, well, no rush. Knowing you, you won't be able to stay cooped up here much longer. You'll probably be running the classes by the end of the month.'

Martha doubted that very much. 'I might go tomorrow.'

'Absolutely. Great. And did you see about registering with the local doctor? Just for a quick chat?'

She shot him a look. 'Don't patronise me, Robert.'

'I wasn't. I just thought—'

'Well, maybe don't. Maybe next time you have a thought, just keep it to yourself.' Martha turned from her husband and followed her daughters into the kitchen.

Orla was hunting through the boxes and Sinead was on her phone ignoring Oscar, who was trying desperately to offer her the paw.

Martha watched them going about their new lives like it was all they'd ever known. Orla pulled a bowl from a box and hugged it like a long-lost friend.

'Old bluey! I forgot about you!'

Sinead was staring out the window into the weed jungle now, preoccupied by the transient concerns of teenage girls.

Martha wanted to grab them. She wanted to shake her daughters by the shoulders and demand to know how they dared to be so fine.

Why aren't you waking, sweating, in the middle of the night? Why don't you jump every time a book falls from the table, or look around for me whenever a floorboard creaks?

But it was just a passing anger. One of those flashes that came on her now and retreated just as quickly.

She cracked the bones of her face up into a smile and tapped her hand on the counter until the two girls looked up. 'Who wants a snack?'

TWO

••••••••••••

'**S**omeone stole the wheels off Fiona Quinn's car.'

Robin Dwyer stopped staring out the sitting-room window and twisted her body around to see her mother, sitting on the opposite armchair, staring down at her phone. The lines on her face were more pronounced. Maybe it was having her twenty-six-year-old daughter back living with her. Or maybe it was just the glow from the screen.

'Can you believe that?' her mother continued, shaking her head at the phone. 'Poor Fiona. She only got the thing a few weeks ago. Bit flashy for a family vehicle but still, no call for swiping the wheels.'

'Who's that?'

Carmel, her mother, looked up from the screen and peered over the rim of her glasses. 'Fiona Quinn. Across the road at number ten. Works part time in an insurance company out by the airport, obsessed with property prices, calls everyone "hun". You know her, you do. Two kids; twin girls. The husband works in London half the week.'

'Vaguely . . .'

It was hard to distinguish the neighbours from one another. Half of them hadn't been here when Robin left home eight years ago. She said hello to some of them, when calling Jack in for dinner or bedtime, but generally went for a middling level of familiarity – unsure if she was supposed to recognise them or not.

Her mother's phone beeped again and she guffawed. 'Would you – the cheeky scuts! Four of them. Trish Walsh says they came up at five this morning and had the whole thing done in less than ten minutes. Trish caught it on her CCTV camera. On a cul-de-sac, can you believe that? No way out. As brazen as you like.'

'The Walshes have their own CCTV camera?' Robin did remember the Walshes. She used to be friendly with their daughter, Laura. She couldn't remember exactly why they'd drifted apart but no doubt it was her fault. Last she'd heard Laura had married the son of a property developer and was living on some leafy square in London.

'They had it installed after all that trouble between Ted Walsh and the Morrissey daughters. Remember? I told you about that. You don't listen, Robin, that's your problem. I might as well be talking to the wall.' Carmel sighed, lifting her glasses on to her head. 'There was a big fight over parking – what's new? says you – and Shay Morrissey's two girls – of course, they're women now – came out of their dad's one night and threw paint stripper all over Ted Walsh's car. They said they didn't but they did; sure, we all know they did. You know what the Morrisseys are like, rough as a New Year's Day hangover. So anyway, after that the Walshes got the security camera installed.'

'Right . . .' Robin's own phone beeped. The Facebook Messenger icon flashed. Eleven unread messages. When would he quit? She switched it to silent and threw it across the room on to the beanbag. 'And sorry – they stole the wheels? Why not the car? How do you steal wheels from a car?'

'Trish says . . .' Carmel frowned as she scrolled rapidly back through the seemingly never-ending conversation between the women of Pine Road. The WhatsApp group had been set up to coordinate their monthly poker game, but its real function was the circulation of gossip. 'Bernie Watters-Reilly is still going on about this rat hole she found in her garden. How she can tell a rat hole from any other kind of hole, I don't know, but she has everyone convinced the whole road is infested now. She's organised a discount for residents on rat poison at Island Stores and is monitoring who's availed of it. Where the feck is it . . .? Here! Now. They . . . They put the thing up on blocks! Had the four wheels whipped off in a matter of minutes. Can you imagine?' Her mother shook her head. 'And nobody heard a thing. Porsche wheels are very in demand – or at least that's what Edie is saying here now. Edie's up in the corner house, a young one. Her husband's a mechanic, so she would know.' Carmel tutted. 'Dreadful altogether.'

Robin twisted back around on the sofa. It was hard to imagine a gang of thieves sneaking past their house in the dead of night, while she slept in her childhood bedroom, Jack on the camp bed beside her, and her parents snoring softly down the hall. That kind of thing didn't happen on Pine Road. She gave an involuntary shudder and told herself it was an expression of horror and not a thrill of excitement.

Two girls wearing the school uniform Robin had once sported pounded up Pine Road, shoving each other as they went. They turned into the garden of the house directly across the street; the one her mother was keeping tabs on.

'We have movement.'

'Hmm? Oh!' Carmel heaved herself out of the armchair and scurried across the living room. She stood over Robin, peering out the window. 'That's the two daughters. They started in Saint Ornatín's at the beginning of term even though the family hadn't moved here yet. They were enrolled at the last minute, despite Saint Ornatín's already being full. Apparently – and Bernie Watters-Reilly told me this now, so it's between you, me and the four walls – there was an emergency order . . . *from the Department of Education.*' There was nobody else in the room, so her mother dropping her voice was for absolutely no reason but effect.

'What's an emergency order?' asked Robin, watching as the sisters squabbled over who got to put their brand-new key into their rather rickety-looking door.

'Well, I'm not sure,' admitted Carmel, returning to her seat as the girls disappeared inside their new home. 'But Bernie says it's serious. And she'd know. She's chair of the Parents' Association. Now you definitely know Bernie Watters-Reilly – she's always in the papers or on the telly, going on about what a brilliant parent she is and how everyone else is raising future Hitlers.'

Robin had a hazy memory of her mother shouting at some woman on the radio the other morning that she'd be better off spending her time learning how to park.

'Bernie has been known to exaggerate,' continued Carmel. 'Always going on about her bloody daughter. *Sylvie.* How a woman called Bernie gets away with calling her daughter Sylvie, I don't know. The only thing French about Bernie is her Merlot habit. And the husband's not much better. I feel sorry for her son – I can't even remember his name, that's how little attention he gets. But no, on this Bernie's probably telling some version of the truth. As Parents' Association chair, she's on the school board, and she told us in the strictest confidence at the last poker game that the Department had made an emergency order on behalf of the new neighbours. Of course, Bernie only said all this because Trish wasn't at the game.'

'Who's Trish again?'

Carmel opened her mouth, agog. 'Trish bloody Walsh! With the CCTV camera. At the top of the road. The principal of Saint Ornatín's. You used to be friendly with her daughter, Laura. Jesus Christ, Robin. Do you need me to get it tattooed on my forehead?'

Robin's head was spinning. She had enough concerns of her own without trying to find the mental space to process Pine Road gossip. A man in a navy wax jacket was striding up the road now, briefcase in hand. Robin glanced back to the new neighbours' place and changed the subject.

'Isn't number eight Mrs Ryan's old place? The woman with the cats?'

'Ah-ha,' said Carmel. 'Let's just hope the smell died with her, that's all I can say.'

'Oh, hang on.' The man in the navy jacket had stopped at number eight. 'I think I have another one.'

'Is it the mother?' Carmel yelped, scurrying back over. 'Ah no. That must be the husband. What age would you say he is? Hard to tell from the back. Fiona and Ruby have already seen him. It's the wife we want, Robin. Nobody's spotted her yet.' Carmel moved her head from side to side, as if some better angle might allow her to see through the brickwork. 'Is he just going to stand there or what? Maybe it's not his house at all.' She gasped slightly. 'Maybe he's casing the place. That'd be a great disguise if he was; a suit and a briefcase. It could be the same people who stole the wheels from – ah no. Never mind. In he goes.'

The man struggled with the key until he fell against the door and it finally opened.

'Right,' said Carmel. 'Dinner. Come and give me a hand.' She held out her hands to Robin. 'I'm not charging you rent on your bedroom, but I didn't say anything about that couch.'

It had been two and a half months since Robin and Jack turned up unannounced, and unexplained, on her parents' doorstep. It wasn't the first time it'd happened, but it was the first time they'd brought all their stuff. Robin had been grateful not to be asked any questions, but she feared that grace period was about to expire. Already this morning her mother had shown her a job she'd found online.

'Telephone sales,' Carmel had said, passing her the iPad. 'Isn't that what you were doing before?'

'Sort of . . . I'm actually thinking about getting into something new . . .'

'And won't this do in the meantime? Send them in a CV and a reference and you should be grand. You'll have to do something if you're going to support yourself and Jack.'

And Robin had dutifully scrolled through the notice, not wanting to explain to her mother that the job she'd been doing before didn't exactly come with a reference, and not entirely ready to admit to herself that she was the breadwinner now.

She grabbed her mother's hands and pulled herself up from off the sofa.

'Hallelujah! She walks!'

A light shone from the folds of the beanbag and her phone shifted slightly as it vibrated against the coarse material, but the two women ignored it. With one last glance towards the window, they headed down to the kitchen.

'Where's that grandson of mine?' asked Carmel, her head already in the larder cupboard. 'He likes to whisk the eggs.'

'Upstairs.' Robin raised her head to the ceiling, listening for the sound of Jack playing on her bedroom floor. 'He's settling a dispute between his farmers. One of them stole the other's cows.'

'Oh. Farm business. Better not disturb him, so. Maybe you'll do it for me?' She slid the carton of eggs across the counter to her daughter.

Robin hadn't been particularly close to her mother growing up, and they'd drifted further when she moved in with Eddy all of two months after they started going out. When Robin told Carmel she was pregnant, her mother pleaded with her to come home and Robin said she wasn't about to let Eddy abdicate his responsibilities that easily. She was also in love with him – besotted, even – but she hadn't said that. She only ever said it to Eddy when she was being dramatic, over the top, and often drunk. She meant it, but she never said it like she did. 'I'm *besotted* with you,' she'd announce, mordantly, before swooning histrionically into his arms. And Carmel could never stand him. But after Jack was born, they stopped fighting about Eddy. They met on neutral ground and quickly grew closer.

'Is it broccoli or leek Jack doesn't eat? I can put either in this quiche, so whatever our little man wants.'

Her mother pulled vegetable after vegetable from the drawers at the bottom of the fridge. This was what a good mother looked like: selfless, kind, always putting her children, and grandchildren, first.

Carmel held a head of broccoli in one hand and a leek in the other.

'Well?'

'Broccoli,' said Robin, clearing her throat and cracking the last egg into the bowl. 'He hates broccoli.'

Carmel placed the vegetables on the counter, walked around the peninsula and wrapped Robin in a hug. She squeezed her tight.

'I'm grand, Mam.' She wasn't going to cry. Carmel knew well her daughter never cried.

'Shut up now, Robin, like a good girl.'

Her mother's perfume filled Robin's nostrils. This she remembered. She'd smelled the same since Robin was a child.

'You know I love that son of yours,' said Carmel, 'and your brother and your father, but you're my only girl. So you're my favourite. It's terribly sexist, I know, but there you have it. And if you tell the others I said that, I'll bury you alive in the back garden and say I haven't a notion where you've got to.'

Robin gave a half-laugh that came out like a snort.

The sound of a key in the front door and the wheels of a bike being ridden in.

'Yo!' Johnny, Robin's brother, had finally moved out of home for the first time last summer, only to move right back in two weeks after Robin and Jack had turned up on the doorstep. His first long-term relationship couldn't stand the pressure of cohabiting, much to his relief. Johnny felt no need to prove his independence; he loved living at home.

Carmel gave her daughter one last squeeze and separated, shaking the leek at her. 'Not a word.'

Johnny came into the kitchen, his face red and slightly shiny from the cycle. 'Did you hear about the Quinns' car?' he said, not even trying to keep the excitement from his voice.

'How did you hear that?' asked Carmel indignantly.

'Met Ted Walsh at the end of the road just there.' Johnny shook his head. 'Mad stuff.'

'Ah,' declared Carmel, brandishing the leek once again. 'I knew it an hour ago.'

Johnny and Robin grinned at each other. Their mother prided herself on being the first port of call for all local gossip in the Dwyer household.

'The women's poker group, wha'?' Johnny came around the peninsula and nudged his helmet against his mother's arm. 'Better than any communication system the guards have come up with, anyway. I'm surprised one of you wasn't out to apprehend them.'

Carmel shoved her youngest child away. 'Don't be getting lippy with me, mister. You left this place in a state this morning. Rasher fat drippings across the floor, the chopping board covered in crumbs. What did I tell you? What did I say to you when you moved back in here? Clean up . . .'

'. . . or clear out,' Johnny and Robin sang in unison.

'Yes,' said Carmel, hand on her hip. 'Exactly.' She played up to this, the role of the put-upon mother; in reality she had little interest in domesticity. 'Now get ten potatoes out of the sack behind the door and chop them into chips like the good son that you are.'

Johnny threw his helmet on the table and went over and started pulling potatoes from the bag. 'Watch it!' The door opened again.

Jack sauntered in, carrying a small plastic cow in each pudgy fist. Carmel peered over her glasses. 'How are negotiations going?'

Jack placed the animals on the counter and rested his chin against the cool marble. 'I don't like them trees, Granny,' he said, and tried to headbutt the broccoli but it was just out of reach.

'Those trees,' corrected Robin, ruffling his tangled, clammy hair.

He pushed her hand away. 'I like the other trees. The big trees!' He wandered over to his grandmother. 'Them trees!' He pointed up at the leek.

'*Those* trees, Jack.'

Carmel hit herself on the forehead. 'Silly Granny.' She shook her head. 'I forgot.'

'That's okay.' Jack climbed up on to the stool beside her and patted her arm benevolently. 'Old people forget things sometimes.'

'That's very true,' said Carmel, bowing slightly at his absolution. 'How did you get to be such a clever boy?'

'Daddy told me,' said Jack, leaning over to the fruit bowl and plucking a grape from the stalk before anyone could tell him not to. 'Granddad forgot his keys and Daddy said it was okay because old people forget things sometimes.'

The room fell quiet as everyone's movements slowed – everyone except Jack, who had realised nobody was telling him off and so was rapidly shoving grapes into his mouth.

Carmel cleared her throat. 'When did Granddad forget his keys?'

'Yes-ter-day!' Jack threw his head back, half laughing, half gurgling, and brought his hand to his forehead just as Carmel had done. 'You forget *everything*, Granny.'

A small piece of grape skin stuck to Jack's lower lip. Johnny and Carmel looked at Robin. She shook her head. She hadn't a clue what he was talking about.

'Mick did forget his keys yesterday,' said Carmel, quietly and without intonation as Jack continued to make light work of the grape punnet. 'He had to ring the bell when they came back from the park.' Then, loading her voice with serenity, she almost sang: 'When were you talking to your daddy, Jack?' But Carmel's eyes were on Robin.

'At the swing! Daddy can make it go much higher than Granddad. Granddad gets too scared.'

'In the park?' said Robin, finally finding her voice. 'When you went to the park with Granddad?'

Jack nodded, his mouth now too full of grapes to speak.

Maybe Jack was getting his days mixed up. He wasn't great with time yet. Surely her dad wouldn't have let Eddy talk to Jack. Or at the very least he would have told her about it. And what was Eddy doing in the park? Had he followed them? Had he been waiting to get Jack alone?

'What did he say?' demanded Robin, her mind suddenly racing. Had Eddy been watching them? Was he still watching them? 'What did your daddy say, Jack?'

Jack pointed to his mouth and bobbed his head from side to side. He reached for the fruit bowl again but Robin caught his hand mid-grab. 'Stop messing now. Swallow that.'

She sounded crosser than she'd intended and Jack's eyes grew wide and worried.

'Spit it out,' she said, opening her palm and spreading it below his mouth. 'Come on. Just spit it out.'

'Robin,' her mother warned, and Robin saw that her son was on the verge of tears. She withdrew her hand and waited for him to swallow. When he did, he was panting, his fat little tongue stained purple.

She tried again. 'What did Daddy say?'

'He said he loved me and he loved Mammy.' Jack's lip quivered. He looked around at the adults. He knew something had changed. He didn't like the way they were looking at him – but he did like that they were looking at him. He rallied under the attention. 'Daddy said when we go home after our holiday with Granny and Granddad, he's going to get me a tractor. Not like the one I got from Granddad, Mammy. A big one! Like on the television.'

'Robin,' said her mother, but Robin had already turned and walked out of the room. The kitchen door slammed behind her as she strode back into the sitting room, reached into the beanbag and grabbed her phone.

*** Pine Road Poker ***

Bernie:
Warning!!! Sylvie was bitten by a dog outside Island Stores today, circa 2 p.m. An adult male fled the scene with the attacker. Be on the lookout for an unfamiliar large black dog. If you see one please let me know but do not approach. Regards, Bernie Watters-Reilly

Ellen:
That's awful, Bernie. So sorry to hear it. Pets that aren't kept under control should be taken out and shot.

Love to Sylvie xxx

Bernie:
Thank you, Ellen. And I'm inclined to agree. I actually wrote about it recently and got some great feedback from readers.

Link: independent.ie/BestParenting/PetsArentPeople

We're debating going to the police. She's quite traumatised.

Ellen:
The poor chicken. Let me know if I can do anything. xxx

Carmel:
Sylvie seems to have all the bad luck. Is that her third dog bite since the summer?

Bernie:
Fourth, Carmel. She's just too trusting. She loves animals and always thinks the best of them.

Carmel:

That must be it.

Fiona:

OMG Poor Sylvie!! Will keep an eye out and tell my two to stay away from any dogs. Tnxs 4 the heads up hun!! XXXX

Ruby:

I think the new neighbours have a dog . . .

THREE

· · · · · · · · · · · · · · · ·

Edie Rice shifted slightly as her phone went silently berserk in her back pocket. She was about to excuse herself to go to the bathroom and check it – leaving people waiting made her anxious – when Daniel's mother clattered one of her good plates down in front of her with an aggressive sigh. The chicken, wrapped in bacon, bounced.

'Before you say it, I know you're a *vegetarian* now.' Mrs Carmody's tone suggested she would have drawn quotation marks in the air if she hadn't had a plate in her other hand. 'Daniel gave me that bit of information after I'd already forked out for the meat. So,' she sighed again, 'I've given you the smallest piece.'

The bacon coat, still sizzling, slipped from the chicken breast and slid a greasy path across the plate. Edie's throat closed over.

'It's perfect,' she enthused when she could manage. 'And those potatoes look delicious. Thank you, Mrs Carmody.' She beamed up at her mother-in-law.

Her phone was still buzzing. Oh gosh. She hoped the Pine Road women hadn't realised she was the last one to put down rat poison. It was so unlike her, but this particular task kept slipping her mind. *Baby brain*, she thought, wishfully.

'Yeah, well,' Mrs Carmody harrumphed, Edie's positive response clearly a disappointment, 'I spent all day making that so don't go insulting me.' Then she carefully placed the other plate in front of her son.

'Thanks, Ma,' said Daniel. Edie didn't like to think badly of her mother-in-law, but his dead bird wrapped in dead pig did not look any larger than hers. He squeezed her hand below the table.

'Everything all right, Edie?' asked Mrs Carmody.

Edie gave her another enthusiastic smile. 'Perfect,' she repeated, glancing around at Daniel's father, sister and older brother. 'Thank you.' When the others started to eat, she picked up her fork and scraped out a couple of uncontaminated beans from beneath the chicken breast.

Daniel carefully constructed a forkful of dinner so there was a bit of everything on it. You wouldn't think it to look at her husband – a tank of a man regularly covered in car oil – but he was a gentle perfectionist. He was thorough and exact and believed if something was worth doing, it was worth doing right. It had taken him a month to propose because he wanted to do it with breakfast in bed and was waiting for the perfect morning light. But Edie had always been far too curious and she found the ring the day he bought it. She felt terrible for ruining the surprise and didn't tell anyone, including Daniel. Although her nail technician guessed; nobody gets refills that often unless they're expecting their hands to take centre stage in multiple social media posts.

'Since when are you a vegetarian, Edie?' asked Daniel's sister.

'Since last year,' she said, doing her best not to hear the sneer in Rachel's voice, and glancing at Daniel who quickly looked away.

But Peter, Daniel's older brother, had caught the look. 'No more steaks for your dinner, Two Straps?' he said, needling Daniel, though his gaze was on Edie as he chewed, mouth opening slightly wider than necessary. 'I wouldn't be putting up with that.'

'I'd say you've lots of time to cook, Edie,' said Mrs Carmody, waving her fork. 'No kids to look after, just your little job to go to.'

Edie, who had started nodding eagerly before her mother-in-law had finished, continued to smile, though her insides were contorting. Daniel rubbed his leg against hers.

She'd stopped eating meat the month they were supposed to start trying for a baby.

'Edie actually got a promotion last week.'

She beamed. He was still proud of her. He loved her. The rest was just a phase.

'Is it more money?' asked Daniel's father, stabbing at his own meat combo.

'A little, I guess, but it's more of a title thing. I'll be going from day receptionist to—'

'How much?'

'Of . . . a pay increase? Oh, well,' Edie looked to her husband, 'about eighty euro extra a week? I think.'

'For answering phones?' said Mrs Carmody incredulously. 'Sure, a monkey could do that. I've been doing it for free all my life.'

Edie did her best to take it as a joke, but Rachel's sharp laugh scraped the smile from her face.

She knew Daniel's family hated her and that the more effort she put in, the worse it got. But she couldn't help it. It had always mattered to her what other people thought.

'You're practically a kept man now, bro,' said Peter. 'First she buys you a house, now she's bringing in the bacon. You'll be able to make up for the economic fuck-ups of Two Straps here, Edie.' Peter nudged Daniel. 'Isn't that right?' Peter nudged him again. 'Two Straps?'

'I didn't buy Daniel a house,' she said, desperate to get out of this kitchen without a fight. 'I inherited it.' Though Peter knew this already.

'Yeah, but who owns it?' asked her brother-in-law. 'Whose name's on the deeds? Ha? Not Two Straps.'

Edie ignored him. 'And Daniel doesn't need me to *keep* him. My husband is an excellent provider. He gives me everything I need.'

Suddenly everyone was oohing and sniggering.

'No, I didn't mean—'

But Mr Carmody brought his fists down on either side of his plate. 'No smut talk at the table!'

Edie reached down for Daniel's hand but he kept them both above the table. Peter continued to grin at her as he picked up his fork. A familiar knot returned to her stomach. They always got to him. No matter what she did, there always came a moment in this house when she felt Daniel loving her a little less.

'Actually, Two Straps,' said Peter, 'I need you to mind Rocky next weekend.'

Rocky was Peter's designer dog, although he spent as much time at her and Daniel's house as he did at Peter's.

Daniel took a sip of his coke. 'You just picked him up from ours yesterday. And we're busy next weekend.'

'Another dance class, is it? Haven't you mastered the cha-cha-cha yet?'

Rachel tittered.

'We did three dance classes for our wedding, because Edie wanted to. A year ago. Stop fucking bringing it up.'

'Daniel,' exclaimed Mrs Carmody. 'Don't swear at your brother.'

Peter slapped Daniel on the shoulder. 'I'm joking! Relax. It's only one night. I'll be back for him Sunday, yeah? Anyway, bro,' Peter winked at Edie, 'you owe me.'

Daniel owed him absolutely nothing. He was forever doing favours for Peter and his brother just acted like he was entitled to it all. Edie didn't like to think badly of people – she really didn't, it gave her a pain in her stomach – but her in-laws made it very difficult.

'Happy birthday, Ma,' said Peter, raising his can in Mrs Carmody's direction as everyone else lifted theirs.

'Ah, thanks, son.' Mrs Carmody beamed as she tucked her greying hair behind her ear. 'It's lovely to have all my family here.' She looked around the table, Edie's face lighting up as she caught her eye. 'And Edie, of course.'

'We got you a cake,' said Peter.

'Ah, now! What did you go and do that for? Don't be wasting your money on me.'

'Nonsense, Ma. What better thing would there be to spend it on?'

Edie looked from Peter to Daniel, momentarily confused. 'We got a cake too.'

'Two cakes!' Mrs Carmody clapped her hands to her chest.

'No, Ma,' said Peter evenly. 'It's the same cake. Edie's just trying to make me look bad, because I didn't physically *buy* the cake. If it's about money, Edie, just let me know what I owe. I'm not working at the moment but I should be able to cobble something together. Or maybe I could pay you in instalments.'

'I wasn't—'

'Don't be ridiculous,' interrupted Mrs Carmody. 'Surely you're not asking for his money, Edie? And Peter out of work? Surely you're not that hard up that you can't spare a few euro?'

'Of course I'm not,' Edie started to insist. Peter was the one trying to make her look bad; he must have seen her and Daniel carrying the bakery box into the house. And Peter might be technically unemployed but he'd just bought a new car – with a discount from Daniel.

But Mr Carmody brought his fists down on the table again before she could get any further, and Peter was back grinning now everyone else's attention was fixed on her.

'What the fuck are we talking about money for?' barked Daniel's dad. 'It's your mother's birthday. Get out the cake, and keep the grubby talk for later.'

Mrs Carmody sniffled slightly. Peter got up from the table, went over to the fridge and produced the carrot cake Edie had carefully chosen and ordered three days earlier, then picked up – and paid for – this morning. It should have been Daniel, at the very least, lighting the candles.

'Ah, son!' Mrs Carmody clapped her hands, an actual tear in her eye at the sight of her name spelled out in icing. 'You personalised it and everything.'

Rachel led them in a chorus of 'for she's a jolly good fellow' but Peter got the sole peck on the cheek. The cake was cut and slices doled out to everyone except Edie.

'Ma,' said Daniel.

'What? Oh, sorry. Can you eat cake, Edie?'

'Of course she can eat cake.'

'How was I supposed to know that? It's hard to keep up with all her regimes.'

'That's okay, Mrs Carmody. It's just meat I don't eat. Everything else is fine.' For the first few months she'd cut down on alcohol and caffeine too, until it became clear she was wasting her time. A glass of white wine was a paltry consolation prize, but it was better than nothing.

But Daniel's mother had already gone back to her other son. 'It's lovely, Peter, just gorgeous.'

Edie watched the clock above the sink and listened as Mr Carmody gave out about the family who'd moved in next door. He didn't know where they were from, but they weren't Irish. Edie reminded herself of generational differences and unintentional biases and the need to be understanding, but it was no use. There was only so long she could spend in this house before she felt herself becoming a worse person. Everyone was finished eating and they'd been there two hours. She pushed back her chair.

'I'll just help with these,' she said, gathering the empty plates to carry to the dishwasher. 'Thanks for dinner. I'm afraid we have to get going.'

'Oh no,' Rachel deadpanned. 'Don't go. You're such great craic.'

Peter snorted so coke came out his nostrils. The familiar knot expanded in Edie's stomach.

'You won't stay for a cup of tea?' said Mrs Carmody, a small quiver creeping into her voice. 'Daniel?'

Edie did not look at her husband but she knew he was looking at her.

'We'd love to, Mrs Carmody, but I'm afraid I have a couple of things to get before the shop closes and Daniel—'

Daniel's father hit the table again and everyone jumped. 'It's my wife's birthday and if she wants you to stay for tea, you're staying. Now sit down there and give us another fifteen minutes of your precious time. You' – he pointed at Peter – 'stick on the kettle.' Peter instantly rose from his seat. 'And don't drown the bloody thing in milk.'

The kettle rumbled and Peter rooted in the press for mugs. Mr Carmody leaned forward and gave Daniel a smile that contained no humour. 'How's my garage going? I hope your wife's not making all the decisions about that too?'

Daniel had worked in the family garage full time, and for peanuts, since the day he finished school. His dad retired three years ago and sold the place to him at full market value. It was entirely, and officially, Daniel's. Yet Mr Carmody insisted on referring to it as his garage and Daniel, who wouldn't let himself be undermined in any other circumstance, never corrected him.

'Fine,' he said. 'Everything's going fine.'

'That's interesting now.' Mr Carmody scratched his beard. 'Because Peter tells me things were a bit slow there before Christmas.'

Edie tensed. The queasiness in her stomach grew stronger. The slow year at the garage had been the cause of everything. It was why they still had cracked tiles in their bathroom and why a greater fracture had threatened to split the two of them.

'No,' her husband replied evenly. 'Everything's fine.'

'Are you sure now, son?'

'I'm sure.'

'You know, I had that place for four decades?'

'I know, Da.'

'And I never once came close to shutting it down. I never once made a loss, even.'

'What's that?' said Peter, carrying over two cups of tea and offering one to his father – 'Get that away from me; it looks fucking anaemic' – and another to his mother – 'Oh no, don't mind me; look after yourselves first' – before giving one to Edie and putting the other in front of Daniel.

'I'm just reminding your brother that my garage has been in the family for forty years without any problems, so he better not be the one to fuck it up.'

'You were the best mechanic in all of north Dublin, Da,' agreed Peter. 'It's a lot for any young buck to live up to. But Two Straps is doing his best, aren't you, little bro?' Then the thirty-year-old man reached for the arm of his twenty-eight-year-old sibling and quickly twisted the skin.

Edie threw the tea down her throat so fast she knew she'd be peeling the skin off the roof of her mouth for days. But she didn't care. She could see the Carmody poison starting to worm its way into Daniel. He was too good for them. She had to get him out. When the cup was almost empty, she brought it over to the dishwasher, went into the hallway, got her coat and the faux-fur colour-block scarf that she thought looked very chic but which Mrs Carmody said made her look like 'a streetwalker'. Then she came back and stood in the kitchen doorway.

'We're off now, thanks again.'

Daniel stood and the rest of them, who were laughing at some video Peter had gotten up on his phone, didn't argue.

As she left the house, Edie imagined the bad feelings falling from her body. She shook herself silently before opening the car, discarding the last of the ill will on the driveway, and when the passenger door was closed behind her, she took a deep breath of unpolluted air.

'Home we go.'

Daniel didn't say anything. He just stuck the key in the engine and checked the rear-view mirror.

She glanced over. 'You all right?'

'Grand.'

She watched him, lost in the concentration of driving, frowning at some invisible grievance on the horizon. Had they gotten to him? They usually did. Was he back to worrying, to beating himself up and taking her down by association, to coming up with reasons not to give her what he'd promised?

'You know you're my favourite?' she said.

His mouth twitched and his head lifted. 'Of my family? I'm not sure that's much of a compliment.'

'Of everyone.'

He gave into the smile then.

Rows of identical houses whizzed past as Edie rolled back her shoulders and felt the knot in her stomach loosen. She loved him and he loved her. It all came back to that. They could let the scaffolding fall because the walls they'd built underneath were sound. That was the gist of the poem she'd read out at their wedding in place of making a speech. She took a deep breath and went for it.

'I know the last few months have been stressful for you, work wise and everything, and we agreed we'd leave it till the new year . . .'

His eyes flickered from one mirror to the other. They hadn't actually agreed, so much as he'd left her with no choice.

'. . . but January is already over and . . . it's coming up again.'

'Already?'

A brutal memory of standing in a new nightdress – she did a lot of window-shopping at Victoria's Secret, but this was the first thing she'd actually bought – and him saying he had a headache.

'Yes,' she said tentatively. 'Next weekend. So, since things are back to normal at work . . .'

A *headache*. That was an excuse women usually gave.

'They're not back to normal, Edie. I'm just not losing money.'

When she'd gotten into bed beside him that night, having changed into her pyjamas and resolved to return the nightdress

32

the next day, she'd felt his erection. It wasn't that he hadn't wanted to have sex with her, he just hadn't wanted to . . .

No. She couldn't go there.

She pulled a strand from her ponytail and wound it too tightly around her little finger. 'Well, I thought we could try again.'

Her voice cracked slightly on 'again' and Daniel turned. A look of sympathy and something else: Guilt? Regret? Resignation?

She sat, half holding her breath, waiting for him to rehash the old excuses of money and security and yada yada. But instead he took his hand off the steering wheel and placed it on her knee.

'I'm sorry,' he said, his own voice threatening to break.

He meant it. She knew he meant it. She just wished she could understand it.

'That's okay.' She placed her own hand over his and squeezed tightly, then she took a deep breath and put on her best, most Edie-like smile. 'At least we're guaranteed a fun weekend.'

FOUR

● ● ● ● ● ● ● ● ● ● ● ● ●

'**H**ang on!' shouted Edie, as they turned up Pine Road and the car came to a sudden stop. 'Rat poison! I nearly forgot, again.' She scrambled to undo her seat belt.

'Rat poison?' Daniel looked at her, alarmed. 'Do we have rats?'

'No. It's just . . . It's precautionary.' Daniel had no interest in the goings-on of Pine Road. He wasn't looking to make new pals, whereas Edie – whose friends had moved out of Dublin, had babies and lost her number – was attempting to build an entire social circle. Being invited into the Pine Road Poker Group had been a big moment. She wasn't going to risk getting kicked out. 'I'll see you up at the house. Will you stick on the heating when you get in? Thank you!'

She closed the car door so quickly she nearly clipped her scarf. She should have known not to wear this to Daniel's parents' house. But then there was barely an item of clothing that Mrs Carmody didn't think 'did nothing' for Edie.

She turned from the car and walked straight into a woman – tall, thin, in wide-legged burgundy slacks – also heading for Island Stores.

'Sorry, sorry! Wasn't looking where I was going.'

The woman smiled – defined cheekbones lifting, brown eyes twinkling – and Edie felt her mouth open. She was in her forties, probably, with a long, dark bob that kinked slightly to the left. She wore a cashmere jumper with her statement trousers; very simple, very chic, very . . . French. Oh, and her purse! It was lovely! Just like something from *Vogue*. *French Vogue*. Edie ripped pictures of women like this from magazines every time she went clothes shopping, but then she got distracted by seasonal trends and came home with yet more prints and sparkle. All of which was to say, this was just the sort of woman whose acceptance Edie craved.

'I like your trousers, they're—'

'Do you live here?' the woman asked at the same time.

Edie abandoned her statement – it was a social tic of hers, using compliments as icebreakers. A woman like this would never do something so needy. A woman like this would be aloof. Oh, how Edie yearned to be aloof.

'On Pine Road? Yes. Just up near the top, there, in the corner.' Edie squinted up the road to see Daniel getting out of his beloved BMW. He always angled the car so precisely. For all the parking animosity on Pine Road, nobody could ever accuse them of taking up two spaces.

'We just moved in,' said the woman. 'Number eight.'

'You—'

Edie couldn't believe it. She was never this lucky! This was the woman behind the mysteriously quick move, the one who'd gotten her kids into Saint Ornatín's at the last minute, even though tons of local families couldn't. Fiona at number ten never stopped talking about how her twins were still on the waitlist for next year despite living five doors down from the principal. Trish said she couldn't interfere on behalf of neighbours but, at the last poker game, when Trish wasn't there, Bernie told them someone had interfered on behalf of this woman, someone very *senior*, and that's how they'd gotten into the school.

Edie's first thought had been international witness protection, naturally. She'd imagined a family of Russian spies moving in to Pine Road, dyeing their hair, wearing coloured contact lenses and distorting their faces with various prosthetics in an attempt to conceal their true identity. Now she met the woman, she was rethinking this. She didn't appear to be wearing make-up, never mind prosthetics.

The husband and daughters had been spotted several times, but Edie would be the first with a report on the mother! She started storing away details. Were those boots Kurt Geiger? She was almost sure they were.

'Number eight! Oh gosh, yes, hi. Hello.' Her fingers instinctively went to her hair, flattening fly-aways and tightening her ponytail. 'I'm Edie Rice.' She yanked her hands from her head and extended the right one towards her new neighbour. 'We're at number nineteen, we've barely been there a year, me and my husband, Daniel. Carmody. Different names, but we're married.' Edie always added this now, since Ellen Two Names had been so confused when they first moved in.

The woman smiled. Good skin, no sign of Botox. Edie planned to look into fillers when she turned thirty, unless she was pregnant. Thinking about that stressed her out. She wanted to have two children by thirty.

'I'm Martha Rigby.' The woman took Edie's hand. Her skin was lovely and smooth. She probably used hand creams. Edie had never seen the point of hand creams but she was open to reconsidering. 'I kept my name when I married too,' said Martha. 'My husband and daughters are Costello.' So much in common already! Maybe Edie was more sophisticated than she gave herself credit for. 'And I've an older son, Ellis, from a previous relationship. Different surname again.'

Edie's eyes widened at this extra, intimate piece of information. Her new neighbour said it like it was nothing, but Edie would never be foolish enough to treat it as such. She took confidences very seriously. It was a big deal to be vulnerable with a stranger, and it deserved reciprocation.

'We don't have any children,' said Edie eagerly. 'But we're hoping to have them soon. We're trying, actually, at the moment – to get pregnant, I mean.'

'That's great, Edie,' replied Martha, barely missing a beat.

'Yes.' Edie hoped there were no bits of beans stuck in her teeth. 'We're super excited about it. Martha.'

She was delighted to have remembered her name. Edie was usually so busy concentrating on making a good first impression and getting her own name right that she entirely missed the part where the other person introduced themselves. Martha Rigby. A strong, sophisticated name. It suited her perfectly.

Martha smiled. She seemed to be having a good time. Which was good. Unless of course she was laughing *at* Edie rather than with her . . .

'Tell me, Edie . . .' said Martha, in a way that settled Edie's insides. She'd always found deep voices reassuring. 'Where did you get such a gorgeous scarf?'

• • • • • • • • •

Martha had been in danger of letting yet another day slip through her fingers. But after the third identical hourly news bulletin, she'd coaxed herself up from the kitchen table, put on her boots and headed down to the local shop to get weed killer and dogfood.

Robert and the girls had gone to visit his parents, but she said she had things to do around the house. She didn't want to be in that car with him and she didn't want to go back to Limerick. Ellis had mentioned calling around, but it was well after lunchtime and there was no sign of her son.

She had been about to turn into Island Stores when she stopped abruptly to check there was money in her purse and collided with a young woman in a loud scarf climbing out of a shiny black car. The woman immediately started apologising, though the collision had almost definitely been Martha's fault. She found the young woman's enthusiastic way of speaking rather adorable. It was as if with every sentence, she was beseeching you to see how *interesting* life was.

Martha told the excitable woman, Edie, where they'd moved from and what Robert did. She in turn told Martha about her procreation plans – Martha did her best not to look taken aback by the bluntness of this – and about how her husband was a mechanic and she worked as a receptionist at the Shelbourne hotel. 'I've just been made receptionist-slash-supervisor,' Edie added. She was disproportionately delighted when Martha congratulated her – although not as disproportionately delighted as when she complimented her scarf – but what Martha was really wondering was how a mechanic and receptionist-slash-supervisor could afford a home on Pine Road. And Edie had pointed to the top of the street, where the houses were slightly bigger.

'What age are your girls?'

'Twelve and just gone sixteen. Orla's in first year, Sinead's in fifth.'

'Sixteen! Great!'

Martha nearly laughed. Ageing: it's just so damn exciting.

'At Saint Ornatín's, right? I went there. I met my husband there, actually. Are you all settling in okay?'

'So far so good,' she said. 'There's still a lot of unpacking to do, and we don't have much storage. We need wardrobes and shelves, but also pillows and possibly a mattress . . .' She was overcome by a sudden urge to go back to bed, but she smiled politely. 'It'll all get done eventually.'

'Have you heard of Interiors World?' asked Edie in a breathless half-whisper, as if she were asking whether Martha had heard of the secret to eternal youth. 'It's an *amazing* place on the Long Mile Road. It's massive and it has *everything*. I spent half my life there last year. We were supposed to get work done to the house, a whole new bathroom, and I had all these lists of what we were going to get and, well, it didn't work out but . . .' The girl's ears started to pink. 'We're going to do it another time. After the baby, maybe. No rush, like. But anyway, it's the most amazing place. Although' – she glanced up at Martha – 'it might be a bit basic for you. You're probably more into bespoke furniture and one-off pieces.' The girl's ears were fully red now.

Martha grinned. She liked this woman. She made Martha feel like her old self: calm, collected and in charge.

'Would you like to go, Edie?'

'Oh.' Edie looked around. 'Sorry. I've kept you. I do that. I ask too many questions, and I—'

'No, Edie. I mean would you like to go to Interiors World? With me? Someday next week, maybe?'

'With—' Edie looked around again and then back up at Martha. 'Yes. Yes, great. That'd be great.'

'Great,' agreed Martha.

'I work shifts but I'm free Thursday? Does Thursday suit you?'

'Thursday morning,' decided Martha. 'Say nine thirty? I can drive.'

It felt so natural, so familiar, to be the one making plans. This was who Martha Rigby was: a woman who made things happen, not a woman to whom things happened.

'Should we ask some of the other women, do you think, from the road?' The smallest frown line appeared between Edie's coloured-in brows. 'There's a group of us, we have a WhatsApp group, you could probably join—'

'I'd rather keep it small.' Bit by bit. Wasn't that what Dr Morten had said? We rebuild bit by bit.

'Right, yes, absolutely . . .' Edie looked up, already wincing apologetically. 'I just wonder if we shouldn't say it to Bernie?'

'Who's Bernie?'

'Bernie Watters-Reilly. She's sort of in charge. Well,' Edie winced again, 'not *in charge*. Although she is head of the Parents' Association at Saint Ornatín's and sometimes she's on the telly talking about how to be a good parent. But no, she's . . . Bernie likes to know what's going on. Most stuff on the road goes through her. She's . . . she's sort of the Pine Road gatekeeper.' Edie reddened. 'At least, that's how I think of her.'

Martha laughed. 'Surely she doesn't have to sanction everything?'

Edie's blush deepened. 'Oh, of course not, no.' She paused. 'But I wouldn't recommend getting on her bad side. Or Ellen's – Ellen is sort of her sidekick. They're a bit . . .' Edie looked around nervously, then spoke louder. 'But they're fine when you get to know them. Bernie just likes being the organiser. You know how some people are like that.'

'I do,' said Martha, who'd had enough dillydallying now and wanted to get in out of the cold. 'I'm one of them. And I'm organising this trip to Interiors World. So if you want to come—'

'Yes,' yelped Edie, visibly weighing up her options, her loyalties, and coming to a rushed conclusion. 'Yes, for sure. Absolutely. I'd love to go.'

'Wonderful. I'll see you Thursday so.'

Then Martha turned and headed into the warmth of Island Stores while Edie, who had clearly been on her way into the shop too, stood awkwardly outside, pretending to read the noticeboard.

*** Pine Road Poker ***

Ellen:
Number 8 alert! New woman spotted. I was cleaning my upstairs windows and I saw her leaving her house. No coat on her.

Ruby:
So she does exist.

Fiona:
OMG! Is this the first sighting? XXX

Ellen:
Yes, Fiona. Of course it is. I wouldn't be telling you otherwise.

Fiona:
YASSS KWEEN!!! Well done, hun! XXX

Carmel:
Where was she going, I wonder? It's freezing out.

Ruby:
Probably going to report the woman a few doors up pretending to clean her windows while she spies on her ...

Ellen:
She went to Island Stores. Must have been a leisurely trip because she returned approximately thirty minutes later. She was carrying two large bags of household products and I spotted Island Stores' own-brand dogfood. (@BernieWattersReilly)

Fiona:
No flies on you, Ellen. (Or your windows!) XXX

Rita Ann:
She didn't happen to have a newspaper tucked under her arm, did she? I find the timing of their arrival and this thievery suspicious, to say the least.

Carmel:
What did she look like?

Ruby:
I'd say she's good-looking, if her husband is anything to go by.

Fiona:
And judging by the daughters, I'm thinking dark hair! XXX

Ruby:
Agreed.

Ellen:
As the only person who's actually *seen* her ... She's tall, pale, late forties, bit gaunt, not unattractive.

Edie:
Good spot, Ellen! I was actually chatting to her outside Island Stores. That's probably what held her up – my fault. We were nattering away! Her name's Martha Rigby, but the rest of the family are Costello. She's a grown son with a different name again. Very modern! They moved here from Limerick. I thought she was gorgeous. Clothes are v glam!

And I'd definitely say early forties. x

Fiona:
What age are her girls, Edie?

Edie:
12 and 16. First year and fifth.

Fiona:
And what does the husband do?

Edie:
Works in Bank of Ireland.

Carmel:
A report worthy of a Pine Road veteran.

Ruby:
I'm afraid she has you beat there, Ellen!

Rita Ann:
Did she mention anything about a newspaper?

Fiona:
Never mind, Ellen. You can't win them all. XXX

FIVE

· · · · · · · · · · · ·

Robin stepped out into the night air and shut the back door gently so as not to wake Jack, who had finally fallen asleep, albeit in her bed.

'Stop calling.'

There was a crackle down the line and the sound of Eddy breathing. Deep, rhythmic breaths, the kind he released on to her skin when he woke in the night and reached for her, searching her body until she too was awake.

'Hi, babe.'

'Stop – stop calling. I mean it, Eddy. And don't come around here trying to talk to me, or Jack. And if you ever intimidate my dad again, I'll . . .' She trailed off. She had no threat to make.

'I didn't intimidate your old man. I would never. Your family is my family. I just happened to bump into them.'

'Yeah right.'

'You don't believe me? That hurts, babe.'

Robin's father had explained that he'd been supervising Jack from the park bench. He'd glanced at his phone for a minute, just to check the latest scores, and when he looked back up Jack was on the monkey bars and there was a man standing under him. When Mick got closer, he saw it was Eddy. He hadn't said anything because he didn't want to worry her. Although when Robin confronted him about it, he'd seemed relieved to be getting it off his chest. He'd seemed a little worried himself.

'I miss you, Robin. I love you.'

'Stop.'

The rasp of his voice said he was sorry but he wasn't going to *say* he was sorry because he was still the man she wanted him to be.

'I miss your hips . . .'

'No.'

'And your ass.'

'Don't.' Robin closed her eyes and she hated herself. Nobody else in the world would have described her as needy, but around Eddy she was.

'I miss how your nipples grow hard in my mouth.'

She felt that familiar ache. She thought of him and she craved him.

'Come back, babe; we'll sort it out. I'll be done with all that stuff if you want me to be. I was only ever looking out for us, for our family. You, me and the little man.'

Robin didn't say anything. She couldn't go back to him. She knew she couldn't.

'You never asked me to stop before – we never spoke about it. But if you do, I will. I'd do anything for you. I'm your man.'

Robin opened her eyes. She turned to face the house she'd grown up in. She looked up towards her childhood bedroom and watched the shadows thrown on the blind by Jack's nightlight. She thought of Jack.

'You took our son with you.'

'Babe, it was a one-off.'

'He missed preschool, Eddy! I didn't know where he was and I couldn't call the cops because, you know, obviously, and . . .' Robin pushed the phone away from her face for a moment and gathered herself. 'Jesus Christ!'

'I'm sorry about that, Robin.' His voice was quieter now, more serious. 'It couldn't be helped. I told you that. It just came up. He was fine. He was asleep in the back of the car the whole time. I would never let anything happen to him, or to you. I'm addicted to you.'

That's what Eddy always said. *I'm an addict, babe, and you're my fix.*

'We just need to get this mess sorted and then we can go back to normal.'

'What mess?'

'That night, when I was out with Jack, there's a bit of a misunderstanding about where I was and someone's saying I was somewhere I wasn't. I've told the guards we were at home watching *Hocus Pocus* – that's your favourite, isn't it? See, I remember. You just have to tell them the same thing.'

'The guards, Eddy?'

'It's nothing. But if they ask you about it – you say the same thing, yeah? The three of us were watching *Hocus Pocus* and then we got up the next morning and Jack wasn't feeling great so we kept him at home. That's all. It'll be over then and we can go back to normal.'

'To normal . . .'

'The way it was before.'

'I'm not lying to the guards for you.'

'Oh now, Robin.' She could hear him smile. She pictured the skin of his lips slowly stretching until smooth and pale. 'Sometimes I think you've really convinced yourself you never did anything. When we both know that's not true at all.'

· · · · · · · · ·

In the few hours since Martha had returned from Island Stores with weed killer and dogfood, she'd had three callers. And every time someone new rapped on the door, she dropped whatever it was she'd been holding.

The first person to come knocking was Ellis. The only upside to their whole ordeal was that she was now living near her son again. Of course, she didn't know it was her son at the door until she opened it. She dropped a photo frame that time.

'I'm here to help unpack,' he declared, hanging his bag on the bottom of the banister and allowing her to hug him tightly.

'I'm not unpacking boulders, sweetheart.'

He followed her gaze to the steel-toed safety shoes peeking out from under his black trousers. 'I've got an hour before my shift. But I'm not here to talk about work so don't say a word.'

'I wasn't going to.'

Ellis was a waiter with vague aspirations to write. But he could be much more. Martha had managed to successfully broach the subject the last time they met and he told her he was considering going back to college. She thought she'd reacted with enough enthusiasm that he might actually see it through this time.

The second person to come calling was a neighbour named Ellen Russell-Something. Her angry knock cost Martha a perfectly good slice of toast. She declined a cup of tea but stayed for half an hour anyway, asking persistent questions and informing Martha, while sizing up Oscar, that a child from the road had recently been maimed by a rogue dog. The child was the daughter of Bernie Watters-Reilly. Martha only recognised the name because of her conversation with the saucer-eyed girl outside the shop, but Ellen took it as a given that she was intimately familiar with this woman's work. Things were cordial enough until Ellen mentioned a road-wide drive to lay rat poison. All Martha said was she'd have to check it was dog-friendly, but Ellen seemed to take this as a slight, not so much on her, weirdly, but on this Bernie woman. She spent a lot of time looking around Martha's kitchen and offered phone numbers for a fumigator, gardener and various cleaners.

When she left, Martha closed the blinds in the kitchen, but still she couldn't shake the feeling of being watched. The hairs on her body refused to lie flat. When the knocker went for the third time, Martha sent the entire cutlery drawer clattering to the floor.

'Jesus fucking Christ,' she muttered before plastering on a smile and shunting open their banjaxed front door.

Carmel-From-Across-the-Road declined the offer of tea but said she'd have a glass of wine. So Martha produced a bottle from one of the few unpacked boxes.

Carmel – red-faced, friendly, probably about sixty – told Martha that her information was being carefully compiled by the women of Pine Road's WhatsApp group.

'We've even got the hours at which your husband goes to and returns from work,' she said. 'If he's having an affair we'll probably know before you do.'

Martha did her best to smile at this.

'And don't be surprised if an older woman comes calling asking about missing newspapers. In fact, she might just help herself and start rooting through your recycling bin. Might actually be an idea to keep the bins in the back garden for a bit, if you put anything personal in there.' Carmel downed the wine with a smack of her lips, as Martha tried to figure out if she was joking or not.

Robert and the girls arrived home just as Carmel was giving her the lowdown on Ellen 'Two Names'. At the sound of the front door opening and the children squabbling, Carmel got up to leave, still talking. 'The woman spends her whole life cleaning her house. She was plain old Ellen O'Toole until Bernie started using two surnames – only because it takes up more room on TV screens and in the paper, that's the kind of ego we're dealing with here – so Ellen went and added the Russell. Bernie is a C-list media personality, at best, but Ellen acts like she's living two doors down from Beyoncé.'

'Oh, pardon me,' said Robert, walking into the kitchen as Carmel went to walk out. Martha caught a glimpse of Sinead stomping up the stairs. Orla walked right past the stranger, as if she was part of the furniture, and headed for the fridge.

'This is Carmel. She lives across the road. Carmel, this is my husband Robert.'

Robert smiled widely. 'Lovely to meet you. My favourite aunt was called Carmel.'

'It's an old person's name,' the woman conceded.

'So what are you doing with it?'

It took Carmel a second, then she started to laugh. 'You charmer. He's a charmer!' She looked back at Martha whose cheeks creaked reluctantly upwards.

'I was just seeing Carmel out.'

In the hallway, Carmel gave Martha some parking tips and explained that nobody paid any mind to the man at number one Pine Road who used old furniture and traffic cones to stop people parking in the open yard beside his house. 'We call it the Occupied Territory,' said Carmel. 'Shay Morrissey says his deeds give him the right of use to nine feet out from his property but nobody's ever seen these deeds so we just move the stuff out of our way. You'll find parking is a bit of a Pine Road obsession.'

In a spur-of-the-moment decision, Martha invited the woman on their Interiors World excursion. For the old, organised her, arranging social outings had been a particular speciality.

'You and Edie?' Carmel looked up from buttoning her coat. 'That wasn't on the WhatsApp chat.'

'We're going Thursday morning, leaving around nine thirty.'

'Sure,' she said. 'I'll bring my daughter. She's been lying around the house moping over her ex for weeks. It'll be something to do.'

When the woman was across the road, Martha closed the door.

The kettle boiled in the kitchen and she heard Robert remove it from its stand. Martha wondered if she was always going to hate her husband.

• • • • • • • • •

Robin made a sound somewhere between mirth and laughter, or at least that was what she was aiming for. 'I took a few calls, Eddy. That was it. I never touched anything or saw anything – I was busy minding *our* child – and I have nothing to do with wherever you were that night.'

'I'll tell you where I was, if you like.'

'I don't want to know. You have nothing to do with me any more. You're only calling because you need an alibi. Well, I'm not lying to the guards for you.'

'That's not why I'm calling. Didn't I come looking for you in the park before this? I'm only asking a small thing. It's fucking nothing. The guards are just looking for something to do.'

The remorseful tone was gone and, from inside the house, Robin could hear the front door slamming and her mother calling.

'I have to go.'

'Hang on.'

'It's Mam. She's going to wake Jack.'

'But you'll tell the guards we were at home, yeah? If they call. The three of us watched *Hocus Pocus* then we stayed at home the next day because Jack was sick.'

Robin pulled the phone away from her ear, took a breath, and returned it.

'So all right, yeah? Okay?'

'Bye, Eddy.'

She hung up just as the back door opened.

'Robin!' The wind chime jangled freely and her mother appeared, framed by the kitchen's harsh fluorescent light. 'What are you doing out here?'

'Mam! Shh. You'll wake Jack.'

'Oh right, yes, sorry.' She dropped her voice slightly. 'I've had a drink.'

Robin stuffed her phone into her pocket and followed Carmel inside.

'I don't know what you're doing out there. It's feckin' freezing.'

Robin closed the door gently behind her. 'What is it?'

'Guess what we're doing Thursday morning?'

Her mother did indeed seem a little merry. Although it didn't take much to send Carmel from sober to tipsy. One year she'd made a potent Christmas pudding and knocked herself out before they'd cleared the table.

Robin worked her way through the TV schedule. 'Watching *Dr Phil*?'

'I do not watch *Dr Phil* every Thursday,' admonished Carmel in a hushed tone. 'I have it on in the background if anything, and if you go spreading that fib about the road, you'll be looking for somewhere else to stay.'

'All right, got it. So what are we doing?'

'Interiors World!'

'What?'

'Interiors World. On the Long Mile Road. I just called into the new neighbour – Martha Rigby, number eight.'

'The Russian spy family,' Robin nodded.

Carmel tutted. 'That was only a theory, Robin, and it wasn't even mine, it was Edie Rice's. You need to stop taking everything I say so literally. Anyway, no. I don't think that any more. I called over to her there and the accent was very convincing. And actually, her and Edie – do you know Edie? She was a couple of years ahead of you at Saint Ornatín's – they're going to Interiors World on Thursday morning and I said we'd go too!'

Carmel beamed. Robin rubbed her eyes.

'I'm going to bed.'

'Your father will mind Jack. I need to order a few tiles for the kitchen and maybe get some sheets. We can get a lift with Martha.'

Robin, tired and desperate to be lying alone in the dark, or as alone as she could get sharing a room and probably a bed with Jack, gave Carmel a kiss goodnight. 'Thanks, Mam. I appreciate the thought. But it's not for me.'

'It's not a request, my dearest,' her mother said sweetly, returning the kiss. 'It's a condition of continued tenancy.'

*** Pine Road Poker ***

Ruby:
Okay, ladies, we're all set for Friday. Madeline's going to clear out for the evening. The stakes are high, so bring your A game.

Fiona:
I still feel bad about making Madeline leave her home. Technically, the rule is No *Husbands*, so if Madeline wanted to stay ...

Ruby:
It's grand, Fiona. Don't worry about it. My darling wife has more interest in the male anatomy than she has in poker.

Edie:
Really looking forward to it, Ruby! Thanks so much for hosting x

Carmel:
Looking forward to taking all your hard-earned cash, ladies!

Ellen:
Monthly reminder that you've never won, Carmel ...

Carmel:
Just call me Carmel the Card Shark.

Trish:
Hope to make it, Ruby, but very busy at school this week.

Carmel:
Running scared already, Trish? We sharks can smell fear.

Ruby:
Isn't that dogs?

Fiona:
Should we invite the new woman? XXX

Ellen:
I doubt she'd be interested. She struck me as lacking a community spirit. Not to mention a basic understanding of dusting.

Rita Ann:
I won't be playing cards with anyone until my newspapers are returned. This has gone beyond a joke. I'm one Tuesday Health supplement away from calling the police.

Bernie:
Everything okay at the school, Trish? Anything the chair of the Parents' Association should know about? Regards, Bernie Watters-Reilly

Trish:
Everything's fine, Bernie.

[Is typing]

[Is typing]

Thanks.

SIX

· · · · · · · · · ·

The list had been up for an entire day before anyone thought to bring it to the attention of the principal. Or at least a supposedly responsible adult had known about it for an entire day. It could have been up longer; they couldn't say for sure when it had been etched into the back of the third stall in the first-floor boys' bathroom because they didn't know who had written it. But Paul Watson, the gormless PE teacher now sitting in front of her, had been made aware of it yesterday. Yesterday! Twenty-four bloody hours! Trish Walsh wished being principal gave you the power to sack someone on the spot.

'What I don't understand,' she said, leaning forward in her swivel chair, elbows on the desk and death stare firmly focused on one of the simpler teachers to have passed through the doors of Saint Ornatín's Secondary School, 'is how I am only hearing about this now?'

Gormless Paul hesitated. He looked around the small grey office as if someone might step in and provide him with a satisfactory answer. But it was only the two of them and she had told Rebecca, her secretary, that under no circumstances was anyone else to enter. She had to keep this contained until she figured out how the hell she was going to make it right.

'I . . . I wasn't sure what to do.' His Adam's apple quivered as he spoke. He was very thin, which she supposed was a good advertisement for physical education. Though teenage boys were no longer interested in being thin. They all aspired to buff now, even the smart ones. She went back to wishing she could fire him.

'So, you thought you'd just do nothing? Is that it?'

Stuck for anything constructive to say – though that didn't usually stop him – Paul shrugged helplessly and gave a little laugh. It was more a whimper than an actual chuckle, and she knew it was largely the result of nerves, but it was still the entirely wrong response and she brought both hands down hard on the desk. If she could have gotten away with it, Trish would only ever have hired female staff – they had more basic cop on – but the rest of the board was always reminding her that this was a mixed school and boys needed role models too.

Well, thought Trish, leaning back in her chair as Paul's face continued to flinch between worry and jocular, if this was the kind of role model Saint Ornatín's had to offer its male students then maybe she shouldn't be surprised they were in the situation they were in.

Trish already had more than enough on this week. Two girls in sixth year had now been hospitalised after fainting from a lack of food and the year head was at a loss for how to stop the epidemic from spreading. Trish had arranged for the Department of Education to send in two counsellors, but of course they had yet to arrive. A boy in second year had smacked another with a hurl after school on Monday, lamentably while still on school grounds, and broken his right leg; both lads said it was an accident but the invalid's parents were threatening to sue. They also had an unprecedented number of new students joining them this term – including two girls who had moved on to her road – and though they were now a month into it, Trish hadn't had a chance to introduce herself to any of them.

And then there was the fact that they'd become the latest victim of the garden rat epidemic on Pine Road. There was a general relief among the neighbours that the rats had yet to make their way inside – and indeed Trish had no desire to arrive down for breakfast to find a dining companion already in situ – but she took such pride in her garden that the thought of the little fucker burrowing through her winter flower beds was a source of great distress.

'Show me it,' she said finally, rising to her feet and pushing back the chair. 'I presume the bathroom is blocked off?'

Gormless Paul scrambled to his feet too. 'Well, I wasn't sure if—'

'Jesus Christ! Students are still using it? Have been using it since *yesterday*?'

'I . . .'

She threw up her hands. 'We're going to have to say something publicly. There's no way parents haven't heard. I'm surprised the media hasn't already been in contact. This is just the kind of thing that would have the *Sun* or the *Daily Mail* launching a campaign to increase the level of supervision in schools.' Trish halted at the side of the desk as her insides gave an involuntary lurch. She had said that to frighten Gormless Paul but as soon as it was out, she realised she wasn't exaggerating. That was exactly what would happen. She'd read about it if it was somebody else's school. God, she wished it was somebody else's school.

'Go and get Brendan,' she barked, letting go of the edge of the desk. 'Tell him to bring the keys for the bathroom, and I'll meet you both up there.'

There were twenty minutes left in the current period so the corridors were all but empty. A new student passed her on the stairwell – Trish recognised every teenager who had been in her charge before this term – but she hadn't the time to stop and introduce herself.

'Have you a pass?'

The girl held up a toilet break card.

'Right,' she allowed, striding on. 'Back to class.'

Trish walked with confidence, stopping twice to pick up loose copybook pages and a well-chewed pen lid. She folded the lined paper and slid it into her back pocket and kept the lid for the bin. Her steps echoed along the first-floor corridor.

When she got to the boys' bathroom, she paused. She knocked loudly on the door. As expected, there was no response. Still, she did not enter. After another couple of seconds, she crossed the corridor to the classroom opposite and peered in. Mrs Leech, teaching sixth-year history. There was a trend for pink hair this year – neon dye and anorexia. A virus would take longer to spread through Saint Ornatín's than a craze.

She turned at the sound of echoing footsteps and watched as Gormless Paul and Brendan came towards her; Paul talking away, Brendan nodding slowly. The caretaker was carrying a large collection of keys in one hand and a massive workbox in the other.

'Mrs Walsh.' He inclined his head as they drew closer.

'Hello, Brendan,' said Trish, smiling. Brendan had been at the school longer than her and was one of the few faculty members she never had to worry about. 'How's Laurie?'

'Arra,' replied Brendan, throwing his head up and sniffing slightly. 'Same as she ever was.'

'That's good.' Although Trish wasn't sure if it was or not. Brendan's wife went through bouts of depression. She looked from the caretaker to the PE teacher. 'Right. Shall we go in?'

Emboldened by the presence of the others, she pushed open the door of the bathroom. The scent of teenage boy permeated the entire school but, as the door flapped back, the distinctive mix of aftershave and sweat intensified. Trish avoided breathing in through her nose.

'It's just–' Paul side-stepped awkwardly around her, his Adam's apple vibrating in his long, thin neck. He pushed open the door of the third stall. 'Here.' He stepped back, leaving plenty of space for Trish to enter the toilet cubicle. She glanced at Brendan who watched her blankly. She was the principal; of course, she would go in first.

Trish stepped into the stall and caught the door as it went to swing shut behind her.

There it was.

Scrawled in black permanent marker on the cheap metal of the bathroom door. The handwriting was as scrawny and childish as the boy who'd no doubt written it, but the size of it, the confidence with which it took up so much space, made her stomach lurch again.

She read through the list without taking in any of the names and only when she got to the end and exhaled loudly did she realise she'd been holding her breath. There was no mention of her youngest daughter.

'Can I?' Brendan raised his eyebrows and Trish shuffled out of the stall. 'Jesus Christ,' muttered the caretaker when he'd squeezed into the cubicle and closed the door slightly. 'You think boys are getting better and then . . .'

'So what should we do?' asked Trish.

Brendan shook his head ruefully. She didn't even bother looking at Paul.

'I think first things first, we paint over it,' she said. 'Yes?'

'If you think so.'

Brendan's expression was impossible to read. Trish was terrible at taking orders – she'd identified a reluctance to delegate as her biggest weakness when interviewing for the principalship four years ago – but in this instance, she wished someone would just tell her what to do.

Would painting over it be seen as destroying evidence? (Evidence! Oh Christ! Would they have to get the guards involved?) But she could hardly leave it up for students to see, and she couldn't shut off an entire bathroom for more than a couple of hours. Every other toilet in the place would be blocked by lunchtime tomorrow. And she was not about to shut the school.

'We'll take a photo of it first,' she said. 'I'll keep that as a record and I'll make the board of management aware. But then, yes, I think we paint over it.' The two men watched her; Gormless

59

Paul twitching. It was herself she was really convincing. 'Good. And we'll lock this particular bathroom until the paint dries. Stick an out-of-order sign on it and hopefully by the morning, anyone who's seen the thing will have forgotten. Boys tend to forget. You haven't heard the students talking about this? Have you, Gorm — Mr Watson?'

The PE teacher, who was now pointlessly staring at the frosted-glass window, jumped. 'No. No, I haven't heard anything. Well, not since yesterday, when one of the students mentioned it to me.'

'Yesterday?'

Trish raised a hand to Brendan, closed her eyes and shook her head. 'I know. I know.'

The caretaker let out a low whistle and Gormless Paul at least had the good grace to look sheepish.

'Well,' said Brendan, 'I've got a small thing of white paint here. I could paint over it now.'

'Okay, yes.' Trish paused. Was she doing the right thing? If she made the parents aware of it, she'd risk making a deal out of some immature prank that would otherwise be forgotten. But if she didn't acknowledge it and word had already spread, she could be accused of a cover-up. She'd take a photo, send it to the board of management; that way she'd have acted responsibly and the burden of knowledge would be spread around a bit.

She reached for her pocket only to remember her phone was charging in her office. 'Have either of you got your mobile on you? We need to get a photo first.'

The two men shook their heads.

'I, eh, I have a pen, if you wanted to copy it down, maybe?' That was Paul, with his first useful contribution of the day, if not the school year.

Trish remembered the loose paper she'd found on the corridor and pulled a sheet from her back pocket. 'Right.'

Paul handed her a fountain pen and she returned to the cubicle.

'I can do it if you like.' Brendan's voice from the other side of the metal door.

Trish smiled. She needed to see about getting that man more money.

'I'm fine. Thank you.'

She allowed the door to swing shut fully as she leaned the paper against the stall wall. She read through the list again. All the names belonged to fifth- and sixth-year students – as if that somehow made it better.

The last one on the list: Sinead Costello. Wasn't she from the new family on Pine Road? Trish felt an irrational wave of guilt. The poor girl had only been here a month.

Trish paused and cleared her throat. Then, ignoring the tremble in her hand, she began to write.

SEVEN

• • • • • • • • • • • • • • • •

'**Y**ou know Mrs Ryan used to put her cats to bed? One night she forgot to close her curtains – the curtain rail may actually have fallen down – and myself and Mick saw her, in her bedroom, putting one of the cats into a cot. An honest-to-God human baby cot. Mad, or what? Very mad. Well, we thought it was mad anyway . . .'

Martha was only half listening to Carmel's ramblings as she navigated the station wagon down the narrow strip of Pine Road not occupied by parked cars. Getting off this road without clipping a wing mirror was stressful enough, never mind having three residents who possibly owned some of those wing mirrors in the vehicle with her.

'Did she?' gasped Edie, leaning forward from where she sat behind Martha and sticking her head in between the two front seats. 'I never heard that.'

'Oh yes,' said Carmel, twisting about in the front passenger seat. 'She used to take them on holidays with her too. Ruby, at number thirteen, met her one afternoon wheeling a suitcase out of her house and she got an awful fright when she heard this whining sound coming from the bag. "What've you got in there, Mrs Ryan?" she asks. And Mrs Ryan unzips the suitcase to reveal eight cats. Eight! All reaching up to Ruby with their little trafficked claws. She was off to stay with her sister in Carlow and she was taking the whole lot with her.'

'Am I going right now, Carmel?'

Her co-pilot glanced back to the road. 'Yes, right and then right again at the very end of the main stretch. Eight little kitties in the suitcase, and nothing else! Not even a toothbrush. Literally, mad as a bag of cats.'

'Gosh,' marvelled Edie. 'I hope it wasn't an expensive suitcase.'

Martha was out on Forest Avenue now and feeling a little more relaxed. It had been nice to wake up this morning and have somewhere she had to be. It was only slightly ruined by how enthusiastic Robert had been about it. If he hadn't said anything, if he just never talked to her, she thought she could go the rest of her life without thinking about what had happened.

'Lovely car,' observed Carmel, running her hand over the dashboard, then down along the side of her seat. 'Some good quality material in this.'

Martha kept her eyes on the road. 'Thank you,' she said, the words sticking in her throat. 'We've had it a while.'

'And why wouldn't you?' agreed Carmel. 'Nowadays people get new cars at the drop of a hat. When we first moved here, there was probably four cars on the whole of Pine Road. Now, it's more likely to be four cars per household. The only upside in my two never bothering their arses to learn to drive is now they're back living with me, they haven't brought extra cars with them.'

Martha glanced in the rear-view mirror and caught Carmel's daughter's eye before she went back to staring out the window. Robin hadn't said a word since they'd gotten in the car.

'I noticed that man you were talking about, with the planks of wood and the chairs?'

'Shay Morrissey.' Carmel nodded. 'What I'd like to know is who he thinks he's reserving the parking spaces for. He hasn't a friend to his name, and once his daughters moved out, they never looked back. He tries to charge for the parking spaces on match days. The tight git.'

'I thought Daniel was going to deck him the other day,' Edie piped up, her eyes like expanding pools. 'Daniel sees him laying out his stupid planks and he goes mental. Red rag to a bull, especially if there's nowhere else to park. And as soon as Shay utters the words "nine feet out from my property", Daniel's face actually starts to balloon. It can take hours to return to its normal size.'

'Daniel's a lovely chap,' explained Carmel. 'He's a great mechanic. Isn't that right, Edie dear?'

'Oh yes! He's the best.' Edie stuck her head back into the gap between the two front seats. 'He has his own place up in Glasnevin – Carmody Motors – but if you have any immediate trouble you should knock up to us. He'd be delighted to help.'

'And tell me this now,' said Carmel, 'is he still trying to impregnate you?'

'Mam! You can't ask that!'

Martha glanced in the rear-view mirror. Robin had torn herself away from the window and was looking at the back of her mother's head in disgust.

'Oh, calm down. Edie's the one who told me. She doesn't mind talking about it. Do you, Edie?'

'I don't mind at all,' agreed Edie.

Martha thought this was probably an understatement; she'd only met the woman once and even she knew about her procreation plans.

'I'd say I dream about being a mam more nights than I don't. The little toes and fingers! And Daniel will make a great dad. He's not as obsessive about it as me, but that's probably better. He's a perfectionist. Doesn't like to do anything by halves. Always wants everything to be just right.'

Martha came to a line of large retail centres. 'Is it this turn?'

'That's it,' said Carmel, 'straight through to the end of the complex. What are you after today anyway, Martha? A mattress, Edie was saying.'

'And maybe a wardrobe. The ones in our old house were all built in.'

'Where was that again?'

'The house?' Martha checked her blind spot. 'Limerick.'

'I know, but where in Limerick?'

'Just . . .' Martha frowned at a point somewhere between the speedometer and petrol gauge. 'Outside the city.'

The seat behind her creaked.

'Well, it wasn't a cheap move anyway,' said Carmel. 'The price of houses in Dublin is unbelievable. Fiona at number ten nearly wets herself every time the Dublin home value report comes out and Pine Road is up, but if you sell you'd have to buy somewhere else to live, so what's the difference? Are you from Dublin originally or why was it you moved?'

'We fancied a change.' Martha pulled into a parking space.

'Ah yeah, yeah,' replied Carmel, her tone clearly saying, *Cut the crap*. 'Why Dublin, though?'

Martha cut the engine and glanced in the mirror. Edie was leaning forward. Even Robin was watching her. Martha searched for a truthful answer that wouldn't invite more questions. She'd been asked it already, casually, by plenty of people: the school, the estate agent, the guys with the moving van. But it was harder to dodge when they had her surrounded.

'My husband got a promotion,' she said finally.

'Bank of Ireland, isn't it?'

'That's right. And the new job was in Dublin. Right.' She unclipped her seat belt. 'Everyone good to get out?'

'Our career guidance teacher was always pushing the bank,' said Edie, closing the car door after her and brushing down her pink, faux-fur coat. 'Nursing for the girls, engineering for the boys, and the bank for all.'

'You know Edie was in Saint Ornatín's at the same time as you, Robin?' said Carmel, zipping up her windbreaker.

'You probably don't remember,' said Edie quickly, blushing. 'I was two years ahead.'

Robin shook her head. 'My memory is fried these days. But I've heard all about you. Great hair, sunny disposition, excellent collection of Agatha Christie novels.'

'Oh, well,' said Edie, clearly thrilled as she ran her fingers through her long, thick ponytail. 'I don't know about that . . .'

'My mother's a big fan. Aren't you, Mam?'

'The daughter I never had,' agreed Carmel. 'So anyway,' she turned to Martha, 'you moved here for his promotion . . .'

'Jesus, Mam,' said Robin. 'Can you not take a hint?'

'You'll have to excuse my daughter. She's not used to engaging with the outside world.'

Robin rolled her eyes.

'She was dumped a couple of months ago by an absolute chancer and, somewhere between moulding the shape of her arse into our settee and eating dry cereal, she seems to have forgotten how to behave in company.'

'I wasn't dumped, Mam. I left him.'

'And you should be glad you did. A toe-rag.'

'You don't even know him.'

'Arra, you'd know it just by looking at him. He had toe-rag eyes.'

'What was wrong with him?' asked Edie, eyes wide, voice hushed.

'Nothing,' said Robin.

'Everything,' said Carmel at the same time.

Martha smiled politely. She didn't like it when people bickered in public, even if it was in jest. 'Shall we go inside?'

The double doors slid open and the women were hit by generic elevator music and the scent of various aromatic diffusers. Martha surveyed the sea of beds, couches and dining tables that stretched as far as the eye could see. Two shoppers – or possibly just tired passers-by – were sitting on one of those L-shaped sofas that seemed to be all the rage as three staff members shuffled aimlessly nearby.

'I love these places,' whispered Edie. 'They're so peaceful.'

'They're peaceful because everyone's doing their shopping online,' said Carmel, as they walked up the central aisle.

'But don't they just make you feel *calm?*'

Carmel looked doubtful. 'No. They make me feel like I'm being fleeced. And it's not a church, pet; you don't have to whisper.'

Robin started reading out the prices of some of the beds. No matter what number she said, Carmel reacted with breathless indignation.

'Jesus tonight!'

'*How* much?'

'Christ almighty!'

'Is the house included in that?'

'But look how much you're saving,' said Edie, stopping in front of a four-poster pine bed and reading out the price-tag, where the text giving the amount saved was printed three times larger than the actual, astronomical amount due.

'Mmm.' Carmel lowered her glasses to read the sign herself. 'It's amazing how you always manage to be saving money in these places. They'd have you thinking they were running a charity.'

'Oh!' called Edie. 'The bathroom section!' She looked beyond Carmel's disapproving head to the far right-hand side of the store and let out a swoony sigh. 'I'll be in Tiles if anyone needs me!'

'I'm off to look for sheets,' said Carmel. 'See if they can't convince me I'm actually *making* money.'

Carmel strode purposefully through the dining tables in the direction of Linen and Martha glanced back at Robin.

'Not so into homewares?'

'Not really,' said the young woman who, Martha thought, looked more like her than she did her own mother. Robin was tall and thin and good-looking in a way that was both plain and striking. Not that Martha would have called herself good-looking, not out loud, but you don't get to forty-four without knowing how other people perceive you.

'Your mum said you and your son are staying with her for a while?'

'Mm-hmm.' Robin looked around with the bored expression of the desperately cool.

'It's tough being a single mum.'

'Excuse me?'

'I was one, for four years before I met Robert. I know what it's like.'

Robin frowned. 'Oh no, I'm not—' She stopped herself, looking at Martha now. 'Shit.'

'You all right?'

'I'm a single mother.' Then again, under her breath with more emphasis: 'I am a single mother.'

'I didn't mean to startle you.'

'No.' Robin shook her head. 'It's grand. I just hadn't thought . . . Single mother. Right, okay.'

'Well, if it's any consolation, I loved being a single mum.' The four years she and Ellis had spent living in a rented room in Limerick city felt like a fairy tale now, the curve of his little body in the rickety bed, the heat of him, curled into her, legs to the left, just as he had lain in her womb. 'I almost resented Robert when he came along.' Martha laughed. 'Not for long, of course. We had the girls a few years later. You don't have favourite children, of course, but,' she smiled, 'it's hard to compete with that sort of bond.'

Martha was suddenly self-aware. It was very unlike her – the old or the new her – to be so forward with personal details.

'Anyway,' she said, smoothing down her coat, 'I'm going to check out the mattresses.'

The mattress section was expansive and Martha read through the differences between pocket spring, innerspring, memory foam and pillow top. She didn't have much of an opinion either way, though Robert was very vocal in his preference for a hard mattress. The one they'd brought from Limerick was fine, she thought, but he was convinced it had gone soft in the middle. 'Nothing fancy,' he'd said that morning, excited by the possibility of 'a good night's sleep' and his wife miraculously returning to the person she once was. 'Just something with a bit of structure.'

Still wearing her coat and shoes, Martha lowered herself on to the most expensive mattress and spread her arms and legs like a starfish.

Helen and Audrey had sent a photo from their weekly Abbyvale hike yesterday. She supposed they thought it was the right thing to do, to show they hadn't forgotten about her. *Greetings from the summit!* the text read. Martha had stared at the photo for several minutes, then she'd put it away without replying.

She felt a presence to her right and opened her eyes. A man in a short-sleeved uniform shirt was leaning over her.

'Worth every euro, isn't it? The softest sleep you'll ever have.' He patted the mattress with such gusto that Martha found herself rocking. 'Like dozing off on a cloud. These bad boys are an extra five hundred at Bed City. So you're saving already.'

She closed her eyes again.

'What do you reckon? Are you tempted?'

She forgot about the salesman and pictured Robert's reaction when he felt how soft it was and saw the price.

'I'll take it.'

'You . . .? Brilliant. Excellent choice, ma'am. It comes with a two-year warranty, you know, and a mattress protector . . .'

Martha's eyes stayed shut. Why was he still there, selling? The deal was done.

'Excellent. Really excellent. You won't regret it. I'll go and get the delivery form.'

He scurried off and she tried to erase his greedy stare. She used to enjoy that side of being attractive – men turning in the street, women looking her up and down – but now she found it mildly distressing.

She was worried the girls weren't coping as well as she'd thought. Yesterday, Sinead had arrived home from school taunting Orla about the possibility that she might have worms and that she was always hungry because they were wriggling about her stomach sucking up her nutrients. The two of them were always arguing but this one had clearly been going on a while. Orla was on the point of tears and, more troublingly, Sinead was relishing it.

Martha told Sinead to take it easy but it escalated into an argument where her eldest daughter got so mad her face and neck became blotchy and she was yelling that Martha didn't care about them, that she was a coward, that she had ruined everything. Martha had let her yell and scream and stomp up the stairs.

Sinead was right. She hadn't phoned the guards since before Christmas. She hadn't checked in once. How could it be that she – who had harangued sports coaches over keeping her daughters on the bench, and fought with the county council until the Abbyvale bin collection was made weekly – just did not want to know?

There was a loud crash and Martha's hand went to her chest.

Her eyes sprang open. 'Jesus!'

'Sorry, sorry.' Carmel was a few metres away, reaching down to pick up two porcelain containers. 'Diffusers,' she said, holding them up. 'You burn incense in them. We had a sewerage leak last year and they worked wonders.'

Martha took a deep breath and waited for her heart to calm down. She never realised how close she was to the edge until the most innocuous thing gave her a nudge. 'What are they for this time?'

'Oh, they're for your house,' said Carmel. 'Maybe it doesn't smell any more, and I'm not accusing you of anything so don't look at me like that, but when Mrs Ryan was in the place . . . Jesus! The stink.'

Carmel dropped the diffusers at the end of the mattress and the thing almost swallowed them up. It was like a cloud. She'd give the salesman that.

'There was a bit of a smell,' Martha conceded. 'But I think we got it. The garden is trickier.'

'Oh, I know. Many a child was reduced to tears when their ball went over the lane and into Mrs Ryan's nettle forest. She never once gave back a ball. And if a kid knocked on her door looking for it, she'd go and complain to their parents that they were harassing her. A battle-axe of a woman.'

'I take it she's not missed, then?'

'I'd say they buried her upside down in case she tried to dig herself out.'

Edie and Robin came towards them, with the salesman not far behind.

'Good afternoon, ladies.' He handed a clipboard to Martha. 'Free delivery is included with this mattress, so you're saving yourself sixty quid there. And we'll take away your old one, free of charge. That's usually forty quid, so another saving for you.'

Martha read through the form, took the pen from the holder and filled in her new address.

'You're buying this one?' exclaimed Carmel, reading the sign for the luxury mattress. 'Fifteen hundred euro!'

'That's the amount saved, Mam.' Robin put her finger on the large red figure and then slid it across to the smaller black one.

Carmel looked at her, aghast. 'Martha! Four *thousand* euro?'

Edie peered over Carmel's shoulder. 'You could do up a whole bathroom for that,' she said wistfully.

The salesman gave Carmel the indulgent smile people generally reserved for small children. 'It's an excellent price for a life-changing mattress.'

'It'd want to do more than change your life,' exclaimed Carmel. 'It'd want to be making me money while I sleep on it for that price.'

Martha handed back the form. 'I'm going to take a couple of pillows as well. Soft ones.'

'We have a buy-two-save-twenty-euro-on-a-third offer currently running.'

'Fine.'

'Excellent! I also wanted to let you ladies know about our daily deal. We're offering an Ultra Safety 3000 house alarm for four hundred and twenty euro. That's a saving of more than fifty per cent on the system. You'll also save on installation fees, which we offer for just twenty euro – a saving of eighty euro. And it should save you another forty quid every year on your home insurance.'

'Does it come with garda call-out assistance?' asked Edie. 'Or is that separate?'

'No, it's built in. So, you're saving on that too.' He looked around at the group, clearly delighted with his sales pitch. 'Any questions?'

Carmel raised her hand.

'Yes?'

'Is your annual bonus dependent on how many times you can get the word "save" or "saving" into a conversation?'

The man turned his attention back to Martha. 'The Ultra Safety 3000 is fool proof. Any hint of an intruder and the police will be notified.'

'That's not true.'

'Excuse me?'

'It's not fool proof. No alarm system is fool proof.'

The man smiled, nodding, like he was on Martha's side but also had so much to teach her. 'It's unbelievable but it's true, and, all in, you'd be saving about five hundred euro.'

'It's like a cult,' muttered Carmel.

Did these people go through customer service training? The customer is always right – and in this case she really was. Martha had real, lived experience. What did this slippery little upstart have? What did he know, except how to maximise his commission by taking vulnerable people for idiots?

'It's not true,' snapped Martha, a familiar flash of anger coming over her, heat rising in her body. 'So please, stop saying it.'

The salesman gave a small awkward squeak of a laugh, like when someone stood on Oscar's chew toy. 'Pardon me, ma'am, but it is.'

'I had that system in my last home and it didn't work.' The flash of rage was slower to leave this time. It burned up her arms, on to her shoulders, spread all the way around her neck. 'Five men broke into my home without that alarm so much as beeping. So don't you tell me, or anyone else, that it's fool proof. That's false advertising and I won't hesitate to report you. I will make an official complaint to the consumer protection agency.'

His smile dropped. 'I'm sorry. It's what we're told . . .' He glanced down at the form Martha had filled out. 'I'll just go and get this processed.'

The young man left and Martha brought the back of her hand to her throat in an attempt to cool it. She felt a rim of sweat forming along her hairline. Just as she went to sit back down on the mattress, she remembered the other three women.

'Your house was burgled?' said Robin, watching her.

'By five men?' whispered Edie.

Martha pulled her handbag from the end of the bed and hauled it up over her shoulder. 'Four or five,' she said, pushing her hair behind her ears. 'I can't fully remember.' *Lies*. She was just like Robert now. 'They came in one morning just before the girls went to school.'

'In the morning?' echoed Edie, then quieter: 'Who breaks into a house in a morning?'

'Did they take anything?' asked Carmel.

'No.' Martha looked her in the eye, to show she wasn't lying, that she wasn't like Robert. 'They took nothing.'

'That's unusual,' mused Edie. 'What were they after, I wonder?'

She shouldn't have mentioned it. She should have kept her mouth shut.

'Still, you must have gotten a fright.'

Martha shrugged. 'These things happen.' She snapped her bag shut. 'It's just part of life. Right. I'll pay, and we'll hit the road.'

'Is that why you moved?'

She hesitated. It was more than Robin's appearance that made her think of herself. What was it?

'Like I said, Robert got a promotion.'

A half-truth was still a lie.

She threw her bag over her shoulder and headed for the register. Her heels clip-clopped along the pristine tiles, and she heard their sharp rebuke.

Lies, lies, lies, lies, lies, lies, lies.

*** Pine Road Poker ***

Ellen:
I highly recommend everyone read Bernie's EXCELLENT column in today's Independent if you haven't already done so. Obviously, they're all excellent, but today's might just be life changing.

Bernie:
Thank you, Ellen. I've had some great feedback on it already. It's gotten a few robust debates going on Facebook, to say the least.

Ellen:
I'm sure it has! I've been arguing with myself over it all morning!

You should really consider entering it for some awards.

Ruby:
I hear the Pulitzer is looking for entries ...

Ellen:
I know you're being sarcastic, Ruby, but it really is that good.

Fiona:
YASSS KWEEN!!!

XXX

Ruby:
Go on so. What's it about? They only get the FT into our office.

Bernie:
It's an examination of plastic box versus paper bag in terms of the best way to package a school lunch. I look at retaining freshness, environmental impact and which is easier to clean.

Ellen:
It's absolutely ground-breaking.

If anyone wants to borrow a copy, I have two.

EIGHT

......•......

Edie put the key into her front door and pushed. She wasn't singing any song in particular, just a general hum of giddy contentment. The excursion had been a total success for reasons that had nothing to do with shopping. She hadn't bought a thing, actually, which should show Daniel he wasn't the only one who took their finances seriously. Although she still didn't think having children was as expensive as he made it out to be. Her mother said that until a child was two, you could basically have them sleeping in a drawer.

She dropped her keys into the Waterford Crystal bowl on the hall table that Edie didn't like but felt bad about regifting because it had been a wedding present from Daniel's aunt.

'Daniel? Bae?' she called into the silent house. Still at work. Good. She opened the door to his office and did a little shimmy of excitement.

Edie had been too distracted by the company to think about buying anything. Robin actual Dwyer had followed her into the bathroom department just to chat!

Robin had been two years behind at school but of course Edie remembered her. While she'd been a late bloomer, and a generally unremarkable teenager, Robin had been top of the class, gorgeous and impossibly cool. She wasn't quite the knockout she'd been a decade ago – her face was a little thinner, its edges harder and her wavy hair not as full – and she didn't seem to have done much with her academic ability. Edie wasn't sure if she had a job at all. But she was still beautiful and cool and, essentially, a dream target friend.

And today, Edie had hit that target in the bullseye.

Robin had come looking specifically for her. She'd asked Edie about her job, and the people who stayed at the hotel, and Daniel. All of which was obviously a promising sign that Robin at least didn't hate her. But then, as they were going in search of Carmel and Martha, Robin had invited her to go for a drink. Just like that! Edie hadn't made a proper friend since school, but she was pretty sure that was the grown-up equivalent of knocking on someone's door and asking if they wanted to come out to play.

They were going out Sunday night. It wasn't a lot of time to decide what to wear – Edie always found 'casual' more difficult than 'formal' – but she'd figure it out. Robin actual Dwyer!

'To the Fern, for one or two,' the target friend had said as they'd made their way through the mattresses.

'Cool, yeah,' Edie had replied, doing her best to mirror Robin's free-and-easy, one-shoulder shrug. 'Cool.'

Of course, if everything went according to plan with Daniel, Edie wouldn't be able to drink on Sunday night. Maybe just the one Chardonnay, but that was it. She'd have Sprite Zero. She'd read a lot of conflicting opinions on message boards about whether or not it was okay to drink in that limbo period between trying to conceive and finding out if you were pregnant. But she didn't want to take any chances.

She and Daniel were supposed to have started trying last year. They'd talked about it on their honeymoon: six months of marital bliss, then down to business. Daniel had been as excited as her. He kept pointing out all the cute kids on the beach in Cancun. Even before they were married, they'd talked about kids a lot and it was always 'when' not 'if'. She hadn't imagined that. But then the summer came, and a new garage opened in Glasnevin, and Daniel felt the hit. He was relying on some big contract to save him in the autumn, and to pay for their bathroom renovation, and when that fell through, he was properly stressed. For the first time, he ended a quarter in the red. He started stressing about money, became convinced that they didn't have enough for a family. He stayed up late watching TV because he couldn't sleep and got a prescription for sedatives. Edie tried to reassure him; they didn't earn a lot but how many couples in their twenties owned their homes outright? But when Daniel was stressed there was no talking to him. Business picked up a bit before Christmas, but he didn't seem any less worried. It had shaken his sense of himself as dependable, responsible, prepared. Any time she mentioned kids, he either shut down the conversation or started up about how financially precarious they were. It gave her a sick feeling in her stomach. Like maybe money was just a handy excuse.

But it was fine now. Absolutely fine. They hadn't started trying last month because they'd gotten into a thundering row about it – she tried not to dwell on the overlapping of her ovulation windows and their fights – but they were trying this weekend. That was what they'd agreed. Friday to Sunday was going to be wall-to-wall sex at number nineteen. What man could have a problem with that?

Edie powered up Daniel's computer and wandered over to the window as she waited for the machine to come to life. She looked from the cupid statues in Ellen Russell-O'Toole's front lawn – it was Valentine's Day next week – down to Martha Rigby's more unkempt garden. It was ironic, if that was the right word, because Martha herself was so beautifully put together. Edie often wondered who these women were that looked good in Cos dresses. Well, now she knew. Martha Rigby pulled it off. She was so elegant. She was stylish and confident – and she was generous. She'd given Edie an unopened interiors magazine without her even having to ask.

When they arrived back to Pine Road, Edie had helped Martha to carry pillows into the house – the mattress was being delivered the next day – and she'd spied the publication lying upside down on the hall table.

'Take it,' said Martha, following Edie's gaze to the glossy magazine still in its cellophane wrap. 'I don't know why I brought it with us. I never even open the things. I finally cancelled the subscription when we moved.'

Edie sat down at Daniel's computer and typed in the password: Daniel4Edie. She pulled the magazine from her bag and did another excited shimmy. The only thing better than a real-life mystery was one that came with a clue.

When Martha said her old house had been burgled, Edie's first reaction was sympathy. Honestly. But then her detective instinct had kicked in. And when Martha said they'd broken in in the morning – not the early a.m. but the actual morning, just before the girls went to school – and that there had been five of them . . . Well, she wouldn't be human if her interest hadn't been piqued. Five men, daytime, and they took nothing? Edie's brain had gone full Nancy Drew. She'd had to yammer on about the Pine Road rat infestation all the way home just to keep herself from demanding more information.

Which was why she'd offered to carry in the pillows. Thankfully Carmel had her arms full with sheets. Any Pine Road resident would have jumped at an opportunity to snoop, obviously, but Edie was on the hunt for clues. That was when she spotted the magazine.

'I'll never read it, honestly,' said Martha, flapping her hand. 'Take it.'

And so she had.

Edie had thanked Martha and told her how much she enjoyed interiors magazines. What she didn't mention, however, was that she already owned this edition. The November issue had a thirty-page bathroom special so Edie, who hadn't yet known the big job at the garage had fallen through, had bought it for herself and read it cover to cover.

Edie turned Martha's copy of the magazine over in her hands.

What this copy had that hers didn't was the packaging: the clear cellophane wrap and the white address sticker fixed to the reverse.

Martha Rigby,

Abbyvale Lodge,

Abbyvale,

Co. Limerick

No longer singing her nonsense jingle, Edie laid the magazine to one side and opened a browser. Curiosity had always been a terrible weakness. But she had a good nose for mysteries. Maybe she could help.

Edie glanced at the address sticker one more time and, carefully, began to type.

NINE

· · · · · · · · · · · ·

Trish's mobile was vibrating its way across her kitchen counter. They were trying to decide who was bringing what to Ruby's for poker tomorrow night. Trish would not be going. She couldn't chance sitting at the same table as Bernie Watters-Reilly. She kept expecting everyone to find out at any given minute.

She switched her phone to silent and turned it over so she couldn't see the screen.

Every time it rang in the twenty-four hours since Gormless Paul had wandered into her office and ruined her week – although hopefully not her career – Trish expected it to be a journalist or an outraged parent. That morning an unknown number had flashed up and she had stared at it in horror until it stopped. It took her an hour to work up the courage to listen to the voicemail. In the end, it had been the exterminator – returning her call four whole days after she'd phoned him.

Trish had sent an official email to the head of the school management board outlining what had happened and wondering if they should inform the Department of Education. Then the head of the board had phoned her and had an entirely unofficial conversation in which expletives were used and he said he knew full well she was just sharing the blame around, making sure there was a paper trail to cover her arse, and that of course he didn't want the department involved.

She sat at her kitchen island stirring the long-dissolved sugar into her coffee and staring out into her beautifully landscaped garden. Trish clanged the spoon against the china cup. She would give it a week before she allowed herself to relax.

'Mum?'

She stopped stirring. Emily, her youngest daughter, had appeared in the kitchen, still wearing her uniform. A ladder was starting to form in her right sleeve. 'Did you check if Laura's old school jumper was up in her wardrobe?'

'This is Laura's,' said Emily, opening the fridge. 'Where's Dad? I'm starving.'

'He's gone to get pork chops.'

'Did I tell you I'm considering becoming a vegetarian?' asked Emily idly, closing the fridge and moving on to the cupboards.

'You didn't, no.' There was no chance of Emily becoming a vegetarian; the child hated almost every vegetable. 'How's school going?'

'Fine.'

'Just fine? Nothing to report. No annoying teachers . . . no annoying boys?'

Emily looked at her with mild contempt. 'I'm not ten, Mum. I actually *like* boys now?'

'No gossip whirling around the locker room? No rumours flying about?'

Emily closed the cupboard and brought a hand to her hip. 'Mum, you know you're a double pain, right? As in, a pain in the side and a pane of glass. I can see right through you. I told you before: I'm not your spy. It's hard enough having the principal as your mum, without everyone thinking I'm a rat too.'

'I was just—'

'Nope!'

The bell went and Emily sauntered out of the kitchen, right past the front door and up the stairs, as if that ringing sound had nothing to do with her. Trish sighed loudly as she got down from her stool and went to let her husband in.

On the plus side, she thought as she reached for the latch, she was almost positive Emily hadn't a clue what she'd been attempting to get at.

TEN

Though '**Martha** Rigby' didn't lead to much, the first result for 'Abbyvale Lodge' was an article from the *Limerick Leader* dated 9 November 2018 – three months ago.

Bravery Medal for Abbyvale Tiger Raid 'Hero'

Edie opened it and read the first couple of paragraphs.

'Oh gosh,' she whispered, looking up from the computer and instinctively glancing over her shoulder. She felt like a child pilfering from the biscuit jar. She shouldn't be doing this. She tried to summon up the shame she knew she'd feel later, but it was no good; curiosity overrode everything else.

She kept reading. Her hand inched closer to her mouth as she made her way through the article and connected the people being written about with the ones who'd just moved in across the road.

'Oh gosh, oh gosh.'

Done, she sat there dumbfounded. Then she pressed 'print'. 'Poor Martha Rigby,' she whispered to herself as she waited for the printer to kick noisily into action. But it didn't. She pressed 'print' again. Still nothing. Again, and again, and again, until finally it spluttered into action and shunted out five copies of the newspaper article.

Edie threw the first four in the bin and carried the fifth copy through to the kitchen. She made herself a decaffeinated coffee – they would be getting down to business tomorrow, after all – and pulled out the notebook she used when listening to true-crime podcasts or watching Netflix documentaries and trying to guess the culprit before it was revealed.

She clicked her pen into action, picked up the article and, slowly this time, read it again.

Bravery Medal for Abbyvale Tiger Raid 'Hero'

Reporter: Cathal McMahon

An Abbyvale resident has been awarded a medal for outstanding bravery from the city's lord mayor after thwarting an attempted tiger raid at his home on Thursday last.

Mr Robert Costello, of Abbyvale Lodge, Co. Limerick, was awarded the medal at a private ceremony this week. His wife and daughters were not in attendance and are believed to be recovering from the ordeal. Mr Costello, a manager at the Limerick City branch of Bank of Ireland, thanked Eoghan Ó Mhurchú, the Limerick City lord mayor, and asked for the privacy of his family to be respected at this time.

A so-called 'tiger raid' – where an employee is forced to retrieve company money for a gang of thieves while his family is held hostage – was attempted on the morning of 1 November at Mr Costello's home. An armed gang of five men entered the premises at 7.30 a.m. wearing balaclavas and carrying crowbars. They ordered Mr Costello, his wife and their two children into the living room where they were tied to the radiators. Garda sources told the *Limerick Leader* that the gang threatened to turn on the central heating if any of the family misbehaved.

At 8.30 a.m., Mr Costello, who has worked at the Limerick bank branch for 17 years, was ordered to go to his place of work and remove the contents of the safe. He was told his family would be held hostage by the gang members while he was gone. He was ordered to go about his morning as normal and return home with the cash at lunchtime, at which point his family would be released.

The gang informed Mr Costello that his Volkswagen station wagon had been fitted with a GPS tracker and that a sixth gang member would follow his vehicle. They threatened to do serious harm to his family if he delineated from the instructed path.

However, the brave Mr Costello did not do as the gang said. Several minutes into the thirty-minute drive from his home to the Bank of Ireland branch, he noticed the vehicle that had been shadowing him had disappeared. When he arrived at the bank, Mr Costello raised the alarm with local guards.

Armed detectives from Limerick City's organised crime branch arrived at Abbyvale Lodge shortly after 11 a.m. While the captors managed to escape through the fields to the rear of Mr Costello's home, Gardaí are following a definite line of inquiry and have drawn up a shortlist of suspects. Mr Costello's wife and daughters were unharmed.

Gardaí believe the gang had Mr Costello's home under surveillance for two months before the attempted robbery. They have appealed for any witnesses who saw a silver Renault Laguna with a Dublin registration plate in the area during that time, and particularly on the night of 31 October and morning of 1 November.

'There is nothing as frightening as our loved ones being placed in the path of serious harm, and few people would have blamed Robert Costello if he had complied with the demands of these cowardly criminals. Yet his bravery in the face of such anguish has made not just his family proud, but his city and county too,' said Mr Ó Mhurchú, as he awarded the medal for outstanding bravery.

'Robert Costello is a Limerick hero and he symbolises the best of our great city. His actions send out a message. They tell thugs and gangs that they do not own us, and we are not afraid. Robert's actions also send a message to international enterprises seeking to establish a base in Europe. They say: "Come on in to Limerick

– the home of highly trained graduates, competitive commercial rents and an exceedingly loyal workforce!'

While the Abbyvale raid was not successful, it was the seventh such incident in the county this year, the highest number recorded since the recession.

A postmaster in Adare and a bookmaker in Limerick City were the two most recent targets. In both cases, the perpetrators escaped with large sums of cash. Gardaí have not yet said if they believe the incidents are connected.

*** Pine Road Poker ***

Bernie:
We need to set a date for this year's pre-Easter street party. I am suggesting Saturday 6 April. I am giving the keynote speech at a parenting conference the w/end of April 13/14 so can't do then. Rgds, B W-R

Ruby:
My favourite time of the year. Oh, how I love to get drunk and disorderly in public . . .

Carmel:
Mick got me a 1980s cookbook for my birthday. Hence I'll be making fondue this year.

Ruby:
I'll be drinking gin.

Fiona:
Yum! XXX

(Fondue. Not gin. XXX)

Bernie:
Sylvie's actually allergic to cheese.

Carmel:
I'll make sure not to throw her in it, so.

(BTW, Fiona – like the new wheels.)

Ruby:

Ellen:

Ruby – Sylvie's been through a lot, with the dog bite and everything. As has Bernie. I hardly think that's appropriate.

Fiona:

Will you make your famous walnut cake again, Rita Ann??? XXX

(Thanks, Carmel! Insurance covered them, thank God!!)

Rita Ann:

I'm making nothing until my newspapers are returned.

ELEVEN

••••••••••••••••••

Robin stood at the bar, trying and failing to catch the barmaid's eye. On the small stage behind her, a duetting couple were reaching for the high notes on 'Summer Nights'. She'd felt sorry for Edie that day in the retail park, so eager for friends that she was desperately courting women twice her age, so she'd invited her out. She was happy to have an excuse to go for a couple of drinks. But it had been a while since she'd been to the Fern and she hadn't realised Sunday night was karaoke night.

The barmaid continued to ignore her. She looked over to Edie who waved brightly. Robin gave her a half smile and winced as the duetters summited the crescendo.

'Summer Ni-hi-heights!!!!'

'Excuse—'

But the barmaid strode on towards a customer at the far end of the counter.

Barmen never ignored Robin, but barwomen seemed to go out of their way to leave her parched.

She kept her eyes trained on the woman as she pulled a pint of Guinness. She willed her to look up, to feel the stare on the crown of her head, to know Robin was next.

The woman's head snapped up. Her eyes flickered in Robin's direction. Bingo.

She was putting the head on the pint but Robin didn't break eye contact. She repeated the order in her head until it took on a hypnotic rhythm. It was on the tip of her tongue, ready to hop. *A gin and tonic and a chardonnay, a gin and tonic and a char-don-nay.*

She delivered the pint and returned to Robin's end. 'A gin—'

'Guinness, please! And a red wine. Rioja, if you've got it.'

Robin whipped her head around to see a man about half a foot away, leaning on the polished counter. He smiled at Robin – not a gloating smile or an apologetic one, but worse. His smile, confidently displayed below an equally self-assured and inadvisable moustache, was commiserative, as if they'd both had equal claim to the next order and it could as easily, and as justly, have gone either way. And who pronounced 'Rioja' like that? He sounded like he had a hair caught in his throat. The man's skin was so pale as to be almost translucent. Nobody was going to be fooled into mistaking him for a Spaniard.

Robin glared at him and rolled her eyes as the barmaid took his money and waited for the Guinness to settle before adding the head.

Of course, that was the one time the barmaid did look in her direction and she thought Robin was rolling her eyes at her so when she finally, reluctantly, took her order, she spilled half the gin measure over the side of the glass and made no effort to fix it.

'Right. Thanks,' Robin muttered, pouring the tonic in after it and carrying the two glasses over to their table. The European wannabe disappeared into the lounge area next door, whistling along as an inebriated man in his forties murdered Bon Jovi.

'Thanks,' said Edie, her eyes widening in gratitude as she took the glass. They widened every time she wanted to stress a point, which seemed to be all the time. They were more like quotation marks, really; when you saw them expanding, you knew words were about to follow. 'I'm not supposed to be drinking at the moment because I'm trying to get pregnant, as you know.'

Robin nodded politely. Did Edie actually think conception was good chitchat material?

'But me and Daniel got into a big argument on Friday,' she continued, 'when I was ovulating, of course, and it killed the mood entirely.' Edie took a gulp of wine and made an explosion gesture. 'Another month gone.'

'Sorry to hear that,' said Robin, who had no idea how it must feel to mean to get pregnant. 'I guess there's always next month?'

'Oh yeah,' agreed Edie, blushing slightly. 'It's not a big deal. At all, like. We'll just try next month. You know what they say: getting pregnant is great, but trying is even better.'

Edie flashed her a full-wattage smile, though it didn't look entirely genuine.

'Oh!' she shouted suddenly. 'I have something to show you.'

Robin caught the table as Edie reached under and almost sent it, and their drinks, flying. When she emerged, she was holding two sheets of paper. 'Here.' She handed them over but just as Robin was about to start reading, she slapped her palm down on them.

'First,' she said, eyes popping, 'let me just say that I don't normally go snooping on my neighbours. Okay? But when Martha told us about the burglary, and then I saw her old address on a magazine on her hall table, my curiosity just sort of got the better of me. I love mysteries, you see; I'm addicted to them really and I'm good at solving them – ask Daniel. When we're watching *Law and Order*, I almost always guess the ending. So anyway, I put the address into Google and I know I shouldn't have but I did, and, well . . . yeah.'

Slowly she drew back her hand and bit her lip.

Robin looked down at the pages. It was a printout of a newspaper article. 'The *Limerick Leader*?'

Edie nodded quickly.

She read slowly, squinting in the dim light and angling the pages towards the fluorescent bulbs at the bar. It was an article about a tiger raid at a home in Limerick. Martha's home, she presumed. Martha and her girls must be the wife and daughters.

A gang of men had held them hostage while her husband was sent to work to steal money. Robin came to 'tied to the radiators' and looked up.

'Keep reading.'

Robert Costello, Martha's husband, had thwarted the plan. He had alerted the guards. Gardai believed their home had been under surveillance for two months.

'Jesus,' she said when she'd finished, laying the pages back on the table.

Edie stared back over the rim of her wine glass.

'At least nobody was hurt, right?' said Robin. 'I'm not surprised they moved. Have you met the husband yet? Robert? I saw him through the window once. God, wow. Quite the hero.'

Edie nodded empathically as she took another mouthful of wine. 'She must be very proud of him. Poor Martha. Can you imagine? I can totally understand why she'd have to get out of that house. It says here they were following a definite line of inquiry. That usually means they know who did it, but it's more than three months and there haven't been any arrests.'

'How do you know there haven't been any arrests? Are there follow-up articles?'

Edie shook her head. 'I couldn't find any so . . .' She dropped her voice to a half-whisper. 'I rang the garda press office.'

'You *what*?'

'I telephoned the garda press office.'

'No, I heard you.' They were between karaoke songs. 'But what do you mean you rang them? Isn't that only for journalists and media types? I thought you were a receptionist.'

'Receptionist-slash-supervisor,' Edie corrected her, 'as of this week.'

'Congrats.'

She beamed. 'Thanks.'

'And the press office?'

'It's just something I do sometimes.' Edie drained her glass. 'If I see a case on the news or read about one and I want to know more or think I might be able to help. I ring from the hotel, so if they ever do figure it out, they won't know who it was. We have hundreds of guests staying every night.'

Robin was seeing Edie in a whole new light. 'Do you use your own name?'

'Gosh, no. I say I'm Eileen Brent. She's my favourite Agatha Christie character. And I say I'm phoning from the *Sunday World*.'

'Don't they notice your name's never in the paper?'

Edie shrugged. 'I guess they don't read it. I'm actually kind of friendly with one of the press officers now. Our children went to the same crèche. Well, they didn't obviously, since I have no children, but she thinks they did. I'm much nicer about the place than she is; I had a better experience with the childminders.'

Robin didn't quite know what to say. She was impressed. 'That's almost as surprising as the article. I never would have had you pegged for a con artist.'

Edie gave a little trill of excitement. 'Thanks!'

'And what are you going to do about this?' Robin poked the paper in front of her. 'Are you going to tell Martha you know?'

Edie gathered up the pages and slipped them back into her bag. 'No. Not yet. I'm going to see if I can help with the case first.'

Robin thought she was joking but Edie's doe eyes were full of hope and Robin made a serious effort not to laugh. A friend of Eddy's had been involved in a tiger raid once; they made off with €40,000 each. Not bad for a morning's work. That's what Robin had thought when Eddy told her. She felt bad for being so glib now. This was how everything with Eddy seemed to go: great fun at the time, a source of great shame afterwards.

Edie got more drinks and they talked about her promotion. It didn't really change what she did but meant more money and a different title. Robin admitted that she was between jobs and when Edie asked what she used to do, Robin tried to remember what she'd told her mother. 'Telephone sales,' she said and, though neither of them was quite finished, pointed to their glasses. 'Another?'

When she came back from the bar, she changed the subject to family. Edie was more than happy to spend a good twenty minutes giving out about her in-laws.

'I mean, what sort of cake could a vegetarian *not* eat?' she said, having drunk half her glass of wine almost instantly. 'If it was a mince pie, sure, I could understand the confusion. Although, there's not actually any mince in those. But it was carrot cake. Carrot! Carrot *is* literally a vegetable!'

'Mothers can be hard to please.'

'It's not just his mother. His father, his sister, his brother; they all hate me. His brother's the worst.' Edie narrowed her slightly glassy eyes. Or at least that's what Robin presumed she was trying to do; in reality, they were just an average amount of open. 'He's thirty and he's still bullying Daniel. *Daniel mind Rocky, Daniel give me some money, Daniel—* Actually, no. Peter doesn't even call him "Daniel". He calls him "Two Straps".'

'Two Straps?'

'One day when they were around twelve, Daniel wore his schoolbag on both shoulders and everyone slagged him about it.'

'That's it? And he's still called Two Straps today?'

Edie nodded morosely. 'Poor Daniel.'

Robin snorted. Edie looked at her.

'Sorry. It's kind of funny.'

Then Edie smiled. 'I guess it is. But I don't know . . .' She tilted her glass and swirled the end of the wine. Her brow furrowed. 'I wish Daniel would tell him to buzz off, you know?'

What grown woman said 'buzz off'? It was like something Jack would say. Robin did her best to keep a straight face.

'I think his family stuff stops him from wanting to be a dad. I mean, he says it's money and stability and that, but I don't know. If you had a family like his . . .'

'But I thought he did want to be a dad? I thought you were trying?'

'Oh we are,' said Edie, suddenly snapping out of the wine-tinged haze. She nodded in agreement with herself. 'He does. We are.'

They were fairly drunk now and Edie went to the bar to get a final round as Robin sat staring into space. After their phone call last weekend, Eddy was back to playing good cop. He kept sending her messages saying he missed her and Jack, and sending photos of the three of them in better times. Robin hadn't replied, but she knew that wasn't sustainable. The threat was still there, underlying everything he said: he had something on her, even if she played it down. And Eddy turning up on her parents' doorstep, shouting blue murder and humiliating her was a distinct possibility.

It was easier not to worry when she was tipsy. When she was drunk, she forgot that she'd done everything wrong.

'I think I'd like to sing a song,' announced Edie, placing the two glasses on the table with that bit too much force.

'I would heartily support that.'

Edie's eyes popped. 'Really? Okay!' She squirmed with exhilaration. 'What should I sing?'

Robin scraped back her stool. 'I'll pick for you.'

'Oh, I don't know . . .'

'I won't pick anything difficult, nothing too high or complicated. Cross my heart.' She dutifully did just that. 'I'll be quick. All right? Okay.'

Edie nodded.

'Stay here and don't chicken out.'

Robin took her drink and ran up to book a slot.

'No indie stuff!' Edie shouted, and Robin gave her a thumbs-up. As she did a lavish twirl to face back in the direction of the karaoke booth, she clocked the moustached queue-skipper from earlier. He was back at the bar. She swung her hips as she strode the rest of the way.

'I've got four ahead of you,' said the guy in the top hat and 'karaoke impresario' T-shirt. He slid the songbook in her direction. 'And no more fucking power ballads.'

Robin flipped open the bulky folder, which landed with a thud. The pages were laminated and sticky. Thousands of songs, all listed alphabetically.

'Rap's usually a safe bet.'

Robin arranged her face into the unimpressed, slightly bored expression she had mastered in her early twenties. Then she turned her head to find the queue-skipper standing beside her, an identical order to earlier in his hands. His pale skin was scattered with moles and he had dark hair parted slightly to the right. He was a little taller than her and thin, but with decent shoulders. Nothing worse than a neck that just turns into arms. He wore jeans and a dark green checked shirt, the kind Kurt Cobain used to wear, sleeves rolled to just below his elbow. He was good-looking, which presumably he knew, or he wouldn't have attempted such unflattering facial hair.

She proffered him the book, eyebrows raised. 'You want to go first?'

He moved his hands away as if touching the laminated list of songs might compel him to sing one of them. 'Not drunk enough for that. But if I was, I'd go for rap. That's all I'm saying. It's effectively talking, so it doesn't matter if you're an awful singer.'

'Who says I'm an awful singer?'

Mustachio grinned. 'No one.'

Was this flirting? Or was alcohol impairing her judgement? She went back to the book and moved her eyes over the pages without taking in a word. She didn't usually get flustered with men, but she couldn't think of anything to say. Time kept passing. If she didn't come up with something, he was going to leave.

'You skipped the queue earlier.'

'What's that?'

Shit.

He'd already taken a step away. He turned back awkwardly now, head facing in one direction, body in the other. His Guinness slopped slightly over the edge of the glass.

'Nothing.' She shook her head and went back to the book.

'No, sorry, I just didn't hear you.'

Where was he going anyway? Was he still sitting in the lounge? Who was he here with? Was he on a date? What if the Rioja-ordered-with-extra-throat-phlegm was for a date?

'Doesn't matter.' She shook her head again and tried not to cringe. 'Sorry.'

He looked more confused. 'Sorry for what?'

'What?' *Just leave.* She wanted to disappear. 'Nothing,' she said. 'I don't know.' She turned back to the book. 'Ignore me.'

He said nothing further and when she looked up a few seconds later, she expected him to be gone.

But no.

'I didn't want to pick a song,' he called out as 'Total Eclipse of the Heart' kicked in.

'I know,' she shouted back, really wishing he'd feck off and put them both out of their misery.

'I just wanted to talk to you.' He gave a sheepish grin. A lovely grin, it had to be said.

'Okay, well, what did you—'

But at the same time, he blurted out: 'I think you're gorgeous!'

They both stopped talking, clamping their mouths shut. His eyes were a colour between brown and green, and they were kind.

She burst out laughing. 'Who says that?'

He grinned. 'Me.'

'Ready yet?' The karaoke impresario was back in front of them, arms folded.

'Em . . .' Robin grabbed one of the selection sheets, wrote down Edie's name and then, from the page opened in front of her, selected the first song she recognised: 'Gangsta's Paradise'.

She handed it to the man, who read it and rolled his eyes.

Mustachio grinned. 'You took my advice. Edie.'

'Edie's my friend.' She nodded towards their table, where Edie was scrolling through her mobile. Probably organising a phone tap for the Costello–Rigby residence. 'She's singing. I'm just picking the song. Okay.' Robin pushed back her shoulders and stood a little taller. 'What's your worst trait?'

'Excuse me?'

'Your worst trait, your most deplorable characteristic, whatever. And don't bullshit me. Don't tell me you're too kind or you're too good to your mother or some nonsense like that. Tell me the truth.'

He stared at her just long enough to make Robin think her routine wasn't cute or quirky but actually just a little weird and stressful. She was about to tell him she was joking when—

'I can be spineless.'

'Okay.' She nodded. 'Go on.'

'Sometimes I tell people what they want to hear, even if it means telling different people different things.' He squirmed slightly, moustache twitching. 'Because I want them to like me, I guess? I hear myself doing it and I don't like it. I'm trying to be better.' He paused. 'What about you? What's your worst trait?'

'I'm selfish.' Robin took a sip of her drink and spoke in a blasé tone, as if such a confession cost her nothing. 'I make a show of thinking about other people but I usually just do what suits me. I'm reckless too. And sometimes I turn a blind eye to things that I know are wrong if it means I get what I want.'

A dimple formed where the apple of his left cheek met the bone. 'Can I get your number?'

Robin raised an eyebrow. 'You're just saying that because you think it's what I want to hear, aren't you?'

'Nah. It's the selfishness. Self-involvement and good legs; you're my ideal woman, basically.'

Robin grinned and picked up the karaoke pen. She turned over another of the song selection slips and wrote down her number. Then she added her name. 'Here,' she said, handing it to him. She pretended to blow hair from her face, but really she was cooling the burn from her cheeks.

He smiled back, pocketed the paper and picked up his drinks. 'I better get back.'

'On a hot date?'

'Oh, yeah. I'm in danger of burning myself, it's that piping hot.'

'Sounds dangerous. I'll try to be cooler.'

He grinned. 'I've no doubt.' He really was very good-looking, even with the moustache.

'Well, enjoy your furnace,' she said, turning back towards her table so he couldn't see the smile erupting across her face, but hoping he appreciated the swing of her hips.

Edie bounced on her bar stool as she watched Robin approach – her eyes all but ready to roll out of her head.

TWELVE

· · · · · · · · · · · · · · · · ·

Martha's mood had improved in the past week. The new neighbours weren't exactly her old friends but they were nice enough. She'd unpacked almost all the boxes and made a start on the garden. She was seeing Ellis more, which was always welcome, and she'd joined the book club at the local library. She might even read the novel this time.

The only downside was how happy it all made Robert.

Sometimes she worried about her rage. It was disconcerting to be fine most of the time, and then suddenly incandescent. She didn't like having an urge to scream at her children. Surely that wasn't normal. But it always came back to Robert. He was the reason she felt like this.

That morning he pointed out that they hadn't had sex in three months. Even though, actually, it was three months and twelve days. Yet more proof that she was the only one with that day emblazoned on to her dreams.

'Obviously after the attempted robbery . . .' Robert began. Martha felt her mouth twitch. He always said 'attempted'; focusing on what he had stopped and not what had happened. 'I didn't expect you to be yourself, none of us were, but moving house doesn't seem to have made it any better. I'm starting to wonder if it's something else.' He stopped searching through drawers for where she'd put his ties. 'I'm starting to wonder if maybe it's me.'

Obviously, she wanted to shout. *Fucking obviously*. But he looked at her with his hangdog expression and she realised that he, inconceivable as it was, had no idea. Robert's world was black and white and if their marriage came to an end it would not be because of anything he had done but because she had stopped sleeping with him. That would become the shorthand. 'Robert Costello? Such a catch! Great job, too. Yes, he was married once. His mentally unstable wife refused to have sex with him.'

She thought about telling him to have an affair, to go off and find someone to fulfil his carnal needs. But instead she said: 'In the wardrobe. Top drawer.'

'In the . . .?' Robert opened the old pine wardrobe that had been here when they moved in and pulled out two ties. Then, though she was willing him not to, he came and sat on her side of the bed. He put a hand on her blanket-covered legs. 'I'm not blaming you, Martha. I'm really, really not. I just want to help.'

He stood again. 'Which tie?' He held out a navy blue one that would go with anything and a yellow and red one that made him look like a clown.

She pointed to the yellow and red.

'I'm going to bring you home flowers this evening – those simple white ones you love, you've always had such excellent taste – and then let's talk about a night away, or even just a night out. And maybe you could go and see the doctor here. We have to register with a new practice anyway, as a family, so even just to do that. Okay? All right? How do I look?'

He turned from the mirror, smiling widely. He looked like Ronald McDonald.

'Wonderful.'

Martha waited until he closed the bedroom door before picking up the navy tie and hurling it after him. It barely made it beyond the bed, and her mood became astronomically worse. She heard the click of the front door – Robert never had breakfast now; far too important – and got out of bed.

She worked up a mild sweat pulling weeds but, in the shower several hours later, it was still rage she was scrubbing from her skin.

Then she brought her fingers up to touch her left cheek, lightly, softly, though of course it wasn't necessary to be delicate any more.

It might seem her rage was misplaced, and it was true she didn't dwell on the people who'd broken into her home and terrorised her daughters and refused to untie them even as they struggled to breathe. And yes, it was also true she could have told the police about the one face she had seen. But what could she have said except that he'd been white? She couldn't make out any distinguishing features from that distance.

It didn't matter who they were, not really. They were just men who had seen an opportunity and taken it. It was nothing personal. They had taken nothing – and more importantly, they had owed her nothing. Her family was just business to them. She should not have been able to say the same about her husband.

A bang downstairs and her shoulders shot up, a towel half-wrapped around her. Then the front door gave way and there was the thud of book-laden bags hitting the floor.

'Muh-ummmm! Tell Sinead to stop telling me what to do!'

Martha wrapped the towel the whole way around. She pushed the bathroom windows open and felt the cold air rush in as the steam billowed out.

'I'm not telling you what to do, Orla! I'm saying that you have to protect yourself!'

'Who needs to protect themselves?' asked Martha, hurrying down the stairs, towel tucked into place but her left arm stuck to her side just in case.

'Women,' said Sinead. 'All women need to protect themselves.'

'Well, yes, everyone does, but I don't think you need to be worrying your sister about that today.'

'Oh yeah?' That familiar, glassy triumphalism filled her daughter's eyes. 'Well, they found a list at school in the boys' bathroom, and my name was on it.'

'What kind of list?'

'A sex list,' said Orla, rolling her eyes. 'I know what sex is, Sinead. I am twelve.'

'Oh,' said Martha, remembering a list that went around among the boys in her school when she was a teenager: what girl would you most like to have sex with? She was ashamed to say now that she'd been pleased with how highly she'd scored.

'Not a sex list, Orla,' said Sinead, shoving her sister slightly. 'It was a rape list, Mum.' She turned to Martha, eyes like bottomless wells. 'It was a rape list and I was on it.'

THIRTEEN
· · · · · · · · · · · · · · · · · · · ·

'**I'm sorry.**'

Daniel took a long side step so he was standing between Edie and the television. He had changed out of his work clothes and was wearing the jeans she'd gotten him for Christmas. He shifted slightly as he held out a small bouquet of daffodils. The heads of the flowers drooped. He was gripping them too tightly. He always clenched his fists when he was nervous.

Without looking directly at him, Edie picked up the remote control, reached around his denim-clad legs and pressed pause on *The Ted Bundy Tapes*.

Daniel cleared his throat awkwardly. He was not one for big gestures.

'I'm sorry,' he said again. 'I hate fighting with you. I hate going to work without saying goodbye and not phoning at my eleven o'clock break. I hate making you mad.'

He proffered the flowers further, their sunny little heads bowed. They looked sorry too. But they were her favourites, and Daniel hated buying flowers. Florists depressed him. They made him think of men who cheated on their wives. She could tell he'd tied the bow himself.

Edie didn't like fighting with him either. She was really bad at it. Twice yesterday she'd come downstairs to tell him her thoughts on some cold case she was reading about, and potentially cracking, and then had to pretend she'd desperately wanted a glass of water when she remembered she wasn't talking to him. And he'd clearly noticed because when he came to bed last night, he left a bottle of water, ice cold from the fridge, on her side table without saying a word.

She resented those ungrateful daffodils. His arms were supposed to be wrapped too tightly around her, not them.

But she had felt abandoned and betrayed. On Friday morning he had started up again about how uncertain things were at the garage this year. They were supposed to start trying that night! He'd suggested they wait another while. She'd been so upset she'd had to come home early from work, citing period pains. The other women had all been very sympathetic because as far as they and the rest of the world were concerned, she and Daniel were already trying to put an end to her periods. And as much as she cared what everyone else thought – which was quite a bit – she cared infinitely more about having a baby. At some point, Daniel had stopped caring about the same thing.

She got up from the couch and took the flowers from him. 'Thank you.' He had taken extra care scrubbing his nails, but faint rings of oil stained his knuckles. She loved those useful hands.

No tears, she warned herself. She couldn't turn into a big baby every time something didn't go her way.

There was a vase in the kitchen between the window and a framed photo from their wedding day. Daniel's footsteps followed her and carefully, slowly, she began to arrange the flowers.

Her fertility window had closed yesterday and they hadn't had any sex, never mind a conversation.

In the photo from their wedding, they were standing at the foot of the lake at the hotel where they'd had the reception. Just before it was taken, Daniel had leaned in and said: 'I'm going to make you happy.' He hadn't said it as if it was a line or something he'd seen in a film once. He'd said it because it was the exact thing on his mind. As simple as that.

When had her straightforward husband become so confusing?

'I didn't like how you turned on me,' she said, adjusting the stems one final time before accepting they would never stand straight. 'I thought we had agreed.'

'I know, I'm sorry. I panicked.'

'And now?'

'I'm not panicked.'

A weight lifted from her chest.

Men got panicked. It happened. Everyone said it. Women got to the ready-for-kids stage before men. Her cousin Kim had given up waiting and just pretended to get pregnant by accident. Her fella believed it really was an accident because he watched her take the pill every night. Only it wasn't the pill she'd been taking at all; it was folic acid. All the other girls thought that was very smart, but it made Edie sad. She wanted to make a family with Daniel, not in spite of him.

'Okay,' she said.

'Okay?' he repeated cautiously. 'Okay you forgive me?'

She nodded, relieved not to have to be annoyed any more, and slowly she wrapped her arms around him. She could feel the relief flowing through his body as their arms swapped positions and he enveloped her.

'I'm sorry, bae,' he said again.

'It's okay,' she murmured, nuzzling her head into his neck. He smelled like he always did after work: aftershave and hot, stifled air. 'There's always next month.' She pulled back slightly. 'What?'

'Nothing,' he said.

But she had felt him tense up.

'What is it, Daniel? Do you want to have kids? Yes or no?' Asking blunt questions usually made Edie awkward – she was uncomfortable making other people uncomfortable – but with this, she didn't care.

'Yes,' he said emphatically.

She relaxed again. It would be okay. 'All right then.'

'I just don't know if I'm ready yet.'

'Daniel,' she groaned. He was breaking her heart.

'I just . . .' He exhaled. 'I just want it to be perfect.'

She wanted to kiss him and hit him, to call him a goose and tell him how his more annoying qualities were also his best. But she also needed to clear this up. She needed to know where she stood. 'It *is* perfect,' she said, gesturing between the two of them.

What if they couldn't get pregnant naturally? What if they tried for a year and nothing happened and then they had to go down the IVF route and that didn't work either? She thought of her ovaries as two fat little old-fashioned alarm clocks, constantly ticking.

Daniel tutted, flinching slightly. 'I should be earning more. We should have enough money to get the bathroom done, to pave the garden. I should be building up savings not eating into them. I should never have let things get so bad at the garage. I took my eye off the ball. I fucked up.'

'You did not fuck up. You had a tough few months. It's all right. These things happen.' She reached for his face. 'Jobs fall through.'

He scratched the tuft of dark hair on his forehead with too much vigour. 'I should have handled it better.'

'Stop being so hard on yourself.' *On us*, she thought. *Stop being so hard on us.* She had checked the bank statements. Things weren't that bad now. But there was no talking to him. He was determined to punish himself. 'Who cares if there's not enough money to get rooms done up or to put in a driveway? The baby will sleep in the spare bedroom. And we don't need a driveway.'

'We do as long as that fucker is living at the bottom of this road,' Daniel muttered. He had gotten into several arguments with the man at number one Pine Road in the past year, all over the empty lot beside Shay Morrissey's house. It was because Daniel worked with cars that he took it as such a personal affront when he sometimes had to park his beloved BMW on the next road over.

'We have enough money, Daniel. We own our own house.'

'You own our own house, you mean.'

Another fleck cracked from her heart. 'Daniel.'

'Sorry.' He closed his eyes, sticking his thumb in one socket and the rest of his fingers into the other. 'See? What a horrible thing to say. I'm not a good enough person to be a dad.'

Edie laughed, a big brash honk. Daniel looked up, startled. She felt instant relief. Of all the arguments he could have given, that was the weakest. 'You're the *best* person,' she said, still smiling. Even the fact he was worried about it proved her point.

She stepped back towards the kitchen island. 'I want to have a child, Daniel.' She rolled up her sleeves. Daniel always laughed when she did this; as if she'd learned how to be taken seriously from watching cartoons. He didn't laugh this time. 'Like, I really want to have one.'

He looked at her the way he used to when they first met, like she was some long-held dream that had finally materialised.

'You would be the best mother.'

'And you would be the best father,' she insisted.

'Stop.'

'You're kind and thoughtful and a great provider.' Daniel winced and looked away but Edie moved so she was in his line of vision. 'I'm not going to beg you, Daniel. I'm not going to make you have a child. But if you don't want to have one with me, I need to know.' Saying it out loud made her stomach constrict all over again. She leaned back on to the island. Would contractions feel a little like this?

'I'm sorry,' he said, shaking his head. 'Of course I want to have one with you. I don't know what's wrong with me. I just get panicked. It seems too real, too big. I work it up in my head. I'm sorry.'

'There's nothing wrong with you,' she said, allowing herself to relax. 'You're the best man, Daniel Carmody. Honest to God, you are. And you're a bit of a ride, too.'

He guffawed.

'You are. Avril Coughlan said that to me in third year before I'd even seen you and I thought she was exaggerating. But then I saw you coming down the stairs at Saint Ornatín's and I said to myself, That's Daniel Carmody; that's the lad from pass Irish that Avril said she'd happily give her flower too.'

'Did she really say that?'

She shoved him gently. 'You wouldn't be asking that if you'd seen her lately.' She puffed out her cheeks to emulate the fillers that had taken over Avril's face. She immediately felt guilty. Even though her ex-friend had never been a very nice person, it wasn't her fault she had low self-esteem. Poor Avril. 'Forget that. I'm talking about you. You'll be a great dad. All right, Daniel? Okay?' She poked him. 'Daniel?'

He nodded. 'I believe it a bit when you say it.'

'Good. You should. So are we agreed? We're trying for a baby. Actually trying, not fighting?'

He was looking at her but he wasn't listening.

'Daniel,' she said again, 'this is like talking to you when Liverpool are playing. Three times I've to say anything before it gets through.'

His eyes flickered then. He saw her properly. He nodded. 'Okay.'

'Okay,' she echoed. Everything would be all right. She knew everything would be all right. 'Good.'

She pushed herself in a little closer, so her chest was tight against his. Then she tilted her head up and covered his mouth with hers. She took a breath and kissed him again, slowly, waiting until its effect had spread down through his body.

'You're just making me want you now.'

'True,' she murmured.

'But it's too late. You're no longer . . .'

'I was thinking we'd go back to the old days, when sex was just for fun.'

He growled into her neck and she laughed, giving a little jump as he reached down for her ass. She liked when he was like this: primal and uncomplicated. She liked when things were simple.

*** Pine Road Poker ***

Ellen:
Just home and Cillian told me about this list that was in the boys' bathroom in Saint Ornatín's! Have you all heard?

Bernie, have you heard about this??? I sent you a text as soon as I heard. I assume the Parents' Association is all over it?

What I want to know is how long the school has known. Trish????

Carmel:
What sort of list?

Ellen:
Photos of it are going around the school. I don't know if I can bring myself to share it.

Rita Ann:
What is it?

Ruby:
Release the photos!

Carmel:
Share it with the class!

Ellen:
[Photo sent]

Fiona:
That was in the school bathroom??? At Saint Ornatín's??? My two are going there next year!!!

Trish????? What is going on????

Rita Ann:
I can't read that writing. I've lost my glasses somewhere. What does it say?

Ruby:
It says: 'The Rape List. The girl with the most ticks beside her name will be raped'. And then there's a list of names.

I feel sick just typing that.

Ellen:
Cillian is good friends with three of the girls listed. Their poor parents.

Trish – I can see you've read my first message. What's going on? How did this happen?

Fiona:
I should say my two are *possibly* going there. Although presumably admissions won't be so competitive after this!!!

Rita Ann:
You didn't get that kind of thing in my day, I can tell you.

Trish:
Hi all. I cannot discuss this as it is a school matter. Please do not circulate that photo. Regards, Trish

FOURTEEN

I **● ● ● held accountable.** How can we send our children to a school where they are sharing classrooms with sexual predators? My Sylvie could be sitting beside a rapist every day. Or maybe she's being *taught* by a rapist? We don't know that it wasn't a teacher who wrote this. And this isn't just about my daughter, by the way. This could be anyone's daughter. This could be your daughter, Trish. For several highly distraught parents, this *is* their daughter. It's reprehensible. It's an absolute disgrace. Aside from blaming the school, which I and the entire Parents' Association absolutely do, we have to—'

'Have you spoken to the entire Parents' Association, Bernie? I thought you just found out about this and that the shock of that was why you have ignored standard protocol and come pounding on the door of my private residence outside of work hours.'

Bernie Watters-Reilly's jaw squared as she regarded Trish coolly. 'You can rest assured that the entire Parents' Association will echo my sentiment. The school is supposed to be teaching our children and guarding them. Instead, it delegates more and more of its teaching responsibilities to the internet. I have raised this at several board of management meetings but it constantly falls on deaf – dare I say, uninterested – ears. What do children find on the internet? Porn. And far, far worse. You can rest assured, Patricia, I am no babe in the woods.'

'I never thought you were, Bernie.'

'If teachers just did the teaching themselves, we wouldn't have a system that is actively breeding wannabe rapists. It points to the violence of . . .'

It wasn't that Trish disliked Bernie. Well, she did – but she also felt sorry for her. Everyone knew Bernie was a gold star member of the *Sunday Times* wine club – she brought it up at every poker game – but however much Bernie drank, her husband drank more. If you asked Bernie, she'd tell you he was self-employed, a consultant, but Trish could see their recycling crate from the back windows of her house and she suspected Dermot Reilly didn't do much of anything but drink.

Her daughter was a precocious brat and Bernie did nothing to discourage Sylvie's behaviour, indulging her every grievance. Declan was the only tolerable member of the family. Not that Bernie had much time for her son; Sylvie did a better job of smiling for the camera when *VIP* magazine wanted an 'at home with' photoshoot with the country's top parenting expert. But Trish liked Declan. He was a gentle soul. She did him the favour of ignoring him in school – having the chair of the Parents' Association for a mother, especially one as overbearing and publicity hungry as Bernie, was enough of a social burden without the whole school knowing the principal was your next-door neighbour – and she gave him forty quid every second weekend to mow her lawn and trim the bushes. He always did a decent job.

'Saint Ornatín's does not breed rapists, Bernie,' said Trish, when her neighbour had finally finished. 'No sexual assault has happened. The list would appear to be an entirely inexcusable and pathetically immature joke amongst the male students.'

'A joke?' Bernie recoiled, bringing her hand to her chest. Trish had seen her do this exact same manoeuvre on television. 'You think this is a *joke*? I'll tell you a joke, Trish. Why did the donkey cross the road? Because it was the chicken's day off. *That* is a joke. But female students being put at risk of sexual assault? That is not a

115

joke. The male students should be lined up and questioned until someone cracks.'

Word had started to spread that afternoon. Someone had blown up a photograph of the list and stuck copies of it on different classroom doors. Trish had no idea where the photograph had come from, who'd done it or why they'd waited so long. The entire staffroom was up in arms, never mind the students. The list had been gone a week now, and Trish had foolishly started to relax.

'I am as horrified as you,' she said, keeping her tone empathetic. 'Trust me. It is entirely unacceptable behaviour and the perpetrator will be punished. We have launched an investigation internally. I was somewhat heartened to see that none of the names had any ticks beside them – and so I think this was an isolated incident as opposed to reflective of the male student population at large. In fact, it was a concerned male student who brought it to the attention of the faculty.'

'Internal investigation, my eye. It sounds to me, Patricia, like you were trying to keep the whole thing secret. You were hoping nobody, including the parents, would ever know about . . . *this*!' Bernie pulled one of the photocopied images from her 'Children Aren't A Distraction from More Important Work, They Are the More Important Work' tote bag.

'You really shouldn't circulate those,' said Trish, already envisaging the photo reproduced beside her neighbour's weekly rant in this Thursday's *Irish Independent*. 'We need to protect the privacy of the students listed here. They are all minors.'

Bernie continued to hold the blown-up photograph of the list aloft and Trish struggled to maintain composure. She had two daughters of her own. Of course, she did not think this was okay. 'Bernie,' she said, calmly, conclusively, 'we took our own record of the list as soon as I was alerted to it.'

'How long ago was that?'

'Not long.'

'Very reassuring.'

'We then removed the list from the bathroom door and sent a report on its contents to the board of management. It would have been raised at this month's PTA meeting.'

'Trish!'

Ted was calling her from the kitchen. He never disturbed her when she was in the middle of something, he just kept the dinner warm. But he knew. Ted always knew.

'I'm sorry, Bernie. I have to go. We're having dinner now. If you want, you can phone the office tomorrow.'

She shut the door and, after a minute alone in the hall, followed Ted's voice and the smell of fish through to the kitchen.

'That seemed to go well,' he said, holding out the wooden spoon for her to taste.

'Did she hear?' asked Trish, looking out to their back garden where Emily was playing with a neighbour's cat. Edie Rice's, probably, or maybe Ruby and Madeline's. Ordinarily Trish, who was not a cat person, would have shooed the animal away but ever since she'd seen that rat hole in her flower bed, she was happy to have a feline visitor.

'If it doesn't have paws she's not interested.'

She shot Ted an appreciative smile. Then the doorbell went.

'Not again.'

'I'll go,' said Ted. 'You stir the parsley sauce.'

There were voices in the hallway, then Ted stuck his head around the kitchen door. 'It's not Bernie,' he said, and Trish put her free hand to her forehead in exaggerated relief.

'It's Martha Rigby,' he said. 'From number eight.'

Trish squinted as she tried to think.

'Sinead Costello's mother,' Ted supplied. 'She was one of the girls on the list.'

'The new girl. Right.' Trish nodded. 'Oh crap.' She'd spoken to most of the girls' parents that afternoon – better to play offensive than defensive – but the only contact number they had on file for Sinead was for her brother. Trish had forgotten to pursue it further.

'She's in the front room.'

Trish hurried up the hall and into the main family room where a tall, slim woman with thick dark hair to just above her shoulders was examining a family photograph taken at Laura's college graduation.

'Martha, hi, I'm Patricia Walsh. Call me Trish.' She held out a hand and the stranger turned to reveal a woman in her early forties. Good-looking, just like the WhatsApp group had said, if a little formidable. She reminded Trish of the mother from *The Addams Family*, the name momentarily escaping her.

Martha took her hand, which was something at least.

'I'm very sorry. I meant to get in contact this afternoon but we didn't have a number for you, only your son.'

'Ellis,' supplied Martha.

'That was it.'

'The girls stayed with him the first week of term.'

'Right, well, I thought it best not to discuss this with him before I'd had a chance to talk to you. I'm so sorry I haven't been in touch yet.'

'I wanted to get the facts. Sinead has told me, of course, several times now; she's quite worked up, but she can get . . . lately, she's been quicker to . . .' Martha shook away the half-formed sentences. 'You heard about what happened to her and her sister?'

'It's in their file.'

Martha nodded, the skin at the tip of her chin crinkling slightly. 'I just want the facts.'

'Of course.' Trish gestured for them both to sit, removing Emily's recorder from her armchair. 'I'd say what Sinead has told you is the truth, unfortunately. It's a serious matter and I want you to know we are treating it as such.'

118

Martha nodded again, and Trish continued. She told her how the list came to her attention and showed her one of the photocopied images that had been hung in the school that afternoon. 'We don't know who took this photo, presumably whoever wrote the list. Once they're caught, this is likely to lead to an expulsion.' Trish didn't mention that she had no idea how she was going to catch them. She told Martha the matter had been reported to the relevant authorities and that there was no need to believe it was anything more sinister than a terrible prank and that the male students were just as aware as the female ones that this was no laughing matter.

Only when Trish had stopped giving her speech did she realise it had been a speech.

'All right,' said Martha, taking a moment to weigh it up. 'Thank you.'

'Oh no,' insisted Trish, relieved not to have had another shouting match. 'Thank you for being understanding.'

'It sounds like you're doing what you can.'

'I've only been principal there a few years. I like it most of the time, but sometimes I miss teaching.'

'Like now?'

Trish smiled. 'Yeah.' She nodded. 'Like now.'

Martha stood. 'I should get home before Sinead starts an online petition to get the school shut down. No, sorry,' she said, seeing the horror on Trish's face, 'I'm joking. I hope. No, no, I am joking. But she has most likely called her father and brother by now. I'll go stop her before she calls my mother; she'll give her a heart attack.'

'I was particularly sorry Sinead's name was on the list,' said Trish, walking her to the door. 'It's not exactly a warm welcome from your new school. She'd only been there a month. I suppose she had the novelty factor.' She grimaced apologetically.

'Sinead loves a cause. If there's any positive to this, it's that it'll give her something to focus on.'

Trish wasn't sure she'd have been as understanding if it was her daughter, especially after what this family had been through. She opened the door for Martha and they shook hands again. It felt strange to do something so formal in her hallway. She was suddenly very aware that she was wearing a pair of Ted's old hiking socks. She wished she'd kept her blazer on, at least.

'You'll keep us updated?' said Martha. 'Let us know when you find the student?'

'Absolutely,' said Trish.

She waited until her neighbour had exited the garden and was walking back down Pine Road towards her own house before shutting the door. Then she went back into the kitchen and stood on the tiled floor until Ted came over and engulfed her into a giant hug.

*** Pine Road Poker ***

Bernie:
Apologies for the delay, ladies. As you now know, I was dealing with serious Parents' Association business. I don't want to say too much at this time but I will confirm that the Parents' Association has made advances to senior school staff and we are, thus far, entirely unsatisfied with the response we have received. We won't be commenting further at this time. Regards, Bernie Watters-Reilly

Ruby:
Is that a WhatsApp message or a press release?

Ellen:
This is not a time for your gags, Ruby. I have spoken to Bernie and poor Sylvie is very upset.

Ruby:
Sylvie? She wasn't on the list, was she?

I don't even think she's in the same year.

Ellen:
That's hardly the point. Maybe you'll understand when you have children. Sorry, IF you have children.

Ruby:
[Is typing]

[is typing]

💩

Ellen:
I don't get it. A walnut whip? What's that supposed to mean?

Ruby?

@Ruby ???

FIFTEEN

· · · · · · · · · · · · · · · · · · ·

Robin was dilly-dallying outside the bar, trying to decide whether to go in or to wait at the door, when the phone she was self-consciously turning over in her hands beeped.

> Be there in four and a half minutes. Waiting for the smoke alarm TO DESIST.

Robin grinned. She slid it back into her coat pocket and took the opportunity to give the hem of her dress another tug. She'd wait out here for the Guy from the Bar – that was how she had him saved in her phone. Johnny, who was babysitting Jack, had been unimpressed that she did not know the name of the man with whom she'd be spending the evening.

'Sure, I've slept with women whose names I didn't know. But I've never gone *out* with one, not sober. This fella could be anyone, Robin. He could be an axe murderer.'

'Knowing his first name wouldn't make that any less of a risk.'

'Or maybe he didn't tell you his name because it's really awful,' her brother had mused, as Jack emptied his box of farm animals on to the sitting-room floor. Two sheep went flying under the couch. Robin ignored them. This dress wasn't made for retrieving plastic animals from beneath furniture. 'Maybe his name's Adolf.'

'A twenty-something Irish man called Adolf?'

Johnny shrugged. 'It happens.'

'I really don't think it does.'

123

She hopped from her left foot to her right and gave her dress another pull. He – the Guy from the Bar – was making them dinner. But first, they were going for a drink. This was both practical (he lived above a wine bar) and preferable (it allowed them to start on neutral ground).

Robin watched a group of similarly aged women file into the bar and a couple of men in business suits come out. The door swung back and forth to let them all pass through.

'Mam's always saying . . .'

'. . . London on Thursday.'

'. . . in before next Christmas . . .'

'. . . working for Peter now . . .'

A hand on her shoulder. She jumped.

'Hi.'

Slightly taller than she remembered, he was wearing the same clothes but in different colours; his jeans were dark green and his faintly checked shirt was black. Same sleeve-roll to halfway up his forearms, same hipster facial hair, same nothing-to-hide smile.

'You look great,' he said, and she squinted slightly in the glare of his delight.

'Not really . . .' she said, uncharacteristically self-conscious.

'You do.' He leaned in to kiss her cheek, his face brushing against hers. The hairs of his moustache tickled and he smelled of clean sheets. 'You're cold.' He was at her ear now. 'Sorry I kept you waiting.'

He pulled back and looked at her again. His joy was so genuine, so unguarded – did he know his head was shaking? – that she laughed. It came out like a splutter, all at once. She couldn't help it.

'What?' he said, beaming away, the left cheek dimple back in position. He lifted the collar of his shirt and sniffed. 'Do I smell like dinner? The whole flat stinks of onions. You've been warned. I had to leave the windows open.'

Robin shook her head. 'You smell good, actually.'

He frowned slightly but grinned more. Butt of the joke or in on the joke, it was all the same to him.

'It's nothing,' she said, laughing again. 'I honestly don't know. Don't mind me; let's go inside.'

'You're just deliriously happy to see me? Is that it? That's it, isn't it?'

'Yeah,' she said, taking the door from him and following him inside. 'That's exactly it.'

The wine bar was busy and, as their dinner was simmering upstairs, they only had time for one. Robin didn't think they were going to get a table. They'd have to go straight upstairs. The prospect didn't seem quite so daunting now she was here, but still she'd rather—

'Here we are.' Her date had stopped in front of a high table with a 'reserved' tag. He crumpled up the cardboard sign and pulled out two stools.

Robin looked around. 'Can we just—'

'It's ours. They reserved it for us.'

'For one drink?' she said doubtfully.

But he was already taking his seat. 'The Merlot's good, if you drink red.'

'Hey! Cormac!' cried a waitress, coming towards their table. 'Didn't think we were seeing you this evening.'

'It's just a quick drink tonight, Riley. This is Robin.'

The waitress, Riley, smiled at Robin and she smiled back.

'The Merlot, right? You're mad for that Merlot.'

Her date shrugged. 'It's very good.'

'And for you?'

'Oh.' Robin looked from the waitress to the menu in front of her. She didn't know anything about wine. She only ever drank white and even then, she usually mixed it with 7 Up. 'Yeah, the same. Thanks.'

'All right.' Riley nodded. 'Two Chateau de Vieux-Moulin coming up.'

Blatantly out of her comfort zone, Robin turned to the Guy from the Bar and instantly adopted the tone she used around Eddy and his friends, that sarcastic, detached way of speaking that implied she didn't really care about anything she was saying and thus nobody's response could hurt her. 'So, *Cormac*,' she mocked. 'I'm very impressed.'

'By my name?'

'No, by how you seem to be some sort of aristocrat. With your special treatment at your *local* wine bar and your poncy Merlot ordering.' She flicked her hair over her shoulder. 'You're definitely straight, right?'

He looked at her with bemusement, his smile didn't falter but the rest of his face scrunched in confusion. 'Yeah. I mean, I'm pretty sure . . .'

She shook her head. 'Sorry.' What was wrong with her? It was like she was still trying to impress the kind of person she no longer wanted to attract. 'I don't know what my problem is sometimes.'

'It's probably your selfishness.'

She risked looking at him. He was grinning. 'You're probably right,' she said, relieved. *No more, Robin*. She started again. 'So, you come here a lot?'

'For work, mainly.'

The waitress returned and put the glasses in front of them.

'They're on the house.' Riley winked and headed off again.

Robin sucked in her cheeks and widened her eyes. 'La-di-da.'

Cormac laughed, blushing slightly but still entirely at ease.

'So, what do you do then, for this work?'

'Lots of things,' he said, lifting his glass and clinking it with hers. 'I'm a journalist, mainly.'

'Oh yeah? What kind of thing do you do?'

'I'm trying to get into theatre reviews at the moment. I do a bit, and I'm trying to specialise in them. But I do lots of stuff.'

'And you meet your sources here, right? Like some old black-and-white film.'

Cormac laughed. 'I wouldn't exactly say I have sources . . .'

'Ever interviewed anyone famous?'

'Sure.'

'Like who?'

He took another sip. 'Like . . . Pierce Brosnan?'

Robin gave a mock gasp. 'The star of *Mamma Mia 2*.'

'Yeah, and James Bond.'

'I know,' she said. 'I'm joking.' Though the flippant way she'd said it was still ringing in her ears.

'And you? What do you do?'

Robin paused. How had she not prepared for this? 'I'm a nurse,' she said, taking a long, slow sip, trying not to wince at the bitterness.

'Really?'

'Mm-hmm.'

She couldn't tell him the truth without explaining that she had a child and a complicated relationship with her ex. Surely she was allowed one date before she had to divulge all that? She was working on swapping flippancy for honesty, but she was hardly going to become a new person overnight.

'Paediatrics,' she added, thinking of it as a half-truth. She did care for a four-year-old, after all. She pictured Carmel rolling around the floor in hysterics at that. Her mother, who'd spent thirty-six years as a nurse, said Robin had the bedside manner of a tax inspector.

Cormac went to ask another question, but Robin got in there first. 'So you like the theatre?' she said quickly. 'I'm more into sport.'

Was that even true? Eddy had loved that she insisted on watching soccer matches and found it sexy when she got into arguments with his friends about what manager needed to be sacked. She always found a reason to mention to men that she liked sport because she thought it made her more attractive. She drank beer for the same reason, even though she preferred spirits. But she hadn't watched a single game of anything since she'd moved home and there was no longer anyone to impress.

'Well, I don't know anything about sport, I'm afraid.'

'Plays make me cringe,' she countered. At least that was true.

'Cringe? Why?'

'Too fake.'

'Well, they are acting.'

'I know. But does it have to be so obvious?'

Dimple, dimple, delicious dimple. 'I'll bring you, some time.'

'You're grand.'

'To something good. I promise.'

'All right.' She held out a hand and felt a tingle up her arm and down her back as his fingers gripped around hers and didn't move. He didn't shake on the deal at all; for a second, he just held her hand.

When they had finished their drinks, they walked out of the bar, another waitress waving to Cormac.

'Are you sure we don't have to pay?' Robin whispered as he held the door open for her.

'Yes,' he whispered back.

Robin followed as he turned immediately to the right and opened an adjacent door. She trailed him through the doorway and up the stairs to his first-floor flat.

She was on a date. This man liked her and she liked him and though she didn't like herself a whole lot since she'd left Eddy's flat, she couldn't be completely awful if someone who was so clearly good saw something in her. She watched Cormac climb the stairs, his legs pushing against the material of his trousers, revealing how thin they were. She imagined them wrapped around her, and hers wrapped around him. She pictured his open face taking in her naked body and she did not feel embarrassed. The thought made her want to push herself against him here in the stairwell.

He brushed his dark fringe from his eyes and slotted another key into another lock. The concentration on his face was disproportionate to the task and Robin grinned. He had skin like cream and she wanted to eat it up.

'All right?' he said, dark eyebrows rising, cheeks crinkling as he paused, key in lock.

Robin bit the insides of her cheeks and nodded.

His fringe flopped down again and the latch clicked open.

Three things hit Robin at almost the same time. The first was the sound of Villagers blaring – that was good, she thought, they had similar musical tastes; the second was the overpowering smell of roast chicken – that was okay, she liked chicken, although possibly not as much of it as he seemed to be cooking; and the third was smoke, layers of grey mist billowing out towards them now they'd provided an escape.

'Shoot!' Cormac took a step back. 'I don't understand. I thought I sorted this just before . . . Okay. Just wait here, okay?' And he went in, battling the smoke with his lanky arms like he was clearing a path in a forest. There was something gloriously nerdy about him. She, the queen of sarcasm, liked how earnest he was.

A minute later he returned, his forehead creased apologetically. 'How do you feel about a roast chicken dinner without the roast chicken?'

'Just how I like it.'

He held his fringe back tightly as his face twitched with stress. *Kiss me, kiss me, kiss me.*

'Okay, well. You wait here' – he opened a side door and pushed her in – 'and I'll try to get rid of the smell and salvage some dinner.'

'All right,' said Robin as the door closed behind her. She took in the chest of drawers and double bed. The green checked shirt from the other night was thrown on the floor under the window. This was Cormac's bedroom. A faint smell of smoke and chicken lingered but it was usurped by aftershave. The same scent was masculine on his skin, but awkwardly boyish in the air. Would Jack's room smell like this one day, too?

Robin heard doors and windows opening and Cormac muttering. The blanket on the bed was thin and the sheets were different shades of navy. There were postcards of paintings thumbtacked to the wall and two books on the bed stand: a fantasy novel she'd never heard of and a biography of Harold Pinter. Robin hadn't read a book in ages. She heard Cormac's voice clearer.

'Okay, great . . .'

She moved to the door and pressed her ear against it.

'Yes, fine, thanks.'

There were footsteps and she hurried back to the end of the bed. But he didn't come in, not for another few minutes.

'Sorry,' he said, pushing open the bedroom door with his elbow and carrying in two plates of food. He set them down on the chest of drawers and lifted his shirt to his nose. 'I smell like I bathed in grease.'

'All okay?'

'There are bowls of baking soda all over the kitchen, so they should soak up the smell.' He stood just inside the closed door, his hands on his hips, as if he was trying to decide what catastrophe to fight next.

'I didn't know baking soda got rid of odours,' said Robin, impressed.

'Neither did I,' admitted Cormac. 'I rang my mother. Here . . .' He took a plate off the chest of drawers and proffered it. Robin stood from the bed and, as Cormac extended his arm further, he also recoiled. 'Oh God, I really do stink.'

Robin took the plate from him and placed it back on the chest of drawers. 'Let me?' She took one more step and her face was at his neck. She bent in slightly and sniffed his shirt. 'It's . . .' She moved her head to the other side and breathed in. She could smell their almost-dinner but an inch higher, at his skin, she breathed in the clean aphrodisiac from earlier. His chest rose and fell. She thought she could hear his heart.

'It'll have to come off, I think,' she said quietly, placing a hand on either side of the hem of his shirt and lifting. He helped her pull

130

it over his head. 'Hmm,' she said, taking in a chest that had more definition than she'd expected.

He looked embarrassed and she knew it might have sounded sarcastic but that wasn't how she meant it. 'You look great,' she said as genuinely as she could manage.

His arm was across her lower back. He held her there and raised his other hand to her face. He tilted her chin up. His unmasked affection had her embarrassed now too and she was about to pull back when, ever so gently, he kissed her. Once, twice.

'More,' she whispered.

He dropped both hands to his side and entwined his fingers with hers. He kissed her and kissed her and kissed her, until Robin's lips started to swell and the potatoes were definitely cold. She put her hands on his cool smooth shoulders. They were beautiful shoulders. She stood on her tippy toes and kissed one. He smiled. She kissed the other, and he brushed his hair from his face.

'Do you want . . .?'

They moved towards the navy bed and, on the sheets, they took their time. Indicating to each other when they wanted to remove an item of clothing and not growing impatient when some took more dexterity than others. Lace-up boots had been a terrible idea. Robin didn't think about her underwear with the rip along the waistband until they were all she was wearing. Cormac barely looked at them anyway. Naked, she pulled up the covers and threw them over him.

She pulled him closer and wrapped her arms around him as she pushed her body against his.

'I think you're great,' he said, and Robin went to make a joke about it, to say of course he did now she was naked in his bed. But she didn't. She couldn't. She was overwhelmed by a sudden urge to cry. *I think you're great.* The no-bullshit honesty of it, and all the ways it wasn't true.

She kissed him again, seriously this time, like she needed oxygen or sustenance or just something that was good. Then she guided him inside her. She and Eddy never watched each other during sex, but she looked at Cormac, watching him watching her, and it felt like magic. She loved his eyes and his skin; she loved the breadth of his face and the few brown hairs in his dark moustache. She loved him, she thought; she didn't really, of course, she barely knew him, but in that moment, in that act, she did. He was perfect.

When it was over, he pulled her on to him and still Robin feared she might cry. She never cried, but she felt like a different person here. The rise and fall of his chest, the weight of his arms against her lower back. She felt like he would go to war for her. Wasn't that often how it was after sex? Until someone got up and left the room to pee or get a glass of water or whatever it might be that instantly broke the spell.

Her phone rang then and he shifted. There it was: the practical thing that destroyed the magic. She rolled over, breathing in the last of it, and reached for the pocket of her coat at the end of the bed. She was glad it hadn't fallen to the floor; her worst angle was definitely naked and on her hunkers.

Johnny.

'Sorry, Robin. Jack woke up and said he's allowed two bananas during the night but I wasn't sure if—'

'I'll phone you right back.' She hung up and looked over her shoulder, but Cormac hadn't heard her brother.

'All okay?' he said sleepily, the tranquillising effect of an orgasm.

'I should go.'

And suddenly he was more awake. 'Was that not – did you not want—'

'No, no!' She leapt back up towards him and kissed his lips. 'That was *grrreat*. Tony the Tiger great. I just have to go.'

'I promised you dinner and you got nothing. I'm a terrible host.'

'I couldn't eat another bite.'

'Can we do it again?'

'What? Make dinner plans and then not eat a thing?'

He nodded, scratching at one of those lovely shoulders.

'I'd like that,' she said, allowing herself a big giddy grin as she pulled her dress slowly over her head.

*** Pine Road Poker ***

Fiona:
96FM!!!

Edie:
?

Fiona:
Turn on 96FM!!!

Ruby:
Already listening. 🍿

Carmel:
Got it.

Oh no.

Edie:
What?

Carmel:
They're talking about the bathroom list at Saint Ornatín's.

Bernie:
Oh my God. Trish?? Are you listening??

Ruby:
I'm playing 'national disgrace' bingo. Two mentions so far.

Carmel:
Some girl who was on the list has phoned in. Lots of angry callers.

Bernie:
What kind of mother would let their teenage daughter on this show? The host is so sleazy!

Rita Ann:
She's a great vocabulary, to be fair to the gurdle.

*girl

Ellen:
It's not just 'some girl'. It's Sinead Costello – Martha Rigby's daughter.

Fiona:
Who?

Ellen:
New family at No 8.

Rita Ann:
Is it? Oh Lord.

Ruby:
And again! Bingo!

Fiona:
Trish?? Are you listening?? Trish??

Trish:
As I already said, I cannot discuss this matter.

Bernie:
As neighbours and parents, that's not going to cut it, Trish. That girl is telling the whole city what a disgrace Saint Ornatín's is!

Carmel:
Isn't that what you were doing on Prime Time on Tuesday night, Bernie? And that was national TV, not local radio.

Ellen:
Bernie was raising the profile of poor management at our schools.
She did it in a calm and reasonable manner. Bernie is a trained media
professional.

Ruby:
She was raising the profile of something all right ...

Fiona:
Is this going to affect the school's ranking in the annual league
tables?? Maybe I need to be looking at other back-up schools for my
two! Trish??

Ruby:
She really does have a great vocabulary for a young one. Her mother
must be proud.

Rita Ann:
What's a Patrick Norman when it's at home?

*Practical Worm

*Patriarchal norm

Ellen:
I told you that family had no community spirit.

SIXTEEN

· · · · · · · · · · · · · · · · · ·

Martha was folding sheets in her bedroom when her phone beeped. It was Edie, from up the road.

I think Sinead's on 96FM. In case you don't know . . . x

Martha read the message twice before reaching for Robert's clock radio. The digital face blinked 22:12. Sinead was hardly on the radio. She'd just gone to bed; she was up early Saturday mornings for soccer practice. Martha turned the dial from Newstalk to 96FM.

'. . . not surprised, Frank. When I was a lad, we had respect for women but now why would you bother? You only have to look at how they're dressing to know they've no interest in respect and sure, as the young lady was just saying, she doesn't even like having a door held open for her. This is just the way society's going now, Frank, to hell in a handcart. And that's all I can say on the matter.'

Martha glanced back at her phone and double-checked she had the right frequency. Why did Edie have her listening to this garbage? *Be Frank with Frank.* You didn't have to be from Dublin to have heard of the late-night phone-in show, and it hadn't found fame through thoughtful debate and nuanced explorations.

'All right, Gerry, well thank you for your contribution. We have Mary on the line now and she says, wait for it, she says this kind of thing is happening all over the country! Well, that's a frightening thought. Do we really not know what's going on in our educational facilities? I have to say, it's making me consider my children's

137

school in a whole new light. Go ahead, Mary – be frank with Frank!'

'Hi, Frank. Have to say I love the show. You've a lovely voice.'

'Well, thank you, Mary.'

'Sort of like butter, slipping and sliding all over my radio.'

'Careful now, Mary. I'm a happily married man. Ha ha ha. Do you want to share your views?'

Martha started to compose a response to Edie.

'Oh yes, Frank, well, as I was saying to your nice researcher there, my son actually took my granddaughters out of their school because of this exact kind of thing. So I'm not at all surprised. It's happening everywhere.'

'This exact kind of thing, Mary? I'm shocked. Tell us more.'

'Well, in my granddaughters' school, which I don't mind naming, I'd be only too happy, it was—'

'Please don't, Mary.'

'Okay, right so, I won't. But the kind of behaviour – and this was sanctioned by the teachers. They were only twelve, barely out of national school, and they were told all about s-e-x. One of them came home and started telling my son about erogenous zones. He nearly fell off his chair. As did I when he told me. I didn't know about that until I was married. And why would I need to have known before then? If girls just kept their knickers on . . .'

Martha had had enough. She reached over and was about to snap off the radio when a shaky version of a very familiar voice piped up.

'Why is the blame always put on women? Why – why is Mary putting the blame on women and not on men?'

'That's Sinead Costello there. If you've just tuned in to us, folks. She was one of seven young female students named on a so-called "Rape List" in a male bathroom at Saint Ornatín's secondary school in north Dublin. The list said, can you remind us of the wording, Sinead?'

A pause. 'It – it said, the girl with the most ticks beside her name would be raped.'

'Truly, truly shocking stuff, folks. And some serious questions need to be asked of school management, I think we'd all agree. You said earlier, Sinead, that you weren't surprised by this list either, but for different reasons. Do you want to tell us those again?'

'Well, yes, okay. We – we live in a society where men are allowed to do what they want to women, and they just get away with it. Just because women are physically weaker, they think they can treat us how they like, humiliate us, use us for their amusement. Women are too scared to stop them, but we can't be scared. We have to fight back.'

'Remind us how old you are, Sinead.'

'Sixteen.'

'Six-teen. And at sixteen, have you really experienced these things?'

'Yes.'

'Shocking. Absolutely shocking. And where were your parents when this was going on?'

'W-well, recently our house was broken into while we were at home and my mother—'

'Sinead!'

Martha flung her phone on the half-folded sheets, threw herself out of her bedroom and into Sinead's, where her daughter was sitting cross-legged on her bed in the Harry Potter pyjamas she'd had since she was twelve.

'Get off that right now! Right now!'

Sinead pulled her phone away from her ear and covered the speaker with her hand. 'It's important people—'

'No!' Martha grabbed the phone out of her daughter's hand and hung up.

'Mum! You can't just—'

'I can do what I like; I'm the parent. What you can't do is call late-night radio shows and tell them our business without even consulting me. I thought you were in bed, for God's sake! What were you thinking? Are you stupid?' Martha was fuming, the pent-up emotion gushing out of her as if a valve had suddenly been released. 'These people only want to exploit you. What about when you go into school on Monday? Well? Did you think about that?'

'Someone has to do something, Mum! The school is acting like nothing happened. They're going to forget, they're going to let them get away with it. People should know – they should know what their precious sons are capable of.' The drawstring in her Harry Potter shorts had frayed from wear and, on her chest, a toothpaste stain covered Harry's scar. Why hadn't she thrown out those pyjamas? Had that stain been there since . . .

'I have to call your father.' Robert was at some retirement do, but should be done by now. 'And I'm keeping this.' Martha picked up Sinead's phone. 'Just – just stay there, and keep the shouting down or you'll wake Orla.'

'Why shouldn't I shout? I'm angry. I refuse to be another polite, nice little girl.'

'Chance would be a fine thing,' muttered Martha. She went to retrieve her own phone and tried Robert, the fury rising in her with each unanswered ring. After the third call she spoke into the answering machine through gritted teeth: 'Sorry to disturb you, Robert. It's just your family, who need you desperately, again. But that's fine. Don't worry. I hope you're enjoying your party.' Martha hung up and waited for herself to calm slightly. Then, having no one else, she rang Ellis. She explained as quickly as she could and he said it was fine, he had just finished his shift, he'd be right over.

Less than twenty minutes later, Ellis was jumping out of a taxi and heading up their short garden path. Sinead came down from her room and all three of them sat around the kitchen table. Sinead refused to put on a cardigan even though the kitchen was freezing, but Martha threw a rug at her all the same. She couldn't stand to see the outline of her daughter's nipples against that pyjama top.

'Mum told me about the rape list at school, Sinead. What a disgusting thing for someone to do. I'm really sorry.'

Martha loved her son. She loved his kindness and honesty and compassion.

'Thank you, Ellis,' said Sinead with such restrained dignity Martha nearly rolled her eyes. 'It *is* disgusting,' she added, shooting her mother an accusatory stare. 'And thank you for calling it what it is. Everyone else is being *euphemistic*. They just say The List.' Sinead drew quotation marks with her fingers. 'As if some fifth year wrote his shopping on the back of the bathroom door.'

'Nobody's saying it isn't serious,' said Martha, rising to the bait. 'I know it's serious. The distinction that has to be made, I think, is that nobody was raped.'

'That we know of.'

'Sinead.'

'Well, maybe they were, Mum,' she snapped. 'Maybe they were and we don't know. Maybe they're too embarrassed to talk about it. Maybe they're in denial.' Tears appeared in Sinead's eyes but she continued to stare at Martha defiantly.

Martha seemed to spend half her life being grateful she was no longer a teenager and the other half petrified of the era in which her daughters were coming of age. She looked at her skinny, scrappy, whip-smart, crusading daughter shivering in her favourite pyjamas that were tainted for ever. She wanted to carry her upstairs, wrap her in layers of bubble wrap and store her under the bed until the time came to celebrate her twenty-first birthday.

'I spoke to your principal. She is taking the matter very seriously and they are investigating.'

'That's how power always speaks.'

'Oh, for heaven's sake. She's not power. She's the woman who lives up the road.'

Sinead was shivering now, the rug fallen to her lap. A tear made its way down her right cheek and Ellis reached out to wipe it away, but Sinead recoiled with such kneejerk force that she smacked her elbow off the arm of the chair.

'Sinead! Are you okay?'

The tears came readily now, rushing down both cheeks. Sinead gave a sharp intake of breath as she tried to harden her face. She held her elbow with one hand and wiped at her face with the other.

Martha knew what this was. She looked from her shocked son to her crumbling daughter and she felt her stomach drop. Moving house wasn't enough.

'Should we get you some counselling, do you think, Sinead?'

'You want to punish me?' her daughter screeched. 'Because some asshole wrote my name on a bathroom door, you want to punish me?'

'No,' said Martha calmly. 'Because of what happened in Abbyvale.'

'Nothing happened in Abbyvale.'

'Sinead.'

'What, Mum? I'm just acting like you. Nothing happened. Everything's fine. Nothing was taken. Nobody was injured, not really. And nobody was caught. Nobody! I'm not even allowed to talk to you about it in case you get *upset*.'

'Come on, Sinead.'

'It's true, Ellis. Dad said they've made no arrests but not to ask Mum about it because she doesn't want to know. How could she not want to know? There's a guy in my year and his sister was bitten by a dog and his mother is always calling the guards about it, demanding to know if they've caught anyone yet. A dog! How can Mum not be on the phone to the guards or lawyers or the minister of whatever every day? What's wrong with you, Mum? They touched me.' Sinead spat out the last sentence. Her hands, arms, shoulders all shaking now. 'And yeah, I know they didn't rape me. But how dare they touch me. How dare they! They are not allowed.'

'You're right, they're not allowed. Mum knows that.'

Martha wanted to tell Ellis to zip it. He didn't understand. He would try to, because he was a good man, but he was still a man.

'I am so sorry about what happened,' said Martha, ignoring her son and piercing her gaze into her daughter, just as she had done that day. 'I'm sorry I couldn't stop it. And you have every right to be angry. I dream about it all the time. I hear the sound of them at the back door when I'm alone in this house. I hear anything in this house and I jump. But you can't let the anger overwhelm you. And phoning a shock-jock radio show isn't going to help either. I doubt your school will be very appreciative.'

'I don't care about the school.' Sinead's face was red and blotchy, and Martha could see the energy starting to drain, the cracks starting to show. *Where the hell was Robert?*

'That school took you and your sister at short notice despite being full. Did you think about Orla when you picked up the phone and made an enemy of what is also her new school?'

'Of course I thought about Orla! That's why I did it. Don't you see?' Sinead was shouting again now. It was breathtaking, really, how she could go from nought to sixty in the blink of an eye. 'She's your daughter, Mum. How do you not see? I don't want my little sister to grow up thinking men can do what they like and she has to take it. She's a person, Mum. She's not a joke!'

Sinead was doing her damnedest to look at Martha with hatred, but her true feelings were too extreme to hide. Her eyes shone and twitched and Martha wanted to tell her to hush, that it would be okay. Sinead sat up straight, her face defiant – but her heart and her soul and her youth were kicking and screaming on the kitchen floor, crying out for help.

'Your principal is nice. Give her a chance. Let her do her job.'

Her daughter looked away.

'They even have a suspect.'

Martha instantly regretted saying this. Partly because she had made it up, but more so because of the double-take her daughter did. Before Sinead could question it, Martha pressed on. 'I think you should go to bed now. It's a miracle Orla is still asleep.'

And then, right on cue, her youngest daughter appeared at the kitchen door: 'Why are you all shouting? I am trying to get my beauty sleep.'

Ellis grinned. 'Well, it's definitely working.'

Orla, whose left eye was glued half-shut with sleep and who had encrusted drool on her lower lip, gave a modest curtsey.

Sinead clambered up from the table and shunted out of the kitchen, knocking her sister off balance as she passed.

Orla winced. 'So – many – emotions.'

Ellis got up from his seat, rotated his youngest sister and led her back to bed. 'Come on, beauty queen.'

Martha sat blank faced at the table and stared straight ahead of her until the footsteps on the stairs stopped. She felt the satisfying instant crumble of her face, like a magician whipping a tablecloth from under a fully set table. She cried ugly, silent wails for several seconds and then, just as abruptly, she stopped. She sat right there, not moving, concentrating on her breathing and waiting for the puffiness to subside. By the time Ellis reappeared downstairs, she had regained full composure.

'Sinead's started listening to Dylan, I see.'

'She was sitting at this table the other morning reading the lyric book of one of Robert's old CDs for about an hour.'

'We've lost her so.'

Martha smiled at her son. 'How was work?'

'Grand. The till didn't add up and there was panic for a while but I had a look over it and it was just that the coffees that came with the evening special hadn't been put through as free.'

Her beautiful son was too smart to be waiting tables. He should be a counsellor; she'd always thought that. But she was too tired, too grateful to him, to get into it again tonight.

She walked Ellis to the front door and gave him the sort of hug she never gave anyone else, not even the girls. It was hard to explain this bond; he was the only child who belonged to her alone. It made her think of Robin and little Jack across the road. Was that the connection she felt to the young woman?

'I love you,' she told Ellis, holding him tight. 'And I love having you so close now.'

Back upstairs she heard the silent vibrations of her phone in the half-folded sheets. Six missed calls, all from Robert, and two text messages.

Sorry. Phone was in cloakroom. Tried to call back.

On my way home. Be there asap.

Martha stood for a moment in the middle of their new bedroom in their new house in their new reality and let it wash over her. She closed her eyes and saw her family, as they had been that day and as they were now.

She saw Robert frowning as he woke that morning. She saw Sinead shivering at the kitchen table. She saw Orla refusing to get out of her old bed. She heard the creak of the decking that she'd presumed was Oscar. She heard the smash of the glass. She saw Robert smiling out of the newspaper with his medal. She saw Orla's wrists growing red. She saw Ellis standing in their old house after all the guards had left, hands on waist, trying to find a purpose. She saw the glimmer of a black watchstrap as a hand reached out for Sinead. She heard the collective male laughter. She saw Sinead paralysed with fear. She felt the sting on her own cheek. She felt herself paralysed with fear. She saw Robert smiling out of the newspaper with his medal. She saw Sinead sitting at the old kitchen table, struggling. She saw Sinead sitting at the new kitchen table, struggling. She saw Robert smiling out of the newspaper with his medal.

And she heard Robert. She heard him outside their house now, loudly telling the taxi driver to keep the change. She felt herself reaching for an unfolded sheet, stuffing it into her mouth. She felt her vocal cords stretch as she screamed into the creases. It was the same maddening sensation as getting a filling; all this screeching in her head that no one else could hear. When she could no longer breathe, she removed the sheet. Then, as she heard the front door open, she switched off the bedroom light.

*** Pine Road Poker ***

Ellen:
I've discussed it with Bernie and given that she obviously has a lot going on at the minute, I'll be taking over as coordinator of this year's Pine Road pre-Easter street party.

Fiona:
YASSS KWEENNNN!!!!

Ellen:
Thank you, Fiona.

T minus five weeks folks.

Ruby:
Shouldn't there be a vote or something? What if someone else is interested in the job?

Ellen:
I don't think anyone else is interested in the job, Ruby, so it's simplest, and quickest, if I just take it.

Ruby:
That's the kind of attitude that led to 10,000% inflation in Zimbabwe.

Ellen:
Are you comparing me to Mugabe?

Fiona:
Who's Mugabe?

Ellen:
An African dictator.

Fiona:
Oh. That doesn't sound very nice, Ruby.

[is typing]

XXX

Ruby:
You're right, Fiona. I apologise.

[is typing]

[is typing]

xxx

Ellen:
We could confirm the details at the next poker game? Rita Ann, I believe it's your turn to host?

Rita Ann:
Can't. I'm getting the bathroom done up. And I'm STILL missing my newspapers!

Ellen:
Weren't you getting the bathroom done up last time it was your turn?

Rita Ann:
[is typing]

[is typing]

The other bathroom.

Ruby:
I'm starting to think you're hiding dead bodies in your house, Rita Ann ...

Ellen:

So, we have Carmel making fondue, Ruby supplying gin and tonics, and me doing a pig on a spit.

Fiona:

A pig on a spit, Ellen??

Ellen:

Oh, it's nothing. You know me, I'll probably just throw it together last minute on a wing and a prayer! BTW, Carmel, we were wondering could you maybe do a cheese-free fondue too, for Sylvie? With everything she's been through I think she'd appreciate it.

Anyone else?

Edie:

I'll do dessert x

Ellen:

Okay. There will be lots of kids there so obviously no nuts, dark chocolate where possible and minimal sugar.

Fiona:

I can make an alcohol-free punch! XXX

Ellen:

Perfect.

Ruby:

What's the point of that???

Fiona:

We should ask if Shay Morrissey might use his parking blockages for good and help us cordon off the road for the day.

I can also provide music.

Ruby:

Just make sure it's sound-free ...

Ellen:
Nobody finds you humorous, Ruby.

That would be great, Fiona. Thanks. Remember to keep the music child-appropriate. No rap-rap.

Edie:
Will I mention it to the new neighbours?

Ellen:
Number 8? I'm not sure they'd be interested.

Fiona:
Oh do! I haven't met them properly yet.

SEVENTEEN

●●●●●●●●●●●●●●●●●●●●●●●●●●

On **Friday** afternoon, for the first time in the twenty-seven years she'd worked at Saint Ornatín's, Trish took a taxi the 700 metres home from work. It was after six when she was finally done – nothing like a media frenzy and a courtesy visit from the guards to add an extra two hours to your day – and even then, she didn't want to chance bumping into a parent.

After word of the list got out, there had been a few pieces about it in the papers and on telly. The *Daily Mail* was considering an 'Are Our Schools Safe?' campaign and the *Sun* had nicknamed the school 'Saint Horny Teens'. Bernie Watters-Reilly had never been one to refuse a call from a journalist but now she had a personal connection to a story, her stock had rocketed. The story was petering out by the end of the first week, but then Sinead Costello appeared on that bloody stupid radio programme and it had started up again, only worse. The list had gone viral and several of the girls on it had been forced to shut down their social media accounts because of harassment. Three of the girls had lawyers for parents and, while they'd yet to say anything, Trish had a bad feeling about it. At least two Sunday newspaper columnists had written about how hearing Sinead's voice had humanised the story and awoken them from their apathy.

Trish wished to God they'd all go back to sleep.

She used her mobile phone to virtually hail a taxi and waited inside the school doors until it pulled up right at the entrance, then she scurried out.

'Where are you off to?' asked the heavyset lad in the front seat, reversing the car on the gravel and turning the volume of the radio down slightly.

'Pine Road, please.'

The man looked at Trish in his rear-view mirror. 'Pine Road? As in, Pine Road just around the corner?'

'Yes, that's the one.'

The man said something under his breath and turned the radio back up. Eventually, reluctantly, the car moved.

Trish fell back against the leather of the headrest and tried to do a minute of breathing exercises. The most important thing with mindfulness was to keep it up, no matter what else was going on. The taxi driver, however, had other ideas. He was determined to make Trish pay for this journey, one way or another. 'That's your place,' he barked at the mirror.

'Pardon?'

'That's Saint Ornatín's they're talking about. They've been on about it all day. A national disgrace. Are the culprits going to be expelled or what?'

Trish glanced down at the radio – a local station – and heard her name.

'. . . a Mrs Walsh who has yet to make a public statement although she is understood to have spoken to the parents of the girls involved. We need accountability. We need action. Where is the school board on this? Where is the Department of Education? Indeed, where is the minister?'

The minister is up my arse, thought Trish grimly. *He's been living there since last week.*

'We did ask the minister if he would come on and speak to us but the offer was declined.'

'Could you turn that off please?'

'I've two nieces,' said the driver, ignoring her request. 'If it was up to me, I'd get the lads who wrote it and I'd cut off their mickeys.' He eyeballed Trish in the mirror. 'Is it up to you?'

'I can't discuss that, I'm afraid.'

'I'd do it for free.' She wished he'd keep his eyes on the road. 'No questions asked.'

The car approached Island Stores. 'Just up the top, please.'

'Not a chance,' the driver harrumphed. 'You couldn't swing a cat on this road with all the cars, never mind do a U-turn. So, if your ladyship could stomach a thirty-second walk . . .'

Trish glanced up the road and considered all the possible landmines between here and her house: an in-person demand for an update she didn't have from Bernie Watters-Reilly; an unexpected meeting with Sinead Costello's mother, or father, or indeed Sinead herself. The girl was camped outside Trish's office during every lunch break and free period, badgering her secretary and reading out extracts from the Human Rights Charter and the Freedom of Information Act. Then there were the other Saint Ornatín's parents living on Pine Road, not to mention the neighbours with no vested interest other than the acquisition of good gossip.

Trish handed over the exact change, gathered her things and, stepping out of the car, slammed the door shut. She hurried up the road, looking nowhere but right in front of her. She felt like a character from one of Laura's old computer games, jumping from rock to rock, avoiding the cracks and the monsters that might emerge from the shadows. She opened her garden gate, winced at the creak, and made it to her front step. She was rummaging rapidly in her pockets – why hadn't she gotten the key ready in the taxi? – when she heard her name.

Busted.

Trish turned from her door to the right, in the direction of the female voice, to see Edie Rice, the smiley young woman who'd moved into number nineteen last year. As landmines went, it wasn't the worst.

Edie had been on her way into her own garden, wearing her uniform – was she a receptionist, Trish tried to recall, at some hotel in town? – under a pink faux-fur coat and a multicoloured fluffy scarf. She stopped at the gate and Trish waved across at her. 'Oh hi, Edie. How are you?'

'Good, thank you. I was just moving the car. No space earlier, had to park it on Oak.'

The girl had eyes like a deer. Talking to her was like shining a flashlight in them.

'It's a nightmare,' agreed Trish, turning back to her door. Just as her hand hit upon the keyring in her coat pocket, she heard the clackity-clack of heels growing closer. She plastered on a smile and turned back.

'I just wanted to say' – clack, clack, closer clack – 'I hope our cat hasn't been bothering you? I've called her a couple of times and she always seems to come from the direction of your garden. Sorry about that. My brother-in-law's dog has been staying with us on and off and she gets spooked when he's about.'

'Oh, don't worry about it,' called Trish. 'Emily loves playing with her. And it's good for keeping the rats away.'

'Maybe that's why we haven't had any,' said Edie, then added quickly: 'Though we did put down the poison.'

'Oh right, great,' said Trish, physically taking the key from her pocket now and holding the Credit Union keyring up in Edie's direction. 'I actually have a bit more work to do . . .'

'Oh grand, right, don't let me keep you.' There was a pause but no sound of footsteps leaving. 'I hope you're doing okay with all the hassle at the school. It can't be easy.'

'I'm coping. Thanks.'

'Well, if you feel like a glass of wine, I'm having a couple of women over this evening – just a couple, Carmel and Robin, like, not Bernie or anyone like that. Not that there's anything wrong with Bernie, of course,' hurried Edie, 'but just if you were looking to avoid all that . . .'

'Yes, no – thanks, Edie. Probably not tonight but I'll keep it in mind. Thanks,' she said again. 'Have a good evening.'

'You too, Trish!'

Finally, the footsteps started up, growing fainter, and Trish stuck her key in the lock. When the door opened, she heard the familiar blare of music from Emily's bedroom, but she did not feel the usual surge of irritation or concern for the neighbours. *Turn it up*, Trish thought, picturing Bernie next door, a glass of wine in one hand, the other clacking over the keyboard as she sent off yet another 'Dear All' to the parents of Saint Ornatín's student body.

Trish turned on the kettle and powered up her laptop. She had her own 'Dear All' to send. The Department of Education had emailed through instructions right at the end of the day – they always did that so Trish wouldn't have a chance to come back with queries until the morning – or in this case, after the weekend. But Trish wouldn't be leaving it until Monday. She was sending off the calming – she hoped – missive tonight.

Brrring!

The doorbell went and Trish heard Emily thundering down the stairs. She mustn't have heard her mother come in. Emily never bothered to open the door, or answer the phone, if someone else was in the house to do it. Her argument was that it was never for her. 'Only old people don't message before they call,' claimed Emily. 'It's basic manners.' It was a relief, at least, to know she did bother to answer when she thought she was alone.

Trish moved closer to the kitchen door and stood to the side so her shadow wouldn't be detected through the frosted glass. She couldn't make out the voices over her daughter's music, which was louder now she'd left her bedroom door open. Then she heard the front door close again. Presumably Emily had told whoever it was that Trish wasn't home and sent them off. She was about to go inform her daughter that she was in fact here, though no need to spread it around, when the kitchen door opened on her.

'Oh!'

'Oh!'

'Sorry, Mrs Walsh, didn't see you there.'

'Mum. I didn't know you were home. What are you doing?'

Emily and Declan Reilly, Bernie's son from next door, came through the kitchen door just as it collided with Trish. Her daughter was still wearing her uniform, though Declan had changed into a tracksuit and was carrying a shovel and a large container of something industrial.

'The garden, of course,' said Trish, ignoring her daughter's question as she sidled out from behind the door. 'I completely forgot. Thanks for calling.'

'Well, you're here so I'll just . . .' And Emily sauntered back out of the kitchen without bothering to finish her sentence. It was amazing to think Declan and Emily were in the same year. Not only did Emily look older, but she acted like a woman who'd seen all the world had to offer and was bored by it already, while the only bit of the world Declan seemed to see was whatever few inches of it were in front of his feet.

Trish smiled kindly, lowering her head slightly in an attempt to catch Declan's eye. 'Everything all right, Declan? You doing all right?'

'Yeah, sound,' he said, glancing up at her, then watching his shoes shuffle again. 'Will I . . .?' He inched towards the back door.

'Please. Thanks, Declan.' She watched him cross the kitchen towards the patio doors, dragging his feet slightly. He'll be good-looking, she thought, when he's older; he looked like his father and while Bernie's husband was a lazy lout who'd lie on the floor if there was work in the bed, he was handsome. Drink hadn't ruined that. 'How are your parents?'

What was wrong with her? The last person she wanted to talk about was Bernie Watters-Bloody-Reilly.

Declan stopped at the back door. 'Yeah, sound.'

Trish nodded and turned her attention back to her laptop, happy to leave it at that.

'You know I told Mr Watson about that list in the jacks? In the toilets, I mean.'

'Did you?' said Trish, casting her mind back to the day Gormless Paul came to her office and started this ongoing headache. She'd never asked which student had told him about it. She closed her laptop and looked at Declan, still standing at the back door, still staring at his feet. She felt sorry for him. We don't choose our families, do we? 'Well, thank you, Declan. That was the right thing to do.'

'You haven't caught anyone, have you? I heard there were suspects.'

If only rumours came from truth. 'Not yet, no. But we're investigating.'

'Does my mam know?'

Trish almost laughed. 'About the list? Yes. She definitely knows.'

'No. That I'm the one who found it?'

'Didn't you tell her?'

Declan shrugged.

Trish frowned. 'Do you want me to tell her?'

Declan shrugged, and Trish waited. 'She's pretty mad about it,' he said.

'I know.'

'And she's even more obsessed with my sister now.'

'With Sylvie? But she wasn't on the list.'

Shoulders up, shoulders down.

Trish imagined what life must be like next door. The two women always shrieking and shouting about something; Bernie's husband pretending he couldn't hear any of it; Declan trying not to disappear in the middle of it.

'She's gone to the police.'

'About the list?' You wouldn't think Bernie had a day job, but she did. She worked part time at an old folks' home up the road, as well as writing her column. Anyway, she could join the queue. The guards were more pissed off than anything else that they were being dragged into what they saw as a school affair. Even if the list had been written in a public bathroom and they had the culprit right in front of them, there wasn't much of consequence they could charge him with. While relieved to know she wasn't dealing with a criminal situation, Trish hadn't been entirely happy with their attitude.

'No, about my sister. And the dog.'

'The—' Trish recalled some talk of Sylvie crying wolf, or dog, from the Pine Road Poker WhatsApp thread. She largely ignored that conversation; she was in too many group chats as it was. If it wouldn't have made her a social pariah on Pine Road, she'd have left the group long ago. There were several times this week when she'd been seriously tempted. But Sylvie was always exaggerating about everything. She'd accused Ruby's sausage dog of biting her last year and Madeline, Ruby's wife, had nearly decked Bernie when she threatened to have the animal put down.

'Sylvie didn't even want to go but Mam said she had to. They went and made a formal complaint but when they came home, Mam was even madder and was calling the guards all these names. Sylvie said the officer in charge had laughed at them.' Declan grimaced, something between irritation, embarrassment and hurt. 'They said they couldn't do a lot without a better description of the animal, so Mam got this sketch artist to come around. He's there now. He's asking Sylvie exactly what the dog looked like and then Mam's going to make posters.'

Jesus. That woman. She'd be on the wine now too. Trish must have done something seriously bad in a previous life to end up with the head of the Parents' Association for a neighbour.

'That's . . . a lot.'

'Yeah,' agreed Declan. 'That's why I'm early. She said I had to get out so Sylvie could concentrate.'

'Well, I'm delighted to have you here, Declan.'

The boy looked up at her. He smiled hesitantly, then flinched.

'Nobody does as good a job on the garden as you do – not even Mr Walsh.'

Declan gave a full grin now. 'I was going to do the weeding and put down a bit more poison. No sign of a rat now for weeks, but you can't be too careful.'

'Exactly what I was thinking,' said Trish, smiling now too. 'And you know if there's ever anything you need to talk about, you don't have to be gardening to call in.'

Declan pushed open the patio doors and lifted the shovel after him. 'I'm sorry the whole bathroom thing happened.'

'Not your fault, Declan.'

The boy nodded as he hunched forward and stepped out into the garden.

EIGHTEEN

Edie carried the glasses carefully into her living room. She'd broken out the special-occasion champagne flutes, even though this was definitely a casual get-together. 'Impromptu drinks,' was how she'd put it to Robin, in her best breezy voice. She'd been dreaming of having the kind of neighbour friends she could invite over for 'impromptu drinks' since they moved to Pine Road.

The glasses had been a wedding present from Daniel's cousin – the son of the woman who gave them the Waterford Crystal bowl. Edie wasn't that gone on these either, but the cousin had yakked on about their 'unique origins' for so long that Edie was now an expert on the things. She thought they looked deformed, not that it mattered; other people seemed to love them.

Carmel took two glasses from Edie and handed one to Robin. Martha carefully extracted the flute that was wedged between Edie's elbow and waist. She'd really rather have used a tray but the only one she could find had an oil stain down the middle of it. She'd almost texted Daniel when she saw it – he had a steel tray specifically for his tools, why did he always have to use the good ones? – but they'd been on a fight-free streak for a couple of weeks now and today was the first day of her fertility window.

'Cool glasses,' said Robin. 'Retro.'

'They're art deco. From the Rhone region, of France, circa 1921.'

Robin made a face that definitely said she was impressed.

'Cheers!' Edie beamed as she raised her glass. 'To impromptu drinks of a Friday evening.'

Edie had met Robin in Island Stores that morning and asked her over for a glass of bubbly on a whim. When Carmel emerged from the cereal aisle, she invited her too. Then she thought it might be weird if it was just her, a target pal and that target pal's mother, so on the way home, she knocked into Martha and asked her around for a drink too.

Edie could scarcely believe she was now the kind of person who 'knocked into' neighbours!

The three women followed her lead and sat. Edie had cut a bit of lavender from the garden, tied it with ribbons and left it in a jar on the coffee table. She was considering handing it out as party favours but wasn't sure if that would undo the free-and-easy vibe she had spent an hour cultivating through strategically placed 'clutter': fashion magazines positioned at an angle, blankets thrown on the arms of couches, a selection of good shoes taken from the bedroom and lined up by the front door. Would party favours be too much? She'd play it by ear.

'Where is this famous husband of yours?' asked Martha, settling into an armchair. Edie had been considering getting that chair reupholstered but now Martha sat in it, honest to God, it looked like those worn bits of leather were *supposed* to be there. 'The best mechanic this side of the Shannon, by all accounts.'

Edie beamed. She loved when people said nice things about Daniel. 'He had to meet his brother for a bit,' she said, trying to copy the elegant way Martha positioned her legs, not so much crossed as draped, one over the other. 'I'm meeting him for a drink at eight.' One drink here, one drink in the pub – that was her limit – then home for some strategic love-making. Everything was so much nicer now things between them were good again. 'Sorry to have to kick you all out so soon.'

'I love coming to things with an end time,' said Carmel. 'Otherwise you don't know where you are. Is it just the one drink or am I going to be scuttered? Do I need to have dinner beforehand or can it wait? If I put the potatoes in the oven, will I be back in time to take them out? With an end time, you know where you stand. Anyway, I'm on babysitting duty. Lover Girl here has a hot date.'

'The hipster journalist?' enthused Edie, clapping her hands. 'You're still seeing each other?'

'Oh, so he's a hipster, is he? Well, well . . . You didn't mention that. She tells me nothing.'

'You don't even know what a hipster is, Mam.' Robin raised her glass to her mouth but it didn't quite mask her smile. 'This is our fourth date.'

Edie beamed. 'How did he take it when you told him about Jack?'

'No deal breakers so far, so . . .'

Edie knew it. She was good at reading people – that wasn't her being boasty, everyone said it; it was her detective gene – and she knew a decent lad when she saw one, even if it was from a distance, when slightly inebriated, in a badly lit pub.

'I'm just happy she's not seeing that other pup,' said Carmel.

Robin rolled her eyes. 'Mam's not a fan of Jack's father.'

'He's a toe-rag,' said Carmel, draining her first glass of prosecco and pushing it, not so subtly, towards Edie. 'A two-bit thug who thinks he's Al Capone.'

'You know when you had Jack . . .' called Edie, hurrying into the kitchen to fetch the bottle and cursing herself for not having a second one cooling in the fridge. Everyone would think she was stingy. And there was nothing worse than being stingy. 'Did you . . . did it take much persuading of Jack's dad?'

'To what?'

'To . . .' Edie blushed as she returned to the room and tipped the bottle into Carmel's glass. 'To make a baby.'

'Little more, Edie love, little more . . .'

Robin laughed. 'It wasn't a decision. Both of us nearly shit ourselves when we found out I was pregnant.'

'Little more . . .' Carmel only put her hand out to say 'stop' when the prosecco was about to go over the brim.

'Oh,' said Edie. 'Of course.' She should have known Jack hadn't been planned. Robin must have been twenty-one when she had him, and she hadn't seemed like the kind of girl who was chomping at the bit to start a family. She'd been far too cool for that. Unlike Edie.

'Does Daniel take a little convincing?' asked Carmel gently.

'No,' Edie replied immediately, wrinkling her nose and shaking her head. 'Gosh no. No, no. He wants a kid. Definitely.'

'But maybe sometimes he's not so sure?'

'Well, I mean, maybe he's questioned it once or twice, but not now . . .'

'That's normal,' said Carmel decisively. 'That's just men. Mick didn't think he was ready either. But they're easily convinced. When we were trying for Robin, if Mick wasn't in the mood, I used to put on this pair of red—'

'No,' shouted Robin, holding her hand up in the direction of her mother. 'No! No! No!'

'So what's this hipster journalist like, Robin,' asked Martha, undraping and draping her long legs. 'Is he good-looking?'

Robin gave a half-smile. 'I would describe Cormac as very handsome, yes.'

'Oooo, *Cormac*,' cooed Edie and, though Robin rolled her eyes, her face had gone full grin. Edie remembered how exciting it had been to say and hear Daniel's name in the early days – even 'Two Straps' had made her giddy back then. 'He was very good-looking as I recall,' she said, only too delighted to big up her target pal's new man. Who knows? If things went well on all fronts, she might end up invited to Robin actual Dwyer's wedding. Maybe she'd even have to arrange a babysitter so she could go. *Imagine!* She was giddy now. 'Tall, dark and handsome,' she confirmed.

'Well, tall-ish,' allowed Robin.

Martha gave a murmur of contentment. She'd finished her prosecco too. 'Robert's barely my height. The only place I get tall, dark and handsome is at the cinema.'

'Oh, actually,' said Carmel, 'I meant to say, I switched phone providers last week and now get free cinema tickets for Monday nights – only myself and Mick go dancing on Monday nights. So if any of youse ever want them . . .'

'That'd be great,' said Martha.

Edie was practically bouncing in her chair. This was going brilliantly. Look how relaxed they all were! In *her* house, at *her* impromptu drinks. And then, as if things couldn't get any better, Carmel uttered those eight magic words . . .

'Will we start a WhatsApp group for it?'

'Yes!' Edie just about caught her glass as her knees leapt up. Robin frowned at her; she composed herself. 'That's a great idea.'

'I have your number, Edie, so you just put yours in here . . .' Carmel handed her phone to Martha. 'How, ah, how is Sinead getting on? I heard her on the radio.'

'I think the whole road heard her,' said Martha, returning Carmel's phone. 'She's fine. She's threatening to organise a mass school boycott if feminist studies aren't made mandatory for all male students but other than that, she's fine.' Martha reached for the bottle Edie had left on the table. 'Can I?'

'Oh yes, of course.' Edie winced as Martha poured the dregs into her glass. Why, oh why, hadn't she put another one in the fridge?

'It's given her something to focus on, at least. She had a rough enough time before we came here.'

The silence that followed that declaration was enough for Martha to look around at the other women. 'After the burglary,' she clarified.

Edie stared at the empty prosecco bottle and concentrated on trying to remember the Harry Potter spell that made vessels fill with liquid. She was acutely aware that nobody else was talking either.

'Ah ha,' said Carmel, so pointlessly that everyone turned to look at her. She brought her flute, already empty again, to her lips.

The prosecco in Edie's own glass fizzled.

Carmel made a faint humming sound.

Somewhere, a floorboard creaked.

'We know!' Edie blurted out. She'd never been able to keep secrets, not even her own. They ate away at her until they burrowed a route to her mouth.

'Excuse me?'

'I'm sorry but we know, about the tiger raid. I looked it up online and I found an article about what happened and Robert getting that medal and it sounded awful and I'm sorry, for what happened but also for invading your privacy. I didn't mean to invade your privacy; I just thought I could help. Although it would be disingenuous to say I wasn't also being nosy. When I get the whiff of a mystery, something takes over, and when you said about them breaking in in the morning . . .'

'And then she told me,' said Robin, holding up a hand, instructing Edie to relax. 'Well, she showed me the article. You must be proud of your husband.'

'And Robin told me,' added Carmel. 'But I haven't told anyone, except Mick. But he's probably forgotten already. He was only half listening because a repeat of *At Your Service* was on TV. Jesus, but that man loves Francis Brennan.'

'So does Robert,' said Martha.

Carmel considered this. 'What's that about, I wonder?'

'I don't know.'

'So, you're not mad?' said Edie, eager for absolution. She was also eager for more details, but not at the risk of losing target friends and possible participants in future impromptu drinks.

'No,' said Martha. 'Of course not. I might easily have done the same.'

'I'd say it was terrible,' sympathised Carmel. 'We'd someone break into our place once. They stole all the DVDs except *The*

165

Bridges of Madison County and I couldn't be in the place alone for days.'

'And they still haven't caught anyone,' said Edie, avoiding Robin's quizzical look. She'd meant it to sound more like a musing than a statement. She'd only phoned the press office one more time. The guards still had nothing to report. It didn't sound like they'd done a tap.

'I actually phoned the inspecting officer yesterday, for the first time since we moved here, to see if he'd any update.'

'And?' asked Edie eagerly.

'Nothing.'

They fell quiet for a moment, then Martha spoke again: 'I saw one of them.'

'You what?'

'One of the men who came to the house, I saw his face. He was outside, in the car. I never told anyone.'

Edie gasped. 'The article said they were wearing balaclavas.'

Carmel shuddered. 'I wouldn't like that now, at all at all.'

'This man was supposed to follow Robert to the bank. He was sitting in the car and it was far enough away but he pulled up the balaclava just as he started the engine. I'm positive he saw me. For a second, we were just sitting there, looking at each other, and then he left.'

'Why wouldn't you tell anyone?' Edie's head was set to explode. There she was thinking it was a dead case, and now she had a piece of information even the guards didn't have. She put her hand to her chest and instructed herself to calm down. All the mother-to-be message boards agreed that relaxed was the best state in which to conceive. 'Not even Robert?'

Martha shook her head and emptied her glass.

'I watched a true-crime documentary recently about a serial rapist in America and in the end, they caught him because one of his victims described him to the press and some woman was out on her lawn one morning, reading the newspaper, and she recognised the description as the guy who was cleaning her pool right at that very second, right in front of her!'

'Nope.' Carmel shook her head. 'Would not like that, at all at all.'

'I felt sorry for him.' Martha ran her finger lightly along the hair that framed her face.

'What?'

'He looked worried. Probably because he was driving back roads, or because he thought he might get caught.' She closed her eyes. 'I can still see him, his face. It's . . .'

Edie reached for a pen on the coffee table. But Martha's eyes flew open again and she snapped out of it.

'I don't think I could describe him, not in any meaningful way. I have no idea of his build or how tall he was, and the balaclava was covering his hair.'

'But if you had to?' pressed Edie, eyeing her notebook lying on top of the television.

'Soulful eyes?' offered Martha eventually, covering her mouth as she spluttered out a sudden laugh. 'I don't know. White, Irish-looking, maybe stubble, sort of dangerous-looking. Although that might just have been the context. I don't even know what colour his soulful eyes were.'

Edie couldn't mask her disappointment. She didn't bother with the notebook.

'I know,' said Martha. 'It's not a lot to go on.'

'No,' sympathised Carmel. 'I wouldn't say you'd be getting your day out in court with that description. I don't get why you wouldn't tell Robert, though. I treat Mick like my own personal worry doll; I lump him with everything that's bothering me, and then I float off to sleep.'

Martha shifted a little, folding her legs in a manner that suggested she was done talking about it. 'I think I just wanted to forget.'

Edie glanced at the clock on the television. 'Oh gosh! I'm already late.'

She leapt from the armchair and the others got to their feet, gathering their things.

'Sorry to be kicking you out!' She carried the empty Prosecco bottle into the hall and grabbed the hairbrush from the table. She was wearing her hair in a high pony, just how Daniel liked it. She gathered their coats from under the stairs and started doling them out.

She marvelled at the cleanliness of Martha's jacket. How did she wear wool without attracting any lint?

'Thank you for coming,' she enthused. 'A lovely, spur-of-the-moment get-together! We should—'

But before she could suggest consulting their diaries to find a good date for their next impromptu drinks, the doorbell went.

A silhouette appeared through the frosted glass of Edie's front door. Robin, who was positioned nearest, leaned forward and pulled it open.

'Oh, hello.' Bernie Watters-Reilly was standing on the doorstep dressed, as she always was, impeccably. Edie wasn't into skirt suits *herself*, but Bernie really pulled them off. 'Sorry to disturb. I didn't realise you were having a party.'

'We're not,' called Edie quickly, standing on her tippy toes to be seen behind the others. 'It was impromptu.'

'We were just leaving actually,' added Robin, making to slide past Bernie.

'Here.' The blonde woman pressed a sheet of paper into Robin's hand and smiled widely. She reached into her bag. 'I have one for everyone in the audience.' She handed three more to Carmel.

'What is it?'

Robin peered at the page. 'Is it . . . a drawing of a dog?'

'It's an artist's impression,' corrected Bernie, smile still at full wattage. Edie ran her tongue self-consciously along her own teeth. 'Of the dog that bit Sylvie outside Island Stores last month.'

Carmel, who was still hoarding all three printouts, snorted but when Bernie's eyes shot in her direction, she pretended to be sneezing.

'So you're taking this quite seriously, then,' said Edie, more tactfully.

'Oh, we are. We've talked to the guards but, as usual, they're doing nothing.' Bernie pulled her jacket tighter. Edie wanted to invite the woman in out of the damp, but she really did have to go. 'This new garda commissioner was supposed to be about reform,' she hooted. 'I'm not seeing a damn sign of it. It's always the same: nothing they can do. Not about parking, not about that catastrophe up at the school, and not about mangy dogs roaming the streets, attacking innocent children.'

This time Carmel exhaled loudly and didn't try to cover it up. 'Still, at least you'll get a column out of it.'

'If it was your grandson, Carmel Dwyer, it'd be a different matter.'

'My grandson doesn't go sticking his hand in dogs' mouths in the hope of a little attention.'

'How dare you!'

'I'm just saying, do you not think this is a bit much? I saw Sylvie out on the road lecturing Fiona's twins on how to dance to Taylor Swift last night. She seemed grand.'

Bernie's showbiz smile tightened. 'She survived this attack, yes, but what about the next one? And what if this beast attacks someone else's child? I wouldn't be able to live with myself.'

Edie tried to take one of the sheets from Carmel. She also thought it was a bit extreme to get an artist's impression of a dog, but she wanted to stay on the good side of all her neighbours, especially the powerful ones. Also, she was intrigued by the possibility of identifying the animal. A mystery's a mystery.

But Carmel folded them over, placed them on the hall table and moved the Waterford Crystal bowl on top, making it clear to Bernie that she would not be taking hers with her.

'Thank you, Bernie,' called Edie, back on her tippy toes. 'I'll take a good look at that and keep an eye out. I'm good with faces.'

'Lick arse,' mumbled Carmel.

Bernie surveyed the group. 'The famous Martha Rigby, am I right?' She flicked her blonde hair behind her shoulders and smiled. 'I've just been to your house. Met your husband. Nice man. And I heard your daughter on the radio last Friday.' She set her teeth to dazzle. 'Very articulate.'

'Right, well,' declared Robin, 'I've a play to get to.' She skirted past Bernie and down the garden path. 'Thanks for the drink, Edie.'

Bernie's eyes flashed back to the trio still standing in the hallway. They narrowed slightly as they landed on the empty prosecco bottle on the hall table. Edie blushed. It had been impromptu!

'Well,' said Bernie slowly, sucking in her teeth. 'Continue to have a nice weekend, ladies. And remember' – she pointed inside, to the folded pages on the hall table – 'stay vigilant.'

Then she turned and left.

The three women stood in silence until they heard the creak of the next garden gate being opened.

'The artist's impression is *signed*,' whispered Carmel dramatically. 'Is she planning to sell it afterwards? What is she like? Quarter to eight on a Friday night. Surely there's a mirror somewhere she could be practising that big TV smile of hers in?'

'Quarter to eight! Oh gosh. I am officially late. Okay, bye!' said Edie, shimmying her coat up both arms and grabbing her keys from the hall table and her handbag from the floor. The other two women were already in the garden. She closed the door and hurried after them.

'Bye.' She waved manically as Martha sailed across the road.

God, she admired that woman's ability to pull off a mid-length skirt.

'See you, Carmel!' She rubbed the older woman's shoulders and hurried down the road ahead of her.

She didn't want to be late for Daniel. She didn't want to risk doing anything – and she meant, anything – that might interfere with their harmonious love nest for the next three days.

*** Pine Road Poker ***

Edie:
I talked to Martha. The Costello/Rigbys are a yes for the Pine Road pre-Easter street party!

Carmel:
Hang on a sec. I seem to have missed last week's thread. Cheese-free fondue?? Is that a joke? The whole bloody thing is cheese!

Edie:
(Martha will make a Pavlova. X)

Carmel:
Cheese-free fondue would be a bowl of air. Is that what you're looking for, Ellen? Cause no problem. I can bring a nice big empty bowl and Sylvie can dip bread in that to her heart's content. One actual fondue for actual people, and one nonsense fondue for nonsense people. How about that? Would that work?

NINETEEN

•••••••••••••••••••••••

'**A**dmit it. You brought me to that play to get me in the mood.'

Cormac snorted so the foam from his Guinness sprayed up on to his face. 'You got me. I thought, "Detailed study of the repressed psyche of the Irish male? She'll be putty in my hands."' He placed the pint on the low table between them. They were sitting in a pub across from the Abbey but given that the wine options had made Cormac opt for Guinness, she doubted it was big with the theatre crowd. 'I thought you were going to unscrew the seat you were wriggling so much in the first act.'

'It took forever for something to happen.'

'It was pensive,' he countered.

'It was slower than Mass. The halftime break couldn't come soon enough.'

He grinned. 'It's called an interval.'

'Whatever.' She smiled back.

So, okay. She hadn't actually told Cormac about Jack, yet – but she hadn't told Edie she had either. She'd kept her answer evasive and Edie had heard what she wanted to hear. She was going to tell him, tonight, just not yet.

'I was impressed by the crowd,' she said. 'Lots of famous people.'

'It was opening night. Nobody there paid for a ticket. It's the great, the good and the critics.'

'What do you call yer man with the wig from the telly? Your pal.'

'I wouldn't call him my pal . . .'

'He greeted you by *name*, Cormac. And you knew what he was going to order!' Robin waved away his modesty. 'So you're basically his best man.'

Cormac laughed into his pint. Robin leaned over and wiped the foam from above his lip.

'Wait till I tell Dad I was sitting behind Bono,' said Robin. 'He's going to love that.'

'Is he a fan?'

'Of Bono? God, no. Although it's hard to know which he hates more, Bono or the sunglasses.' Robin took a sip of her wine. 'I don't know how he saw a thing. The place was pitch black.'

'Maybe he was snoozing?'

'Wouldn't blame him.'

Cormac flicked a beermat in her direction but she deflected it.

'Well, I loved what it had to say about fatherhood, the way the briars started to unravel. I found that very affecting,' said Cormac, his hand stopping halfway through his hair. 'Why are you smiling?' Though he was smiling too. She *loved* that. She loved that he didn't mind potentially being the butt of a joke.

'Nothing,' she said, 'I just like how earnest you are.'

'No, you don't,' he scoffed.

'I do, really.'

He blushed, then pointed at her empty gin glass. 'Another?'

'Go on,' said Robin, pushing it towards him. 'But then I have to go.'

'Go . . . back to my flat?'

Cormac grinned and Robin grinned more.

'No. Go home, to my own home.' Now was the perfect time to tell him. *Tell him you have to go home to your son*, Robin admonished herself. *Say: 'There's something I've been meaning to tell you . . .' and be done with it. It'll be fine. And if it's not fine, it's better to know.*

But Robin wasn't sure if she really believed that. She liked him.

Like, feel-it-in-her-tummy amounts; butterflies before she met him, hollowness when she had to leave. What if she ruined it? What if fully embracing honesty left her with no man, no job, no qualifications, and little choice but to return to Eddy?

But before she could say anything, Cormac was leaning across the table, giving her a long, slow kiss that she was sure was drawing the eye of a few of the auld lads at the bar. She felt her body slump as he pulled away. 'I'll convince you when I get back.'

She hadn't heard from Eddy in more than two weeks. Maybe he'd found someone else to provide an alibi? Would she be missing him more if she hadn't met Cormac? Because she didn't miss him, not any more. Eventually she'd arrange some way for Jack to see him but she'd wait for whatever this latest mess was to blow over.

'A nightcap before we retire,' said Cormac, placing the gin and tonic in front of her. Robin drank slimline when she ordered for herself, but she never stipulated that when the man went to the bar; he'd think she was obsessed by her weight. 'And by retire, I mean get naked in my bed.' He was clearly unused to talking suggestively and she enjoyed the awkward effort he made in spite of it.

'I really have to go home to my own house. I'd invite you to come but, you see—'

'You're staying with your mother, I know,' said Cormac, cutting her off. She took it as a sign from the gods to enjoy a few more deep kisses before breaking the news.

A group of young lads came in and took the table next to them. Robin inched her stool closer to Cormac, so they could squeeze past, then she moved it closer still.

'Did you find the ending believable, when the medics arrived and immediately knew there was nothing they could do?'

'How do you mean?'

'Like, as a nurse,' he said. 'Would that really happen?'

'Oh.' *Shit shit shit*. She'd totally forgotten she'd told him she was a nurse. She needed to start writing down what lies she told and to whom. 'Well,' she tried to remember the final scene. 'Well, in real life they probably wouldn't have brought a surfboard. But I guess that's artistic licence.'

'I think that was a spinal board.'

'Well, whatever. I don't know the exact terms. I like my sports with balls.'

'No, a spinal board, as in for carrying patients. Like in a hospital?'

'Right. Yes.'

She winced.

Cormac's forehead creased.

'I'm not actually a nurse.'

'Oh.'

'Yeah.'

'But you said . . .'

'I know.'

'So you're a . . .?'

'Unemployed.' *Un-qualified, un-skilled, un-desirable*. 'The last job I had, if you'd call it that, was working for my ex-boyfriend. We were going out for, like, five years. But it's over now,' she added. 'He did bits and pieces, dodgy stuff mainly, and I helped out on the phones.'

'The phones?'

'Yeah.' She swallowed the end of her gin and tonic. She should have drank it slower. 'He was selling these knock-off boxes that allow you to get all the TV channels without subscribing to Sky or whatever.'

'Dodgy boxes.'

'Yeah. Except his were called Bye Bye TV Bills Dot Com.' Robin caught Cormac's eye and laughed. 'I know. But it worked. People remembered the web address. They'd look it up, then ring us. Or, well, ring me. I took the orders.'

'So you were in telephone sales.'

'That's what I say,' she exclaimed, before dropping the smile. 'It's embarrassing. You've got this very impressive job and I'm just a . . . I never finished college.' She considered this. 'I never finish *anything*.'

Cormac chewed lightly on his lower lip, mulling it over. 'Could your ex do us a deal, do you think?'

Robin looked up at him.

'Currently, I only have the terrestrial channels, but if we're going to go out, I should probably look into watching more sport . . .'

She got up from her seat and went over and kissed him for long enough that the young lads at the table beside them started to cheer.

'Get a room!' they shouted.

'I tried,' implored Cormac, turning to them. 'But she tells me she has to go home.' Robin buried her face in his jumper though she wasn't really embarrassed. She loved the smell and feel of him.

He walked her to her bus stop but the next 41 wasn't for twenty minutes so she said she'd walk home, and he said he'd walk with her, even though it was in entirely the wrong direction. She didn't put up a fight. She liked interlacing her fingers with his in the cold and the discombobulating feeling that came with walking a route she'd taken thousands of times before with someone new. She pointed out her secondary school and the pub where she had her first summer job. He knew the area a bit and liked the houses.

They turned on to Forest Avenue and Robin went to say goodnight. She could make it the rest of the way herself. But right in front of them were two people standing about a foot apart.

'Edie?' called Robin, squinting to see.

She and Cormac took a couple more steps towards the silhouettes and Edie turned, her face switching so quickly to her trademark doe-eyed enthusiasm that Robin almost missed the distress that had been there before.

'Hello!' she exclaimed, looking from Robin to Cormac. 'The hip . . . Cormac! The guy from the bar. You probably don't remember me. I was the one Robin requested a song for the night you guys met!'

'Oh right, yes. Edie. I remember the name.' Cormac raised a hand to wave to the taller man Edie was with, but the man – Daniel, presumably – was still frowning at his wife. They had interrupted a row. Cormac did that awkward thing of turning a snubbed wave into a head scratch. Robin grinned. She wanted to reach out for the spurned hand. 'How, ah, how did you find singing "Gangsta's Paradise"?'

'I didn't. We left before they called it. Robin, this is Daniel, my husband. And Daniel this is Robin, Carmel and Mick Dwyer's daughter.'

'Hi,' said Robin.

'Hello.'

Robin sympathised with Daniel. She also found it hard to plaster on a smile when annoyed. Edie, however, was clearly a master. 'How was the theatre?' she enthused, eyes widening as she looked from Robin to Cormac. 'Robin said you were going. What a civilised way to spend an evening.'

'I'm going on, Edie,' said Daniel, and he lumbered off before his wife could respond.

'Sorry,' said Robin when he'd left. 'I was calling you before I realised . . .'

'Oh my God, no,' gushed Edie. 'It's fine. We were just . . . Nothing.' She smiled brightly, her eyes glinting against the streetlights. Had she been crying? 'Just a stupid squabble. So really, how was the theatre?'

Cormac talked earnestly about the play and Edie nodded enthusiastically but Robin could see her zoning out when he started describing the 'soundscape'.

'That sounds wonderful!' she said. 'Okay, well, I'll leave you lovebirds to it.' She kissed them both on the cheek, which took Cormac by surprise, and headed off after her husband.

'She's . . .'

'Enthusiastic?'

'Yeah. Nice, though.'

'Very nice,' Robin agreed. 'She's a good person.'

'Yeah,' said Cormac, shifting slightly. 'I could tell.'

They both looked at each other, Cormac stuffing his hands into his pockets as he shuffled silently on the footpath.

'Did you know it was Valentine's Day when we went on our first date?'

'No.' He looked momentarily panicked, as he worked his way back through the dates. 'You're right, it was. God, sorry. I should have given you a card or something.'

'No,' Robin insisted, almost laughing. 'I hate Valentine's Day. It's stupid. I just wanted to admit that I noticed and, even though I think it's stupid, I took it as a good sign because I like you.' She took a deep breath. *There. Now. How hard was that?*

He looked at her in that unembarrassed, awe-filled way, like he'd just discovered some other part of her face and he liked it a lot.

She would like, very much, to see herself through his eyes.

'What?' She grinned, knowing the answer could only be good.

'I like spending time with you.'

'Even though I'm a two-bit criminal.'

He tilted his head slightly. 'That just made you sexier.'

'Next time, I have something else to tell you.'

'Something bad?'

'No. Just something I should have told you.'

Cormac thought about this. 'Well, me too, so.'

'Really?'

'Not bad,' he clarified, 'but if we're laying our cards on the table, there's something I should tell you too. A secret for a secret. We'll swap.' He lowered his head and kissed her softly. She was getting used to that mouth. 'Bye.'

Robin thrust her own hands into her pockets and swung her jacket open and shut as she bounced along Forest Avenue, past

Elm and Oak Road and turned on to Pine. She licked her lips gently. It had been forever since she'd done enough kissing for them to be so puffed up. It was a pity kissing took a back seat as you got older. When you were a teenager there was months of the stuff. There was a lot to be said for chasteness, Robin decided. Well, a bit of it anyway.

The gate to her parents' garden was open and she turned in, swinging herself slightly on the hinge. She was about to pull the key from her bag when she heard a familiar voice behind her.

'Hey, babe. Where've you been?'

TWENTY

....

Martha hurried from Edie's house across to her own as a breeze whipped around her ankles. Maybe it was the alcohol, but Pine Road looked particularly charming this evening, the windows all aglow behind heavy curtains. Popping into neighbours in Abbyvale had required a ten-minute walk and a high-vis jacket. Here, she was barely outside long enough to need this wool coat.

She pushed open her gate and bustled along the cracked garden tiles. Only when she was met with the resistance of their warped door did she remember that her new home wasn't all positives. When the door finally gave way to reveal Robert standing at the other end of the hall, blind hopefulness across his face, her good mood evaporated entirely.

'You said you'd get that fixed.' She closed it firmly behind her and skirted past Robert into the kitchen where she switched on the kettle. In the bright lights and responsibility of her own home, the effect of the alcohol doubled. 'Where are the girls?'

'Orla's doing her homework in the office, and Sinead's upstairs.' Robert returned to the stove where he had three pots on the boil and a dozen dirtied bowls sitting on the worktop. 'They ordered pizza. So . . .' Robert rotated a cookery book, lying open on the counter, so Martha could see it. 'I thought I'd make us dinner.'

Martha made dinner every night, as Robert knew well. She did the shopping in advance based on a weekly meal plan. She had the makings of tonight's dinner, for all four of them, in the fridge, and now it would go to waste. And while Robert would make a grand gesture of cooking, he wouldn't do the mundane, and far more appreciated, task of washing up. That would be left to Martha. When she cooked, she cleaned as she went and used about a third of the number of implements Robert did – so the workload was never divided evenly; the bulk always fell on her side. She filled a glass of water and took her time downing it. 'What's Sinead doing?'

'Don't worry,' said Robert, mildly wounded as he turned the ignored recipe back around. 'She's not starting a campaign to overthrow the establishment. I checked. She's reading.'

Marx? Martha thought to say, as she would have once, knowing it would make them both laugh. Now the idea of seeing him smile turned her stomach. So instead she said: 'You didn't give her back her phone, did you?'

'No,' said Robert, in that irritating, drawn-out way that let Martha know he was being excessively patient. 'We told her two weeks. I do know how to see a punishment through.'

He tasted a sauce from one of the pots and when he spoke again it was more light-hearted. 'A woman called,' he said, raising the statement at the end as if inviting questions. But she didn't ask any. She just took a mug from the draining board and reached for a teabag.

'She wanted to see our dog. She was on the hunt for a vicious hound that maimed her daughter or something, and for the animal's male owner; she thought poor Oscar and me might be to blame. Sinead was out walking him when she called but I assured her it was not the same dog. Look.' Robert grabbed a flyer from the counter and held it out for Martha. 'She even had these made.'

'I saw it,' said Martha, keeping her gaze on her mug. 'She called to Edie's too and handed them out. I suppose if your daughter was harmed you would be looking for justice.'

Deflated, frustrated, Robert put the sheet back on the counter.

For about thirty seconds neither of them spoke and Martha wondered what he would do, what he would say, if she just screamed. He'd never heard her scream. He'd rarely seen her cry, until last year.

'Are you hungry?'

Martha shrugged, even though Robert's back was turned to her as he concentrated on the cooking. He looked over his shoulder.

'Well?'

She shrugged again.

'Right,' he sniped, turning back.

After another twenty seconds, he spoke up. 'You know, if you—'

'Da-ad!'

Orla's voice travelled from the office through to the kitchen. Robert put down the wooden spoon. 'What?' he shouted back and Martha felt a flash of rage at how he, the adult, couldn't just go into the next room and speak to her. It didn't matter, though, because next thing Orla appeared at the kitchen door. 'The printer isn't working! It keeps flashing and saying "job queued". I did all my science homework and now I can't print it out!'

'Did you check that there's paper in it?'

'Yes!' shouted Orla, pushing her hair out of her face and adjusting her glasses. 'I have a very high IQ, you know.'

Robert looked at Martha and it took everything she had not to smile. 'Do you really need the printer?' he asked.

'Yes! I've made this whole presentation on atoms and I need to print it out.'

'It'll just be a backlog. I'll fix it when I'm finished here. Okay?'

'But I have to go to bed *soooon*,' Orla whinged.

The printer was always getting jammed. It was another thing Robert had said he would fix but hadn't. 'Your father will get it going again and then he'll leave the presentation outside your door. It'll be there in the morning. All right?'

Orla gave an exasperated sigh.

'All right, Orla?' Martha pushed.

'Fi-*ne*.'

'You know why you should never trust atoms?' asked Robert, relieved not to have to leave his precious once-in-a-blue-moon gastronomic masterpiece.

'Why?'

'Because they make up everything.'

Orla scrunched up her face. 'Why do you even try to be funny? You're old. It's embarrassing.'

Then she left the room and Martha heard her heading upstairs.

They ate dinner in relative silence. Robert started out telling her anecdotes from his day and Martha made noncommittal sounds until he, thank God, gave up. After dinner, they told Orla to go to bed and switched between the channels before settling on some movie starring Richard Gere. Well, Martha did. Robert was mainly on his phone.

'Who sends a work email at ten p.m. on a Friday night?' he said, shaking his head at his mobile.

'Who checks their work email at ten p.m. on a Friday night?'

Martha felt Robert looking at her but she didn't take her eyes off the TV.

Sinead came downstairs to say goodnight around 11 p.m., allowing her parents to kiss her on the cheek. She had soccer practice in the morning. She seemed happy enough, didn't she? All things considered and determination to take down her school aside.

Martha did worry she'd noticed the rift between her and Robert. It really couldn't go on like this much longer.

'Are you going to fix the printer for Orla, or . . .?' Martha said when Sinead was gone and Richard Gere had moved on to his second love interest of the film.

Robert groaned as he pushed himself up from the sofa.

Martha was glad she'd phoned the police. They'd had nothing new to impart but she could tell her phone call had caught them off guard. It might be enough for them to take another look at the thing. She felt she'd done something for her daughters, at least.

Robert started banging around next door and Martha turned up the volume. Gere's new girl was looking at him like he was an ice cream on a hot day and Martha felt a sudden flash of envy, not for Richard Gere, she'd always found him a bit slimy, but for that lustful emotion.

'Fuck!'

The ads came on and Martha went in to tell her husband to be quiet. She opened the door to find him down on his hunkers under the desk. The only visible part of him was the arse of his suit trousers and the very slightest builder's crack.

'You'll wake the girls.'

'I banged my head,' came his muffled response. 'There's a couple of . . . pages . . . stuck!' The buzz of the printer started up. 'There! Now, it should . . .' Robert wriggled back out from under the table and rubbed at his head. 'A backlog,' he said, peering down at the page coming out of the printer. 'From whoever was too impatient to wait. Sinead, probably.' He picked up the first couple of sheets. 'No atoms project yet, maybe—' He frowned down at the pages.

'Just leave it to print. Orla can get her sheets in the morning.'

But Robert stayed where he was. He held out the pages towards her, still staring at them. Martha, irritated by how slowly he worked, grabbed them.

'Is that the list?' he asked. 'From the school?'

She looked at it. Then she shook the page and looked again, as if it was a Magic Eight ball and she could just give it another go if she didn't like the first fate she'd been designated.

It was the exact photo Trish Walsh, the principal, had shown her the day Martha called to her house. It was the exact photo that had been printed out and posted on classroom doors all over the school.

'Why was Sinead printing that out?'

Martha didn't answer him.

'Martha?'

'Where's Sinead's phone?'

'Where . . .? I don't know. You're the one who took it off her.'

A panic rose in her. She stormed into the kitchen and rooted around in the larder press behind the various canned goods until her hand tightened around her daughter's confiscated Samsung. She powered it on and entered her password – she had the same password on all the family phones.

'What are you looking for?' asked Robert, before finally spotting his self-combusting soufflés. 'Oh, bollocks! I forgot all about dessert!'

Robert did his best to rescue the elaborate sponge and Martha scrolled through her daughter's phone until she found the gallery. Selfies, photos of Pine Road in the early morning, on her way to school presumably . . .

Then, there it was.

Or there they were, to be precise. Two photos of the list on the bathroom stall wall. The exact same as the image on the sheet she was holding in her other hand.

'What?' Robert had turned off the oven and was mopping at sponge that had spilled down on to the floor of the cooker. He was only making it worse. He looked at his wife as he wiped, flicking half the stuff out on to the floor and making hissing sounds every time his hand came close to touching the hot surface. 'What? What is it?'

Martha leaned against the larder cupboard and let her arms fall to her sides. She spoke quietly. 'Sinead took the photo of the list.'

'What?'

'Sinead took the photo of the list and then she stuck it all over the school.'

Robert guffawed. 'That doesn't make sense.'

'Yes, it does.' Martha was surprised at how easy it was to accept. 'I should have known.'

'Why would she want to publicise a *rape* list . . .' Robert dropped his voice. It was the same tone he used when he talked about *sanitary towels* or *tampons*. It was very irritating. '. . . that had her name on it? Why would she want people to see that? There's no way. No, no way.' Robert came over and reached for Sinead's phone. 'Let me see.' He took another step. 'Show me what you mean.'

Martha clutched the phone to her chest. She looked at Robert and felt the fury raging within her. 'It's a call for attention,' she said. 'For justice.'

Robert looked from Martha to the printout that had now fallen to the floor and back to his wife. 'Will you please,' he said, reverting to his excessive-patience voice, 'for just two minutes, stop looking at me like you're willing me to burst into flames and tell me what you're talking about. Our daughter did not take a photograph of a *rape* list with her name on it and plaster it all over her brand-new school where she has yet to make any friends. You're acting crazy.'

'You don't get it,' Martha snapped. 'You're so entirely self-involved that you can't even begin to try to understand how anyone else in this family might react to a situation. Sinead made the list public knowledge because she wanted something done about it. She wants men who do bad things to be punished. She wants the world to show her that she doesn't always have to be a victim.'

Robert contorted his lips into an expression that was dangerously close to a smirk. 'You sound hysterical.'

'And you sound like a smug, narcissistic arsehole!' That wiped the smile from his face. 'And if I do sound hysterical, Robert, then it's your fault. This' – Martha picked up the printout from the floor and waved it in his face – 'is your fault!'

'I don't think that's fair—'

'None of it is fair!' Martha was so full of rage now she could barely get her thoughts into sentences. 'You have no idea what your daughters, and I, went through when you were off playing the hero.'

'I know you—'

'You don't know anything! I have never felt so powerless in my life and Sinead . . .' The thought of it, the memory of her daughter. 'Sinead was humiliated.' *She would not cry.* She let this sink in. *She was done crying.* 'It was horrendous and we are all struggling to come to terms with it, and Sinead can't. She thinks all men are out for themselves, that they're a threat to her, and she can't see anyone contradicting that.'

'I don't know what you mean by that, but I am certainly not a threat to my daughter.' Robert was angry now too. *Good*, thought Martha. *Show me you're not okay! I know I'm not being fair to you. I know you're not that bad. Don't just take this shit; throw it back at me!* 'I do the best for Sinead and you and Orla. I took a massive risk and you act like—'

'You put *us* at risk!'

Robert jumped at the ferocity. She was screaming now, screaming aloud for all the times she had done so silently into whatever material was lying about.

But she did not want to wake the girls. She took a deep breath and calmed herself.

Robert, too, spoke more calmly. 'I know you blame me for what happened and I get it,' he said. 'They wouldn't have come to our house if I didn't work in the bank. I was the target and you were collateral. But I don't think it's fair, Martha. I didn't ask for this.'

Martha looked at him, shaking her head in disbelief. 'I don't blame you because they came to our house, Robert!' How did he not get this? How was he so bloody obtuse? 'I blame you because you left us! We should have been in it together but you were in it for yourself. You saw the chance to play the hero and you took it.'

'And it worked.'

'Yeah! But what if it hadn't? What if your risk hadn't worked?'

'I knew—'

'Stop saying that! You didn't know. None of us knew anything. You said it yourself. You took a risk – you. On your own. You took a risk with our lives. You couldn't just do what they said. You couldn't just be the subordinate one for once, for me. For the girls. For *your family*!' Martha closed her eyes and waited.

It fizzled up, bursting to the surface. 'You lied! You said you would go and get the money and come back, but you lied, to me. You lied to me!'

'I lied to the crooks. I was saying what they wanted to hear.'

'No, Robert. You were speaking to me. You lied to me! I thought – we thought—' She saw her girls falling to pieces, tasted the sick in her mouth. Those few minutes, when it was technically all over, when they still didn't know.

'Everyone thinks you're the hero and it sickens me so much that I can't even look at you.' She spoke softly, watching the words pierce Robert, relieved at least to know he could still hurt. 'You put us in jeopardy and then you were the one rewarded. Medal, promotion, all of it, everything worked out for you. But me and the girls, we're still struggling.' She picked up the printout off the floor. 'And some are struggling more than others.'

Robert opened his mouth but in the time it took to formulate a response, Martha had left the room. She climbed the stairs, Sinead's phone in hand, but stopped herself when she got to her daughter's door. It was nearly midnight. Sinead would be asleep and it wouldn't do any good to wake her. It would still have happened in the morning and Martha would be a little calmer.

She diverted her path towards her own bedroom, catching her reflection in the mirror. Lines showed around her eyes, and new ones formed at the side of her mouth. She smiled, then dropped it. Smiled, then dropped it again. She sat heavily on the bed and exhaled loudly. For a moment, she let her hands cover her face. Aware, then, that the curtains were still open, and how Carmel across the road had once been able to see right into this bedroom, she walked across to the window.

She put her hand on the curtain and glanced outside. She went to pull the thick material across, but she froze.

Her insides tightened and her arm, outstretched towards the curtain, went rigid.

She stared and she stared but the vision did not change.

Out there, on her new street, was the man with the soulful eyes.

*** Pine Road Poker ***

Fiona:
Anyone see a blue hairbrush on the road? Willow thinks she dropped it earlier. If y'all could keep a lookout, maybe check outside your houses, that'd be great. Thanks, gals! XXX

Carmel:
Didn't see one.

Fiona:
OK. Thanks anyway, Carmel XXX

Ruby:
Had a look outside our gate, no sign.

Fiona:
Thanks for checking, hun! XXX

Ellen:
I swept our path this evening and didn't see anything.

Fiona:
Thanks, Ellen. XXX

Edie:
Just home. No sign.

Fiona:
Thanks for looking, Edie hun. Hope you had a fab night. XXX

TWENTY-ONE

'**J**esus Christ, Eddy!'

Robin brought her hand to her heart, but kept her keys clenched in her fist as she turned to face her ex. 'Why are you creeping about outside my house?'

She caught her breath and watched as Eddy stepped out from the side of the tree. He was wearing the coat she'd bought him last winter. She'd bought it but, just like everything else, he'd paid for it.

'I told you not to be stalking my parents' house.'

Eddy looked up at her parents' bedroom window. 'How's my son?'

'He's asleep. Everyone's asleep.'

'You're not,' he said, looking her up and down. 'Out somewhere nice?'

'That's none of your business. If you want to see Jack, then fine, phone me tomorrow, at a reasonable hour. But other than that . . . we don't have anything to say to each other.'

Eddy just kept nodding. Robin clenched her keys tighter.

'So that's it? I look after you and your kid—'

'Our kid, Eddy.'

'—for five years and then, that's it?'

How had she been so in thrall to this man, and for so long? When Robin and her college friends started going to club nights, they'd met Eddy and he'd invited them back to his place for after parties. He had a penthouse. They thought it was the coolest fucking thing, and when he put his eye on Robin she was honoured. It was like she'd proven the thing that mattered so much to her – that she was sexier, more desirable, *cooler*, than all the others.

She knew why she'd been in thrall for so long. She'd had a nice life, and she'd done nothing to earn it.

'What do you want, Eddy?'

'I asked you to do one thing for me. Do it and I'll stop turning up like this. It's nothing, Robin. Just say we were watching films Halloween night. I've already told the cops I was with you, so if you don't go to them, they're going to come and ask for your side, sooner or later.'

Even though he wasn't saying anything new, something about it niggled.

'You, me and Jacko watching *Hocus Pocus*, your favourite, then we went to bed and woke up together, happy families, on the first of November. It's easy, Robin. Do you hear me?'

'November first?'

'Halloween to November first, yeah. No big deal.'

'You need me to cover for where you were on the morning of November first.'

'Right, and the night before, yeah.'

Robin looked across the road at Martha's house where all the curtains were closed and the lights off. What were the chances? Surely not. Still, she pulled Eddy back behind the tree.

'I thought it was to do with the Bye Bye TV Bills Dot Com boxes. But—'

'It doesn't matter what it's to do with, babe.'

Fuckedy fuck.

'Did you rob a house, Eddy?' she hissed. 'Did you? Do you need me to cover for a fucking robbery?'

'It doesn't matter what it was,' he said emphatically. 'You don't need to know. It's easier. I promise it was nothing bad. I swear on Jack's life.'

'Do not swear on his life, you shit! Oh Jesus. Was it a . . .' But if she said 'tiger raid', he'd know. Presumably he had no idea his victims had moved in across the road. Poor Martha and the girls.

'You just go into the station and tell them—'

'Do you swear it wasn't a robbery?'

'Jesus, babe. It doesn't matter what it was . . .'

Oh fuckedy fuck fuck fuck.

'I have to go in.' Robin turned back towards her house, but Eddy caught her arm.

'Ow, Eddy. Christ!' She tried to reef it from his grasp.

'I'm not fucking around, Robin,' he whispered. 'The guards will be asking you to verify my whereabouts and you better not let me down.'

'Let *go*,' Robin stressed, yanking her arm away. She marched back up the path and, ignoring the tremor in her hand, pushed the key into the lock and opened the door.

She got inside and she leaned against it. Deep breaths, nobody panic. She was okay. She was fine.

She wasn't fine. Her heart was pounding.

An armed gang . . .

Balaclavas . . .

Tied to radiators . . .

She put her hand to her chest to stop her heart busting out.

· · · · · · · · ·

Martha whipped the curtains across so quickly she worried she might pull them down.

How had he found them?

Was he here because she'd seen his face? Was it because she'd gotten in touch with the police again? Were they closing in on him? Had he come to shut her up?

The bedroom door opened and Robert walked in, already starting to unbutton his shirt.

'Martha? What are you doing?'

She looked at her husband but she couldn't speak.

'What?' he said, dropping his hands from his shirt. 'What is it?'

*** Pine Road Poker ***

Fiona:
False alarm, gals! Willow just found the brush in her schoolbag.
Thanks for checking everyone. You're all KWEENS!! xxx

TWENTY-TWO

•••••••••••••••••••••••••••••

The snap in the backyard is the first thing. The familiar sound of Oscar padding back to the house post morning pee, trampling on a twig, breaking it under paw. Martha will let him in in a minute, when she is done assembling lunches and straining her vocal cords in an attempt to rally the rest of the house.

'Come on, girls! You're going to be late!'

She grabs three oranges from the punnet beside the fruit bowl – she really needs to clear out that bowl and start actually using it for fruit – and fires them into the lunchboxes: Sinead, Orla, Robert.

Each easy-peeler lands neatly in its intended plastic container. Hat-trick.

'Robert! Don't forget your shirt is hanging in the hot press!'

No butter on Sinead's sandwich, crusts off Orla's, extra ham for Robert.

'Orla! Sinead! Let's go!'

Tinfoil around the sandwiches and the right one dropped into each box: Sinead, Orla, Robert.

The sound of movement upstairs – *finally* – and then another stick breaking in the yard, this one closer to the back door. Martha goes to turn to let Oscar in but Sinead enters the kitchen then, halfway through a sentence – 'There's no conditioner . . .' – and Martha is annoyed to see she's still in her pyjamas. In the same moment Martha remembers she hasn't let Oscar out for his morning pee yet. The dog is still asleep where he shouldn't be, upstairs at the foot of Orla's bed, and so there is no pet to be breaking twigs at the back door.

Sinead is staring beyond her mother and Martha turns instinctively, not yet having time to be concerned. Glass smashes and she sees what her daughter sees. A man with impenetrable black where his face should be turning the handle of their back door – the door Martha chose when they had the kitchen redone so it was almost entirely glass and thus let in more light – and behind him two, three, four more men, all without faces, all coming into her home.

'Oh.' Martha's hand flies to her dressing gown, as if these are breakfast guests who've arrived early and caught her before she's had time to fix herself.

'Robert,' she says timidly.

But her husband isn't with her. He's two storeys above in the master bedroom, searching everywhere but the hot press for his shirt.

'Get out!' Sinead shouts, waving her arms in front of her, like she's batting away flies. 'Get out!'

Her daughter's outrage jolts Martha to life. 'Robert!' She shouts it this time. Then she roars: 'Robert!!!'

The first man grabs Martha, twisting her hand until she drops the lunchbox lid – Robert's lunchbox lid – and placing her in a headlock. Another man grabs Sinead, who starts kicking and screaming: 'Get off me! Get off me!' The other three run past, through the kitchen, and Martha hears them on the stairs. The last one bangs the door against the wall and Martha, whose head is now bent downwards, sees the handle dent the wall and a shard of paint fall to the tiled floor.

'Robert!' she screams as best she can with such pressure on her neck. 'Call the guards!'

The man holding Sinead slams the kitchen door shut. Her daughter tries to wriggle free and he takes his hand off the handle and slaps her across the face. It's so swift Martha wonders if it happened at all. It seems incongruous. Nobody has ever raised a hand to her daughter. But the whole room is still now. Sinead goes quiet, limp, and Martha feels the sting on her own cheek.

Two of the other three come back through the kitchen door, the first shoving Orla ahead of him – Orla throws her mother an indignant look, as if this is all Martha's doing, as if the battle to get them up for school on time has been taken up a notch – and between them, they're holding Robert. Robert is wearing his suit trousers, shoes and a vest.

Three times she told him his shirt was in the hot press. Three times.

She's glad Orla at least is in her uniform. Sinead's threadbare Harry Potter pyjamas look so much flimsier against the thick black material of the men's jumpers and balaclavas.

'They locked Oscar upstairs. He hasn't had his pee.'

'Get in there,' the one holding Robert growls, distorting his voice with depth. 'Get the fuck in there.'

All four of them are shoved into the living room, Orla's jumper catching on the door handle. 'Ow!' She is crying now. 'You hurt me.'

'Don't hurt her!'

But they all ignore Martha. Or maybe they didn't hear. Her own voice sounds so far away. The one holding Robert throws pieces of rope around and Martha watches as they start to tie Orla to the radiator.

'No! No! No! N—'

A hand across her own face now and this time the pain is real: sharp, stinging, blinding her momentarily. She is shoved on to her hunkers, and then falls fully to one side. They are all being tied to the radiators. Her and Orla on one, Robert and Sinead on the other.

'The heat,' she stutters, wondering if her jaw is broken.

She opens and closes it. Sore but working.

'The heat will come on in a minute,' she says louder, her voice still sounding like she's left it echoing in the kitchen.

'Shut the fuck up,' growls the man tying up Robert, the one clearly in charge.

Orla whimpers gently, in that sorry-for-herself way she does when she's finished with the real tears but isn't quite ready to shake hands. Her hair falls in sheets over her face so Martha can only catch glimpses of the blotchy skin beneath.

Sinead stares into space, lost in a daze. It seems unnatural, even in this environment. Sinead always has something to say. Perhaps that man slapped the words out of her. *If I'd known that I might have tried it sooner*, Martha thinks, by way of a joke, and feels suddenly, violently ill. She can see the outline of her daughter's breasts beneath Harry Potter's face. There's a toothpaste stain over the wizard's scar. She wants to tell her daughter to lean forward slightly, to slacken the material, not to remind them of what she is, of what they have.

Martha looks at her daughter's long, scrawny legs, the knees scratched from soccer, and is suddenly livid. *Why didn't you put on a jumper? Why didn't you cover up?*

A couple of the men leave the room and one returns with Robert's shirt. He found it in the hot press without her having to say a thing. He unties her husband and watches as he dresses.

The man in charge is telling Robert what he has to do. He has to go to work, take money out of the safe – €240,000 is what they're expecting, they don't say how they know, just that they do – and bring it back to them.

'Simple,' says the boss man. They use that word a lot and Martha starts to believe them. Robert will return with the money and then the men will leave. Robert won't breathe a word of it to anyone, and the men won't kill his family. Simple.

Orla watches the men as they speak, her head like an umpire at a tennis match, and Sinead continues to stare into space.

They won't turn on the heat if he comes back with the money, the boss man says. They won't slit his wife's throat, they won't take turns fucking his little girls. 'It's simple, Robert.' So, so simple.

Robert looks from one man to another, and Martha knows what he's doing. He's wondering if this is an inside job. He's studying their eyes to see if he recognises them. There's no point, she thinks, you'll only make them mad. Who cares about the money? It's not their money. Martha didn't realise how similar eyes were until now; body shape is the only way she can tell these men apart.

'Just do what they say,' she tells Robert, not realising she's been crying until the words get caught in phlegm. In her head, she is exceedingly calm and she's surprised to find her limbs are shaking, her throat contracting, that her body has betrayed her.

Robert looks down at his family. Orla is quieter now, maybe it's seeing her daddy fully dressed, standing on his own; one thing back to normal. The men have turned off the radiators, which is good, but also means the room is freezing. Sinead's nipples push against the material of her pyjama top. Martha is convinced everyone has noticed. She does her best not to look.

These men must have weapons. Five against four isn't much of an advantage. What if they'd had people staying last night? She looks around and yes, right there, in the hand of one of the quieter men, she sees a gun. Was it there all along? Her throat starts to close over. She is suddenly very, very scared.

'Robert.'

It comes out like a high-pitched whine, like the air being let out of a tyre. Her husband kneels down and holds her hands and two of the men stand over him.

'It's okay, Martha.' Robert is scared, she can tell, but he holds her eyes the whole time and speaks loudly.

Two of the men by the door laugh. She could have sworn they glanced at Sinead.

She grips Robert's hands tighter. She cannot tell him her premonitions, so she says, 'Do exactly what they say,' and hopes he understands.

'I will.'

'Exactly, Robert. Do it exactly.'

'I will, I will. I'll go and get the money and I'll come right back to you. Nothing else. I swear.'

'You swear?'

'I swear.' He holds her eyes. 'It'll be fine.'

Her breathing returns to normal.

Through the window, she watches Robert walk down the gravel to the station wagon. He's wearing the wrong jacket. It's navy while his trousers are black. Two of the men flank him, both talking in his ears. He looks like a reluctant child, being accompanied by his parents on his first day of school.

You'd think the men were reassuring him, if you didn't know better, and if it weren't for the balaclavas.

A silver car pulls into the drive and another man in a balaclava steps out. Did they buy them in bulk or did they each have their own? There isn't much cause for owning a balaclava in a temperate climate like Ireland, unless of course you are a terrorist, unless you need one for your next terrorising session. She decides to say this to the police when it is all over and done with; they should start with the balaclava shops.

The new balaclava man talks to one of his accomplices and then gets back in the car. Robert starts the engine of the family station wagon. She hates this car now. She wills Robert to be okay. Her eyes flick back to the silver car, a Renault Laguna. The man starts that engine. The car staggers slightly and, just before he pulls out of the driveway after Robert, Martha sees his face.

He rolls the balaclava up like a hat and frowns at the gearstick. Then he looks back towards the house. And before she knows what she's doing, she's smiling at him. He snaps his head around and the car moves forward. Martha turns her head just as quickly and she catches two of the men looking at Sinead. She doesn't need to see beyond the balaclavas to know what's written on their faces and she strains her wrists against the rope.

•••••••••

'Did you girls dress up for Halloween?'

The man sitting on the couch with his legs spread and his head leaning back has been doing all the talking since Robert left and everyone else went quiet. The same man was perusing their framed family photos on the mantelpiece earlier, knocking a couple for good measure, so they smashed on the floor beside Sinead.

There are three men in the living room. The boss man went through to the kitchen with another one about an hour after Robert left and hasn't been back. Martha wishes she could see her husband. She worries about his asthma, then reminds herself that he is good in emergencies. She says it all the time, not realising how much she means it: she would trust Robert with her life.

'Did youse? Ha? Did youse go trick or treating?' He laughs, though nobody else has said anything and his own questions are hardly witticisms. 'Fucking knocking on doors and dirty old men asking if you've been naughty or nice.'

'That's Christmas. That's not Halloween.'

Orla has blown the hair back from her face and is speaking in that patient teacher voice she uses when explaining something to Martha and Robert that, at their 'advanced age', they really should know.

The man pauses and Martha's heart hammers. Then he looks up at his accomplice standing by the door and he howls. 'She's fuckin' right!' He laughs too loudly, smacking his thigh too violently. 'She's smart, this one. Well, whatever the fuck. What did you dress up as?'

Always a sucker for a little intellectual praise, Orla accedes with an answer. 'I was Marie Curie.'

'Who's that?'

'The scientist woman,' says the lad by the door. He's younger. Martha can tell from the self-conscious way he stands. 'I did her at school. What did she invent again?'

202

'Radium,' replies Orla, shaking the hair from her face, her hands tied to the rad. 'And she didn't invent it, she discovered it. It already existed. She was the first woman to win a Nobel Prize.'

'Told you she was smart,' says the man on the couch, spreading his legs a little farther. 'And what did you wear, Brainiac?' He winks at his accomplice.

'I wore a white laboratory coat.'

'And nothing underneath?'

Orla frowns. She looks to her mother, and Martha, who can hear the blood rushing in her ears, shakes her head.

Don't mind him, she tries to convey. *He's a bad man. Don't listen to a word he says.*

The bad man whistles. 'Very sexy,' he says, throwing his head back again. 'What do you think? Should we get you to show us your costume? A white coat and nothing underneath. Have you got fishnets? Maybe some high heels. I'd say your mammy could lend you some.' He winks, this time at Martha, and starts laughing again, hooting away to himself. 'And what about you?' He leers down towards Sinead. 'What did you dress up as? And careful now, 'cause I'm already feeling a little throb in me jocks.'

Sinead doesn't speak. What if her daughter has gone into shock? What if she's been scarred for life and she never talks again? But no, it's okay. Sinead is moving; she's chewing the inside of her cheek.

'I'm talking to you, Leggy. Didn't your mammy teach you that it's good manners to answer someone when they're talking to you?' He slips down from the couch, on to the ground, and sort of crawls towards Sinead.

Martha's stomach threatens to give way.

'What did you,' he inches closer still, 'dress up as?'

Martha knows what he's looking at; she knows what he sees.

'Tell him,' she snaps.

Sinead looks at her mother. She hesitates. Her eyes on Martha's, she finally says: 'I'm too old to dress up.'

The man starts to honk uncontrollably, as if this is the funniest of all the unfunny things that have been said so far. His laugh is so loud, so oppressive. He's taken the oxygen from the room and he's used it all up on this horrendous cackle.

Martha wants to shut her eyes but she doesn't. She keeps them trained to Sinead's.

'You're a big girl now, are you?' says the man. His face is in Sinead's but she keeps her eyes on her mother and Martha holds the stare right back. She sees a string of drool, emitted during the Great Laugh of 2018, running down her daughter's pyjama top. She fucking hates those pyjamas. Sinead's teeth are worrying the inside of her left cheek and in the corner of her right eye Martha sees the man's gloved hand moving, slowly.

No, no, no, no, no.

She desperately wants to shut her eyes, desperately, desperately . . .

He removes the leather glove and rests his hand on her daughter's left shoulder. A black, patent watchstrap shows. Sinead's right eye twitches but she doesn't move. Martha goes to exhale – not in relief, just because what goes in must eventually come out – but then, almost gracefully, the man slides his hairy, overgrown claw under the cream material of her daughter's top and down on to her breast. He gives a murmur of satisfaction but the noise is far away, like it's back in the kitchen with her own voice.

Sinead's body begins to vibrate. Her wrists bang quietly against the radiator pipe. Still, the girl doesn't move.

'Mum.'

Orla's voice, quivering beside her. Martha forgot she was there.

'Mum,' she says again, more urgently this time.

She gives Sinead what she can and keeps staring at her. Eyes on eyes. Nothing else exists.

Look at me, baby. Just, look, at, me.

There's a crash from the kitchen and everyone jumps. The man with the oppressive laugh and life-destroying hands is stumbling to his feet, slipping back on his glove. The door bangs open and the men gather. One of them is holding some sort of radio. It crackles but no words come out.

She can't hear what they're saying.

'Muh-ummm.'

'What,' she snaps, suddenly finding her voice. 'What is it?'

She looks to Orla and Orla nods back to where she has just been looking, at Sinead. Only it's not Sinead she is nodding at, it's lower. It's below Sinead. It's the grey carpet turning black and, between her daughter's scrawny legs, the dark circle pooling out.

The boss man breaks away from the huddle and comes at Martha so fast she flinches. 'Where the fuck is he?' he says, waving the radio at her.

She goes to wipe the saliva from her face but, of course, her hands are still tied.

'Where the fuck is your husband?'

'He . . . he's coming.'

'I don't think so. I don't fucking think so!' He stands and turns back towards the men.

'What's wrong?'

The boss man ignores her, speaking to his collaborators instead. 'Why isn't that gobshite answering his phone?' Nobody responds. 'Fuck!'

Martha is worried. She is really seriously worried. What happened a moment ago at least came to an end, but this feels like something that won't be over, something very bad, something beyond this room, something worse than all of this.

Where is Robert?

Why don't they know where Robert is?

The man's shoulders hunch as he paces the room. 'Fuck!'

Orla starts to whimper again. Sinead's vibrating wrists clang faintly against the radiator. Her daughter's cheeks and neck are red. Because of what she's done, not because of what has been done to her. Her daughter is mortified, while the men haven't even noticed the piss.

Something awful has happened to Robert.

'You're fucked now,' the man shouts at Orla. 'Your old man doesn't care about you. Whatever happens now has nothing to do with me. All right? It's your dad. He's left you behind.' The man draws back and spits in Orla's face.

Martha feels her bowels shift. Her stomach heaves. A dry retch. She sees Robert in the car, dead. She knows where the accident has happened, that turn off the second road, the blind spot.

She doesn't want to think it, but the thought is there already; *The only reason he isn't here is because he can't be.*

The radio crackles and the boss man holds it up. Words splutter down the line. All numbers and locations. Is it a police radio? Martha thinks she hears 'Abbyvale' and she thinks she hears 'accident'.

Another dry heave. She can't help it. Orla is keening now.

Then the radio is gone, and the men. They're out the door, into the kitchen. The back door opens and there are heavy, quick footsteps.

'Where's Dad? Mum? Where's Daddy?' Orla is banging her head against her mother, her voice increasingly aggravated. 'Where is he? Where is he? Where is he?'

The sound of cars, outside, on the gravel.

Orla stops headbutting her. Martha gasps. Her heart stops then starts again.

'He's here! It's him. He's here!'

The front door is forced open. Footsteps. The living-room door flies back.

'No . . .'

Her heart stops all over. The air leaves her. She thinks she will faint. It's not Robert.

Two men wearing helmets and thick black vests over jackets. 'Garda' is written across their backs. Neither man is Robert, because

Robert is dead. Her husband is dead. He's dead. Her children's father is dead.

Martha vomits. She hasn't eaten today so it's just bile. She swallows most of it back down, but there's a trickle down the collar of her dressing gown.

Orla starts to hyperventilate.

The men in helmets run into the kitchen and out the back door.

And all she sees is Sinead shaking, not vibrating but a proper fit. Her wet pyjama shorts cling as her body clangs against the radiator. She sees Sinead understanding what she already knows.

I'm sorry, baby, but your daddy's dead.

*** Pine Road Poker ***

Ruby:
Public service announcement: Have youse seen what Shay Morrissey is holding?

He's out on the road now.

Ellen:
What? A new plank of wood?

I'm in the middle of polishing a tricky knob.

Carmel:
Glad to know Joe's having a good Saturday, anyway.

Ellen:
I expect that kind of crude humour from Ruby, Carmel, but not from you.

Carmel:
Sorry, Ellen. Couldn't help myself. Won't happen again.

Rita Ann:
Is it my newspaper, Ruby? Is he holding several back issues of the Irish Times? Because really now, this has gone on long enough. It's well beyond a joke.

Edie:
Looking out the window but can't see from up here. x

Rita Ann:
What is it??

Ruby:
Sorry – was making lunch. A pneumatic drill! Like one of those massive professional yokes you see builders with on the street. I'm watching him from the window now.

Oh! Oh!!

Carmel:
What???

Ruby:
He's heading around the side of his house!

Ellen:
Oh my God WHO gave that mad man a pneumatic drill??

Ruby:
He's disappeared from sight. Maybe he's drilling through whatever cars dared to park nine feet out from his property?

Fiona:
Oh lordy. I think Kevin parked ours around the side last night.

Ellen:
Should we call the police?

Carmel:
I'm going out for a look.

Edie:
Wait, Carmel! It may not be safe.

Ellen:
I don't even want to imagine the mess he'll make ...

Ruby:
G'wan, Carmel! Tell him he's a nutjob from me!

TWENTY-THREE

'**C**armel! Wait!'

Edie tripped slightly on the bit of footpath outside Ruby and Madeline's house that had been pulled up by the root of a tree. They'd called the council several times about it, and Bernie had gotten them all to sign a petition at November's card game, but nothing had been done.

'Coocoo, Carmel!' She was trying to do up her coat one-handed as she jogged down the road. Carmel Dwyer was out her own gate, turning left down towards the Morrissey place at the end of the road and left again on to the Occupied Territory.

Just as Edie reached the Dwyer house, Robin stepped out the front door, wearing an oversized hoodie and carrying a packet of cream crackers.

'Oh, hi, Robin.' Edie was already breathless. Her GP told her some intermittent cardio could help with conception but after a day of walking to and from work left her with blisters, she'd shelved that advice. What did it matter anyway, when she and Daniel were too busy fighting to do the only sort of cardio that really mattered? 'Sorry about last night, bit embarrassing really.'

'What? Oh, that.' Robin waved away her concern. 'Did you see where my mam went? She muttered something about Israel and the Middle East and just marched out of the house.'

'It's Shay Morrissey,' said Edie, still catching her breath. She really was shockingly unfit.

'That bully?' Robin rolled her eyes. 'When we were kids, he used to scream at us if we bounced a ball off his wall. He was worse than Mrs Ryan. Mam ate him once. Told him that was what happened when you bought an end of terrace; you got the massive bonus of not having to bring your bins through your house in exchange for kids occasionally using your wall as a goal.'

'God, that's true,' said Edie, having a mini-epiphany. 'I never thought of the bins benefit. It'd be great not to have to drag them through the house, or leave them in the front garden. I think it looks terrible when people do that.' Then quickly: 'But no offence to Madeline and Ruby.'

Robin reached into the packet and produced half a cracker. She looked tired.

'Anyway, sorry.' Edie shook her head. 'I think your mother is about to *eat* Shay Morrissey again.'

'What did he do this time?'

'Well, I don't know exactly. Ruby sent a message to the WhatsApp group saying he was out here with a big drill.'

Robin laughed, a shard of cracker spraying from her mouth. 'Oh, we have to see this. The bloody mentaller!'

'Where's Jack?' said Edie, trailing Robin down the road.

'My dad's taken him into town. They both needed to get new shoes.'

They rounded the corner on to the side of Shay Morrissey's house where they came to a sudden stop.

'Oh gosh,' murmured Edie.

Robin gave a low whistle. 'Mental, mental, chicken oriental.'

The brick wall at the side of his house had been painted with three massive words: MORRISSEY PARKING ONLY.

Each letter was about as long as Edie and the white paint at the bottom of the 'Y' had run to such an extent that it pooled at the base of the wall. Beside the pool of paint was a stack of bottle-green poles wrapped in cellophane.

'White paint gets very dirty,' murmured Edie, who still regretted the eggshell colour they'd gone for with their porch when they first moved in.

Robin tilted her head. 'It looks like a seagull shat it out.'

Standing on the gravel in front of the sign – a spot where Daniel had left their car on several occasions – was Shay Morrissey. He was dressed in jeans, a greying wife-beater and construction goggles pulled firmly over his eyes. A pair of ear mufflers were slung around his neck and a look of determination consumed his face as he straddled a massive jackhammer.

'I'd say he's freezing.'

Edie was wondering how he'd managed to reach the top letters. Their own ladder wasn't high enough to get to the eaves of the house. They'd never cleaned out the gutters. Not once since they moved in. She must remember to ask Daniel to sort that out. If they were still married.

Daniel and Edie had gone to bed not talking and woken up the same way. It had happened *again*. First day of this ovulation cycle and he'd started up with the doubts. She could tell he was in a mood the second she arrived at the pub. And within an hour, he'd gone back to the money excuse. They owned their own house, for God's sake! And then, to make matters worse, Robin and her new man had caught them arguing on the street like a pair of fishwives.

Daniel had headed off at the crack of dawn this morning without a word to her, as if *he* were the one with a reason to be cross. She had a sinking suspicion that things weren't going well at the garage again. But even if they weren't, she couldn't let spreadsheets dictate her family planning.

When Daniel came home and saw the mural that now marked the entrance to Pine Road, Shay Morrissey would do well to not be standing in the vicinity of a veritable weapon.

'Shay Morrissey, put that down right this minute!'

Carmel, who had disappeared and reappeared in a high-vis jacket, was walking straight up to him, waggling her right index finger in his goggled face.

Shay, who was still gripping both handles and had the jackhammer pointed towards the tarmac, looked from Carmel to the two younger women behind her. Edie gave him a wave. She felt bad about how often Daniel got into fights with the man.

'No!' he shouted back, although there was an edge of uncertainty to his defiance.

'He looks like a suicide bomber,' whispered Robin, pulling another cracker from the packet.

'Which makes your mother the peace negotiator.'

Robin guffawed. 'We're all in trouble so.'

Carmel resumed jabbing her finger in the air in front of Shay's face. 'What in the name of all that is sane do you think you're doing?'

'I . . .' Shay glanced behind Carmel. Edie smiled at him. 'It's none of your business!'

'It is so my business, Shay Morrissey! I live on this street and I'm not going to let you drill holes in it wherever you please. What would Muriel say, God rest her soul, if she could see you out here defacing the side of her beloved home and making an absolute spectacle of yourself? For God's sake! Would you not even put on a feckin' shirt?'

'Don't you bring Muriel into this!' Shay's grip on the drill tightened.

'For the love of Jesus, will you—'

'This is my land! Mine! I have the right to use for nine—'

'Nine feet out from your property. Yes, yes, we all know. And so what?' Carmel rolled up her sleeves and Edie watched her transfixed; she wasn't quite like the negotiators talking suicidal people down off ledges, too aggressive, but she could be a terrorist interrogator. 'You're going to blow a big hole in the ground here? Is that it? Rather it was a crater than allow other people to park on it?'

'No!' retorted Shay, sounding more confident now. 'I'm putting in retractable bollards.'

'Retractable what?'

'Bollards. Like you see in the city centre. I can secure them into the ground and when I need to park I can lower them. And then when I don't, I can raise them up.'

Carmel only faltered for a moment but it was all the permission Shay needed. Suddenly Edie was stumbling backwards and the ground around them started to shake.

'Jesus!'

The sound of the machine pummelling into the concrete reverberated all around and Edie brought her hands to her ears. She could just about make out fragments of what Carmel was screaming.

'. . .have you committed . . . turning in her grave . . . right now . . . hope you catch your death . . .' Carmel's arms were by her side as she leaned forward and roared into the deafening clamour. She was still screaming when the noise came to a sudden halt. '. . . not enough mourners to carry your coffin!'

Shay looked down at his machine and frowned. 'The arsing wattage.' He dropped the drill and followed its cord around the corner and back into his house.

Edie lowered her hands from her ears.

'Are you all right, Mam?' called Robin.

Carmel was inspecting the jackhammer in Shay's absence. She gave the thing a few kicks, then started to tug at the wire.

'Mind, Mam. Jesus.' Robin walked over to her and Edie looked around to see that the drilling had brought several neighbours out. She waved up the street at Ruby, who was standing at her gate, eating a bowl of something. Martha was making her way down to the bottom of the road from the opposite side. Edie walked over to her.

'I heard the noise.' Martha was dressed all in black with a chunky silver necklace. She looked a little worn out but still great. What was bags under the eyes on Edie was heroin chic on Martha. 'What's going on?'

'Shay Morrissey,' said Edie, nodding over to his house.

'The planks of wood fellow?'

'Yep,' nodded Edie. 'He's taken it up a notch and is now installing parking bollards.'

'Is he allowed do that?' Martha asked, only sounding half-interested.

'I just hope he either gives up or has it done before Daniel gets home. If Daniel sees— Robin!' Across the road, Carmel was heading back into her house and her daughter was following. Robin glanced over at Edie and Martha but kept going. Edie waved her over, but her target friend hesitated. 'Robin!' she shouted again. Eventually – reluctantly, Edie thought – she crossed the road.

'Hello, Robin,' said Martha, stifling a yawn. 'Excuse me.'

Edie gave her a sympathetic smile. It couldn't be easy at the moment, with Sinead and everything.

Robin was still looking across the road, even though there was nothing to see but a discarded drill. 'Hi.'

'Has Carmel given up?' asked Edie.

'I doubt it.'

'Oh, Martha!' said Edie, suddenly remembering. 'Do you know who I ran into last night?'

'Who?'

'Robin,' she beamed. 'With her man.'

'My what?' snapped Robin.

'Your new man.' Edie frowned. 'Cormac.'

'Oh, right.'

Martha smiled, but Robin went back to squinting across the road.

'He seemed nice,' said Edie. 'Very handsome up close, which is good.' Still, Robin continued to look away. She was being quite rude. 'How was the rest of your night, Martha? Did you have chicken for dinner in the end?'

'Hmm?'

'Last night,' repeated Edie. 'Did you have the chicken? You were saying you were going to make it for dinner?'

'Robert made dinner. It was . . .' She trailed off.

Edie could be relied on to keep a conversation going – she hated for anyone to feel awkward and she was rather good at filling dead air – but it did help to get a little feedback.

'Is everything okay, Martha?' she pushed, since Robin clearly wasn't going to ask.

'I saw him,' she said quickly. 'Again. Last night. I saw the man from the robbery.'

Edie gasped. 'You *saw* him? Where? *Here?*'

Martha nodded. Edie looked to Robin who at least had the manners to look shocked. 'What was he doing?'

'He was . . .' Martha shivered. 'He was standing out on the road.'

'On *Pine* Road?' Edie exclaimed, looking with dumbfounded shock from one woman to the other. They were equally pale. 'Are you sure?'

'I was standing in our bedroom, about to close the curtains, and he was just . . . he was right there.' She pointed to the middle of the road, the space between her house and Robin's. 'Robert knew there was something up but I couldn't tell him. I'd have to admit that I saw him the first time.' She paused, the lines around her eyes pronounced. No wonder she was tired. 'Should I tell the guards?'

'Of course you should tell the guards!' exclaimed Edie.

'I don't know . . .' said Robin at the same time.

'What are you talking about? Of course she should tell them.' Edie turned back to Martha. 'Do you think he tracked you down?'

'I don't know.'

'Was he . . .?' Edie lowered his voice. 'Was he looking at you?'

'No. I don't know. It was only a second and then I just . . .' She mimed closing the curtains. 'Maybe I was mistaken, but I don't think so. Or maybe it was a coincidence. Except this is a cul-de-sac so where else could he be going?'

Edie thought of a true-crime podcast she'd listened to recently, about a man in Colorado who served fifteen years in prison only to get out and murder the witness who put him away. He didn't even go to see his mother first, or stop for some lunch. It was literally the first thing he did. If Edie knew she was going straight back to prison, she'd at least have had a Cornetto.

She wasn't about to worry Martha by telling her that, but it was a true crime; these things did happen.

'You have to tell the police,' she said decisively. 'If nothing else, it might prompt them to give a bit more attention to the case.'

Beep!!!

A car horn caused them all to turn. Shay Morrissey was back on the road, lifting his drill. There was no sign of Carmel but a car had stopped at the bottom of the road.

'Oh gosh,' murmured Edie. It was Daniel's car.

A teenage girl walked up the road past them. She was dressed in soccer shorts and a jersey and carrying muck-covered runners.

'Sinead,' called Martha and she turned to follow the girl without a word of goodbye.

Beep!!!

'Oh gosh,' repeated Edie. 'Talk to you later.' She left Robin standing alone and made her way over to Daniel, catching the driver's door just as it flew open.

TWENTY-FOUR

Martha heard Sinead's soccer boots and kit bag hit the floorboards – even though they had a coat stand and cubbyholes now – as she followed her into the house and watched her disappear upstairs.

'I need to talk to you.'

'Shower!' her daughter called and kept walking into the bathroom.

Martha picked up the kit bag and carried it down to the kitchen. Placing it on the table and unzipping it, she heard the electric shower kicking in upstairs. The bag was full of soccer vests. It must be Sinead's turn to wash them; meaning it was Martha's turn. She opened the washer and tossed them in. Then she threw in a tab and set it to 60 degrees. The washing machine kicked in, vying with the shower above it for attention, and Martha walked over to the kitchen window.

Robert had cut back the weeds. When had he done that? When she was over at Ellis's place or up at Edie's? It must have taken a while. For the hundredth time in the past twelve hours, Martha wondered if she should tell Robert what she'd seen. What did the man want? Did he know she'd checked in with the police? Was he trying to scare her?

If she told Robert she'd seen the man's face last night, she'd have to tell him she'd also seen it at the time. Robert could admonish her; he would be perfectly entitled to lay into her for withholding evidence and thwarting any chance of them getting justice. But he wouldn't do that. At the peak of her rage last night, traces of lost compassion had returned. Just traces, but enough to see her husband as a human made up of more than one event. Robert didn't hold grudges. He never blamed her for their children's shortcomings. He was more forgiving than her.

The washing machine lulled and the shower came to an abrupt stop. Martha reached into the drawer by the sink and produced the printouts Robert had pulled from the printer the night before.

If she had said something about the man she saw at the time, might the culprits have been caught? She doubted it. She could recognise the man – or at least she now knew she could – but she couldn't describe him in any meaningful way. 'Soulful eyes' was hardly going to make a Wanted poster.

The bathroom door opened and Martha listened as her eldest daughter banged around her bedroom. Robert and Orla had left early for a sprinting competition in Offaly. Robert had texted to say they'd be back by three.

The washing machine kicked back in and Martha gave a start. 'Christ!' she muttered.

Had she really seen him? Could she be 100 per cent sure?

'Did you take my—' Sinead came bustling into the room, dressed in what she'd informed Martha were called 'Mom jeans' and an oversized black net sweater. She peered into the kit bag. 'Did you take the vests?'

Martha nodded to the washing machine. 'You're welcome.'

'You really shouldn't go through my things.'

'Excuse me?'

'I don't go through your things, so I don't think you should go through mine. Privacy is a basic right. It's recognised in the United Nation's Declaration of Human Rights.' Sinead walked over to the washing machine and stared in to the rapidly turning drum. 'Great,' she muttered.

Martha wanted to ask what bad could possibly come from someone else doing your washing but that was a sure fire way to get sidetracked and, as much as she'd like to put it off, Martha had to talk to Sinead, today. Now.

'Sinead.'

'Martha.'

Martha pursed her lips. 'Sit down,' she said sharply. 'And less of your lip.'

Sinead pulled out a chair and flopped her body down. She mimed zipping her mouth shut and put her hands on her knees, under the table.

Martha took a deep breath, picked the A4 pages up off the draining board and walked over to the table.

Please let me be wrong, my darling girl. Please just tell me I'm wrong and I'll believe you.

She pulled out her own chair. 'Your father was fixing the printer last night, because Orla needed to print something off for her homework . . .'

Still pretending to have her lips zipped, Sinead widened her eyes in mock fascination.

'. . . and he found this.' Martha opened one of the sheets, picture side up, and put it on the table in front of Sinead. 'Three identical ones came out, actually.'

Sinead didn't touch the page. She just stared at it.

'I checked your phone.'

Sinead's eyes shot up from the page to her mother. For a moment they burned with outrage, but that fell away too. Martha went to the larder press and took out her daughter's mobile. She sat back at the table and powered it on.

'I found photos of the list.'

She put the phone in front of Sinead, but she didn't touch that either. Martha watched as she chewed the inside of her cheek.

'Did you make the poster?'

Sinead nodded.

Martha's body tensed.

'Did you stick them up around the school?'

'Mum, I—' Her lips unzipped. 'I did it for a reason. I did it to raise awareness.'

Martha closed her eyes. 'Sinead, Trish – Mrs Walsh – has the police involved. This is serious. Why wouldn't you just tell a teacher about it? Or me? Why would you make a big public campaign instead?'

Sinead watched her mother, pupils dilated, her jaw still worrying at her cheek. 'Does Dad know?'

'Of course,' said Martha. 'He found the printouts.'

Now it was Sinead's turn to squeeze her eyes shut. 'Are you going to call the police?'

'On you? No. Of course not. The school might have something to say, and we should probably tell Mrs Walsh, but you haven't broken the law. Sticking up posters isn't a crime – even if it was an incredibly stupid thing to do.' At least Martha didn't think it was a crime. It could possibly be considered littering. But was that actually a crime? Or obstructing an investigation, if an investigation into the list was already under way? But Martha doubted a little postering was going to interest the boys in blue.

Sinead took her hands out from under the table and reached for her phone. She opened the gallery and lifted it up to her mother. It was the photo from the printout.

'Yes, I know.'

Sinead flicked her finger across the screen so it shifted between the two identical images of the list written on the bathroom door.

'I saw them last night, Sinead, and I can see it right now.' She tapped the blown-up image lying on the table. 'I really don't need to be reminded.'

'No, Mum. Look.'

Something in the tininess of her daughter's voice made Martha's body tense. She looked at her daughter, the worry undeniable. She grabbed the phone from Sinead and flicked between the two images. At first, she could see nothing different from the photo lying on the table in front of her.

'What am I looking at? It's just—'

And then she clocked it.

She paused on the second photo, then flicked back. She flicked forward again. They were not the same. The first image was of the same list, but it was not complete. The last name – Sinead's name – had still to be added. The second image, and the one on the table, was the finished job.

'No.' She looked up from the phone to her daughter, who recoiled under her gaze. Martha's body strained with tension. 'Is this . . .? Did you write this, Sinead?'

Sinead opened her mouth to speak, then shut it. And resignedly, so faintly that her neck barely moved, she nodded her head.

TWENTY-FIVE

'**M**am! Stop! What do you think you're doing?'

'I'm putting a stop to this mad man's reign of terror,' said Carmel, wrestling the shears back off Robin, who was coming up their garden path just as her mother was exiting it. 'This road has gone loopers. Rats, dogs, stolen tyres. It's time for some sanity!' Carmel chopped the air with the giant scissors and pulled the garden gate open.

Robin shut it again. 'You'll electrocute yourself if you cut through that wire.' Carmel pulled at the gate but her daughter wouldn't let go. 'Edie's husband is talking to him now. Look.'

Carmel slackened her grasp on the gate and they both turned towards the Occupied Territory. Shay Morrissey was back, although now wearing a duffel coat over his vest – 'You must have gotten to him, Mam' – and he was shaping up to the man Robin had seen Edie with last night. He seemed to have things under control.

'All right, Carmel?' called a woman standing in a garden two doors up from them, eating a bowl of soup.

'Oh, hi, Ruby!' Carmel called back. 'How's it going? One of the lesbians,' she murmured to Robin. 'I told you her and Madeline got married after the referendum? Myself and your father were invited to the afters.'

'I remember.' Her mother hadn't shut up about it. She'd still been working at the time and was the first nurse on the ward to attend a same-sex wedding. You'd swear she'd won an award.

'It was incredibly stylish, Robin. Both of them in these gorgeous off-white jumpsuits and the cake was just rows of little cakes. Very modern, as you'd expect. But they still did salmon or beef so, you know, a nod to tradition.'

Several neighbours were out now, watching from the safety of their gardens. The only people actually out on the road were Shay, Edie's husband and, a few yards back, Edie. Robin glanced across the street but there was no sign of life from number eight. Martha and her daughter had both disappeared inside.

'Oh, feck me! Daniel just put his hand on Shay's shoulder! Jesus, but he's a braver man than me.' Carmel sucked air in through her teeth as they watched the two men square up to each other. 'Give us one of those crackers, Robin. You know how nerves make me hungry.'

'I talked to Martha.'

'Mmm.' Carmel munched away, crumbs falling from her woolly jumper into the flower bed. 'What's Shay saying, I wonder?'

'I don't feel good about it, Mam. I think I should say something.'

'Whatever it is, he's saying a lot of it. And with feeling.'

'I think I should tell her.'

'Is Daniel . . .? Is he leaving? Oh, no. Feck me! He's going for the boot.' Carmel shoved her hand into the packet again and stuffed another cracker into her mouth. 'He goin' foh da boothhhh!' A cream-coloured spray soaked the garden.

'Are you listening, Mam? I think I should tell Martha about Eddy. Or else I should go to the guards before they come to me.'

Carmel snapped her head around, wiping the crumbs from her chin. 'The guards, Robin? Are you mental? No.' Robin had been in the middle of telling her mother about Eddy's midnight visit and the connection to Martha's tiger raid when Carmel got a WhatsApp message about Shay and went barrelling out of the house. 'For all you know, you put two and two together and came up with five.'

Behind her, Daniel was taking what looked like bolt cutters out of his boot.

'All you know is that Eddy did something stupid, and okay probably illegal, around the same time that all that happened to Martha. But thousands of people do stupid things every day. You have no proof that there's a connection.'

'She saw him, Mam. When he came here last night. She saw Eddy on the street.'

Carmel let this sink in and was still struggling to find a counter-argument when there was a roar from behind. 'Oh my God, he's got a bolt cutter! Well, good man, Daniel,' she said, flinging her own shears on to the porch with a clatter. 'That should get the job done, anyway.' Transfixed, she reached for another cracker.

'Is Shay making progress with that drill, Carmel?' shouted her soup-eating, lesbian pal. 'That tree is blocking my view.'

'I don't think so, Ruby! But he's giving it a good shot!'

'The missus will be raging she missed this,' said a man standing in the garden next to the soup-eater. 'Yep! Here she is now – texting me to take a video for her!'

'I'm going inside,' muttered Robin.

'Don't say a word, Robin,' said Carmel. 'Eddy's a waste of space but he's your son's father. You don't want the hassle, not when you can avoid it. Ah, ya bowsie, ya!' And she was back to the action, just in time to see Shay get a bollard an inch off the ground and sort of lever it in the direction of Daniel's back wheel. 'Ah, now. Not the BMW.'

Robin closed the front door, leaving it on the latch. She could hear her mother shouting – 'Ya bowsie! Ya bowsie! Ya blue-bollocked bowsie' – as she headed into the kitchen. Her dad and Jack would be in town for another while and Johnny had stayed with friends last night. Or at least he'd told Carmel he was staying with friends; Robin presumed it was a girl.

Robin pulled out her phone and opened the Irish Jobs app. She'd applied for a few positions over the past couple of weeks but had yet to get as much as an interview. Not that she was surprised; she

225

wouldn't have given her an interview either. She scrolled through the notices but there was nothing new.

And just like that she was hit by a memory of flirting with a friend of Eddy's, drunkenly, in their flat one night. It was a nothing memory, just something stupid she'd done once, but this kept happening. She'd be in the middle of doing something entirely unrelated and out of nowhere she'd have a flashback to something she'd done in the past, nothing awful, just something she was ashamed of. Now that she was no longer living that life, it turned out she was ashamed of a lot.

She knew why she shouldn't tell Martha what she knew, but she also knew why she should. She needed to talk it through with someone.

Cormac.

She wanted to tell Cormac.

It had only been a month but he had listened when she told him about Eddy and he hadn't judged. She liked him a lot. A lot a lot. And she needed to tell him about Jack. She wanted her conscience clear.

Her phone started vibrating in her back pocket and she pulled it out, willing it not to be Eddy. She looked at the flashing screen and grinned. Cormac. She took it as a sign.

'I was just thinking about you.'

'That's good. I'm always thinking about you.' She could almost hear the dimple forming on his cheek. 'How's it going? I'm just on my way home from the barber's.'

'You got a haircut?'

He laughed. 'Don't worry. It doesn't look any different. My mum thinks the barber sees me coming. She's convinced he never takes anything off at all.'

'Glad to hear it,' said Robin, leaning back on the counter. 'I like your hair.'

'I like yours.'

Robin cringed into her free hand. They were disgusting.

'So, how've you been in the twelve hours since I last saw you? Sleeping, breakfast, don't skimp on the details.'

'Quite a lot has happened, actually,' said Robin.

'Really? Want to tell me about it?'

'Yes.' *Yes, yes, yes.*

'Today?'

'Yes please.' She thought about Jack, who was due home around three. She needed to tell Cormac about his existence before then. 'I have a few hours now . . .'

Cormac was good. She knew this. He was the sort of person she wanted in her life. She would trust him. She would tell him about Jack, then maybe explain about Eddy and Martha.

'Great. Will I pick you up? We could go to Howth for a walk? And you can talk the ear off me.'

Robin grinned. 'That sounds perfect.'

'What's your address, exactly?'

'Nine Pine Road, off—'

'Oh, I know it.'

'Do you now?' said Robin, impressed. 'And you not even from Dublin.'

Cormac said something but it was lost to the roars from outside. Robin leaned forward and peered into the hallway but the front door was closed and she could see nothing.

'Sorry,' she said, covering her other ear. 'Say that again.'

'My mother lives there. They just moved into number eight; her, my sisters and my stepfather. Martha Rigby. Do you know her?'

TWENTY-SIX

'**D**aniel, just calm down. It's not—' But Daniel was out of the car, pulling his arm away before Edie could get a grasp on it, the seat belt snapping into its holder behind him and the car door left wide open, as he bulled his way over to Shay Morrissey.

'Oi! Morrissey!'

The owner of number one Pine Road was walking down his garden path, having heard some of what Carmel had said, at least, and added a jacket to his working-man ensemble.

'What do you think you're playing at?' Daniel pointed up at the MORRISSEY PARKING ONLY sign. A few of the other letters had started to run and there was a lot of white paint at the base of the wall.

'I'm asserting my right to land,' replied Shay, not even looking at Daniel as he continued along the route back to his jackhammer. 'I will not be bullied out of it. This is nine feet out from my property and I have a right to insert retractable bollards if and when I wish.'

'Bollards?' repeated Daniel. His eyes fell on the green poles still in their packaging. He glanced back at Edie, who winced.

'Daniel, don't—'

'That's right. Bollards. Retractable ones.'

Daniel was a foot taller and about forty years younger than Shay, but to be fair to their neighbour he stood his ground. His eyes darted about as Daniel moved closer – unlike Edie, he was probably glad to have so many witnesses gathered on the road – but he didn't move from his spot.

'I don't care if they retract up your arse,' said Daniel, quieter now but still perfectly audible from where Edie stood, as he put his hand on Shay's shoulder. 'You're not putting them on my street. Am I clear?'

He sounded like his brother, or his dad, the way she'd occasionally heard them talk to Daniel. This was the Carmody temper. Daniel rarely let it flare up. When they had rows, like they had last night, Edie was the one who got worked up.

Yet again, Edie felt sorry for Shay Morrissey. He wasn't the real reason Daniel was so angry, he just happened to be in the wrong place at the wrong time.

'Daniel,' she called, trying to be heard by her husband but not the rest of the neighbours. Robin and Carmel were standing in their garden, and a few of the others were out too: Ruby, Rita Ann, Liam Chambers from number eleven. At least Martha had gone inside. Edie could forget any chance of ever being mistaken for chic – for *French* – after this. Brawling on the street was about as unsophisticated as it got.

'Come on! We've other stuff to talk about. And Peter was looking for you,' she added. 'He rang. He couldn't get you on your mobile so you should probably—'

'Yeah, he got me,' replied Daniel, still looking at Shay.

'Right. Well . . .'

Ruby waved from up the road. Edie lifted a hand meekly in response.

'Do what your little lady tells you,' said Shay, smiling up into Daniel's face. 'And get your scum hand off my shoulder.'

'What did you call me?'

Shay paused, confused. 'I didn't call you anything.'

'Scum?'

'No, I called your *hand* scum, not you.'

'My hand is part of me.'

'Well, technically, yes, okay, but that's not what I meant—'

'That's what it sounded like.'

'It wasn't my intention. But look, if you want to take it like that, then go ahead. I won't stop you.'

'Come on, Daniel. Get back in the car.'

'Come on, Daniel. Get back in the car,' mimicked Shay. Then he leaned slightly to the left of Daniel. 'No offence, love!'

Daniel turned from Shay and walked towards her. Edie breathed a sigh of relief. 'Good. Let's just drive—'

But he wasn't going for the car door, he was going for the boot. He popped the trunk. Edie rushed over.

'This is ridiculous, Daniel,' she hissed. 'You're annoyed about last night, although I don't know why. I didn't do anything, except presume that what we had agreed still stood. I never went back on my— Oh, for heaven's sake. What are you going to do with those?'

Daniel had produced a pair of bolt cutters and was shutting the boot again. The thing was full of all sorts of crap from the garage. A few of the neighbours started to whoop and cheer when they saw the massive scissors. It sounded like Ruby was yelling 'Take off his mickey!' but the woman was a practising solicitor so that seemed unlikely.

Daniel took the potential weapon and walked over to Shay. Then he swerved slightly down towards the drill. He was going to cut the cord. Edie caught a sob in her throat. Was there *anything* that didn't make her think of having children?

'Get away from that,' shouted Shay and he made a jump for Daniel but her husband spun around, wielding the bolt cutters.

'Daniel!'

He wasn't listening. He was a man possessed. Poor Shay. He was at risk of losing a limb and it wasn't even about him – or at least, it was only a little about him.

Shay was roaring now, but Daniel just kept on cutting. Then Shay started dragging one of his new bottle green bollards across the tarmac of Pine Road. Oh gosh. He was heading for Daniel's car.

'Daniel!'

'I'm busy,' her husband fumed, not looking up from the cord that was proving difficult to sever.

Edie couldn't help but see it as a metaphor.

The neighbours were having great chats and Edie felt a mixture of mortification and jealousy. She didn't want to be the spectacle. She wanted to be part of the audience; standing in her own garden, shouting across to the other spectators; solidifying her place in this community; making friends!

'Everything okay, Edie hun?' shouted Fiona, coming halfway down the road, but when she saw that both men were now armed, she quickly retraced her steps. 'Give us a shout if you need anything, hun!'

Daniel was grunting and cursing over by the laneway as his implement refused to cut through the wire, while Shay was doing similarly disgruntled huffing and puffing as he tried to lift the bollard and fling it at Daniel's car. He had set the bollard up like one of those yokes they threw in the Olympics. On his second try, Shay made contact with the body of Daniel's car. Edie couldn't see the assaulted side of the vehicle from where she stood but from Carmel's excited roars – was she calling him 'bossy'? – she knew damage had been done.

Edie was on the verge of going home and leaving them to it – Daniel was her husband not her child. Another sob. Christ. *Get a grip, Edie!* – when Bernie Watters-Reilly turned the corner on to Pine Road.

Edie clamped her eyes shut. This was it. It was all over for her now. She'd be kicked out of poker and the street party and general Pine Road acceptable society, and she and Daniel would become such social lepers that they'd be forced to move.

She didn't want to move! She'd started to make real friends. She was now in *two* WhatsApp groups!

But Bernie didn't look at her or Daniel or Shay. She just marched on up the road like a woman on a mission. Was she going home?

Or calling to Trish, maybe? Poor Trish. Edie observed Bernie quick-stepping it up the road, when a cacophony of sound came out of nowhere. She spun around just in time to see Shay – who was sixty-five if he was a day – pulling down his jeans and – was he? Oh gosh, yes, yes he was – he was mooning her husband.

Carmel and Ruby had gone into hysterics and were whooping and hollering from their gardens. She could have sworn Ruby shouted, 'Take it off.' Daniel was sitting on the pavement, speechless, sweat pumping from his forehead and the massive scissors paused at an angle. He couldn't seem to take his eyes off the insubstantial, forlorn looking arse as it wriggled its ghostly pallor from side to side.

Edie couldn't hear what Shay was heckling over the neighbours' roars but whatever it was, Daniel was up on his feet, charging at the older man and his naked behind. Shay barely had time to wipe the jeer from his face, never mind pull up his jocks, before Daniel's fist collided with it.

'K! O!' hollered Ruby. There was no mistaking it this time.

That was it. Edie was a forgiving woman but she'd had enough. Her heart was broken and this was ridiculous. She marched over, grabbed the keys from Daniel and told him to get up to the house before someone called the police. Then she returned to his car, noted the scratch to the paintwork above the rear wheel, and climbed in. She drove it slowly up the road and parked outside Ellen's, the only available spot. She ignored the twitching curtain and the sight of Ellen Russell-O'Toole yet again cleaning her windows as she strode across the road, up the garden path and into their own home. She barely had her jacket off when Daniel came storming in behind her.

'Did you see what that fucker did to my BMW? I'm going to get the hammer, go down there and smash his car window in. See how he likes it, the—'

Edie spun around, so furious she couldn't stop the tears. She couldn't speak. She just stood there, blinking at her husband and gave a big, loud, ugly sob.

'What?'

'What?' she echoed. 'What?' She pulled down the sleeve of her good cotton blouse, which she had pulled out of the back of her wardrobe after seeing Martha wear something similar, and drew it across her face. 'You've just humiliated me in front of all my friends!'

'They're not our friends, Edie. They're our neighbours.'

'They are my friends!' shouted Edie, more vehemently than the statement really warranted. She didn't really like Bernie Watters-Reilly, if she was being honest, but the woman was a gatekeeper, and she liked Ruby, although she didn't know her surname. 'What did you have to go and hit him for? He might call the police! And you're not even annoyed about the parking! You're just annoyed about last night. You don't even care about Shay Morrissey.'

'I do so care about Shay Morrissey. I care very fucking deeply. I hate the fucking arsehole.'

'Okay fine, you hate him. But that's not why you're annoyed.' Edie threw herself down on the stairs. 'I don't even think you are annoyed about last night. I think you're annoyed because I want a baby and you don't.' She wiped at her nose. She was calling his bluff, looking to be reassured. 'I thought you wanted kids but you didn't. You don't. That's it, isn't it? It's that simple.'

'I just see the realities, Edie. I realise how unsteady running my own business can be. I saw how easily a bad year could leave us broke.'

Edie's mind flashed to her favourite fantasy – her, Daniel and two kids, one girl, one boy, curled up in bed on a rainy Sunday afternoon watching *Up* – and she started to sob again. She brought the collar of her shirt to her nostrils and blew. She'd have to wash it at 40 degrees now, and the instructions said no higher than 30. Why didn't she have a tissue? Someone like Martha would have a tissue.

'Please stop crying.'

'I don't know why this is happening.' A dull ache expanded in her chest. 'We used to talk about having kids, years before we were married, it was always the plan.'

'I'm sorry, Edie,' he said, though he didn't sound sorry. He sounded cross, bored even. He didn't sound like her Daniel. 'How many times do I have to say it? I'm sorry. Things happen. People are allowed to change their mind. And I'm not saying I never – I just – there's a lot to consider. I'm not sure I'm the right person to be looking after a child. I'm not responsible enough.'

'What are you *talking* about?' Edie shrieked, flinching at her own pitch. 'Where is this coming from? You're just making stuff up now!'

'I'm stressed enough as it is. Jesus!' Daniel put his two hands on top of his head. 'I don't need this!'

And before Edie could shout at him to stop being such a bloody martyr, he was storming into the kitchen. She heard the back door open and slam – as if they hadn't given the neighbours enough to talk about already – and knew he was going out to throw around tools in his shed.

Another ovulation weekend ruined.

Edie sat on the stairs and felt the potential child evaporate into the ether.

*** Pine Road Poker ***

Rita Ann:
Was that the guards just leaving Pine Road?

Fiona:
WHAT???

Rita Ann:
Squad car just left. I took its parking space. Anyone see what house they called to?

Fiona:
I actually feel a bit faint.

This cannot be good for property values.

Ruby:
Probably calling to Shay Morrissey about this afternoon's land grab.

Unless you finally filed a missing report on your newspapers, Rita Ann?

Ellen:
I presumed they were heading for you, Fiona, about the stolen wheels.

They weren't going to Morrissey's. They were walking up the road.

Fiona:
Definitely nothing to do with us! You saw them, Ellen?? How far up the road did they go? Was it our side or the other side??

Ellen:
How should I know how far they went? I have better things to be doing than standing on my doorstep all afternoon.

I'm in the middle of a serious spring clean.

My money's on the new people. I always thought their sudden move had something to do with C R I M E.

Ruby:
You realise spelling out words doesn't work in text, right, Ellen? Like, literally, makes zero difference.

TWENTY-SEVEN

●●●●●●●●●●●●●●●●●●●●●●●●●●●●●

'**H**ey,' **said** Cormac, stepping forward just as Robin pulled back.

He turned the thwarted kiss into an uncertain smile. 'Everything okay?'

'Of course,' she replied, still holding the door. 'You're early.'

'Maybe a few minutes . . .' He glanced at his watch. 'I like your house.'

'It's exactly the same as your mam's house, no?'

'I don't know,' he said slowly. 'I haven't been inside this one yet.'

'Sorry.' She forced her hand off the bolt. 'Come in.'

She stood to one side and Cormac entered. He kissed her on the mouth.

'Hi.'

'Hi,' she replied, smiling, then immediately feeling awful again. 'Martha said her son's name was Ellis. I remember because the first dog we ever had was called Ellis. He was terrified of birds.'

'Is that Mick?' Carmel's voice from the kitchen. 'Did he get Jack— Oh, hello.' Carmel stopped in the doorway between kitchen and hall. 'Who's this, then?' she said, advancing quickly.

'This is Cormac. Or possibly Ellis.'

'Cormac,' Carmel cooed. 'We've heard a bit about you. The hipster journalist. Aren't you handsome? Moustache wouldn't be quite to my taste, mind, but still.'

'Mam.' Robin closed her eyes.

'I know, I'm old. I don't get why you'd want rips in your jeans or to wear runners without laces, but sure look. Nice to meet you, Cormac.'

'Nice to meet you too, Mrs Dwyer.' Cormac pushed back his fringe and held out a hand.

'God, I remember when your father had hair like that. The sort of mane you could lose your fingers in, or more if—'

'Mam, *please*.'

'You from around here, Cormac?'

'I'm from Limerick, originally . . .'

'Very nice, very nice . . .'

'But I've been living up in Dublin for seven years, since I went to college.'

'Cormac is Martha Rigby's son,' said Robin, not wanting to invite a thousand questions but knowing Inspector Carmel would hit upon the key piece of information eventually.

'Martha Rigby? Across-the-road Martha Rigby? Get away. I didn't know that. Did you know that, Robin? You didn't tell me that. She tells me nothing, Cormac.'

'I just found out.'

'Get away,' Carmel said again. 'I didn't know – oh wait, I did know she had an older son, but hang on now. It wasn't Cormac . . . What was it?'

'Ellis,' provided Cormac-slash-Ellis.

'That's the one.'

'My family are the only ones who call me Ellis. Everyone else uses my surname. Cormack. It's my dad's name.'

'Ellis Cormack,' said Robin, silently adding the 'k' to how she'd been hearing it. Cormack the surname, not the first name.

'Three different surnames in the one family. You're practically American! Of course, Pine Road has always been very progressive. We've two lesbians at number thirteen. Married. Did Robin tell you that? *I* was invited to their wedding. Very classy affair, gorgeous salmon. There's a civil partnership on Elm Road, but what's that to boast about? It's not 2015, people. No, Pine Road is very diverse, we have *two* families with double-barrelled names, although their children won't necessarily thank them for that bit of "progression", especially if they already have ridiculous Frenchy first names . . .'

'Okay, well, we might just go for a walk . . .'

'Ah no. No, no, no. Youse go on into the kitchen. I'm going upstairs anyway to do my correspondences.' Carmel waved her phone at them. 'We had a bit of drama on the road today – over parking, of course. This yoke has been leaping ever since. Right, good luck,' she said, heading for the stairs.

On the third step, Carmel stopped. 'You're *Martha's* son.' It dawned on her, finally.

'Yeah. Martha's son. I just found out.' Robin widened her eyes, telling Carmel to zip it. No matter how stealthy her mother thought she was being, she never was.

'Right, well, let none of us do anything we might regret, especially when we don't know anything for sure and it wouldn't achieve anything anyway. As the old saying goes.' Then Carmel winked at her daughter. Except the only place Carmel could wink was in her head. In reality, she just leaned forward and blinked, slowly.

Robin grimaced.

'*Is* that a saying?' whispered Cormac as they made their way down the steps into the kitchen.

'Don't mind her. She drinks at lunch. So. Tea?'

'Yeah, great, thanks.' Cormac stood beside the kitchen table, his hand idly rubbing the surface. 'It is like my mum's place. Different décor – they've got wooden floors, which make the stairs noisy, especially when my sisters are pounding up them – but the layout's the same.'

Robin busied herself with the kettle and cups. 'We have coffee either,' she said, opening and closing cupboards, even though the tea and coffee were already out on the worktop.

'Tea is fine.'

'Two teas. All right. Coming up.' Robin glanced over her shoulder to see him flicking through one of her brother's kayaking brochures. She opened the fridge and retrieved the milk.

'So, do you know my mum, then?'

'I wouldn't say I *know* her. We have some biscuits too, if you like?' An hour ago, Robin was dying to talk to this man about Martha. Now, there was nothing she wanted to discuss less.

'My sister Sinead is finding it hard to fit in, but Dublin seems to be growing on Mum. She had such a busy social life in Limerick. It was a tough move, for all of them.'

'She mentioned the tiger raid, all right,' said Robin, handing him a mug of tea. She went to sit but was too fidgety. She leaned against the cooker instead.

'She told you about that?' Cormac was taken aback. 'You must know her well enough, then.'

'Well,' said Robin, doing her best to shrug off the conversation, 'another neighbour came across an article about it. Your mam only mentioned it briefly. Anyway, how are you? How was your Saturday morning? Oh! You got your hair cut. I didn't even notice.' Robin took a long loud slurp but the tea was far too hot. 'It suits you,' she managed to squeak out as her throat and mouth burned. 'Very . . . short.'

'Thanks?'

'No problem.'

'It's good to see you.'

'You saw me last night.'

'That was good too. I like seeing you. I like you.'

She couldn't do this. She couldn't carry on like she didn't know anything. She liked him too – she really, really liked him – but it wasn't right. Right?

'How's the tea?'

'Good.'

'Good, good.'

'Everything okay, Robin?'

'Yeah. Fine. Why?'

'You seem jumpy.'

Robin pursed her lips and shrugged. Maybe she should just tell him; just go ahead and tell him that she knew who had done that to his family.

'Is it this secret you're keeping?'

'What?' barked Robin, the tea slopping in her mug. 'There's no secret. I'm not keeping any secret.'

'Last night you said you had something to tell me, and I said I had something to tell you. A secret for a secret, remember?' He got up from his seat and walked over to her. 'It's okay,' he assured her, half-laughing. 'It can't be that bad.' He took her face gently in his hand. 'I'll be able to take it.'

Jack. He meant Jack.

'I like you, Robin.'

'I like you,' she whispered, in spite of herself. And when he kissed her, she leaned in; she pressed her body against his and waited for his arms to reach around her. She let herself sink into the kiss. *Why don't people kiss more?* she thought for the umpteenth time since meeting him. Cormac gave excellent kisses.

'Better now?'

The kindness in his voice and on his face bolstered her. She would tell him about Jack. She would start with that and then she would see.

'Okay, come on,' she said, picking up their barely touched mugs of tea and throwing the liquid down the sink. 'I can't sit in here, I can't concentrate.' She grabbed a jacket from the pile on the chair. 'Let's go for a walk and swap secrets.'

Cormac followed her out of the kitchen and up the hall. 'And that's how you make an unappealing conversation sound romantic.'

*** Pine Road Poker ***

Ruby:
Madeline says she saw them too. They definitely didn't go to the new people because when she spotted them, they were across from us and still walking up.

It must be someone at the top of the road.

Ellen:
Well, it certainly wasn't us.

Fiona:
Did they call to you, Trish? Was it to do with the school? Or to you, Bernie? Or Edie?

[Fiona is typing]

I just hope everyone's okay XXX

Carmel:
Hello all. I did not see the coppers but I *did* just meet Robin's new man. Very handsome!

Ellen:
Is that little Jack's father, or another man?

Fiona:
That's great, Carmel hun. Delira for Robin XXX

(Did he see anything, maybe? XXX)

Carmel:
Fiona – thanks. Ellen – it's another man; I'll draw you a chart so you can keep track.

Re: The Fuzz: It was probably about earlier. Maybe they called to Edie and Daniel? Whoever it was, it's none of our business.

Ellen:
I couldn't agree more. Nothing as unseemly as gossip.

Fiona:
I just hope everyone's okay XXX

TWENTY-EIGHT

Trish's phone was hopping. All the yelling had died down and everyone had gone back indoors, but the post-match analysis was only beginning.

Fiona thought it was like an episode of *Ireland's Crime Feuds* and Ruby, who pointed out that Fiona hadn't been there for the whole thing, said it was actually more like *Gang Wars*. Ellen said Ross Kemp looked quite like her Joe and Ruby had responded with a long line of those stupid crying-laughing emojis. Things were rarely crying-laughing funny.

Trish would not be getting involved. Ted had gotten into an argument with Shay Morrissey's daughters about parking once and the next day all the colour had been stripped from the bonnet of their car. She'd like to have put her phone on silent, but she was waiting on the call.

She'd phoned the board of management chair that morning, not wanting to wake the man last night when Emily had come into Trish and Ted's bedroom and told them what she knew. Normally she wouldn't say anything, her daughter had said, making it clear this was a one-off and she was not spying on the student body for Trish, but several of the girls on that list were her friends.

It actually hadn't been that late. It was probably just after 11 p.m. when Emily came home from a party at a friend's house and sat at the end of their bed and told them who'd written the list. A lot of gossip flew around Saint Ornatín's – both the staffroom and the classrooms – but her daughter believed this story, and unfortunately so did Trish.

She could have gotten out of bed there and then, gone downstairs, unplugged her phone from the kitchen and phoned Norman Roster, the management chair. But she hadn't. She'd given herself the night to toss and turn and dwell on it. Even this morning when she finally brought herself to pick up the phone, she tried putting it off, tried telling herself it was a Saturday and to leave it until Monday. In the end, she had done the right thing – and the best thing for her career.

She'd had as brief a conversation as she could, supplying Norman with the basic facts; he said he'd look into the best course of action and get back to her. So now Trish was playing the waiting game. Sitting at her kitchen island, staring out the glass walls into her beloved garden and willing the phone both to ring – so she could get it over with – and to spontaneously combust – so she could ignore the whole thing a little longer.

Today had been the first day that Saint Ornatín's had not appeared in any newspapers – although Virgin Media was making a documentary about Ireland's Sexed-Up Teens, so no doubt they could look forward to a mention in that – and it would be good to draw a line under it. If nothing else it would be the end of Bernie Watters-Reilly banging on her door demanding answers whenever she felt like it.

At that, the knocker pounded and Trish jumped from the island stool. Had she invoked the devil through thought alone?

But no, padding up the hallway in her stockinged feet, she could see through the frosted glass that it was two people, both too tall to be Bernie. She undid the latch.

'Oh, hello.'

'Hello,' replied Martha Rigby, her eldest daughter standing half a foot behind her. 'Do you mind if we come in?'

TWENTY-NINE

'**S**hay.' **Edie** was still pressing the heel of her hand into the puffy skin beneath her eyes when she opened the door. 'Eh . . . Hi.'

Her neighbour stood on their step, scratching awkwardly at his face. The red shine to the left of his nose was already on its way to becoming a bruise. A lamentably vivid memory of his sad, pale arse flashed before her.

'The guards weren't calling to youse, then no?' he said, raking his upper lip with his teeth as he peered into the hallway.

'The guards? No. Why?' Had he called the police? She told Daniel this would happen. This was exactly what she said would happen.

What would Bernie Watters-Reilly say when she saw a squad car pulling up outside their house, sirens blaring? What would Fiona say? She was hosting the next poker game. Edie could forget about being invited to that, not once Fiona started looking up the effect residential disputes had on house prices.

'Should we be expecting the guards?'

'Oh, I didn't call them,' said Shay. 'Just thought someone else might have. I saw a couple of them walking up the road. Thought I'd come and see.' He stopped scratching. 'Your hubby's an animal and I'd be only delighted if his finger got stuck in his nose and the nail continued to grow but, you know, we're neighbours.' Shay shrugged. 'I wouldn't go ratting him out to the coppers.'

'So you didn't call them?'

'No.'

'Okay. Phew.' Edie exhaled. 'Thanks.'

He nodded. 'No bother.'

Edie looked out on to the street. The guards had been on Pine Road? Did the others know about this? She patted her pockets. Her phone was still in her jacket.

'It's the neighbourhood code.'

'Absolutely,' agreed Edie, then she paused. 'What's that?'

'You know: what happens on Pine Road stays on Pine Road. Blood is thicker than water, but neither's as thick as mortar.'

'Right. Yes. Absolutely.' Edie thought about it. 'That's quite good, Shay.'

'Yeah. I dabble in verse.'

'Do you?'

'Haiku mainly.' Shay gnawed at his lip again. 'Anyway, I think I saw the coppers crossing to the other side of the road, but thought I'd come and make sure.'

Edie peered out to the other side of the street. She'd text the group as soon as she was done here. Pine Road was having quite the day.

'Edie! Bae?' The back door slammed shut and Daniel's voice called out from the kitchen. He was making his way up through the house. 'I'm sorry! I'm an idiot. You should just ignore me. If you want to go upstairs and make a baby, I'm ready. My little man might need a few gentle strokes to get him standing to full salute, and maybe a few nibbles on your yum-yum num-nums—'

The kitchen door opened into the hallway and Edie, who was doing her best not to pinch her eyes shut, watched as a look of unadulterated pleasure spread across Shay Morrissey's face.

'Hi, Daniel,' he called cheerily, lifting a hairy hand and waving it into the hallway behind her.

There was no response and Edie didn't dare to turn around.

Shay's smile grew even wider. The level of euphoria bordered on the obscene.

He leaned to the side and called down the hall again: 'Everything good with you?'

'Shay just called in to see if the police had been to see us, Daniel. Apparently, there were a couple of them on the road.'

'I didn't want you getting into trouble on my account, Dan-Dan.' Shay's voice had a mild squeak to it. His cheeks were puffed like balloons.

Daniel didn't respond. Shay wiggled his eyebrows at Edie, mouth still plastered with delight.

'Daniel,' called Edie. 'Come up here and say hello. And sorry. See if we can't be friends again.'

She smiled at Shay who was having a great time.

'Daniel.'

The floorboards creaked and her husband slowly made his way up the hall to the front door. His expression, as was always the case when he was embarrassed, was thunderous.

'All right, neighbour?'

Edie wanted to reach out and burst Shay's engorged cheeks.

'Where were the police going?' said Daniel eventually.

Although he had directed the question towards Edie, Shay was only too delighted to respond. 'Not sure,' he said.

'Maybe it was something to do with Fiona Quinn's wheels?' suggested Edie.

'Whose wheels?'

'Fiona Quinn,' Edie told her husband. 'Someone stole the wheels off her car a while ago.'

'I didn't know about that.'

'I think they were headed for one of those houses.' Shay pointed across to the opposite corner, where Bernie's and Trish's houses were. 'Might have been to do with that dog Bernie Wackers was littering my letterbox about.'

Edie had forgotten all about Bernie's sketch artist and the printouts. They were still on the hall table.

'Although if the coppers are wasting their time on that when I'm constantly reporting non-resident cars on this street, they're even more useless than I thought.'

'I didn't know about any of this.'

Edie ignored her husband. He'd been made to feel foolish and now he was sulking. He had no interest in what went on on the road. He barely knew the neighbours' names. And how was she supposed to tell him anything anyway when they spent all their time arguing and making up?

'Are you going to apologise to Shay, Daniel?'

Shay's eyes lit up and he went back to unabashed grinning. Edie knew Daniel was annoyed at her but she didn't care. She'd worked too hard to fit in on this road, she wasn't going to have him ruining it all.

'Daniel!'

'I'm sorry I hit you.' She could hear the clench in his jaw.

'Not a bother, neighbour,' replied Shay with grandiose graciousness. 'We all get a little wound up from time to time. And aren't we lucky if we, eh, have ways to release all that pent-up energy?' Shay sucked in his cheeks in a half-hearted attempt to stop himself laughing and Edie felt her husband square beside her. 'I'm leaving the bollards for today anyway, you'll be glad to hear. Going to see about getting a professional to put them in later in the month.'

Daniel went to say something but Edie put an arm firmly on his.

'Anyway, I'll leave youse to it. Good luck with, ah . . . whatever it is you get up to for the afternoon.' He turned and walked down the path. 'Up! Ha. I didn't even mean it like that. I'm off to have my tea. Yum-yum num-num!'

Daniel opened his mouth but Edie had the door closed before he could say a word. She gave him a good solid stare, daring him to start yet another argument. But instead he sulked off, back towards the kitchen and presumably the shed. Edie stood alone in the hallway and sighed.

She took her phone from her jacket pocket. Thirty-two new WhatsApp messages! She read through the thread and replied, hoping the delay hadn't made her look like a suspect. Was she being a grass by mentioning Trish and Bernie? Surely not. Those two would have nothing to hide and anyway they were long-term residents. She was still a blow-in; a criminal rumour like this could follow her around for the rest of her Pine Road days.

She pressed send and threw the phone on to the hall table, beside Bernie Watters-Reilly's 'Wanted' posters. She'd forgotten all about them. Edie pulled one of the sheets out from below the bowl and unfolded it. There was an actual 'Wanted' masthead at the top of the page and the sketch was signed, just as Carmel had said. How much had Bernie spent on this?

Then Edie focused on the actual drawing and her amusement faltered.

She knew that dog.

That was Rocky. It was a picture of Peter's dog.

'Edie?'

Daniel came back through the kitchen and into the hallway. She folded the sheet quickly and pushed it back under the Waterford Crystal bowl.

'I'm sorry,' he said. 'I know I keep saying that but I am, I'm sorry. I don't know what's wrong with me . . .'

'It's okay.'

'It's not. I want to explain exactly but I can't—'

'Daniel,' she interrupted. 'It's okay. I get it. I understand.'

He opened his mouth to disagree but she took a step forward and kissed him, slipping her tongue gently between his lips.

'I understand,' she said again, moving away and pulling him after her up the stairs.

Because now, finally, she did understand. Daniel had been minding his brother's dog when the animal bit Sylvie Reilly. He was the adult male who'd fled the scene. If she'd been minding a dog and it bit a young girl, Edie would be questioning her suitability to be a parent too. She'd be doubting how responsible she really was and if she should be entrusted with a child's welfare.

Dear, sweet Daniel, always so hard on himself.

It finally made sense and Edie was overcome with relief.

*** Pine Road Poker ***

Edie:
Hi, ladies. Sorry for the parking tiff earlier. Daniel is a bit stressed at work and I think he just saw red. I'm the one who's red now, though! V embarrassing! Sorry again.

And no. The guards were definitely NOT calling to us.

Shay Morrissey (long story) said it looked like they went to Trish's or Bernie's. He lost them behind the tree.

x

THIRTY

'We're here,' said Martha, having refused refreshments and now sitting upright at Trish's mahogany kitchen table, 'because Sinead has something to tell you.'

'All right,' replied Trish, interlinking her hands and resting them on the gleaming wood. 'I'm listening.'

Her face was unreadable and Martha wondered if, faced with a student, Trish had consciously gone into teacher mode, or if this was just what a long-term career did to you.

Martha could feel Sinead look at her, but she didn't turn. It was up to her daughter to explain.

'It's about the list on the bathroom door,' came the small voice beside her. 'I took the photos of it.'

Martha kept her eyes trained to Trish's face as her daughter spoke, but there was no discernible change.

'I printed them out and I stuck them up around the school.'

Trish nodded. It was the same thing you saw with doctors, an unflappable expression of calm, mild interest.

'Tell her the other bit,' said Martha.

Her daughter shifted beside her and Trish's face softened a fraction.

'And I wrote it,' said Sinead. 'Not all of it. But my own name. I added my name to the list.'

Martha, though she had heard this qualifier an hour earlier, breathed a sigh of relief. For an awful few seconds that afternoon she had thought her daughter, just weeks into her new school, had written the whole thing. Adding her own name was still a definite cause for concern, but at least she wasn't bringing others down with her.

'I was in English and I heard two boys talking about the list. They weren't laughing, but they didn't think it was a big deal either. I just wanted to see it for myself first, to make sure it was really there . . .'

Sinead repeated all that she had already told her mother. Although now, on its second telling, the sentences were clearer, the story without gaps. Martha continued to watch Trish as Trish watched her daughter. She didn't interrupt Sinead the way Martha had or demand clarification or ask her to repeat herself.

'. . . So the next day, I asked to go to the toilet but I went into the boys' bathroom instead of the girls' one. I found it on the back of the door and I added my name to the bottom. Then I took a photo. I saw you on my way back from the bathroom, Mrs Walsh. I think you were going to remove it, because it was gone by the end of that day. If I'd left it even till the next class, I might have missed it.' There was an edge of pride to Sinead's voice, and she must have caught it too because she quickly brought the tone back to remorseful.

'I know it's a sicko thing to do,' she pleaded, though the principal had yet to make any objection. 'But when I heard the boys talking about it, I was so angry. They weren't going to tell a teacher. I really was. I was going to report it. But when I saw it, I got even madder. I felt sick. I . . .'

I felt like I did that day in Limerick, Sinead had told Martha an hour earlier. *I had to do something this time.* In the principal's kitchen, however, Sinead left her own experience out of it. She didn't mention all the ways she had conflated the two events.

'You painted over it,' said Sinead, her tone now verging on accusatory. 'If I didn't do anything, everyone would just act like nothing had ever happened . . .'

Like you do, Mum, Martha added silently, *like how we all act like nothing ever happened.*

254

'. . . So I took the photos and I stuck them everywhere and sent them to the newspapers and radio stations.'

Oh, Sinead.

But as Martha listened for the second time to her daughter purging and trying to rationalise her actions, she found herself beginning to understand. She knew what it was to have misplaced rage; to be angry about one thing and to direct it at something – or, in Martha's case, someone – else because they were right there, and they were wrong too, and it's easier to lash out than to accept that something awful was done to you and you may never get the chance to right it.

'I thought it was wrong,' stated Sinead. 'That list shouldn't have existed, and I wanted people to know about it. I added my name because I knew people would take me more seriously if I was one of them – one of the *victims*. Being an activist isn't enough. People like their victims to have a face. It had to be personal, about me. That's how I could make it right.'

And then there was silence. She was done. Martha turned, finally, but Sinead was no longer looking to her for guidance. Her gaze was fixed across the kitchen table, on the school principal.

When Trish moved, it wasn't much, just a slight shift of her body and the relaxing of her face. 'Is that it all?'

'Yes.'

Trish nodded. Her hands separating now as she pulled herself up a little straighter. She didn't seem shocked by what Sinead had said. Was that possible? Was it not shocking? Perhaps this was always her demeanour.

'I'm sorry,' added Sinead. 'I know it's not your fault.'

'No, it's not,' agreed Trish. 'And it would be true to say that I could have done without a journalist from the *Mirror* doorstepping me two days in a row last week, or the *Sun* branding the school "Saint Horny Teens".'

Sinead laughed. Then stopped abruptly. 'Sorry.'

'It's very catchy,' Trish agreed. 'We'll be a while living that one down.' She sighed. 'But it's not your fault either, Sinead. Not really.' She leaned back and stretched her neck with a loud crack, then she smiled at them both.

Martha and Sinead looked at each other. 'Is . . . Is that it?' asked Sinead, taking the words out of her mother's mouth.

Trish gave a rueful laugh. 'No, that is not it. God, I wish it was. But as far as you're concerned, I think it is.'

'You're not going to punish me?'

'No,' replied Trish, as if she'd been mulling it over for longer than ten minutes and this was the last word on the matter. 'I don't think that'd do anyone any good. There are other things that might help.'

Trish glanced at Martha, who nodded. They could all benefit from some therapy. She knew that already, she had just been reluctant to acknowledge it.

Martha's surprise at how relaxed the whole thing had been must have shown because Trish was now regarding her with a reassuring smile. 'Look, we've nearly drawn a line under the whole thing now, and the bigger issue is not who spread the list, though of course' – she glanced at Sinead – 'I wasn't delighted about that, but the bigger issue is who wrote the thing in the first place – the whole thing.'

'Have you caught the person who did it, then?' asked Martha, speaking for the first time since her daughter had started to divulge her story.

'Possibly,' said Trish, avoiding her gaze. 'But I can't go into that just—'

A phone on the table started to flash and vibrate.

'Sorry,' said Trish, scooping it up. 'I have to take this.'

'No problem.' Martha pushed back her chair and gestured for Sinead to do the same. 'We'll see ourselves out. Thanks for . . . Thanks.'

'Thanks for letting me know,' said Trish. 'See you Monday, Sinead.' Then she turned from them and walked towards the rear patio doors. 'Hi, Norman. Thanks for returning my call.'

Martha ushered her daughter into the hallway. She would find someone for Sinead to talk to and she would tell Robert about the man she saw, both from their new bedroom window and that day in the old house. She imagined telling him and she didn't feel annoyed. She felt relief. It was exhausting to hate him.

In the hallway, she handed her daughter her coat and then, without really intending to, she hugged her.

'It's okay, Mum.'

It wasn't Robert's fault or hers; what happened in Limerick was not the fault of anyone in her family.

'I'm sorry we don't talk about what happened more,' she said, parting from Sinead.

Her daughter looked at her. 'Sometimes I feel his hand on me.'

'Sometimes I felt his hand on you too. I get a pain in my chest, just here.' Martha brought her hand to her left breast. 'And sometimes my cheek stings so much, I look in the mirror and am convinced it will be glowing red.'

'He wasn't allowed to touch me like that.'

'No. He wasn't.'

The faint sound of Trish's voice and a clock ticking from the living room to their right. They stood in the unfamiliar house, looking at each other, just as they had that day, when Martha's role of protector had been so diminished she no longer had the power to make things better with words.

'I was worried I liked it,' said Sinead, all of a sudden. 'I mean, I don't think I did. I couldn't have. I just . . . I felt something stirring inside me and I wondered, you know, if that was me being turned on.' She scrunched up her face at the awkward-sounding phrase. 'And then when I . . . when I wet myself' – again rushing through the words – 'I felt glad. I was almost happy it happened, happy I *wet myself*, because then that could be the thing that was stirring. I . . .' Her face was pleading with Martha to make it better, to fix it for her, to tell her it would be fine. 'Sometimes I still worry I did like it . . . and I hate myself.'

'That's a completely normal reaction,' said Martha, barely allowing her daughter to finish her sentence before responding and not caring an ounce if it was true or not. 'When we're in danger our bodies are no longer logical. Instinct takes over. It's not up to you any more. Your brain isn't in charge. None of it is your fault. All right? Sinead?'

Sinead nodded and her breathing quietened.

When she spoke again, it came with the familiar, crusading tone. 'I was just trying to make the school a better place, Mum. For me and for Orla, and for everyone.'

'I know, honey,' said Martha, kissing her firmly on the forehead and finally pulling open the door, her arms shaking slightly. She was relieved to step out on to the top of Pine Road, where the daylight was rapidly fading.

Halfway down Trish's path, Sinead tugged at Martha's sleeve. 'Look, Mum. Is that Ellis?'

She peered down Pine Road, raising her hand to her forehead to shield the afternoon sun. Ellis was standing across the road from their house. Was he *in* the Dwyers' garden?

'You never said Ellis was coming over. Ellis!' Sinead shouted. 'Hey, Ellis!'

'I didn't know,' said Martha, as Sinead headed for her brother and Martha followed, trying to make out who he was talking to. A woman, with long, dark, wavy hair. 'Is that—'

But before Martha could say 'Robin Dwyer', someone else was calling for the same young woman, albeit using a different name.

'Mammy! Mammy!' shouted Jack, running across the road towards Robin and Ellis and tripping over a shopping bag almost as long as him. 'I got shoes with four laces and a zillion million colours and they have lights! Mammy, want to see? Want to see, Mammy?'

*** Pine Road Poker ***

Bernie:
Dear all. Guards called to our house this afternoon. Nothing to worry about – and nothing that will affect house prices. It concerned the dog that bit Sylvie. All fine. Thank you for the concern. Regards, Bernie Watters-Reilly

THIRTY-ONE

'**Mammy, want** to see? Want to see, Mammy!'

Robin honestly could not remember her son saying 'Mammy' so many times. Even when he first learned the word, he used it sparingly, doling it out like a treat for when she did something right, like giving him another mini box of raisins.

'Mammy, Mammy! Look, Mammy!'

All right, Jack. We get it. You own me.

Robin watched her four-year-old run across Pine Road, almost taking himself down with the shopping bag he was carrying. His new runners must be in there; he would have insisted Granddad let him carry it. Jack's latest obsession was with his ever-increasing maturity. It started when she informed him he was now four and three-quarters. Every morning he asked her if he was more yet. He called quarters 'waters' and took them very seriously.

Jack came to a stop inches from her knees and she stared down at his little panting face. He had Eddy's nose, but everything else was hers. What would happen if she denied him? If she turned to Cormac and said: 'Nope. Never seen this child before in my life.'

'Hey, Jacko,' she said, bending down to help her son with the paper bag that was already turning his pudgy cheeks red as he tried in vain to tear it apart. 'We'll just take the box out, all right?'

Down on her hunkers, she saw Cormac's legs shift. She couldn't bring herself to look up.

'I was about to tell you,' Robin began but then her out-of-breath father caught up – 'That boy is putting me to shame. His nose runs faster than I do' – and someone was calling Cormac, or rather Ellis, from the other direction.

She looked up at her father: 'You're early.'

'I am not,' he said indignantly. 'One shop, two pairs of shoes, home. It's your mother who thinks a basic cash-for-goods transaction should take an eternity, not me.'

'Ellis!' The girl she recognised as Sinead Costello was throwing her arms around Cormac. 'What are you doing here?' Sinead smiled down at Jack. 'Hello. I'm Sinead. What's your name?'

Momentarily frozen under the pressure, Jack looked to his mother, and Robin, being the grown-up in the situation, knew she would have to be the one to look the girl in the eye. 'This is Jack,' she said, getting to her feet. 'And I'm Robin, his mother.' She continued to avoid Cormac's gaze. 'I live here.'

'Cool,' said Sinead, still hanging on to her brother. She smiled at Jack and Robin watched her son thaw. Once he acclimatised, Jack basked in the attention of adults. 'I like your shoes.'

Jack nodded kindly – as if to say 'Well, obviously' – and twisted himself slowly from side to side. 'I'm four and three waters.' He fluttered his eyelashes at the girl. 'Very soon I'll be more.'

Give him five minutes and he'd be tap dancing.

'Ellis. Hello, my love.' Martha Rigby had reached them now and was kissing her son on the side of his face not blocked by Sinead's arm. 'What a lovely surprise.' Robin watched genuine affection flood Cormac's face. She hoped she and Jack would be like that one day.

'Hi, Robin.' Martha's gaze moved among the various members of the Dwyer family. Her expression was ostensibly friendly but there was a wariness to her tone. 'Do you all know each other?'

'This is Jack,' said Robin, eyes on the boy instead of Martha.

'Yes, I've seen him riding his tractor up and down the road . . .'

'I have two tractors!'

'And this is my dad, Mick.'

'Hello, Mick. I'm Martha, we're in number eight.'

'Ah right, yeah. Carmel mentioned. How're you getting on with that back garden? Find any cats in there yet? No skeleton claws sticking up out of the soil? No? Ha?' Mick gave a loud, lonely laugh. 'Right, well, I'll head in.' And he hurried off up the path, into his house.

'Mammy!' shouted Jack, who was wrestling with one of his new shoes.

Cormac looked down at him as if he'd never seen a child before and Robin went to help her son but Sinead was already on the pavement, undoing the Velcro and laces.

'Do you . . .?' Martha waved a hand between Cormac and Robin.

'This is Robin,' said Cormac, dragging his eyes away from Jack.

'I know this is Robin, Ellis. I live across the road from her.'

'This is the girl I was telling you about, the girl I was seeing.'

'The girl . . .' Martha trailed off, tilted her head slightly.

'We just found out you live across the road from each other,' said Cormac. 'I guess you know each other, a bit? Robin said . . .' *Robin said she knows all about what happened in Limerick. What she didn't say is that she also knows who did it.* 'She said you've met a few times.'

Robin's eyes flickered from this new neighbour to Cormac. She didn't want to be here. She watched Sinead help her son put on his new shoes and felt a sucker punch of guilt.

Martha searched Robin's face and she offered a watery, apologetic smile in return.

'And this is the man you were seeing. The hipster . . .' She let the sentence peter out.

Was Martha remembering how she'd swooned at the idea of Robin's dark, handsome, tall-ish stranger that was in fact her son? Robin wanted to disappear. Why didn't the parking fiascos ever happen when you needed them?

And wait. Had Cormac said 'was seeing'? The girl he '*was* seeing' – as in, not any more?

'I didn't realise it was the same person,' said Robin, pointlessly.

Cormac broke into that stupid adorable half-smile, half-frown. 'Do you think I'm a hipster?'

'I didn't actually say that, it—'

'It's the moustache,' came Sinead's voice from below. 'It's post-ironic.'

The teenager was pulling the tissue from Jack's second shoe. She was what Carmel would call *a great girl*. Robin, meanwhile, was a fraud.

'Hipster journalist, you said,' questioned Martha.

'It was actually Edie who used that term; I never—'

'But Ellis isn't a journalist.' Martha's searching glance shifting to her son. 'You're not a journalist.'

'Just in case you didn't know, Ellis,' said Sinead, doing up Jack's laces. The shoes really were very colourful.

'No, but Ellis is a waiter,' said Martha. 'You're talking about going back to college but you work in a wine bar.'

'All right, we get it,' said Cormac, his face reddening. 'I know where I work.'

'In the wine bar we went to? Where they know your name?'

'That's what I was going to tell you.'

The staff had been so friendly that night, and Cormac said he went there for work. How had he put it exactly? But they'd gone to the opening night of the theatre, where nobody paid for tickets so he must have gotten them somehow, and then Cormac had known that C-list celebrity at the bar, the guy with the wig. Cormac knew what he was going to order – Oh. Of course.

'I am doing journalism too,' he said. 'I'm doing reviews and some interviews for a couple of websites. I'm building up a portfolio. I'm just in the wine bar until I can make that pay.'

'I thought you were going back to college,' said Martha.

But Cormac kept talking to Robin: 'I was reviewing that play we went to . . .'

Jack clung to Robin's legs as he pulled himself up.

'I'm sorry. I was going to say.'

'It's fine.'

'I didn't mean to hide it . . .'

And then, in case they'd all lost sight of who had actually hidden the bigger secret, Jack was on his feet and jumping as hard as he could on the pavement.

'Mammy, look! Look at all the colours!'

Except Jack wasn't even the biggest secret, was he? He was small fry compared to what Robin was keeping from this whole family.

Cormac grinned down at the child – 'That's great, Jack!' – then back up at her. 'He's great.'

The wave of shame that hit Robin then could have knocked her to the ground. Two flashbacks in rapid succession: her laughing at Eddy laughing at someone else, and her turning the music up when the neighbours below had politely complained. They were nothing memories – they were so much less than what was right in front of her – but her whole body was alight with shame.

She wasn't just keeping secrets, she was pretending to be a different person. She wasn't like Cormac. She was pretending to be good and decent, when she wasn't. Even when she thought she had stopped, she was still always acting.

Jack found a crack in the pavement and was jumping from one side of it to the other, the heels of his runners lighting up every time he landed. 'I'm!' Jump. 'Four!' Jump. 'And!' Jump. 'Three!' Jump. 'Waters!'

Robin bent down slightly and put her hands on his shoulders. Jack didn't need her interference, but she needed his. She couldn't look at any of them.

'Okay, Jacko, calm down,' she said, using her child the way she used to use rolling cigarettes: something to do with her hands when she couldn't think of what to say.

Sinead clambered to her feet. 'Is this your girlfriend?' She was trying to slag her brother but she was the one blushing. Robin remembered how difficult it was to talk about that stuff when you were sixteen.

Cormac smiled at Robin, dimple on his left cheek showing, nose crinkling slightly. The shame churned inside her. He could never have kept a proper secret. His face would never have allowed it.

Jack started tugging at Sinead's hand and she let him lead her into his grandparents' garden.

'Watch,' he instructed the teenager, as he climbed on to the low step at the front door and jumped back on to the path. 'Watch!' And he did it again.

'Wow,' said Sinead. 'That's really cool.'

'Yes,' agreed Jack. 'I'm very good at it, amn't I?'

The teenager looked back from where she was dutifully applauding the lights on Jack's runners and smiled at Robin. Imagine being sixteen and having five men in balaclavas break into your house. She must have been terrified. And then she was on that horrible list at the school too. It wasn't fair.

'I'm sorry if I've said something I shouldn't have—' began Martha.

'It's fine,' Robin interrupted, not wanting to hear this woman apologise to her.

Until recently, Robin hadn't felt shame in years. She thought she'd left that emotion behind. But she hadn't lost it, she'd just been storing it up, and it came crashing back like a rogue river bursting through a temporary dam.

'Wow! Jack! That was a big one.'

She couldn't do this.

She looked straight at Cormac, the culpability oozing from her. Surely, he could see it.

'I should take him in.'

'I thought maybe we'd still go for a walk . . .'

'I can't. Sorry.' Robin started gathering up the shopping bag and tissue and shoebox. 'He probably hasn't eaten.'

'Robin . . .' Cormac looked from his mother to her and opened his mouth to show all the things he couldn't say. 'I . . .'

'I'll talk to you later, okay?' She bundled the shoe packaging in her arms and stepped around Martha. 'Sorry.'

She pushed the front door open and threw the packaging inside, then returned for her son. 'Okay, Jack, come on.' She caught him post-jump and dragged him inside, leaving Sinead still kneeling on their garden path and closing the door before Jack started irately informing her of his age.

ONE MONTH LATER

*** Pine Road Poker ***

Ellen:
Okay, ladies. The wait is over. Clear your diaries and clear the road!
The PINE ROAD STREET PARTY is THIS COMING SATURDAY!

We'll need as many cars as possible PARKED ELSEWHERE. I've
spoken to Oak who will be expecting a few extra vehicles. I have yet
to hear back from Elm – which won't surprise anyone.

I've also negotiated a one-day armistice with Shay Morrissey RE: the
Occupied Territory. SO PLEASE USE THAT AREA FOR PARKING!

Everyone is down to bring something. DO NOT FORGET YOUR DISH.
Rita Ann is back on board, supplying her popular walnut cake, so
@EdieRice, we no longer need your dessert.

I want this year to be our BIGGEST and BEST Pine Road PRE-EASTER
STREET PARTY so I'm thinking we crack it up a bit. And yes, that
is a pun. Because I have decided to design ... AN EASTER EGG
TREASURE HUNT!

I will be doing the clues and the 'chocolate' eggs that serve as the
treasure at the end of the trail will, of course, be low-sugar. I'll need
several of you to volunteer your HOMES and GARDENS for use as
hiding places for the clues. PLEASE LET ME KNOW THIS WEEK.

I AM ALSO STILL LOOKING FOR A GENERAL VOLUNTEER.

Ruby:
WHY ARE YOU SHOUTING AT US, ELLEN?

Ellen:
Is that a joke? Because I really do not have time for your jokes this week, Ruby. T MINUS FIVE DAYS.

Fiona:
Rita-Ann's Walnut Cake? YASSS KWEEEENNN! XXX

Rita Ann:
I told you before not to call me that, Fiona. I had relatives who died in the War of Independence and I find any reference to the monarchy deeply offensive.

I will not be volunteering my house for any hump

*hunt

Ruby:
How come you're back in, Rita Ann? Did you catch the newspaper bandit?

Rita Ann:
It has been dealt with. That's all I'll be saying on the matter.

Ruby:
Settled out of court? Non-disclosure agreement? Good for you, Rita Ann.

Edie:
No biggie at all on scrapping my dessert, Ellen! I've had three practice rounds at that vegan cheesecake you suggested and still can't get it right, so probably for the best. I'll find another use for the boiled dried seaweed!

What can I bring instead?

x

Ellen:
You could source the eggs for the treasure hunt.

Edie:
Absolutely. No problem at all!

Ellen:
They need to be dairy-free, low-sugar (no sugar if possible), circumference of 11mm x 17mm, wrapped in biodegradable foil. 70 should do it, four different colours for wrapping, avoid gender-specific shades. I need them Friday evening at v latest.

Also, Rita Ann: could you make the walnut cake without walnuts? We want to be sensitive to nut allergies.

I'll be calling to homes tomorrow looking for volunteers, and for homes and gardens where we can hide the clues. I'm thinking rhyming riddles.

Ruby:
What was that noise?

Ellen:
What?

On the street?

I don't hear anything.

Ruby:
Thought I heard a chorus of doors being double-bolted and keys thrown away. My mistake. Never mind!

THIRTY-TWO

'The short answer, Doctor, sorry, Lorna, is that I'm here because my husband wanted me to come. We could probably spend the whole hour talking about that statement within itself given that up until a few weeks ago, I wouldn't have done anything because my husband wanted me to; more likely, I'd have tried to do the opposite.

'I bought this ludicrously expensive mattress two months ago, the softest thing you've ever felt. I would never have paid that much for a mattress except I knew how much he wanted a hard one. Four thousand euro, just to spite him. At that time, if it meant giving him an eternity of awful sleeps, it seemed like a bargain. Only the joke's on me now, because I hate the thing. It's like lying on marshmallows. I wake up feeling sticky.

'It's a long story. But the short version: our family home, in Limerick, was subject to a tiger raid last year, the day after Halloween, and it was awful, obviously. Robert, my husband, works in a bank so that's why they targeted us. They made him go to work to get the money, and they kept me and my two girls tied up in the house. Sometimes it feels like it happened yesterday and other times it's like it happened in another lifetime, another dimension, to another person – or not another person, but another version of me. Does that sound crazy? Because I think that a lot. The Martha Before and the Martha After. Don't read too much into that. I'm actually a very rational person.

'So yes, it was awful. And we moved to Dublin afterwards because, well, because I couldn't sleep in the house any more. Who could? It wouldn't have been good for the girls to stay there either. So Robert got transferred to Dublin and we came up here. He got promoted, actually. And he got this medal from Limerick City, for bravery. You see, he didn't follow the thugs' instructions; he didn't go to the bank, get the money and come back like he was supposed to, like he told me he was going to – he went rogue. And it paid off. Well, it paid off for him, and for the bank. He raised the alarm and the guards came and the men scarpered without a penny. All hail Robert.

'Everyone thought he was a hero, except for me. I hated him. I'm sure you get wives saying that about their husbands all the time in here, but it's not an exaggeration. I absolutely hated him. And it's mad, because I loved him the day before it all happened. As quick as flicking a switch. On, off. Here, gone. Love, hate.

'I didn't hate him because the men came to our house; I don't blame him for that, I don't even really blame them. It wasn't personal. We could have been anyone, so long as one of us worked in a bank. I'll tell you how I think of it. You know when you're younger – or maybe it still happens to you, Doctor, Lorna – and lads are driving by in a car – never one lad, always several of them – and they roll down the window and shout something at you. Like "hey, sexy" or "nice legs" or "show us your tits" or whatever. Well, it's kind of like that. Those lads in the car don't see you. It doesn't actually matter if you're sexy or have nice legs, you might not even have tits at all. If you stood in front of them later that same day, they wouldn't recognise you. Because they don't see you. You're not real. You're not a person. It's not personal. In the moment where they roll down the window and shout at you, you're not a human being. You're an object that exists solely for their amusement; a reflective surface off which to bounce their own good time.

'Sorry. Wandering. I haven't talked this much since . . . Maybe since I went hillwalking back in Limerick. You can't beat a walk-and-talk. Sorry, can I . . .? Is that water for me?

'I didn't hate Robert because they came to our house. That wasn't his fault. I hated him because he abandoned us. He looked me in the eye and said he was coming back. And then when it all started to go wrong and he didn't turn up, I was convinced he was dead. It was the worst moment of my life. Even though now, obviously, I know he was fine. In that moment, I was convinced. I thought: The only reason he could possibly not be with us is because he's dead. It was like my insides dropped from my body into a pit of fire, but all the nerve endings were still attached. My daughter wet herself, for Christ's sake.

'I never used to get angry, but there you are. Or well, here I am. Anyway, that's all a bit beside the point because I'm not so angry with him now. It's hard to explain, though no doubt you'll make me, but there was other stuff with my daughter more recently and it made me realise that maybe some of my anger was misplaced. And then – oh yes, and this is probably the nub of why I'm here – I saw one of the men who'd carried out the tiger raid. I saw him on our new road, in Dublin, a few weeks ago.

'Although now I say that out loud, I start to doubt it. Maybe I didn't see him at all. I don't know. I told Robert about it. Not straight away – I hadn't told him I saw one of their faces in the first place – but I started to get paranoid that maybe the police were involved, or that Robert was in on it, all this mad stuff that made no sense, so eventually I just told him. I had to. And it was the strangest thing because suddenly I felt less angry at him. We had a common enemy again, you know? It was like I reached the peak of hating him and then it sort of . . . evaporated. And talking to him made me question if I really did see the man at all, or if it might be a coincidence, and I guess I'm here because I want to either accept that I didn't see him or accept that I did and move on. Because that was several weeks ago now and nothing has happened. No rocks through our windows or death threats in the letterbox. And I like our new home so I'd like to be able to stay.

'The girls have settled down now, I think, and we're talking more, which is great, and important. Sinead, my eldest, is seeing a counsellor, which was when Robert suggested I might go too. That I considered his suggestion was progress, never mind that I followed it. I have an older son who lives in Dublin, and I love being near him. We live on a nice road – although some of the neighbours are a bit intense and in ways it's a lot gossipier than living in a small town, which surprised me, I have to say. There's a street party coming up and every day someone, usually the same woman, is knocking on my door about it. It's like she's organising the Met Gala, only with a stricter timetable. But I've made friends and I like some of them. There was an awkward situation a few weeks ago with my son and one of the women on the road. They'd been seeing each other and I'd heard both of them talk about the other but didn't realise they were the same people. It doesn't matter now, because it all sort of fell apart. I'm still not entirely sure what happened. But I know Ellis has been calling and texting, or whatever people in their twenties do, and she's not replying.

'To be completely honest, I'm relieved. I like the girl, but she's not right for Ellis. She has a child, for one thing. And Ellis is too young for that. By the sounds of it she also has a fairly dodgy ex-boyfriend, so a lot of drama. There's something else about her too . . . I got this feeling like maybe she doesn't think Ellis is good enough. She's pretty, no question, but Ellis is beautiful. Maybe it's because he's a waiter, or she doesn't think our family is good enough – that we're damaged? I'm not sure. But I mean, she's the single mother. I don't even think she has a job. Anyway, I don't want to be catty because I do like her, I just don't want it to be awkward, you know? I'm sure it won't. He'll move on. He's probably already moving on.

'And I want the same thing, for myself. To get back to your original question, Lorna. I need acceptance, some closure. I guess I'm here because I want to move on.'

THIRTY-THREE

....

'**D**o I write it down, or how does it work?

'Okay. I'll speak slowly then. It won't take long, right? I don't have much to say. Eddy Dunne, my ex-boyfriend, told me the guards would be looking for me to give a statement in order to confirm his whereabouts last October thirty-first into the first of November. He wanted me to tell you guys that he was with me and our son that night and the next day. I got a missed phone call yesterday from this station. I thought I'd just come down myself.

'Eddy wasn't with me that night. I was at a fancy-dress party with friends, and Eddy was supposed to be at home minding our son. When I got back to the flat, at about four a.m., neither of them was there. He came home around lunchtime the next afternoon, the first of November. I was out of my head with worry. He wasn't answering his phone and I didn't know if Jack was okay. He was fine. And there's zero point you guys asking him anything. He's four. And three quarters. He doesn't remember what he did yesterday, never mind five months ago.

'I could have called the guards, sure. But let's just say, with Eddy, the police didn't seem like a viable option.

'I don't know where he was. I have no idea. He never told me. I couldn't even guess. Seriously. Why would I lie? I've no idea where they were. All I know is he wasn't with me.

'So, is that it? Can I go? My son's at home . . .

'No, we don't live there any more. Like I said, we broke up months ago. Me and Jack are living with my parents at the moment. Nine Pine Road, Drumcondra, Dublin Nine. But hopefully we won't be there too much longer.

'No, there's nothing wrong with it – my parents are great – just I got a job.

'Just office work. Is that . . . is it relevant? Covering someone's maternity leave. Not very exciting, but it's nine months, at least, and the pay is decent. It'll probably take a while to find somewhere to rent – it's like *The Hunger Games* out there at the moment – but yeah, I'll let you know if it changes. Jack's starting school in September.

'Sorry? No, I'm not. Not that it's got anything to do with anything. I'm single. I was seeing someone but whatever, it didn't work out. It's fine. He's better off. I mean, we're both better off. I'm concentrating on Jack and getting my shit together.

'So that's it, yeah? Good. Signature and date. There you go.'

THIRTY-FOUR

'I **would not** ask you if it wasn't a matter of life and death. I respect opening hours more than anything – not literally more than *anything*, but like *a lot*. I'm a working woman too, public-facing job, although I have to say I don't have the same natural aptitude for it as you do. Has anyone ever said you look French? 'Cause you do. And that's not just because this shop makes me think of *Chocolat*. Usually I only really go in for crime and mysteries and stuff but, gosh, I love that film. So *romantic*. I love Juliette Binoche. You actually look a lot like her. I think it's the hair. You've got great hair. Now that I see it, I just can't un-see it. You're actually the image of her. You are! Except younger.

'I work over in the Shelbourne hotel, if you're ever passing. Or if you want to come in for a few drinks some night? I would absolutely look after you, no problem. I'm not *bribing* you, by the way. I'm just saying how much I'd appreciate it if you could just get this one little order done by Friday. I'll pay more for the eggs. You could practically name your price and I'd pay it. Not that I'm rich or anything, because I'm not. But I live on a sort of rich road and I really don't want to turn up with the wrong kind of eggs. I mean the requirements are pretty specific and you were the only specialist chocolatier – I mean, gosh, not the *only*, but like the only one that *everyone* raved about! And I can't give my neighbours anything but the best. Do you know Bernie Watters-Reilly? Yeah, that's her; that lunchbox article was actually very popular. Well, she lives on my road. We're friends. Well, kind of. She knows my name. I think. I'm actually a bit scared of her.

'Wait! You don't know her, know her, do you? Okay. Good. Phew.

'To be totally honest with you, Betty, can I call you— Oh no, right. Mrs Kearney. What? Oh, sorry. *Miss* Kearney. To be totally honest with you, Miss Kearney, I've been having a bit of a difficult time recently. I mean, everything's fine – it's *absolutely* fine. Great, even. Work was just tough for my husband and then there was this whole thing where he was looking after a dog and the dog bit a girl – you definitely don't know-know Bernie, right? – and he felt really guilty about it, even though the girl was fine, it didn't even break the skin. But anyway, we were meant to be trying to get pregnant and he started worrying he wasn't responsible enough – because of what happened with the girl – and it was all a bit stressful. You know?

'That's not me spinning you a sob story, by the way. It's fine now. Like, it's much better. We're back trying! But apparently the police are looking into the biting incident. I'm a bit worried about that, to tell you the truth. I don't want my child to be visiting their dad in the big house. Would you go to jail for something like that, do you think? Anyway, I don't want to tell Da— my husband about the police investigating because I don't want him to start worrying again. I haven't even told him that I know about the bite and about him leaving the scene. And so, yeah, sorry. That's all a bit confusing. You just have such a kind face. I bet people open up to you all the time. No? Really? I'm surprised.

'What I'm basically saying is that I've been a bit up the walls recently and it would really, really, really help if I could get these eggs.

'We're having a big pre-Easter street party and I'm in charge of the eggs and if I mess it up I feel like I'll have messed up the whole party and I, I've actually made some pretty good friends on the road, Mrs – Miss Kearney – and that wasn't easy. It kind of, it took a while and I really don't want to mess it up and, oh gosh,

I'm so embarrassed. I don't usually cry in front of strangers, or not people who are working so damn hard to bring something as good as *chocolate* into the world but, yeah, I've been trying to practise daily gratitude but this party just matters a lot to me and—

'What? Oh my gosh, yes. Thank you! Fifty per cent more expensive, that is absolutely fine, brilliant in fact, and I will absolutely stop talking. Right this second, yes. Thank you, thank you! I'll unzip my purse and zip my mouth.

'Okay. Right now. Zipped!

'And sorry, sorry. One last thing. Your foil doesn't happen to be biodegradable, does it?'

*** Pine Road Poker ***

Ruby:
Wait, I've got it!

Rita Ann – Did they catch your newspaper thief READ handed??

THIRTY-FIVE

· ·

Robin **came** home to find her mother and Edie Rice sitting at their kitchen table with two large baskets of colourful ovals between them. Her mother was wearing one of Robin's berets and gripping a paintbrush, while Edie held one of the objects out to her, as if offering the most precious of gifts.

'Hold still, Edie,' warned Carmel, her tongue poking out the right-hand side of her mouth as she concentrated on whatever it was she was doing. '*You* . . .' she said dramatically, '*are my easel.*'

Edie cupped the shiny oval between her hands and carefully inched it closer to Carmel's brush.

'What are you doing?'

'A little hoodwinkery, Robin, my dear,' said Carmel slowly, her eyes narrowing over her task. 'We are . . . perfecting . . . the art of . . . deception. There.' She snapped her head back up, removing the brush. 'Next!'

Edie placed the object in one basket and rummaged around in the other. Carmel dipped her brush lavishly in a pot of Crayola paint.

'Is that Jack's art set?'

'Myself and Edie are pulling off the greatest con job Pine Road has ever seen,' said Carmel, ignoring her daughter's question and catching her hat as it threatened to tremble off her head. 'Another egg, Edie dear. Come on, come on. We've a lot to get through.'

'Are they . . . are they chocolate eggs?'

Carmel looked up at Robin with a toothy smile of pure, unabashed cunning. Edie's face, meanwhile, was all eyes, and they were filled with the guilt of a woman who'd committed a thousand murders.

'It was your mam's idea . . .'

'Ah now, Edie! Don't go hanging me out to dry already. I am merely volunteering my artistic skills, which have heretofore been shamefully wasted.' Tongue back out, Carmel drew whatever she was drawing on the second egg. 'Next!'

Robin kicked off her shoes and sat down at the other side of the table. 'So what are they for?' she said, peering into the baskets.

'They're for tomorrow's treasure hunt,' said Edie, still shame-faced. 'I was in charge of getting the eggs, which was more difficult than it sounds because Ellen was very specific about what type of eggs she wanted—'

'The woman's a pox,' declared Carmel. 'Bernie's a dose, but Ellen, it turns out, is the real egomaniac. *My pre-Easter street party is going to be the biggest and the best pre-Easter street party.* I would not be surprised if she turns up tomorrow with a crown and sceptre and demands a coronation.'

'I managed to get the eggs she wanted,' said Edie, 'after a lot of running around town, buttering up people who did not want to be buttered. The chocolate world is a cold one, I can tell you. It's not like *Chocolat* at all. But I got them: low-sugar, dairy-free, no pink or blue foil. But the one thing Ellen requested—'

'Demanded,' corrected Carmel, tongue back out as she marked another egg.

'—that I could not get was that the foil wrapping be biodegradable.'

'Is biodegradable foil even a thing?' asked Robin, to the interest of nobody.

'So,' said Carmel, straightening up from the egg with a flourish of her paintbrush, 'we're giving all the wrappings a little letter "B". B for biodegradable.'

'But they're not biodegradable?'

'Who's to say, Robin? What does biodegradable even mean?'

'What?'

'No,' answered Edie. 'They're not.'

'Right. And is "B" normally the symbol for biodegradable?'

'Jesus, Robin, what am I, an encyclopaedia?' said Carmel, exasperated. 'But you can be sure if we don't know, then Ellen Two Names doesn't know either. The woman's as thick as my thighs. At poker last month Ruby mentioned how her sister, who is a musician, had spent six weeks living on the road and Ellen wanted to know if the council had moved her on.'

Robin looked at the two baskets. 'Is it still a big deal, the Easter Street Party?'

Carmel and Edie exchanged a look.

'Eh, yes, dear. It is.'

Another egg carefully placed in the 'marked' basket.

'It all kicks off at eleven tomorrow. Clear your diary and clear the road!' Then Edie frowned. 'I have to get these to Ellen by seven. I took the afternoon off work.'

'We'll get there, Edie, don't fret. The artist is at work!' Carmel dipped her brush again. 'Jack's very excited for the Easter egg treasure hunt.'

'Is he?'

'He is.'

'Is, em, is Bernie taking part?' asked Edie, shifting in her seat as Carmel reached out and snapped the woman's hands firmly in position. 'I haven't heard much from her since the police called to her about that dog biting incident.'

Carmel was deep in concentration, muttering to herself. '*You* shall be my greatest creation.'

'Have you heard any more about that police investigation into the dog? Carmel? Any leads? Any suspects, even?'

'You all right, Edie?' asked Robin.

'Yes fine,' retorted Edie defensively. 'Why?'

'Nothing. You just sound strange. Your voice has gone sort of . . . high.'

'I'm just wondering if anyone has heard anything about the dog investigation. I'm just taking a neighbourly interest. Nothing more. I don't see anything *strange* about that.'

Before she entered this house, Robin had been preoccupied by thoughts of what Eddy might do if he found out she'd contradicted his alibi. She was feeling sorry for herself over the whole Cormac debacle – she hadn't spoken to him since that day outside her house with Jack and Martha – and was generally worrying about what she was going to do with the rest of her life. But now she was here, Robin found it difficult to reconcile the world outside with the things that seemed to matter within these four walls; mainly, Pine Road itself.

'Did you not hear about that?' said Carmel, finally coming up for air. 'Where have you been, Edie?'

'I've been running around the city trying to find eggs.'

'Well, it's been the big news on Pine Road all week. The police weren't calling to Bernie that day about the dog at all. She was fibbing about that. Careful, Edie!'

'Sorry,' said their neighbour, fumbling to stop an egg from falling. 'But I thought that's why they were on the road? Shay Morrissey saw them going into her house.'

'Oh, they were calling to her all right. It just wasn't about the dog.' Carmel drew something indecipherable in the air and the beret finally slid from her head.

'Why were they calling to her then?'

Edie had gone from high-pitched to breathless, and Robin was starting to think there was a sanity test you had to fail in order to get a house on this street.

'It was about the list at the school,' said Carmel, reaching down for the hat. 'That's why Ellen's been able to go full dictator on this street party. Bernie's out of the picture, she's fallen from grace. Her son, Declan – he was the one who wrote the list.'

*** Pine Road Poker ***

Ellen:

Good morning, residents! Today is the day!

The all-improved *NEW* Pine Road pre-Easter Street Party with the inaugural Pine Road Easter Egg Treasure Hunt.

For anyone who somehow missed Monday's booklet – distributed to all homes! – let's go over the itinerary ONE MORE TIME.

8 a.m.: Begin clearing cars. If we could fill the Occupied Territory first and then feed remaining vehicles over to Oak Road. We don't want everyone trying to get off the road at the same time, so if we start at the bottom and incrementally work our way up. Keep your eyes on your windows, ladies. My Joe will be out in a high-vis from 7.45 a.m., ready to assist in directing cars.

8.30 a.m.: Anyone doing significant cooking/baking would want to have their offering in the oven by now.

9 a.m.: Chairs and tables to be carried out on to Pine Road. We expect all residents to bring a chair for themselves, and a few more for visitors. I know several of us have family coming today – and a few select guests from Oak, Elm, Beech and Chestnut. I'm expecting our biggest turnout EVER so *please* be generous with seating.

9.15 a.m.: Commence the stringing of bunting. B.Y.O.L. (That's Bring Your Own Ladder. All acronyms are in Tuesday's booklet.)

9.20 a.m.: Myself and Trish Walsh, who has kindly volunteered to help with the Treasure Hunt, will commence calling to participating houses to hide clues. DO NOT watch where these are placed.

NOTE: I WILL NOT HESITATE TO DISQUALIFY SUSPECTED CHEATERS, EVEN IN THEIR OWN HOMES.

9.30 a.m.: Helium tank delivered to the road.

9.40 a.m.: Commence blowing up of balloons with said helium.

9.55 a.m.: Commence table decoration.

NOTE: ARTIST'S IMPRESSION OF HOW THIS SHOULD LOOK WAS IN THE FINAL PREPARATION BOOKLET DISTRIBUTED TO HOMES ON THURSDAY. PLEASE FOLLOW.

10.15 a.m.: Complete table decoration, bunting and balloon inflation.

10.18 a.m.: Commence laying out of food.

NOTE: COLD FOODS ONLY AT THIS POINT

10.30 a.m.: Commence playing of music. Fiona – Begin at a low level and gradually increase between now and 11.10 a.m.

NOTE: FOR ACCEPTABLE VOLUME, PLEASE SEE MONDAY'S INFORMATION BOOKLET FOR DUBLIN CITY COUNCIL'S APPROVED DECIBEL LEVELS.

10.45 a.m.: Hot food in place. It would be better if this were served gradually, with remainder kept warm in stoves. If possible, do *not* use microwaves. Several Elm residents will be in attendance.

10.52 a.m.: Pig on Spit in position.

11 a.m.: OFFICIAL KICK-OFF. I expect everyone out on the road by 11 a.m., relaxing and having a good time. There is no dress code, this is a street party. But my advice would be smart-casual.

11-11.30 a.m.: Relaxing and light mingling. (Suggested)

11.30-11.50 a.m.: Light snacking. (Suggested)

12 p.m.: THE GREAT EASTER EGG TREASURE HUNT IS GO. Instructions to be outlined before event commences. High-vis jackets will be handed out to all participants to distinguish them from other revellers. There is space for thirty neighbours to participate. I expect strong take-up.

1.15 p.m.: Depending on the mental ability of participants, I expect the winners to be announced around now.

1.30 p.m.: Modest celebration and feting of winners.

1.45p.m.: Spur-of-the-moment speech by resident to thank the organiser of the highly successful first ever Pine Road Easter Egg Treasure Hunt. (Suggested)

2-4 p.m.: Fun party games. Nothing that might cause offence – unlike last year. Chinese whispers has been banned.

4 p.m.: More hot food served.

4.30 p.m.: Preliminary tidy-up.

NOTE: SEE 'HOW TO CLEAN EFFECTIVELY' PAMPHLET DISTRIBUTED WITH THURSDAY'S BOOKLET.

5 p.m.: Low-level, social alcohol consumption.

NOTE: SEE ALCOHOL UNIT RECCOMMENDATIONS DISTRIBUTED ON WEDNESDAY AS STAND-ALONE FLYER.

5-10 p.m.: Mingling and chit-chat.

10 p.m.: Wind-down.

10.15 p.m.: Pine Road Street Party ends.

10.20 p.m.-midnight: Official, high-level tidy-up.

NOTE: ALL TABLES AND CHAIRS THAT HAVE NOT BEEN REMOVED BY 10.40 p.m. WILL BE GIVEN TO SHAY MORRISSEY FOR HIS OWN PERSONAL USE. THIS WAS PART OF THE NEGOTATION DEAL FOR USE OF THE OCCUPIED TERRITORY.

Carmel:

All the beeping!! It's like being in a torture camp!

Could you not have sent this at a reasonable hour?

Or at least as one long message???

Ellen:

You really shouldn't keep your phone in your bedroom, Carmel. It's best to have a digital unwind before sleep.

THIRTY-SIX

It was four weeks since Trish found out from her daughter that Declan Reilly had written the list.

At first, it had all unfolded quickly. Trish had talked to Norman, the head of the board of management, the next day and he'd phoned the police. Two sets of parents had made official complaints and the guards, though reluctant to get involved, had instructed the school to keep them abreast. Two officers called to Bernie's house that same day – the day of the great parking showdown between Shay Morrissey and Daniel Carmody – to deliver a warning. They were leaving any actual punishment up to the school.

And then it all moved slowly. Trish had advocated for a suspension rather than expulsion. The rest of the board thought it would be easier to cut him loose. Trish argued that Declan had alerted Gormless Paul to the list and that by confessing to her daughter he'd practically confessed to her. She spoke to his previous good character and the evils of peer pressure. Initially Bernie didn't help matters by involving a lawyer and holding up the whole process, but in the end, the lawyer probably made the board paranoid about making the smallest mistake and it was decided to suspend Declan Reilly for two weeks and to have him commit to a series of sexual respect courses. Trish wanted to have the other boys who were in the bathroom that day enrolled in the course too but Declan refused to offer up any names.

Declan was now halfway through his suspension and when Trish called to Bernie's to discuss his return to school, she'd found the woman in an alarming state. While the empty bottle of red wine sitting on her counter no doubt had a role to play, it was also linked to Ellen's 'treachery'. Having found out about Declan's suspension, the woman who had once worshipped at Bernie's feet had turned on her former icon with chilling speed.

Not only did Ellen advise Bernie to sit out this year's street party entirely but she told her that should the *Irish Independent* be seeking a more credible parenting expert, she had an A2 in Leaving Certificate English, a successful track record in implementing screen time limits and two children who were not sexual deviants.

'I made this road what it is, and now Ellen's trying to steal it from under me!'

Trish had tried to appease the sobbing woman, telling her she was sure that wasn't the case as she pushed the ignored back-to-school agreement across the counter.

'You don't know her,' spat Bernie, with such ferocity she knocked the pages to the floor. 'I taught her everything she knows!'

In a move she now regretted, Trish had agreed to keep an eye on things. She told Bernie she would volunteer and make sure it wasn't a complete takeover. Ellen, meanwhile, had been delighted to have a helper she didn't have to blackmail.

So here Trish was leaving her house, and her husband, at 9.20 on a Saturday morning with a ring-binder full of treasure hunt clues and instructions from Ellen to barge into people's homes and leave them in very specific locations. Ellen was currently dispersing half the clues on the left-hand side of the road, while Trish did the right. She felt sorry for Declan and, to a lesser extent, Bernie. Trish reminded herself of this as she knocked on the first door.

'Trish! Hello. Lovely to see you!' exclaimed Edie.

'Apologies, Edie. I know it's early, but I'm helping hide the Easter egg treasure hunt clues. I'm sure you saw how tightly Ellen has this thing timetabled.'

'Absolutely,' agreed Edie. 'I'm honoured to be taking part. Isn't it the most glorious day?'

Trish glanced up at a sky she would have described as average. 'It's good it's not raining,' she offered.

'Oh it is, it absolutely is. You're so right! Come in, come in!'

She followed Edie through to the kitchen, and watched as she spun – no, pirouetted – on the tiled floor and landed with her palms on the island.

'Do you know when you have those days where everything seems terrible, hopeless, and then something happens and suddenly everything is right again?'

'I . . .' Trish looked around the kitchen. 'Sure.' She placed the ring-binder on the island. 'So, you agreed to let us put one of the clues in your house . . .'

'Clues!' trilled Edie, clasping her hands together as Trish opened the ring-binder.

'Yep. Clues.'

Trish found Edie's enthusiasm exhausting at the best of times – between the energy and eyes, she wouldn't have been that surprised if the woman had an MDMA habit – but she was surely more hyper than usual today.

Trish pulled out an envelope. 'I have one to hide in this house. And sorry about this, but Ellen wants me to do it without the residents watching, to prevent any cheating or accusations of cheating . . .'

'Absolutely. Whatever you want! I really am just so happy to be part of the Pine Road community.'

This was another point where Trish and Edie differed. If Trish and Ted didn't have so much stuff, and if it wasn't so close to the school, she'd happily have moved. She wouldn't miss living next door to the head of the Parents' Association, or the constant drama and WhatsApp message alerts, dementing her all the livelong day.

'Is Daniel here?' she asked, before she went roaming about their house.

'He had to go out for a couple of hours.' Edie rested her elbows on the counter, her chin on her fists. 'But it's good because it's given me a chance to hide the clues for my own treasure hunt!'

'You're making a treasure hunt?'

'For Daniel. Isn't that fun? I've done five clues and hidden them around the house, and then left his prize at the end.' Edie beamed. 'Rhyming riddles are harder than you'd think.'

'Okay. Well.' Trish was starting to feel like the Grinch. 'If you stand at the kitchen door and maybe cover your eyes, I'll go and hide this.'

'Absolutely!' Edie shimmied over to the corner. 'I feel like we're playing hide-and-seek!'

Trish left the room and headed for the stairs.

'Shall I count to ten or something?' Edie called. 'Or no. I'll sing!'

Trish didn't know what any of the clues said just that each one led to the next and that this particular envelope had a Post-it note stuck to it that said 'leave in Edie's bed'. Feeling like some sort of Peeping Tom, she pulled back Edie's blanket and quickly threw the envelope under.

Right. Done.

In the kitchen, Edie was singing Florence + the Machine's 'Dog Days Are Over' and sashaying from side to side.

'Edie,' called Trish, finally tapping her on the shoulder to get her attention.

'Oh!'

'Thanks. I'm off.'

'Did it go okay? Actually, don't tell me anything. I want to do the treasure hunt. Oh,' Edie paused, the first hint of anything other than drug-induced bliss, 'did Ellen say anything about my eggs for the hunt? Did she like them?'

'She said they were great,' lied Trish. Ellen had actually said they looked like something you'd get in Aldi and lamented how you give someone one simple task and they still managed to disappoint you.

'I think I'm going to wear something fancy to the street party,' said Edie, walking her to the door. 'You know those days where you just want to wear something fancy?'

'Sure,' said Trish, who preferred comfort and found daytime 'fancy' was usually code for 'cheap'. 'See you at the party.'

'I'll be there! Eleven a.m. sharp!'

Ellen was hiding clues in a flower bed across the road. She was already well ahead. Trish hurried into Ruby's garden, placing the envelope, as instructed, in her recycling bin and then into the Chambers' next door, where an envelope was placed in the microwave. By the time she reached Carmel Dwyer's house, she was slightly ahead of Bernie, who was still poking about in Rita Ann's lawn.

'Jesus Christ!'

A massive bunny rabbit was standing at the end of the road. It was bright pink, about a foot taller than Trish and wearing battered Asics trainers with a reflective cycling jacket.

'Hi, Trish,' came a muffled, forlorn voice from within the manically grinning rabbit head.

'Joe?'

'I'm directing cars,' came the voice she recognised as belonging to Ellen Russell-O'Toole's husband.

'You . . . Why are you wearing that?'

'Ellen,' he said stoically, and went back to staring out on to the road, waiting.

Carmel's grandson opened the door, a colourful oval painted on each cheek.

'Hi, Jack,' said Trish. 'I like your Easter eggs.'

'It's my birthday today. I'm five.'

'Wow. Happy birthday. Five is so big.' Trish beamed at him. 'Is your granny here? Or your nanny?' What other names did grandparents go by? 'Your gran . . .?'

Suddenly the boy threw back his head with the dexterity of

something from *The Exorcist* and bellowed at the ceiling. 'Graaa-nneeee!'

'Jack Dunne, stop that shouting right now!' shouted Carmel, appearing from the kitchen. 'You're not supposed to open that door by yourself.' Carmel marched up the hallway but Jack ducked and ran before she could reprimand him any more. 'Hi, Trish. How's it going?'

Trish smiled. 'He was just saying it's his birthday. That's nice.'

'It's not his birthday.' Carmel sighed. 'But he keeps telling people that it is. He has me lighting candles for him to blow out all week and he refuses to go to bed unless someone sings Happy Birthday to him. He's an insatiable little tyrant.'

Trish nodded, not quite sure of an appropriate response. 'I'm just here to hide your treasure hunt clue.'

'Old Two Names caught me on the hop on that one; I was struggling back from Island Stores with three bags of messages and nowhere to hide.'

Trish opened her ring-binder and pulled out the envelope for number nine.

Carmel peered at it. 'That for us?'

Trish covered the Post-it note with the instructions on where to put it. 'It is.'

'What does it say?'

Trish smiled. 'I'm just told where to hide it.'

'I'd say I only need one guess as to where the final clue leads anyway, whose house gets the glory of being home to the main prize.'

Carmel glanced over Trish's shoulder and she also turned to watch Ellen walking up Martha Rigby's path.

'I couldn't possibly say.' The road and its mother knew Ellen would be keeping the glory for herself. 'So, am I okay to go and hide this in yours? Will you wait out here – just to make sure there's no cheating?'

'I would never!'

'Or accusations of cheating.'

Carmel, who was still trying to read what the Post-it note said, acquiesced. She stuck her head back into the hallway. 'Robin! Jack! Johnny!' Then to Trish again: 'Mick's gone to the supermarket.'

Johnny stepped out into the garden in his socks, Robin and Jack following. 'I'm watching something.'

'Come out for a minute. Trish has to plant a bug in our house on behalf of Agent Two Names.'

'What?'

Trish stepped inside, closing the door and tiptoeing down to the kitchen where, as instructed by the Post-it, she placed the clue on top of the fridge.

'All done,' she called, stepping back out into the garden as Jack ran inside and Johnny followed.

The three women stood in the garden, Robin a little farther back. Trish and Carmel smiled politely.

'It's good it's not raining,' said Trish for the third time this morning.

'Is Two Names expecting many people?'

'Oh, yes. She's really dedicated to this being our biggest and best street party. Almost all the residents are coming, a few extended family members, people from other roads.'

'Well, I've got the fondue simmering. Do I still need to bring a bowl of air for Sylvie, I wonder? Are Bernie and family coming?'

'I don't think so,' said Trish. 'I suppose you heard about Declan ...'

'I did. From Ellen,' added Carmel. 'I have to say I was surprised.'

'Me too,' said Trish. 'He's a good lad who did a bad thing.'

'I don't mean I was surprised Declan was responsible, I barely know the chap. I was surprised Ellen was spreading the gossip. I know the woman loves to bitch, but I thought she loved her C-list-celebrity friendship even more. She wanted me to sign a petition to have Bernie removed as head of the Parents' Association.'

'Oh God,' groaned Trish.

'I declined,' added Carmel. 'Not worth the hassle. I suppose she fancies nicking the job. I'd say she's in her element this morning; her bid to succeed Bernie as queen bee well under way.'

'She's fairly wound up, all right.' Ellen had stopped referring to residents by name, only by house number, and had told Trish that the only acceptable excuse for street party non-attendance was a death notice.

'She always has to be the best,' sighed Camel. 'Did you see the Easter decorations in her garden? Jesus on the cross I can handle, just about, but the fountain that keeps his palms constantly bleeding? It's a bit much.'

'I hate the giant wicker rabbit,' said Robin. 'It's the same size as Jesus, and wearing more clothes. That's not cute. It's creepy.'

'I wouldn't look down the end of the road so,' said Trish.

Robin frowned and Trish checked her watch. 'The helium man is late.'

'Two Names won't like that.'

'No,' agreed Trish, watching as the front door of Martha's house opened and Ellen stepped out, two stopwatches swinging around her neck. 'She's already started using the military twenty-four-hundred-hour clock. Oh, hang on now; is that him?'

A young man with dark hair was walking up the other side of the road carrying a bag for life. Trish had envisaged a big cylinder, like something you'd see in a hospital, possibly on wheels. The young man turned into Martha's garden, said a polite hello to Ellen, and looked over at the Dwyers' garden.

He lifted a hand, and Trish waved back as Carmel squinted. Robin, meanwhile, walked straight into her house.

'That's Cormac,' said Carmel, pulling her glasses up from around her neck. 'Or Ellis. Whatever his name is, he's Martha's son.'

THIRTY-SEVEN

· ·

'**D**on't be silly, Ellis,' said Martha, shooing her son into the kitchen where Orla was at the table, making animal ears and flicking through a booklet. 'Family were invited. And you're our family.'

'Hello, brother,' said Orla, looking up from what she was reading just long enough to check if Ellis had brought her anything. She eyed the bag for life with some interest.

'Hello, sister. That beauty sleep is paying off for you. You don't look a day over thirteen.'

'I'm twelve!'

'Oh right. My bad.'

Orla scrunched up her face and Ellis leaned over to engulf her in a half-hug, half-headlock.

'Who's doubting that you're our family?' said Robert, coming into the kitchen from the utility room with a punnet of strawberries. 'Are these the ones, darling?'

'Yes, perfect. Thank you, love,' said Martha, taking the fruit and smiling at her husband. It didn't always come naturally, but Martha was enjoying the effort that went with rekindling their relationship. Forgiving Robert had resulted in a sort of modest second-honeymoon period. There was a lot to be said for waking up in the morning and not loathing the person lying next to you. 'Nobody's doubting it, except maybe Ellis. He's wondering if he should have come.'

297

'Of course you should have come. They're doing an Easter egg hunt. Lots of chocolate. It'll be fun.'

'It's not an Easter egg hunt, Dad,' said Orla, brushing her long hair out of her face as she peered at the booklet. 'It's an Easter egg *treasure* hunt. There's going to be clues that we have to figure out.'

'I thought it was just scrummaging around for chocolate eggs.'

'No.'

'It requires brain power?'

'Yes.'

'Well, in that case, I bagsy being on Orla's team,' said Robert, and his daughter's chest physically expanded with pride.

'Everyone will be dying to meet you,' said Martha, still trying to wipe the worry off Ellis's face. 'You'll be the sacrificial lamb for this particular Easter feast. Expect lots of questions. Pine Road makes the Spanish Inquisition look like an amateur operation. They'll be delighted to have someone new to interrogate.'

'Robin didn't look delighted. As soon as she saw me, she went running into her house.'

'I'm sure you're exaggerating,' said Martha, checking the pavlova base in the fridge. 'Anyway, you'll barely see her. Ellen was just saying she reckons there could be more than a hundred people at this.'

'A hundred people? Out on that street?' exclaimed Robert. 'Jesus. Good thing we moved the car.'

'Mum?' called Orla from the dining table.

'Where did you leave the car?'

'Down in that lot at the end of the road,' said Robert. 'This massive rabbit was flapping his paws at me. I know how to park my own car, buddy.'

'A massive what?' Martha slapped Ellis's hand away from the strawberries – 'They're frozen' – as she emptied them into a Pyrex dish.

'Muh-ummm!'

Martha sighed. 'Yes, Orla?'

'Whose team is Ellis going to be on for the Easter egg treasure hunt?'

'I don't know,' said Martha, tapping in the microwave settings. 'He can go with you and Dad, or me and Sinead. Whichever.'

'It says here it's two per team.'

'It says where? What are you reading?'

Orla held up the booklet so Martha could see the front.

'Pine Road's inaugural Easter Egg Treasure Hunt: The Rules. By founder Ellen Russell-O'Toole.' Martha frowned. 'Did that come through the letterbox?'

'It was in yesterday's pile.'

'Well, I'm sure it doesn't matter,' she said. 'It's a street party, not the Olympics.'

'I think I should just go . . .'

'No,' said Martha decisively, coming around the island to kiss her son on the cheek. 'No way. You're here and you're staying. I'm making pavlova. You love my pavlova. It'll be fine. I promise. Stay.'

Ellis shrugged off his jacket and sat down beside Orla. He watched as she resumed work on the animal ears.

'They're cute. You'll make a lovely Easter bunny.'

His twelve-year-old sister rolled her eyes. 'Rabbits actually have nothing to do with Easter, Ellis. They can be born throughout a large section of the year. And new-born rabbits aren't cute. They have no fur for a week and can't even open their eyes. Like rats. These are lamb ears. They are smaller and go more to the side. See?' Orla carefully fastened the band to her head. 'Seasonally and anatomically correct.'

Sinead would be home from soccer training in a few minutes and then they were all going to a party on their new street, together. All her family was safe and well. Martha allowed her body to swell with contentment.

The boy who wrote the list up at the school had been caught and suspended. Martha thought he should have been expelled but she hadn't pushed it. The family were neighbours and it wasn't really her place; he hadn't actually written Sinead's name. She should probably be grateful Sinead hadn't been in line for a suspension too. As far as Martha knew, Trish had kept what they had told her to herself. Martha, in turn, had signed Sinead – and herself – up for counselling.

Both the girls had come home from school that week with a piece of good news: Sinead had been appointed head of the debating team while Orla had made the mathletes. Some kids might be embarrassed but Orla had already added it to the CV she planned to distribute this summer when she was thirteen and thus, due to an agreement Martha barely remembered making when she was eight, allowed to look for babysitting jobs.

Robert came and leaned against the counter beside her, both of them watching Ellis and Orla. Carefully, she reached for his hand. She'd had two therapy sessions now and was all but convinced the man on the street had been a figment of her imagination, an accumulation of stress.

Things were good. Life was good. She didn't need to dwell on the past.

'Penny for your thoughts,' murmured Robert.

'I was just thinking how happy I am,' she said, reminding herself not to shirk such declarations. They were a team again. She moved closer to her husband and tentatively rested her head on his shoulder. His body grew sturdier under her touch. 'I'm happy with how things have turned out.'

The microwave pinged and Martha straightened up.

'Give me a hand with this, will you, Ellis? I've to have it out on the road in' – she glanced at the clock on the oven and tried to remember the timetable she'd read in one of the early booklets – 'eight minutes.'

THIRTY-EIGHT

It had been a month since she'd last seen Cormac, though she thought about him every day. Several times a day, Robin corrected herself, the back of her neck burning. She didn't just recall things, she invented whole scenarios. She imagined bumping into him on the bus, him turning up at her door unannounced, discovering she had an STI and being forced to tell him; anything that resulted in contact. Every time she received a new message from him, she pounced on her phone, before remembering there was nothing he could say that would cancel out her guilt. She had the power to right a terrible wrong done to his family, and she wasn't going to.

Contradicting Eddy's alibi had given her enough reasons to worry without telling the police where he actually was that night. She would just have to live with the guilt. It would be easier to handle when she stopped living across the road from them.

Robin shook her hair out of the high bun it had been in since the night before and reached for the hairbrush. Her mother came back into the house and Jack went running out from wherever he'd been hiding.

'Mammy, Mammy, Mammy!'

'Upstairs, Jack!' Robin called. His footsteps grew louder until he eventually burst into their bedroom. 'Careful.'

'Can we go to the party now? If we don't go now, all the eggs will be ate!'

301

'Eaten,' said Robin. 'We'll go in ten minutes.'

'Counting to how many is that?'

'It's too many to count for kids, but it's not long. I promise.'

'Cross your heart!'

Robin dutifully did as she was told. 'Ten minutes.'

Jack leapt from her bed to his own and down on to the ground. 'I'll ask Granny to count to ten minutes!' He ran from the room, making vague fighting sounds and banging something against the banisters. Robin winced. This was what he was like before he'd consumed his weight in chocolate.

She opted for a no-make-up make-up look – tinted moisturiser, mascara on the top lashes only, eyebrows filled in – and pulled on the green fitted jumper Cormac had complimented when they went to the theatre but which was plain enough that he probably wouldn't remember. She wore it with jeans and runners, so it didn't look like she was making an effort.

Anyway, he wasn't here for her, she reminded herself as she made her way downstairs. He was here for his family.

'Okay,' said Carmel, standing in the hallway with a large metallic dish in her hands. 'Are we right?'

Johnny was beside her holding what looked like a Bunsen burner, while her dad had a cooler at his feet and a basket of torn-up bread resting on top. Jack was weaving in and out between their legs mumbling to himself and occasionally swiping at the floor: 'One egg, two eggs, three eggs, four . . .'

'I'm just going to get a glass of water.'

'I'll wait for Robin,' said Johnny.

'You will not,' barked Carmel. 'Get out there and make polite small talk with the elderly neighbours. Ask Mrs Birmingham to tell you about how she has no tear ducts now, she'll love that. And wipe that puss off your face. You'd swear you were being sent to a day's hard labour.'

Mick put his hand on the door. 'Are we ready?'

'Yes yes yes yes yes yes!' shouted Jack, running back and forth, banging against the door then the banisters, like their old dog used to do when he knew he was about to be taken for a walk.

Her dad opened the door and Jack went flying out of the trap. Robin went down to the kitchen, filled a glass from the tap and knocked it back. She gave herself a once-over in the hallway mirror – practising a smile and then an I-don't-know-you're-watching-me look – and stepped out on to Pine Road.

Only this didn't look a thing like Pine Road.

In the ninety minutes Robin had been inside, the place had been transformed. There were balloons tied to the street lights and bunting draped across all the trees. A long line of tables had been laid down the middle of the street as if for a wedding banquet and they were covered in pink tablecloths. Some sort of dead animal had been impaled at the very top of the line of tables and was turning slowly over a fire pit. The street was packed with people – eighty, at least – and, most remarkable of all, there wasn't a single car.

Robin ran her eye over the crowd. Jack was messing with two other kids and her mam was cackling away in a group of women. Johnny sat at one of the tables, eating cake and trying to protect it from the spittle of an older woman who was pulling at the skin around her eyes and speaking right into his ear. A few chairs down was someone dressed in a full-scale rabbit costume. He was tapping his paws despondently, out of time with the unidentifiable pop music floating through the air.

Robin was distracted from the anthropomorphic bunny by a door opening directly across from her. Martha walked out carrying a cake and Cormac was right behind her. He was laughing and joking with his sisters. A heat rose in her body. It hurt to look away.

'Edie!' she said with far too much enthusiasm, as she spotted her friend. Were they friends? Well, whatever. She needed someone to talk to. 'Hi, Daniel.'

The couple drew up beside her, holding hands.

'Isn't this amazing!' enthused Edie. 'It's like a different place completely. All the tables have matching tablecloths and oh my God did you see the lamb?'

Daniel smiled at his wife, then at Robin, who grinned back.

'The lamb?' Robin stood on her tippy-toes and peered around. It was hard to see anything with all the people, yet she managed to immediately lock eyes with Cormac, who was looking up from his sister at the same moment. Her insides flipped and she pulled her gaze away. She made a show of searching the crowd now and lifted her hand to shield her eyes, like a sailor seeking land. 'Is that a lamb? The dead thing on the stick with . . . does it have a *tennis ball* in its mouth?'

'Hmm?' Edie followed her line of vision. 'Oh no. That's the pig on the spit, and an apple. No, look.' She tugged Robin's attention so she was peering up the road. 'See? In Ruby's garden?'

Robin peered up the row of gardens until—

'Oh, shit! Look at that!'

It was a real live lamb eating grass from a Pine Road garden. It had a bell around its neck and everything. 'Where did that come from? I have to show Jack.'

'Ruby's sister is married to a farmer and they rent them out for fancy Easter parties. Some social influencer cancelled theirs this morning – she changed the colour scheme for her party at the last minute and the lamb no longer matched – so they let Ruby have it for free. Oh gosh, what time is it?' Edie patted down her pockets before glancing at her husband.

'Twenty-five past eleven,' said Daniel.

'Twenty-five past . . .' mumbled Edie. 'We're supposed to be doing light mingling . . . Okay, perfect. I'd call this light mingling. Five more minutes and then it's time for light snacking. I think. I meant to bring the timetable with me.'

'You seem kind of hyper, Edie.'

'Do I?' she beamed, as if Robin had given her a massive compliment. 'I guess I'm just happy.' She looked at Daniel who smiled back. 'I've had a lovely morning. I made Daniel his own treasure hunt. Have you ever made one? It was so fun.'

Daniel looked less convinced.

Robin excused herself and went to get Jack. She had to drag him away from the girls he was playing with but once she explained there was a real live baby sheep, he moved more willingly.

She asked the woman in charge of the lamb – Ruby – if Jack should approach the animal in a certain way, but she hadn't a clue.

'I'd say don't poke her in the eye or tell her she looks like mutton and you'll be grand.'

'Have you antiseptic maybe?' asked Robin.

Ruby looked around from where she sat on her doorstep. 'I have gin?'

Jack had just worked up the courage to touch the animal, when the deafening, echoing sound of an alarm rang out and everyone – including the lamb – jumped in fright.

'That bloody autocrat . . .' began Ruby as Robin covered Jack's ears and steered him out of the garden.

Edie reappeared beside Robin and they watched as a woman with a megaphone stood on a garden chair and struggled to stick some sort of wire back into what looked like a car fob.

'Is that a rape alarm?' whispered Edie.

'Now that I have your attention,' the woman boomed into the speaker, 'I want to officially welcome you all to the Pine Road pre-Easter street party. We've had a few of these before, but I think you will all agree that today marks the beginning of a new, more exciting, more morally upstanding chapter. For the visitors among you, I'm Ellen Russell-O'Toole and I'm the organiser of today's event—'

'Yes, queen!' came a roar from somewhere in the crowd.

'And for the first time in Pine Road history,' continued Ellen, 'we will be having a Pine Road Easter egg treasure hunt!' She moved the megaphone away from her mouth and looked around until a few people – including Edie – started to clap.

Edie looked at her wrist, where she now wore Daniel's watch. 'Eleven fifty-one,' she marvelled. 'Right on time.'

'The Pine Road Easter egg treasure hunt will begin at noon . . .'

'I love Easter egg hunts!' came another voice from the crowd and a few people hollered in agreement.

'Gonna catch me a couple of those chocolate bad boys!'

'No egg left behind!'

'This is not an Easter egg hunt,' said Ellen into the megaphone, 'this is an Easter egg *treasure* hunt. I want to assure you all, especially the parents among us, that the eggs involved are dairy-free and wrapped in biodegradable foil . . .'

Robin glanced at Edie who studied the ground.

'. . . the colour of the wrapping paper is gender neutral and the chocolate is low-sugar.'

'Mugabe!' came a shout from behind but when Robin turned Ruby was sipping her gin and tonic and staring blankly at Ellen.

'This is the first such treasure hunt,' continued Ellen, megaphone firmly in place, 'so we will need to go over the rules.'

'We just run around and find as many eggs as we can!' someone shouted.

'No,' said Ellen. 'That's an Easter egg hunt. This is an Easter egg *treasure* hunt. It's different. There are clues.'

'Like someone shouting hot when you're near a hidden egg and cold when you're not?'

'Again,' said Ellen, with slightly more edge, 'that's an Easter egg hunt. A treasure hunt has riddles, written on pieces of paper, each one leading to the next until the winner gets to the end of the clue trail where they'll find the eggs.'

'Will Bernie be out to explain the rules?' called a woman from the other side of the crowd, and the road suddenly went silent.

Somewhere a spoon clattered to the ground and the sound reverberated for a good three seconds.

'Lisa Channing,' whispered Edie. 'The family have been in Berlin for six months. Just back last night. They clearly haven't been briefed.'

'Bernie Watters-Reilly is sitting out this pre-Easter street party,' said Ellen, her voice definitely higher now. 'I am in charge.'

Carmel crept up beside them, waved at Edie and dutifully reciprocated Jack's request for a high-five.

'I see your man's here,' she whispered. And though Robin was doing her best not to look at Cormac, her eyes immediately flickered to where she knew he was, beside his sisters. Only this time he didn't feel her eyes on him. He was concentrating on Ellen, who was still standing on the chair.

'I know,' Robin whispered back. 'I saw him going into Martha's earlier.'

'Not him,' said Carmel. 'Your other man, the charlatan toe-rag.' Her mother jerked her head towards the bottom of the road. 'Eddy's here.'

THIRTY-NINE

E die was trying her absolute best to concentrate on everything Ellen was saying but it was hard with so much going on; both on the street – a whole set of balloons had just broken free from the streetlamp outside Rita Ann's – and in her head.

It was difficult to be still, though she was trying, when her body was ready to burst with giddy joy.

'Those participating in the inaugural Pine Road Easter Egg Treasure Hunt will divide themselves into teams of two,' boomed Ellen.

Two, repeated Edie to herself. *Teams of two. Right. Got it.*

'Why do you need teams for an egg hunt?'

'It's not an egg hunt!' Ellen yelled, which, combined with the megaphone, created terrible reverb. 'It's a treasure hunt! All right? An Easter egg TREASURE hunt. It was in the booklets!'

Edie looked to the side to make sure Robin was also paying attention – she pitied the resident who had any follow-up questions – but she was gone. It was just Carmel there now.

'The woman's a maniac,' said Carmel, a little too loudly for Edie's liking. Although she had to agree. She had the utmost admiration for Ellen's preparation skills and timekeeping, but the woman's face was currently going from red to purple. Bernie Watters-Reilly was equally intimidating, but at least she gave the impression of being calm and collected.

Edie looked up towards Bernie's house, where all the curtains were still pulled, and felt a deep pang of guilt. A big part of her good mood was for the same reason that another neighbour was in turmoil. Edie hadn't been glad to hear Declan Reilly was the one responsible for the list, or that the guards had been involved, but she couldn't help feeling relieved – and yes, okay, joyous – to learn that this was why the police had called to Bernie's house and not because they were investigating Peter's dog.

Edie had been having nightmares in which her husband was escorted away in handcuffs while the women on the road messaged one another about it, having set up another, secret, WhatsApp group. But she no longer had to worry. The police were not involved. The relief was immense.

There was no reason for Daniel to fear becoming a father now. The dog bite couldn't have been that bad if they weren't investigating. Edie hadn't mentioned what she knew because things had been great the past few weeks. The garage was going well and Daniel was relaxed again. Even earlier today, when Shay Morrissey took one of her homemade biscuits and eyeballed her husband while declaring it 'yum-yum num-num', Daniel hadn't punched him.

'We have fifteen copies of the first clue, which means fifteen teams – of TWO PEOPLE – can take part,' boomed Ellen. 'The clues are all hidden in houses and gardens around Pine Road. Please be respectful in homes and do not make a mess. When you've read a clue, put it back where you found it so the next team can also have a chance of locating it.'

'Hey, teammate,' whispered Daniel, creeping up behind her and putting his arm around her waist.

'Nope. Sorry, Daniel. This hunt isn't for you. You have your own treasure hunt to do.'

'Edie,' he groaned. 'You know I'm not good at riddles . . .'

This was true. It was why he hated Christmas crackers.

'It's only five clues,' she said. 'And they're not difficult. You'll be done before you know it.'

'And who'll do the treasure hunt with you?'

'I'll find a partner. It'll be good for neighbour team building.'

He groaned. Edie smiled. Things were good.

She pulled a folded rectangle of fancy paper from her back pocket and handed it to him. 'First clue.'

Ellen continued to call out instructions: 'If everyone wishing to participate could come up to this space in front of me, we'll get started.'

Daniel unfolded the note and read. 'When you come in the door, you throw the keys here; the object is heavy, but the material is clear.' He looked up at Edie. 'The glass bowl on our hall table?'

'I don't know,' she said, trying to do that one-shoulder, nonchalant shrug Robin was so good at. 'Go and see for yourself.'

She gave him a final kiss, on the lips, and ran off to stand in front of Ellen Russell-O'Toole and look for a treasure hunt partner. She didn't care about winning, she really was one of those people who just liked taking part, but she did think a morning spent making her own clues might give her an edge; she was already in a rhyming, riddling state of mind.

She was one of the first to reach the marked-off area. Fiona's twins were there, arms linked, and Fiona stood behind them, talking to Rita Ann.

'Will we make a little team, Rita Ann?' cooed Fiona, going to link her neighbour.

'We will not,' retorted the older woman, yanking her arm away. 'Your voice goes through my head. It's like one of those hearing tests. It's a wonder it doesn't set the dogs off.'

Fiona's face dropped. Edie felt terrible. Honesty was important, but not as important as compassion.

'I'll be your partner, Fiona,' she said brightly.

The woman's face spread with relief. 'Oh thanks, hun! That'd be great! I love a little healthy competition. I find it's good for the complexion.' She linked Edie. 'Gets all those red blood cells flowing.'

310

Ellen climbed down from her chair and threw a bag of high-vis jackets over her arm. 'Right. Who's got a team?'

'Me and Fiona!' shouted Edie, throwing her arm in the air.

'Yass, kween!'

'Jesus Christ,' muttered Rita Ann, sticking her finger in her left ear.

'And us!' called the twins.

'Myself and Pat,' said one of the less friendly neighbours who lived on the opposite side of the road to Edie.

'Hang on, hang on.' Ellen picked up a clipboard from the ground beside her chair and started writing down names, handing out the jackets as she went. 'Right, who else?'

Little Jack ran up then, pulling a handsome man behind him.

Ellen looked the man up and down. 'Who are you? You're not from Elm, anyway. Oak? Chestnut?'

'I'm Eddy,' he said, placing a hand on Jack's head. 'I'm Jack's dad.'

So *that* was Robin's ex. Edie could see the attraction – your classic brooding bad boy, really – but personally, she preferred kind and loyal. She hugged herself as she looked up in the direction of their house. Daniel should be on the second clue by now, maybe even the third.

Ellen tapped her clipboard and looked from Eddy to Jack. 'Are you a team?'

'What do you say, Jacko? Are we doing the egg hunt?'

'It's not an egg—'

'YESSSS!' The little boy started running around his father's legs.

Eddy gave Ellen a crooked smile. 'I guess we're a team then.'

I'd say everything's crooked about you, bucko, thought Edie, rallying her loyalty in a bid to cancel out the fact that she found his smile rather charming. Lovely eyes.

'Right,' muttered Ellen, digging in her bag of jackets. 'I've got a kid's one in here somewhere . . .'

Martha's family appeared then – all except Martha herself. 'Me and Mum are a team,' Sinead Costello informed Ellen. 'And Orla, my dad and Ellis are another team.'

'I like your donkey ears, hun,' cooed Fiona.

Orla brushed her long, thin hair from her face and touched her sorry-looking animal ears. 'These are lamb ears. They're anatomically and seasonally correct.'

'Are they?' encouraged Fiona. 'Good for you. My girls are wearing sparkly bunny ears. Willow even made a cute little tail to match.'

Orla frowned; every time she adjusted her glasses, the DIY ears drooping slightly. 'Rabbits don't have sparkly ears. Costumes cause a lot of miseducation. People grow up thinking all rabbits are pink and white and that quadruped mammals have prehensile, multi-fingered hands and feet rather than paws.'

Fiona nodded, smiling, not really listening. 'The girls are dead cute. You'll probably want a pair when you see them.'

Orla looked doubtful. Ellen put her fingers to her lips and whistled.

'Can we stay on track here, please?' She looked down at her clipboard. 'Who's Ellis?'

Martha's son raised his hand. Martha's son who was also the fella Robin was seeing. She'd heard that from Carmel, and also that it was all off between them. Which seemed a pity.

'I go by Cormac, usually.'

'Fascinating,' mumbled Ellen, making notes on her list. 'Well, I'm afraid you'll have to find someone else to be your partner, Cormac. It's only two per team.'

'I *told* you,' grumbled Orla.

Ellen tapped her clipboard again. 'And where is your mother? We're in serious danger of getting behind schedule here.'

'I'll go and get her,' said Robert Costello and he headed off towards their house.

A few more participants came forward and Ellen started physically moving people around so they stood in clearly defined pairs.

'Right,' she said, 'how many teams is that now? Six, seven – you need to find another partner, Cormac – eight, nine . . .'

Robin came flying into the circle.

'Robin, have you got a part—'

But Robin wasn't paying any attention to Ellen; she immediately rounded on Jack's father.

'Why are you here?' she half-shouted, arms straight by her side. 'You can't be here. You have to go. Now.'

'Relax, babe. I'm here to see Jack, and you. I hear you've been telling stories about me—'

'I'm serious, Eddy; you can't be here.' Robin looked around fretfully. 'Where's Martha? Edie?'

'Oh,' said Edie. 'Martha?' Why was Robin looking for Martha? 'I don't know.'

'Robin, if you're not taking part in the treasure hunt, I'm afraid you need to leave the circle. We are really pushing it for time.'

Edie glanced at Daniel's watch. They were three minutes behind schedule. She felt stressed on Ellen's behalf.

Robin turned to Ellen, not even trying to keep the irritation out of her voice. 'What are you saying?' She was either very brave or foolish, or most likely just hadn't been on Pine Road long enough. 'Fine, yes, whatever. I'm taking part.'

'In that case, you need a partner.'

'Jack. I'm with Jack.'

'No, Mammy,' said Jack, shaking his head regretfully, 'I'm with Daddy.'

'Fine then, Edie. Can I be your partner, Edie?'

'I actually already agreed to be with Fiona. Sorry, Robin, if I'd known—' Fiona got a tighter grip on her elbow.

Orla was looking around now. 'I'm going to get Mum and Dad!' And she was off before Ellen could remind her how behind schedule they were. Robin watched her go and then started on her ex, more anxious this time.

'You have to leave, Eddy. Now!'

'I'm going nowhere, babe. I'm hanging out with Jacko, and you and me need to talk.'

'I'm sorry now, Robin, but without a partner, you can't be here. I'll have to ask you to—'

'I'll be her partner.'

Half the circle looked over to the hipster journalist who, Carmel had informed Edie, wasn't actually a journalist at all.

'Who's the fella?' someone half-whispered.

'It's the new woman's son,' said someone else.

'I don't think . . .' Robin began, but Ellen was already putting a hand on each of her shoulders and pushing her over to stand beside Cormac. She threw a fluorescent vest over Robin's shoulder.

'We are now ten minutes behind schedule, people!'

Eddy was eyeing up Cormac, while Jack tried to scale his back. Lucky Robin. Edie knew it wasn't very modern feminist of her, but she quite liked the idea of two men vying for her affections.

'We are now officially in code red of scheduling. I'm sorry, Sinead,' said Ellen, turning to Martha's daughter, 'but we're going to have to start without the rest of your family—'

'Here comes the lamb!' shouted someone.

'Eddy!' shouted Robin. 'Just leave! Please!'

'People! Please! We are twelve minutes behind schedule!'

Orla landed in the circle with a thud, hair tangled around the ears. Edie thought she looked more like a mouse. 'Mum and Dad are fighting,' she said, rolling her eyes. 'I'll be with Sinead.'

'Are they okay?' the hipster non-journalist asked his sister, as Robin started shouting at Eddy again. Jack was whimpering and Fiona's twins were singing along to whatever song was playing.

'That's enough!' roared Ellen, jumping up and down as her face went all grape-like again.

Everyone stopped.

Edie and Fiona exchanged a look. Edie quickly pulled on her fluorescent singlet.

'Everyone gets the same first clue,' said Ellen, handing out the envelopes. 'Do not open these until I say "Go". Each clue leads to the next, until the ninth one, which leads to the eggs. Put the clues back when you find them, and first one to the eggs wins. All right?' Ellen took a deep breath and reached for the stopwatch around her neck. 'Any questions?'

One of the not-so-friendly-neighbours from the other side of the road raised his hand.

'Quick one for you, Ellen.'

She sighed. 'Yes, Pat.'

'I'm just wondering what exactly we need clues for in an egg hunt?'

FORTY

· · · · · · · · · · · · · · ·

Martha had forgotten the serving cream.

She left the dessert on one of the pink tables and went back into her kitchen to grab the carton from the fridge. The electric whisk handles were in the dishwasher, which Robert had already turned on – maybe things weren't just back to normal, maybe they were better; he'd never bothered with the dishwasher before – so she rooted out the hand whisk from the second drawer.

The cream was just starting to thicken when a deafening sound went up from outside and Martha dropped the whisk into the bowl.

'Damn it!'

She picked up a tea towel and walked into the hallway to see what the racket was. She dabbed at her new Rixo shirt, trying to erase the extra dashes of white added by the cream. It couldn't be a car alarm blaring: all the vehicles had been moved.

When she got to the door, the ringing stopped and she saw Ellen Russell-O'Toole standing on a chair with a megaphone in hand.

'. . . marks the beginning of a new, more exciting, more morally upstanding chapter . . .'

Martha's three children were in the crowd, side by side, Orla's anatomically correct sheep ears sticking out rather than up. Robert was a little to the right, talking to another man. She smiled. They were all making friends.

Robert clapped the man on the shoulder and headed back towards their children. Martha, too, was about to go back into the kitchen when the man her husband had been talking to turned around.

The hand that was holding the tea towel shot up to her chest. She froze. He turned, making his way easily through the crowd, but she knew that face. It was him.

Out the door and on to the porch, she looked around but he'd vanished into the masses. Ellen was still yelling into her megaphone and what looked like a lamb was standing in a garden across the road. Martha was about to move out into the crowd when Rita Ann shouted at her.

'Trish says you're getting cream!'

Martha looked over at her neighbour.

The woman shook a plate of something at her. 'We need some over here!'

Martha's eyes darted back to the crowd, but she could see neither her husband nor the man.

'Yes, I . . . it's coming,' she called back to Rita Ann.

Should she go out and look for them, or should she go back in? What was her best move?

'By itself?'

Not knowing what else to do, Martha turned back into the house. She stood at her kitchen counter and tried to get things straight. She had not imagined it. She had seen him twice now on their new road, a place he had no business being. Why didn't he just approach her? She was the one who'd seen his face, not Robert. Why didn't he come to Martha and tell her to keep her mouth shut? Why was he talking to Robert?

Not just talking to him, she thought, absent-mindedly picking back up the whisk; laughing with him, joking with him.

Outside, the echoing boom of Ellen's voice disappeared and the general chitter-chatter started up, spooling slowly from her ear to her brain, like a growing swarm of flies.

She used the hand that wasn't holding the whisk to steady herself at the worktop.

'Martha.'

Her husband appeared in the kitchen and she jumped. But she didn't drop the whisk. That was probably a first.

'The girls are looking for you,' said Robert. 'They're about to start the egg hunt.'

'The treasure hunt,' said Martha, overcome by a familiar out-of-body sensation.

'Right, yes, the treasure hunt. Come on or we'll miss the start. The woman organising is very keen on rules. I don't think she accepts latecomers.'

'Were you in on it, Robert?' She looked straight at him, studying his face as best her concentration would allow. 'Were you in on the tiger raid?'

'What?' Her husband's face contorted grotesquely. 'The raid on our house? No. Of course I wasn't in on it. Why would you ask that?'

'You were talking to him on the road, laughing with him.'

'Who? What are you talking about, Martha?'

'You were talking to one of the men who came to our house that day, the one who drove the car, the one I saw here before.'

'No I wasn't.'

'I saw you, Robert! I saw you just now, laughing and talking with him.'

'I swear to God, Martha, I don't know what you're talking about.'

'Who were you talking to, then? Just now? The man outside that you were having a good joke with? Who was he?'

'I don't know,' said Robert, looking at her like he had in the days after the raid, when he acted as though he might have to have her committed. 'I was talking to loads of people, neighbours, one guy in a massive bunny costume. A couple of others in civvies. I don't know. I was mingling.'

'Muh-umm! Da-had!'

Orla came pounding down the hall, into the kitchen, wearing a reflective jacket, hair flying in sheets behind her. Martha could see her out of the corner of her eye but she kept her focus on Robert. She was waiting for the tell.

'There you are,' their daughter huffed, as if they were the truant children. 'We have to go. They're about to start the treasure hunt!'

'I swear, Martha, I was just talking to some neighbours.'

'Who? Which neighbours?'

'I don't know their names.'

'Come on, Mum! Dad!'

'How do you not know their names?'

'I just don't. Jesus, Martha. There's a lot of people out there. I was making chitchat, not creating profiles.'

'Dad!' Orla pulled at her father's sleeve and Martha switched her attention.

'Go on without us, Orla. Your dad and I are talking.'

'But Dad said he'd be my partner!'

'You can be Sinead's partner. Go on. Out.'

Orla threw her mother a very Sinead-like look. Was this the beginning of the teenager years? But she didn't say anything. She just ran, loudly, out of the house.

'If he's out there, Martha, which I doubt, it has nothing to do with me.'

'He is out there, Robert. You can't convince me I'm imagining it this time.'

'I didn't convince you last time,' he all but shouted. 'You weren't sure. I could only go on what you said.' He took a breath. 'Come on, then. Let's go and see if we can find him. You can point him out to me.'

Martha stared at her husband. Was he mocking her? Trying reverse psychology? But his expression didn't change. He met her gaze, eyes open, face giving nothing away. He moved towards the door and she went to do the same.

Then she stopped and turned. As if on autopilot, she lifted the large ceramic bowl of half-whisked cream from the counter. And she carried it outside.

FORTY-ONE
· ·

Robin watched helplessly as Eddy, now with Jack clinging to his back, ripped open the envelope and began to read the clue.

'*I belong to all, yet I belong to none. But at the bottom of it all, I am claimed by one.*' Eddy twisted around to match his son's cheeky-monkey grin. 'What do you think that means, Jacko?'

Beside her, Cormac was opening their envelope and holding out a card with the same riddle written on it. 'Do you want—'

But Robin didn't have time for clues or awkward niceties. She had to make Eddy leave. She couldn't let Martha see him. The road was busy but not so much that she might miss Eddy altogether.

'Eddy, please. I am begging you. I will meet you later. I'll go with you now if you want to talk. Just not here.'

He hoisted Jack farther up his back and the boy giggled. 'Is this about your new boyfriend?' He nodded to Cormac. 'Don't want me to meet him? Is that it? Well, too late, babe.' Eddy held out a hand.

'He's not my boyfriend,' said Robin, refusing to blush.

'I'm Eddy. This is my son, and this used to be my woman. Until she repaid my years of looking after her by shopping me out.'

'For God's sake . . .'

Cormac reluctantly took Eddy's hand and looked at Robin. 'I'm Cormac. I'm not . . . My mum lives on the road.'

'Good for you, Cormac. Anyway, me and Jacko better be off. We've got some eggs to hunt.'

Jack threw back his head and cheered triumphantly.

'Just give me Jack.'

'No!' roared the boy.

'Okay, Eddy, well done, you wanted to get to me and you have, you've succeeded. You win. Now please – please, please, please – just go. I'll meet you at your flat in an hour.'

'Eggs eggs eggs eggs eggs!' shouted Jack.

The woman with the megaphone was in front of them now. 'Have you two even read your clue? What's the hold-up? Some of the others are on the second one already! Chop-chop! Let's go!'

Robin glanced at Cormac and for a second, she faltered. *Dimple, dimple, delicious dimple.* 'I'm sorry,' she said. 'I'm not in the headspace for this. Why don't you go ahead?'

But Ellen was still in earshot and she came marching back. 'What part of the rules do you people not understand? This is team building. Not glory hunting. No solo runs! Two people PER TEAM!'

Robin turned back to plead with Eddy, but he was gone.

'Whose is this?' Ellen demanded, picking Eddy's fluorescent jacket up off the ground. Of course he wasn't going to wear it. Ellen barrelled off, looking for the culprit. 'All treasure hunters must dress appropriately!'

Was Eddy actually doing the stupid treasure hunt? He didn't know anything about this road. And since when did he participate in party games? He wouldn't even try pinning the tail on the donkey at Jack's birthday last year.

'Robin,' said Cormac, 'about that day, outside your house. I was taken aback. I wasn't expecting Jack and—'

'It's not that,' she interrupted, still searching around her. 'Really.' She didn't have time to explain, even if she could find the words. Jack and Eddy were nowhere to be seen. But there was Martha, back outside her house. She was standing on the pavement, holding a large bowl. She was looking around her.

Martha was going to find Eddy before she did.

'Fine,' said Robin, swiping the card from Cormac. 'Let's do it.' At least this way they could follow where Eddy went. 'What's the clue?' The words were engraved in gold leaf on a solid cream card. How much money had been spent on this treasure hunt? *'I belong to all . . . none . . . bottom . . . claimed by one.'*

Ellen was back and about to rebuke Robin again when someone started shouting in the distance – 'I know where the eggs are!' – and she went flying off in the direction of the voice.

'Who said that? Come on! Own up right this minute!'

Robin felt Cormac's hand brushing her arm and she stopped searching the crowd.

She looked at him properly for the first time since that day outside her house. How had she not noticed before how like Martha he was? Dark hair, pale skin, high cheeks. Her heart ached as her stomach churned.

'I think it's talking about the Occupied Territory, down the bottom of the road.'

'Well, let's go then,' said Cormac, and he held out a hand.

Though she was stressed and fearful and knew it was a bad idea, she reached out and took it. And for a moment, as his fingers interlocked with hers, everything felt a little better.

FORTY-TWO

'**W**hat are you looking around up there for, Edie? She's not Jesus! She didn't write the next clue in the goddamn sky! Get down on your useless knees and help me look!'

Edie didn't know Fiona that well and she had noticed she could get quite stroppy when she had to fold early in their monthly poker games but she had not grasped just how competitive the woman was until now.

Gone was the smiley, squeaky-voiced woman who called everyone 'hun' and fretted about her children and house prices. In her place was a monster, hungry for victory and dairy-free chocolate eggs.

'What are you waiting for?' yelled Fiona, looking up momentarily from where she was scavenging around behind car wheels. She had oil all over her hands, and her hair, which had been perfectly neat just ten minutes earlier, was sticking out in all directions. 'If those little shits find this clue before us, you're going to pay for it!'

Sinead and Orla, who were searching a couple of cars over, slowed down and looked over at Edie uncertainly.

'She's not talking about you,' Edie called back. 'Keep going, girls, you're doing great.'

'I am so talking about them,' growled Fiona, who was now feeling around beneath the wheel of Daniel's car. 'Little upstarts. Since when do lambs wear glasses, hmm? That's not very anatomically correct, is it? Specky-four-eyes, know-it-all donkey . . . Get down here now!'

Edie got down on her hunkers. She was wearing her first ever pair of Cos trousers but reckoned the wool could withstand dirt better than Fiona clawing at it. She had just started to root around – 'I already did that wheel, you half-wit!' – when she heard Daniel behind her.

'I finished your treasure hunt.'

Beaming, Edie scrambled to her feet. 'I'm delighted!' She was standing before she realised Daniel didn't sound as delighted as her. In fact, he didn't sound or look delighted at all.

'It's a pretty sick way of letting me know, Edie.'

'What? Really?' She almost stumbled as Fiona yanked at her trouser leg. Edie shook her off. 'I thought it was lovely,' she said, confused and a little hurt by Daniel's reaction. 'Wait. What did you find?'

'I found the printout.' He was so angry. Why was he so angry? 'When did you find out?' he said. 'Why didn't you tell me you knew?'

'The printout . . .' Edie tried to think. 'I didn't hide any printout. I don't know what you're—'

And then it hit her. Bernie Watters-Reilly's Wanted posters. They were still under the Waterford Crystal bowl. Daniel had found the artist's impression of Rocky, Peter's dog; the dog he'd been minding when it bit Sylvie.

'Oh no, Daniel! That wasn't part of it. That wasn't a clue.'

He was already making his way back up the road towards their house. She ran after him, ignoring Fiona's cries. She grabbed his arm just outside Ruby's house, where the lamb was now sleeping. Orla and Sinead ran up the road past them. They must have found the next clue.

'Daniel, stop! I didn't mean for you to find that, honestly. It wasn't part of the trail I made for you.'

'Why did you even have it, Edie?' he shouted, brushing her off and still moving. 'Why didn't you tell me you knew?'

'Someone gave it to me. I was going to say something but you were in a good mood again this last while. And it's nothing to worry about. I promise. And if it is anyone's responsibility, it's Peter's.'

'It's as much my responsibility as Peter's,' he said, moving to the side as more treasure hunters pushed past. 'It's really serious, Edie. The police are involved.'

Fiona appeared between them, throwing Edie a filthy look. She tripped on up the road, turning and shouting at her as she went. 'Defector!'

'No, no they're not,' said Edie quickly. 'I found out yesterday. The police aren't investigating.'

Daniel stopped again, a couple of metres from their house now.

'Some of the neighbours told me. They heard it from Sylvie's mother.' Edie couldn't stop the grin. 'You can relax, Daniel. The police aren't investigating.'

FORTY-THREE

The road was as busy as it had been earlier but the crowd more dispersed. Martha spied the girls heading out of the parking lot beside Shay Morrissey's house, both wearing those yellow jackets. Ellen stood nearby, holding a clipboard.

The surrounding chitter-chatter dropped to a low hum and all the bodies melded into one. Martha felt like she was floating. She was up with the balloons, looking down on Pine Road, searching the crowd.

'Is that the cream, Martha?'

Rita Ann was sitting at the table, wearing two scarves and chatting to a human-sized rabbit. Martha didn't find this strange.

'I've eaten the pavlova now,' said her neighbour. 'But it'll be good to have some anyway. Have you tried the fondue yet? It's very good. Isn't it, Joe?'

The human-sized rabbit brought one paw to its stomach and patted.

There was no sign of the man from the robbery.

'I'd take some cream for this walnut cake,' said someone sitting on the other side of the table. 'It's a bit dry.'

'Excuse me,' said Rita Ann, heaving herself out of her seat. 'I made that cake and there's nothing dry about it.'

'I only meant—'

'You meant nothing. I'd say you have a saliva deficiency. Your skin does look dry, sort of scaly. You should get that looked at instead of going around insulting people's cakes.'

Martha took a step towards the table, gripping the ceramic dish tightly with both hands.

'I'm actually grand,' said the chastised neighbour. 'I was mistaken. I don't need any cream at all.'

Rita Ann took her seat again and Martha was about to place the bowl on the table when the crowd parted slightly.

And there he was.

He was standing, talking to her neighbour, to her *friend*.

The bowl fell from her hands. It seemed to tumble slowly, turning over and over, the cream too thick to budge. It crashed to the ground, making contact with the pavement just as the music she hadn't even noticed was playing came to a sudden halt.

It's funny how you only notice the constants when they stop.

The bowl bounced once before shattering into three solid pieces, the cream spraying up and a sliver of white appearing on the leg of her dark trousers.

FORTY-FOUR

The music stopped and the sound of everything shattering resounded in Robin's ear. She spun around and instinctively knew where to look.

Martha's eyes were wide, her face pale and her hands held out in front of her, now empty, as if keeping something at bay.

It was too late. There was nothing Robin could do.

Martha had seen him.

Without looking around to see exactly where Eddy was, Robin ran across the road, stepping over three children drawing something on the pavement and ignoring her dad's insistence that she taste whatever it was he was eating. She came the long way around the line of dining tables and stopped only when she was right in front of her neighbour.

Martha eyed her hesitantly. 'I saw . . .'

'I know.'

Cormac came running behind her. 'Mum? Are you okay?' He turned to Robin. 'Is she okay?'

But Robin spoke only to Martha. 'You saw the man who was at your house in Limerick. The same man you saw on this road a few weeks ago.'

Martha nodded, the skin around her eyes starting to crease.

'What?' said Cormac. 'What did you say?'

'I'm so sorry, Martha. I should have said something.'

But Martha wasn't looking at her; she was staring behind,

beyond, her eyes moving up the road. She said something else but the music started up again and the words were lost.

'What was that?' Robin turned to Cormac. 'What did she say?'

But Martha spoke again, and she caught it this time. 'Eddy.'

Her heart pounded. She wanted to vomit, to expunge the expanding dread. 'I'm sorry, Martha, I knew it was Eddy and I should have told you. I wasn't—'

'No,' said Martha, louder now, more abrupt. '*Edie.*' Her voice and awareness returned, as she pointed up the road. 'The man I saw is the man with Edie.'

FORTY-FIVE

•••••••••••••••••••••••••

As **Edie** followed Daniel up their garden path, a stream of neighbours ran ahead, pounding through the front door and up their stairs.

'Tell them to leave,' said Daniel, pushing past a pair of teenagers who had tied their high-vis jackets at the belly button like crop tops.

'I can't. I agreed they could use our house for the treasure hunt.' She followed Daniel into their office and Orla went to push past her. 'It's not in here.'

The little girl gave her a sceptical look, her mouse ears looking even sadder than earlier.

'I promise. It's somewhere upstairs.'

Orla ran back out of the room and Edie closed the door behind them.

'I don't understand,' she said. 'If it's not about Peter's dog, then what is it about?'

'Will you stop talking about dogs?' retorted Daniel, his voice strained and desperate as he paced the room before finally sitting in the armchair by the window. 'It has nothing to do with a dog.'

He lowered his head into his hands. She perched herself on the swivel chair at his desk.

'What printouts are you talking about, then?'

He groaned, face obscured.

'Daniel? You're scaring me now. Tell me what's going on.'

He looked up and she was instantly nauseous. The expression on his face, like he'd gambled their house away or murdered her family – like whatever he'd done, there was no turning back. He pointed at her feet.

'What?' She looked down, bending her legs slightly to the side. 'The bin?' Of course. She had hidden the fifth clue in the wastepaper basket.

'Empty it.'

Feeling queasy still, she picked up the basket and upended its contents on to the floor. Several A4 pages fell out, followed by the folded-up clue he'd been supposed to find. This was the final clue, the one that led to his prize. But he'd missed it entirely.

The A4 pages were duplicates of the *Limerick Leader* article she'd printed off by accident weeks ago. She reached down to pick one up.

'These have nothing to do with you,' she said, scanning the details of the tiger raid again. 'Did I tell you about this?' No, she didn't think she had. 'It's about the new family at number eight.'

'No, Edie,' said Daniel, his voice thick. 'It's about me.'

The office door creaked and one of the not-so-friendly neighbours stuck their head in.

'Upstairs,' said Edie, standing to push the door shut before the person had fully retreated. She didn't want to be rude but she had a very bad feeling about whatever Daniel was going to tell her. She barely recognised him, face drained of colour, fingers digging into the side of his skull. He hadn't even looked this bad when the work stress hit its climax back in November.

'All this time, I've been . . . I've . . .' He exhaled loudly. 'Why didn't you tell me you knew?'

Edie looked down at the printout. Her internal protests quietening long enough to hear what was being said. How could this article be about Daniel? He had nothing to do with Limerick. Unless . . .

She suddenly felt very warm. Her Cos trousers prickled against her legs and she began to scratch at her neck.

She rehearsed the question in her head a couple of times, before finally saying it aloud. 'What do you mean this is about you?'

'What do you want me to say?' He gave a loud exhalation and looked at her, his lovely face awash with culpability and fear and something she'd only ever seen in bed, late at night, when he confessed past sins. 'I did it. Is that it? You want to hear me say it? I was part of the robbery. Okay? You're right. However you knew, you were right.' He groaned quietly, hands down on his knees, just about holding his head up.

Was he going to be sick?

'I agreed to help Peter and some of his mates. He said I wouldn't have to go in. I was the driver. I could just wait outside and follow the man when he drove to work. But I fucked up. I panicked. I was getting into the car and I pulled up my balaclava, just for a second, just so I could see where I was going, and his wife saw me. She looked right out the window at me. There were two kids there too. They were tied to the radiators. Oh, Jesus.' His head was in his hands again and he was rubbing at his cheeks, like the skin might come away, like he might be able to change his face. 'I saw them in there, sitting on the floor, fucking petrified. I still see it, Edie. I can't stop seeing it.'

He was seeking absolution from her, but she was countless steps behind. She was still back in a time when she thought his guilt was linked to a dog.

Daniel leaned forward and pulled up one of the articles. 'Tiger raid. I didn't even know what that meant before this.' He stared at the page, then back up at her. 'Did you find this on my search history? I did my best to clear it but I knew I was going to mess up eventually. It was always late and I was so tired, I couldn't sleep.'

Edie thought of the sleeping tablets Daniel had started taking last year. She'd presumed it was because of the garage, that he couldn't sleep because of stress from work. But of course. She looked at him, into his big dark eyes, and his handsome, handsome face, ready to crumble. This was the stress from work. This was the big job, the one that was going to save them but had fallen through.

Daniel had been involved in the tiger raid. Daniel was the man Martha had seen on Pine Road that night.

'But you've met Martha,' she said vaguely.

'Who?'

Was that true? Martha had been in their house, but Daniel hadn't been here that evening. And she had been on the road that day Daniel drove home to find Shay Morrissey out with his retractable bollards. But Martha had gone inside before Daniel was out of the car.

The night Martha saw the man from the robbery on Pine Road was the night before Parking-gate. It was the night she and Daniel fought on the way home from the pub, and he stormed off as she chatted to Robin and the hipster non-journalist . . . Edie's scalp began to sting.

'I thought you didn't want to have kids because of the dog . . .'

'What dog, Edie?' said Daniel, his voice high. He was growing more stressed by the sentence, blotches of red forming on his pale skin. 'Please stop going on about a dog.' He went back to trying to erase his face. 'I didn't do the job right, I didn't follow the man. His missus saw my face and I panicked. I kept thinking of those girls, on the floor, tied up. I left the motorway. I left the car where they'd told me to collect it and I came home. They were going to break my fucking legs but I thought I could fix it. I have fixed it, I think. Peter believed me when I told him the man got away from me and he convinced the others. I told them I tried to follow him but he swerved off the road, I told them there was a police car, that I didn't want to risk it. I can't stop seeing them, Edie.' His voice broke and for a horrifying moment she thought her rock of a husband was going to cry.

'It's okay, Daniel,' she said quietly, absently. Not sure if it was or not.

'I've been taking tablets, but they don't work. Nothing works. I'm glad you know; I'm glad. I need to say it all. I'm sorry. I keep seeing the family, the children. I just want that picture out of my head.'

FORTY-SIX

. . . .

'**Are you** sure, Martha? Are you absolutely sure?'

Martha stared into her husband's face – it was difficult to look anywhere else, he was that close – and a sliver of the disgust that had been retreating in recent weeks inched back in. Robert had gone back to talking to her as he had after the robbery, like she was a child who kept counting her fingers and coming up with thirteen.

'Yes, Robert,' she said calmly, 'I'm sure. I saw him with my own two perfectly functioning eyes.'

'Did you guys see him?' he asked, turning away from her to Ellis and Robin.

Martha closed her perfectly functioning eyes. *Be fair, Martha*, she told herself and she breathed through the rage. Yet again she was directing it all at Robert when there was a more obvious, more logical target readily available to her. So available, in fact, that he was only a few metres up the road – had been only a few metres up the road since the day they moved in.

'I think she's talking about one of the neighbours' husbands,' Robin replied, though she was looking at Martha. 'Edie's Daniel?' she mouthed, and Martha nodded.

'Mum, will you please tell me what's going on?'

'One second, darling,' she said, putting a hand on Cormac's arm. She felt fine now, perfectly rational and alert. The man with the soulful eyes lived on her road. Well, he had to live somewhere. He was Edie's husband. Daniel. Daniel the lovely man. Daniel the excellent mechanic. That made sense, she supposed; he had been driving a car. 'I have to deal with something.'

She went to stand from the chair that she now realised she was sitting on.

'Hang on,' said Robert, puffing out his chest. 'I'm going to call the guards. You stay right here. I'll just find my phone, call them, and be right back out. Don't budge. Ellis!'

'Yes?'

'You make sure your mother stays right there.'

It must be tough to be so feted and admired and then have it fade away. Robert surely missed being the hero. He did brave well, but when she thought of him on that day in November it was always shirtless, his belly pushing against his belt. She didn't mean to have such cruel thoughts. But there they were.

She never used to question Robert's behaviour, to consider the choices he made might actually be wrong. It made sense that what she'd been through had changed her. She'd worried it had made her colder, but now she thought it had made her resilient, the way she used to be when it was just her and Ellis.

'Do you understand, Martha?' Robert was back in her face now. The slightest bit of spittle catching just below her eye. 'You stay here.'

She smiled and nodded and watched him walk up their garden path and into the house. Then she stood from her chair and began to walk up Pine Road.

FORTY-SEVEN

'Is this why you didn't want to have kids?'

Daniel gave her the look he sometimes gave her now, the one she'd never been able to place. 'I *left* them, Edie. Two little girls with a group of fucking monsters. I knew they were monsters. How could I have just left them?'

Edie went to tell him the girls were okay, when there was an almighty crash from upstairs.

'Sorry!' came a voice through the ceiling.

'Should we be keeping an eye on them?' asked Daniel, his voice changing slightly. 'In case they steal anything.'

And with that absurd aside, it all slotted into place. Daniel had been worried about the garage throughout the summer but his mood swings really only began late last year, around the time of the robbery. That was why he didn't want any publicity for the garage; when she'd talked to Bernie, and Bernie had gotten them a 'small business' feature in the *Independent*, the whole thing fell through because Daniel wouldn't have his photo taken. He'd lost weight, he hadn't been sleeping, he refused to take pleasure in anything. He didn't think he was an unfit father because some dog had growled at a kid on his watch; he thought he was unfit because he'd left two girls, someone else's children, chained to a radiator and at the mercy of a bunch of awful men.

Daniel chewed the nail of his ring finger. His eyes seemed suddenly far apart and his nose oddly flat. She barely recognised him. This was the cause of the tension between Daniel and his brother, not Rocky. The dog seemed so childish now. How could she have thought he was worried about a dog?

'Edie?'

Of course, he didn't want kids. He thought he was a monster.

'Bae?'

Did she think he was a monster?

'I'm sorry, Edie.' His voice volleying, remorse filling the space between the quivering notes. 'I'm so fucking sorry. I didn't want you to know about this. I didn't want you to worry. I didn't want you to know what I'd done. I'm so ashamed. I'm so sorry.'

No. Daniel was not a monster. Daniel was her husband.

She loved him.

Edie was an exceptionally well-behaved citizen. She'd never lied to a guard or cheated on a tax or driven in the bus lane, no matter how late she was. She didn't take soap from hotels in case anyone thought she was stealing and she felt bad when the dentist gave her free dental floss. But she and Daniel were a team. She loved her husband more than anything, even civil obedience. She would lie in official statements for him. She would perjure herself in court, she would allow their lovely new neighbours to suffer silently for the rest of their lives, if that was what it took. She had to adapt to the situation and this was her metamorphosis. She hated him, he had ruined everything, but she always loved him more.

'It's okay,' she said. 'I forgive you.'

The naked gratitude made him childlike. She wanted his child.

'There's something else, Daniel. The–' She was about to tell him that the family he'd helped terrorise were now living on their road and that the wife who'd seen him that day in November had seen him again a few weeks ago, but the door to the office opened again. 'The clue is upstairs!'

Only this time, it wasn't treasure hunters.

And though a blanket of dread descended on Edie and she accepted that it was too late – too late to perjure herself to prove her loyalty, too late for today to be the glorious first-day-of-the-rest-of-their-lives she had envisaged, too late even for the Pine Road dream she'd been working towards – she couldn't help the latent delight that ignited when she saw that she and Martha Rigby were wearing the exact same trousers.

'Hello, Daniel,' said Pine Road's newest woman. 'I don't believe we've met.'

FORTY-EIGHT

' **I overestimated** their intelligence,' said Ellen, throwing herself
down beside Trish at one of the banquet-esque tables and
flicking through the treasure hunt route she had mapped out on
squared paper at the back of her clipboard. 'They should be done
by now but several of the clues have yet to be touched. The haiku at
number nine seems to have thrown them.' Ellen traced her finger
along the route. 'Occupied Territory to number thirteen, fine,
then up to number nineteen without a problem. A few seem to be
floundering when they get to nine but a couple more have made it
over to sixteen then on to eight. . .'

Ellen looked up at Martha Rigby's house while Trish helped herself
to another slice of Rita Ann's walnut loaf. Rita Ann had ignored Ellen's
instruction to remove the nuts – small mercies – and the famous cake
was good, but not quite as moist as Trish remembered.

Ellen tapped her pen on her clipboard and pushed back her
chair. 'We seem to be losing them at number eight. . .'

The majority of residents were still sitting along the tables. Shay
Morrissey was wearing Joe O'Toole's rabbit head and doing his best
Bugs Bunny impression, using a squashed bread roll as the carrot.
Rita Ann was pilfering spoons and napkins and making little effort
to hide it as she stuffed the junk into her bag. Treasure hunters
continued to run in and out of houses. Trish didn't think a couple of
the properties were actually part of the game but she turned a blind
eye. Ted had gone inside to read the paper a half hour ago and she

was desperate to do the same. She needed a break from the noise. It was like being at school.

'Oi!' shouted Ellen, as Fiona's twins approached her garden gate. 'Where do you think you're going?'

The girls looked at each other, then one of them shouted back: 'We're hungry, and tired. We just want an egg.'

'You haven't finished the treasure trail.'

'We followed the riddle in there.' One of the girls pointed at Martha's house, number eight. 'But the clue wasn't where it was supposed to be.'

'Or maybe you just didn't get it right.'

'We did,' the other twin insisted. '*An inherited eyesore that you think they'd have mowed; welcome to the worst garden on Pine Road.* We checked all around the weeds. There's no envelope.'

Ellen pursed her lips. The twins were obviously right. 'Stay away from my house,' she shouted. 'Who says the eggs are in there anyway?'

The girls rolled their eyes at each other and Ellen turned to Trish. 'I'm going into number eight to investigate. Stand guard at my house and don't let anyone in who hasn't completed the hunt. Cheating is contagious, Trish,' she said, gathering her clipboard. 'And I'm sorry to say Pine Road might need to be quarantined.'

Trish popped the last of the walnut cake wedge into her mouth, lamenting that the cream had all been ruined, and reluctantly went to stand outside Ellen's garishly-decorated front garden.

'All right Trish,' called Ruby from across the road. She got up from her step and left a couple of kids in her front garden petting the lamb that someone said she'd won off a social influencer. Ruby crossed the road, one of those fancy gin and tonic glasses that look like goldfish bowls in her hand. 'How's the treasure hunt going?'

'Too complicated. I don't think many people read the booklets Ellen put through the doors this week. We're still getting complaints from residents who thought they were doing an egg hunt, and a few

341

have just given up. Some of the clues appear to have gone missing now too.'

'That's awful!' said Ruby, grinning from ear to ear as she took another sip. 'I'd say that has ruined Ellen Two Names' day altogether. Has the "Bring Back Bernie" campaign began yet?'

Giggling started up behind Ruby and the two women turned to see Fiona's twins running into Rita Ann's house.

'I thought Rita Ann said she wasn't having anyone in her house? *I've* never even been in Rita Ann's house.'

'She did say that,' said Trish, frowning. 'She only let Ellen hide a clue in her front garden.' Trish glanced, longingly, up the road to her own nice, quiet home. But no. She couldn't just leave the road to fall asunder. 'I better go in and make them leave. Will you stay there and stop anyone going into Ellen's house?'

'No way,' said Ruby, hurrying after her. 'I'm not missing a chance to see inside Rita Ann's place. I'm only half messing when I say she might be keeping corpses in there.'

'Girls!' Trish stepped over the threshold of her neighbour's home as she tried and failed to recall the twins' names. How she'd forgotten, she didn't know; Fiona rang the school every week to see if they had moved up the waitlist for next year yet. In the end Trish had actually pulled a few strings to confirm their places, on the condition that her neighbour promised never to phone again. 'Come out, girls! You're not supposed to be in—' Trish stepped farther into the dark hallway. 'Wow!'

Ruby came to an equally abrupt stop. They were squeezing along the only part of the hallway not occupied by towering mounds of boxes and bags and a general assortment of rubbish. 'What is all this?'

The junk was everywhere and it was piled to the ceiling in places. The mounds morphed from one to another, with only their peaks to distinguish them. Trish spied an old filing cabinet, a ball of bed linen and a Scooby Doo wastepaper bin.

'Is that a shopping trolley?' whispered Ruby, reaching into the middle of the mess before thinking better of it and snapping her hand back.

'Mind!' warned Trish as the gin and tonic sloshed towards the brim of her glass.

Ruby arched her eyebrows. 'I hardly think a spillage is going to make a difference.'

'No wonder she couldn't find her newspapers,' Trish muttered, spying a set of gardening tools at the top of one large pile.

'Oh no,' said Ruby. 'Did you not hear about that? She never lost the newspapers at all; they never came. She forgot to renew her subscription.'

The girls giggled in the room to their left.

Trish surveyed the mess further. The stacks continued down into the kitchen and each of the steps up to the first floor was occupied by some sort of clutter. She picked up a packet of tea towels only to find they were stuck to a half-opened tube of flypaper. She quickly put them back. 'Presumably she misplaced her renewal form.'

'Forget renewing her newspaper subscription,' said Ruby, sipping her gin, 'she'd be better off renewing her bin collection.'

Trish didn't really want to go any farther – the thought of Rita Ann living in this place gave her a horrible sad feeling; no wonder she never hosted poker or invited anyone in for tea – but neither did she want this hunt to go on for ever. She looked at Ruby who nudged her on.

'You better get those girls out before they need a tetanus shot.'

They rounded the corner into the living room where there was a bit more space, enough to see from the couch – which was only half covered, mainly in filled plastic bags – to the television. Most of the rubbish was stacked around the doorway, teetering towers of magazines and newspapers and reams and reams of paper.

'She's kept all her bills,' said Ruby, agog, as she tried to read some of the letters without touching them. 'This one's from nineteen eighty!'

'Girls,' said Trish again, feeling a little ill and stressed and not at all like she was on a day off. 'What are you doing? There's no clue in here.'

'Who knows what's in here?' murmured Ruby.

Then from outside, Trish heard Ellen shouting her name. She winced. She just wanted to go home.

Ruby grabbed her arm. 'Ellen is such a neat freak. She will *die* when she sees this place.' She made no effort to hide her delight.

FORTY-NINE

Robin **was** through Edie's front door, Martha just ahead of her, Cormac right behind. There were several people in Edie's hallway, running up and down the stairs, pushing into one other and throwing things around. In their yellow treasure hunt singlets, they reminded her of the protesters who'd progressed to rioting in France.

Martha turned into the front room and Robin went to follow when she spotted Jack and Eddy on the stairs. Her son's face was covered in chocolate and her ex-boyfriend was looking at his phone.

'What is he eating? Is that chocolate?' she demanded, reaching her hand out to cover Eddy's screen.

'Relax, babe.'

'Chocolate *eggs*, Mammy,' said Jack, giving her a big toothy, chocolatey grin.

She looked around at the other treasure hunters, all mid-pursuit. 'Did youse finish the treasure trail already?'

'It's very long, and I don't know what any of the clues mean,' said Eddy, finishing whatever he was typing and shoving the phone into his pocket. 'But there were eggs along the way. He found that one in the wardrobe upstairs.'

'You found—' Robin looked at her ex-boyfriend, this man she had been besotted with for so long. 'They're not for you, Eddy! They belong to the people who live here!'

'It's an Easter egg hunt.'

'No, it's not! It's an Easter egg treasure hunt!'

'I'm going into Mum,' said Cormac, who Robin had momentarily forgotten was there. 'You okay here?'

'Ah, would you look? It's your new fella. Cornelius, was it?'

'Cormac,' said Cormac, only realising as he answered that he shouldn't have bothered.

'I like the moustache. Kiddie-fiddler chic. You go on into your mammy. Robin will be fine with me.' Eddy winked. 'She has been for years.'

'Ignore him,' she said. 'I have been for years.'

Cormac slipped into the front room and Robin went to follow him just as Jack started pounding back upstairs, counting imaginary eggs.

'Jack! I'll be down here if you need me!'

'Hang on,' said Eddy, following after her. 'We still need to talk about you screwing me over.' He shadowed her down the hall and into the front room.

What was the TV room in the Dwyer house had been turned into an office by Edie and Daniel. There was an armchair by the window, where a wan and clammy-looking Daniel was getting to his feet, and a computer desk in the corner where Edie sat, her skin also pale and her big eyes ready to roll right out of her head. Without the usual accompanying enthusiasm, her expression looked eerily hollow. Martha stood towards the centre of the room, with Cormac at her back. Robin couldn't see their faces but she heard Martha's steady, rhythmic breathing and watched her shoulders rise and fall. It was the room's only decipherable movement.

'What the fuck is this?' Eddy half-whispered, having followed her right into the room. 'Musical statues?'

On the ground between them were several copies of the article Edie had brought to the pub a couple of months before: the article about Martha and her family and, Robin processed, also about Daniel.

She looked at the burly man with the kind smile and dark eyes. Soulful eyes. That was what Martha had called them.

'Someone really needs to press play.'

Robin ignored Eddy. As did everyone.

'You live here?' said Daniel eventually, his pale, desperate face moving between Martha and his wife. 'I didn't know. Edie, she lives here.'

But Edie didn't speak.

'The man on the road I was talking to earlier, at the party, I thought he was familiar. Is that your . . .? Was that . . .?' Daniel couldn't stop staring at Martha. 'I didn't know,' he said again. 'I swear, I didn't know.'

'Mum,' said Cormac, an edge to his voice. He reached an arm towards Martha's shirt but she pulled herself away.

Robin stretched out and pulled Cormac, without resistance, closer to her. Eddy made an 'Aww' sound from her other side. She continued to ignore him. Cormac shot him a deathly look.

'The police have been called,' said Martha. 'My husband is calling them right now. They'll be on their way.'

Daniel nodded, as if this was exactly what he'd expected her to say. Edie's face shot up in alarm. Robin thought she heard her give a low moan.

'Okay,' said Daniel, still nodding. There was a beat. Robin could see him considering his next words. 'Are your daughters okay?'

Beside her, Cormac bristled. Robin tightened her grip.

Something on Martha's face must have hardened because Daniel was straight in babbling, clarifying, words pouring from his mouth like they'd been clogged for months.

'I'm sorry. I didn't mean anything by that.' He brought a hand to his forehead. 'I've been thinking about them for months, couldn't stop – Jesus, not like that, not like . . . I'm not like those men. I shouldn't have left them there. I know I shouldn't. I regret it, so much. Were they . . . were they okay?'

But Martha didn't want to discuss that. She was here for a different conversation. 'All the time we've been here, you lived here too, right up the road. I've been in your house!' She glanced at Edie, who was still staring into the middle distance as if the drama was actually unfolding in the space between Martha and Daniel.

Martha paused. 'I saw you that day, in Limerick. I felt sorry for you.'

'I know,' said Daniel quietly.

How could he know? thought Robin. *How could he know what she'd been thinking?*

'I thought you saw me,' Martha added. 'But after, I thought I'd imagined it. It was so far away.'

'I saw you,' said Daniel. 'I keep seeing you. Not really, I mean, not until now, but in my head and at night and when I try to get to sleep and every time I go to do something I might enjoy, I see you and I remember and I stop.'

Edie looked at her husband, as if only now realising he was there, but still she didn't speak.

'Mum?' said Cormac, whose shifting was getting louder. 'Is this one of the men from Limerick?'

No response.

His voice heavier now, Cormac turned to Daniel. 'Are you one of the men from Limerick?'

'What has your boyfriend got against Limerick?'

Cormac whipped his head towards Eddy. 'Why are you even *here*?'

'Do you realise what you did to us?' said Martha, ignoring her son, ignoring everyone but Daniel. 'Do you know what you did to my girls? Why would you do that? Why would anyone do that?'

'I'm so sorry. I didn't know what it would be. I was told you wouldn't be there, that the rest of the family would be gone. I was desperate. I was told it would only be him, your husband.' Daniel's head wouldn't stop shaking. 'You're the new friend; Martha Rigby, always the full name. Edie told me about you. But I didn't

348

know. The articles said Costello. Never Rigby. I didn't know. I'm so sorry.'

'Is this him?' Cormac freed himself from Robin's grip and continued to shift his weight, more erratically now, psyching himself up. 'Is this one of the men who came into your house? Did he tie Sinead and Orla to the radiator? Did he?'

'No,' interrupted Daniel. 'No. Jesus, no. I was driving the car. I never went into the house. I would never . . . I'd never done anything like that. Ever. I was desperate. I was worried, I wanted — Edie — We wanted to have kids. I thought I'd have to close the business. Everything was failing.'

Cormac took a step towards Daniel, his foot landing on the printouts.

'Everything's ruined,' said Edie, so faintly only Robin heard.

Outside, an alarm started to blare.

'Is that the ballbuster with the foghorn again?' said Eddy, losing interest in the immediate drama and peering out the window.

Robin followed his gaze. A house alarm across the street was blazing red and two treasure hunters in high-vis jackets were running away from it, back down the garden path.

'I've been tearing myself apart. I felt so guilty. I'm so sorry. And to you, Edie. You got us this house and Dad gave me the garage and I could provide nothing. But I'm glad you're here, Martha. I am. I deserve it. Call the police. I deserve—'

Cormac lunged for him. Robin reached out, grasping the back of his shirt just long enough for Eddy to move forward and come between the two men. Not that Cormac would have done much damage; Daniel was the size of him and Eddy combined.

'Easy now,' said Eddy, placing a hand on Cormac's chest. Cormac's face started to burn up as he made half-hearted efforts to get to Daniel. Eddy grinned. 'I'd say the only place you're doing much fighting is on the chessboard, am I right, Cornelius?'

It wasn't much of a swing, because he wasn't much of a fighter, but Cormac gave it his best shot. He brought his right arm up from his side and managed, by fluke as much as by design, to clip Eddy's cheek.

FIFTY

● ● ● ● ● ● ● ● ● ● ● ● ●

On the pavement outside Rita Ann's house, Ellen was rebuking Fiona who, to give her fair dues, was managing to look defiant.

'Number ten was caught cheating,' announced Ellen.

'My name's Fiona, as you well know, Ellen, and I was not cheating. It was an oversight.'

'The clue that should have been in Martha's back garden was in fact in number ten's pocket!'

Fiona blushed faintly. 'It was an innocent mistake. My partner abandoned me. I was thinking for two.'

'Well, you don't need to think for anyone any more.' Ellen pulled out her pen and drew a line on her clipboard so heavy Trish could hear the paper rip. 'You're disqualified!'

'You can't do that!'

'You've thrown the entire hunt off, number ten.'

'Stop calling me that!'

'I don't know if we'll be able to come back from this.' Ellen turned on Trish now. 'What were you doing in number twelve? There's no clue in there. I told you to guard the home base.'

If Ellen really was petitioning to get Bernie off the Parents' Association, Trish hoped to God she didn't get elected in her place. She had thought dealing with Bernie was bad, but that would teach her; better the devil you know.

'Fiona's twins ran in to Rita Ann's,' said Trish, nodding to the girls' mother. 'I was telling them to get out.'

'So, the apple doesn't fall far from the tree,' said Ellen, tucking the clipboard back under her arm. 'What did I tell you, number twenty?' Trish realised she was referring to her. 'It's contagious.'

'What's contagious?' demanded Fiona. 'Is Ellen insulting me? Is she insulting my children?'

'Hey! Judas!'

The women turned to see Bernie storming out of her house, down her path and out on to the road. Sylvie was trailing behind her. The former Pine Road ruler had dressed since Trish last saw her and was looking more like her put-together self, but she seemed to have retained the rage.

'Judas! I'm talking to you!'

A flash of terror crossed Ellen's face.

'Ellen Russell-O'Toole, don't you turn your back on me!' Bernie had reached them now and she was right up in her former apostle's face. 'I saw the clue that leads to our gate. I never gave you permission to hide something at our gate!'

Ellen pushed her shoulders back, though Trish could see the tremor in her hands. 'Well, technically, it's just outside your property so . . .'

Bernie yanked a card from her daughter's hand.

'Hey! You have to put that back. Other hunters need to find it. You're destroying the treasure hunt!'

Bernie ignored her former friend and read: '*A son who's been suspended, a daughter whose accusations are outrageous; stop at the gate*' – she looked up – '*because this bad parenting is contagious.*' Bernie flung the card back down by her side and glared at the poison-penned poet. 'You've always been jealous of me.'

'I have not!'

'Yes, you have. And now you're trying to destroy my good name and remove me from the Parents' Association. You were no one until you met me, with your mousy hair and your plain children and your one, pitiful surname! I gave you that double barrel, and I can take it away just as easily. And let me tell you, Ellen O'Toole—'

The woman gasped.

'—you can start all the petitions you like and take over all the street parties, but at the end of the day your wood floors will still be laminate and your *original Victorian crown mouldings* are still stuck on with superglue!'

Most of Ellen's body was shaking now, but she gathered herself and spoke into her former idol's face. 'You're a has-been.'

'And you're a never-been.'

'Ladies . . .' began Trish, as a shriek of laughter went up from Rita Ann's house.

'Get that clue off her,' said Ellen, who looked like she'd been struck. She'd given them all a detailed tour of her downstairs mouldings when she hosted poker back in September. 'I'm going to get the junior Kray twins out of Rita Ann's house.'

'Are you talking about my daughters?' Fiona demanded, but Ellen had already left. 'Is she talking about my daughters?'

Trish gave the small group of disgruntled women her most reassuring principal-like smile, as Ruby slurped on the end of her drink. *Get it over with, and get home.* Trish tightened her smile. 'I'd better help Ellen.'

But as she turned up Rita Ann's garden path, the rest of them followed: Fiona, Ruby and Bernie, all marching after her.

'Oh my God,' said Bernie, as they crossed into the hoarder's house.

Fiona gasped.

'Ellen?'

The organiser of the first Pine Road treasure hunt, which was currently in the process of becoming the last Pine Road treasure hunt, was standing in the doorway between Rita Ann's cluttered hall and her cluttered living room.

'Ellen,' said Trish, more gently this time. She pushed past Ruby, almost sending the hallway mound of junk sliding.

Fiona's girls were running around the front room, one of them wearing a lampshade as a hat and the other using two boxes, full of files, for shoes. Ellen was very pale. Her own house, right next door, was never anything but immaculate.

'It's . . .'

'I know,' said Trish soothingly, rubbing her arm. 'Girls, come on! Out!'

'Don't talk to my daughters like that!' came Fiona's voice from behind.

Then, suddenly, the girls did stop.

'What's that?' said the one whose face was masked by a lampshade.

'It's not me,' said the one with her feet in the boxes.

'What is it?' called Bernie, making her way to the front. 'Let me see.'

'Hey,' said Ellen as her former icon pushed past. 'I'm in charge here, this is my—'

'Shh!'

Ellen, in spite of herself, did as Bernie said.

Then they all heard it. A rustling from the side of Rita Ann's living room.

'There,' said the twin with the cardboard shoes. 'It's—'

Before she could finish the sentence, two rodents emerged from the side of Rita Ann's sofa and zig-zagged their way around the mess and across the carpet to the fireplace.

The two girls began to scream, the first one trying desperately to wrestle the lampshade from her head, as they started hopping wildly. Most of the adults weren't far behind.

'What? What is it?' called Fiona, freaking out from the back of the hallway. 'I can't see.'

'Rats!' shouted Bernie, looking around wildly – for what exactly Trish couldn't be sure.

'Oh my God,' shrieked Fiona. 'Oh-my-God oh-my-God oh-my-God . . .'

'Girls, come out!' called Trish, but their mother was already pushing past, squeezing herself into the too-small space between Bernie and Ellen.

'Careful!'

'Oh my God,' said Fiona when she saw the extent of the mess in the front room. Then one of the rodents reappeared from the side of the fireplace and ran back towards the couch. Everyone started screaming even louder, the twins and their mother springing from foot to foot. Ellen looked like she might faint. Fiona reached across Bernie, who refused to budge – 'Watch it!' – and banged into Ellen, who was easily wrong-footed.

'Mind!' shouted Ruby.

'Mum!' called one of the twins.

But it was too late. Trish watched, aghast and exhausted, as Ellen went stumbling into a tower of magazines right at the entrance to the living room. This had a sort of domino effect that sent the other towers of books and newspapers and bags all banging down, one after another, into a massive pile that blocked the doorway from the hall. The entire living room was obscured. For two whole seconds, everyone was silent.

Then, just as suddenly, Fiona was screaming anew as if the force of her lungs might blow down the wall of rubbish that stood between her and her children.

'This is a complete disaster,' said Bernie, turning to Ellen who was still regaining her balance. 'Never in all my years in charge of the pre-Easter street party has it involved the incarceration of minors.'

Ellen wrapped her arms across her chest. 'They weren't meant to be in here. If people just read the booklets . . .'

'Mum!' came a wail from the other side of the wall. 'I think there's a whole family in here . . .'

'Get them out!' screamed Fiona. 'Get them out! Get them out before they're eaten alive!'

FIFTY-ONE

E**die watched** blankly as Cormac half punched Eddy, half stood on his own foot – and Daniel swiftly switched places so he was now the one keeping two men apart.

'Stop,' he warned gently, holding Cormac at a distance just as Eddy had done. Her husband's hand almost spanned the width of Cormac's chest.

The three men hesitated, momentarily flummoxed about who was gunning for whom. The house alarm continued to blare out on the road. Cormac eyed up Daniel, who loomed over him, and tried to decide exactly how angry he was.

'I was protecting *you*,' Eddy told Daniel, his pride more wounded than his face.

'Mate, I don't need your protection.'

Edie had always enjoyed Daniel's size. Most women wanted daughters and she'd like one too, but she wouldn't have minded a rake of sons. They could form their own rugby team. She felt a surge of love for her husband. Then she remembered how interested she'd been in Martha's mystery and how she'd naively thought she could solve it, and she resented him all over again.

'I might not look like a brawler,' said Cormac, also sounding slightly put out, 'but I've taken a few martial arts classes.'

'You're wily,' concurred Daniel generously. 'I can tell by looking at you.'

356

Edie loved and hated her husband in such shattering, equal measures that she could feel the contradiction cracking its way down her heart.

'You were part of the gang that tied up my sisters at Halloween?' said Cormac, shaking off the perceived slight on his brawn and getting back to the point. 'Is that right?'

'I didn't tie them—'

'Yeah, but you were part of it. You know the other men, don't you? The ones who carried out the tiger raid?'

'I'm sorry. I should have stopped it and I didn't. I—'

'Hang on,' said Eddy, raising a hand as if asking a question in class. He stuck his head around the side of Daniel so he could see Cormac. 'This happened on Halloween night?'

'Morning of November first,' replied Cormac reluctantly.

Eddy looked over at Robin. 'That's why you were asking about a house robbery.'

Robin rolled her eyes. 'This isn't about you, Eddy.'

'I was dealing with a delivery of Bye Bye TV Bills Dot Coms that night. I'd never be involved in something as fucked up as a tiger raid.' He placed a hand on Daniel's shoulder. 'No offence.' Then back to Robin: 'I'm insulted.'

'Why are you talking?' shouted Cormac. 'You don't even live here!'

'Neither do you, pal.'

'I don't understand why you haven't left—'

The door to the office flew open, Martha stepping out of the way just as the handle was sent flying towards the wall. At least Edie knew the doorstops worked now.

Ellen, Bernie and Ruby came tumbling into the room, arriving in descending states of panic.

'Oh, thank God,' said Ellen, breathless as she leaned against the doorframe. Her typically sleek hair was staticky and the heat of her skin was pushing through her make-up. Edie, who suffered from rosacea, had recently discovered an excellent foundation. She'd probably never get the chance to recommend it to her neighbour now. And she loved passing on that kind of thing. She had done so well making friends, ingratiating herself with the neighbours, becoming part of the community. She wanted to take Daniel's face in her hands and scream.

A few hours ago, today had been the first day of the rest of her life. Now, it felt like the last.

'We need help,' said Bernie, side-stepping Ellen. 'Men, preferably. There's a bit of lifting involved.'

'What's going on?'

'There's been—' began Ellen, but Bernie interrupted again.

'Two children are trapped over in Rita Ann's house, with a number of rodents. I think we've found the source of Pine Road's rat problem.'

'Oh gosh.'

'Yep,' said Ruby, surveying the whole new dramatic scene into which she had just arrived. 'Turns out Rita Ann is a hoarder. If you're looking for that electrical goods receipt you lost in nineteen ninety-six, she probably has it. The house is stuffed with junk. And rats.'

'Yes and a whole pile of the junk fell over blocking the entrance to the front room and now Fiona's twins are caught in there,' said Bernie. 'If they're not eaten alive by rats, they're going to hyperventilate from the screaming. We need to get them out. Now.'

Ellen's eyes landed on Robin, then Cormac and Eddy. 'What are you doing? Where are your high-vis jackets?'

The three of them looked at one another.

'Have you *given up* on the treasure hunt?'

'You can hardly blame them,' surmised Bernie. 'The whole thing is such a disaster it's almost impressive.'

'We were doing it, but other stuff got in the way,' Robin apologised.

'I tried my best, I really did.' Ellen's voice was wandering into the hysterical as she threw her arms up in the air. 'But I'm dealing with barbarians and two-bit criminals. Thieves, cheaters, people going into houses that aren't on the route, setting off house alarms. It's not my fault!'

'I thought it was a good egg hunt,' offered Edie gently. She really didn't like to see anyone upset.

'It was not a bloody EGG HUNT!'

'That's all very interesting, but we need to get the girls out,' said Bernie, in a voice so calm and commanding it made poor Ellen look even more unhinged. 'Now.'

The three men looked at one another.

'Come on!' barked Bernie.

Cormac and Eddy moved for the door, while Daniel glanced from Edie to Martha. Edie looked to Martha too and she nodded her consent.

Just as they were following the new arrivals out, Jack came bursting into the room.

'I found it, Daddy! Mammy! I found it!'

He was waving a package back and forth so fast Edie couldn't make it out, but the wrapping was familiar . . .

Robin bent down to her son's level, in the middle of the bottleneck at the door. 'What's that?'

'The prize, mammy!' he shouted, face covered in chocolate, delighted with himself. 'I can read that. I know that word. I know lots of words.' He was speaking to the other adults now. 'It says *prize.*' Jack stuck out his tummy proudly as he looked up at his attentive audience.

Robin took the package from him.

'Oh. No,' said Edie, realising what it was and starting to get up but Jack was louder.

'I won the treasure hunt!'

Ellen frowned, looking down at the box. 'That's not one of mine. I didn't sanction wrapping paper and laminated adhesives. None of that can be recycled.'

Edie had used wrapping paper leftover from a christening gift for her cousin's baby a few months ago. She hadn't had time to go out and get something else. She'd only found out this morning.

'It's mine,' she said weakly, though she knew it was too late. Robin already had the paper off and Jack was looking at the white stick like he might burst into tears. 'Tha-*at's* not cho-o-*lat*,' his voice warbled.

Edie sat back down. She knew how he felt.

'It's . . .' Robin trailed off. She knew what it was. All the women standing over her at the door knew what it was.

'It's a pregnancy test,' supplied Ruby.

'It's mine,' said Edie, the accumulating weight of the injustice getting too great to bear. For months she'd been imagining the way she would tell people, first Daniel then everyone else.

This wasn't even close to what she'd planned.

'It was meant for Daniel. It was the prize at the end of his treasure hunt.' She looked over at her husband. 'That was what you were meant to find.'

It was his fault it had happened this way. And it was his fault that what should have been the best day of her life, the day she found out she was pregnant and got to tell her husband, was now the worst.

'You're pregnant?'

'Yes.'

'Look, this is great,' said Ruby kindly. 'Really. Congratulations, Edie, but we need to get the twins out. So . . .'

Eddy and Cormac followed Bernie from the room, Jack running at their feet.

'Congratulations,' said Cormac as he left, and Edie nodded.

Ruby and Ellen left then too.

'Edie,' said Daniel.

'Go on,' she replied, barely able to look at his joyous, remorseful face. 'All this will still be here when you get back.'

'I . . .' He was going to say 'I love you', she knew he was, but he stopped. He nodded. And then he was gone.

Edie, Martha and Robin were all that remained.

'Congratulations, Edie.'

'Thanks.'

'Yes, congratulations,' said Martha. 'I'm very happy for you.'

The trousers looked much better on Martha; she didn't seem to find them itchy at all. Edie felt foolish for all the time she'd put into today, picking her outfit and doing her hair, making an elaborate treasure hunt so she and Daniel would always remember this day. And they would, of course, always remember it, but not for the reasons she had intended.

Another siren joined the house alarm and Edie didn't need to look out the window to know what it was. Robert had called the guards. They'd all just been waiting for them to arrive.

'I'm sorry for what my family did to yours, Martha,' she said. 'I didn't have any idea until today. But Daniel's a good person. I'd bet my life on it. He shouldn't have gotten involved and he's been suffering. I knew he was. I just didn't understand why. He'll never fully forgive himself. So you know.'

Martha gave her a sad smile as the sirens outside stopped. 'I'm sorry too, Edie. But I have to report it. For my family. I am really happy for you, though, about the baby. It's great news.'

Then she walked slowly, gracefully, out of the house. Edie stayed where she was, staring at the blank space on the wall in front of her as Robin came over, sat at her feet and quietly took her hand.

*** Pine Road Poker ***

Ruby:
Did anyone see who they put in the back of the squad car?

I missed it. I was in at the rescue mission.

Carmel:
What I want to know is where that dog came from?

Ruby:
Was it Martha's dog? Their door was open for the treasure hunt. Just a pity Ellen's was open too.

She's still out there, scrubbing away.

Carmel:
I don't think she'll be getting another Easter out of that crucifix.

Ruby:
Well, at least now we know *all* chocolate makes dogs violently ill – even the no-sugar, no-dairy, no-taste kind.

Carmel:
I didn't see who the cops took away but a woman from Elm said it was 'a tall man'.

Also, I hate to steal Fiona's schtick, but two police visits in as many months? This is not a great look for Pine Road.

Rita Ann:
I may or may not have seen something, but I'll be answering no questions until someone takes responsibility for the destruction to my house. It will take me weeks to get everything back in order.

Ruby:
Order, she says ...

Rita Ann:
And that's to say nothing of the trauma suffered by my pets. I haven't been able to coax them out from under the couch all evening.

Fiona:
They're rats, Rita Ann! Not pets! And what about the trauma suffered by my girls?

Rita Ann:
They're pet rats, actually. House-trained and very friendly. And your girls are lucky I'm not having them arrested for breaking and entering.

Fiona:
I didn't see who was in the squad car because I was SLIGHTLY preoccupied with the welfare of my daughters. But I think I saw Edie Rice driving after it.

FIFTY-TWO

•••••••••••••••••••••••

The last time Edie was in a police station it was also because of Daniel. Only that time, it had been a visit she was excited to make. She'd come to collect his passport. It had taken all of ten minutes and she'd never considered that any of the people waiting around her were there for anything other than joyful holiday preparations.

This time, as she sat in one of the uncomfortable steel chairs, three hours into a wait that the officer at the desk had said could go on all night, she watched the people come and go, and not one of them did she see produce a passport renewal form. Maybe it was the time of the year or maybe she was projecting, but as she waited for her own criminal to be released, suddenly everyone entering and exiting the station appeared to be living a life of crime too.

Two guards bustled in through the main station doors. A young woman walked between them, her shoulders and head down. A few people queuing at the information desk turned to watch.

A man in a pair of trainers so high they went halfway to his knees jogged in a few minutes later. He rapped on the window of the information desk and signed the big ledger that the on-duty guard had been producing for people all day. Then he jogged back out and Edie watched through the glass doors as he hopped into a Land Rover almost as shiny as his shoes.

Four more guards came in, this time escorting two teenagers who began hurling abuse at the officer sitting behind the information-desk window in the middle of reception. Not that the term 'reception' seemed accurate for a place as grey and uncomfortable as this. If they just painted the walls a different colour – from grey to light blue, even – it'd be far more welcoming. Although, Edie considered as she shifted her weight from her left bum cheek to her right, 'welcoming' probably wasn't what they were going for.

'All right, Stephen, Jason,' said the on-duty guard in response to various slights on her mother.

'Fuck you, Maura,' one of the teenagers shouted as they disappeared through the frosted-glass door at the other side of the room. 'Your ma's in the Black and Tans.'

'And your da sells DVDs!' hollered the other.

An elderly couple sitting on the steel chairs opposite Edie visibly stiffened at the language. They didn't look like hardened criminals. She watched as the woman crossed and uncrossed her ankles. Maybe they were the parents of one, or the grandparents, or maybe they were the victims.

Edie's phone buzzed in her back pocket. She couldn't bring herself to look.

She thought of the person she'd been at eight o'clock that morning when the timer on her phone had gone off and she dared to look at the stick resting on the toilet cistern. She'd left and re-entered the bathroom three times, just to be sure wishful thinking hadn't overruled vision and that the little 'plus' symbol really was there. This morning, the biggest hardship in her life was that she'd have to wait three whole hours for Daniel to get back from the garage so she could tell him. Now Daniel had her waiting all over again. Except this time, all the joy had evaporated.

The door off the reception room opened and Edie's heart rose. But no. It was one of the teenagers from earlier, more subdued and sombre as he left the station unaccompanied.

Edie got up and walked over to the on-duty officer.

'Excuse me,' she said quietly, glancing over at the elderly

couple. She bowed her head and generally did her best to appear more like a victim than a perpetrator. 'I'm just wondering if I can check—'

'I told you you'd know when I did,' said the guard, without looking up from her computer.

'I know,' agreed Edie, speaking at half this woman's volume in the hopes that this might encourage her to do the same. 'But could you maybe check if they're still questioning him? Or if there's any idea of when they might be done?'

The guard looked up at her.

'I don't mind waiting. I'd just like to know.'

The woman sighed, reached for her mouse, and shook it. 'Carmody, right?'

Edie all but whispered: 'That's right.'

The guard squinted at the computer screen, then back up. 'Still questioning him.'

'And how long do—'

'Don't know.'

'Would you say an hour—'

'Don't know.'

Edie took a step back. That was all she'd be getting. 'Okay. Thank you. I'll just be over here . . .'

But the guard was engrossed in her computer screen again and Edie wandered back to her spot, avoiding the gaze of the couple.

• • • • • • • • •

Trish was on the way back into her house, having finished helping Ellen hose the last strings of chocolate dog vomit from her railings, when Bernie stepped out her front door. She had no coat on and didn't appear to be heading anywhere. She was there to either receive the gossip or impart it.

She looked at the rubber gloves in Trish's hands and gave a sympathetic pout. 'Quite the unmitigated disaster, wasn't it? I could have told Ellen a treasure hunt was a terrible idea. It's not like in the fourteen years I've been organising the idea never crossed my mind.'

Trish hated Pine Road, her neighbours and basically everything in that moment that was not her family and the inside of her house. 'The police visit was less than ideal,' said Trish pointedly, knocking on her door and willing Ted to hurry up and open it.

'I didn't call them,' said Bernie. 'I don't know why they were here, but I took advantage of their presence and reported a crime. At least now justice might finally be served. We can all rest a little easier knowing that grievous bodily attacks do have consequences.'

Ted pulled open the door and the warmth of Trish's house rushed at her. She almost collapsed into it.

'When Sylvie recognised the dog, and the man responsible for it, I had to act,' continued Bernie, straightening her cardigan. 'It was their fault, coming back to our road again. People have to take responsibility for their pets. It was just fortunate the guards were already here.'

· · · · · · · · ·

'Carmody!'

Edie's head shot up, and the door to the side of the waiting area opened again. She got to her feet and pulled on her coat. Finally. She was relieved to be done waiting, if not to see him.

'Peter,' she said, approaching her brother-in-law who was being led to the information desk to sign forms.

'What're you doing here?' he said gruffly.

'What were you doing on our road, more like?' she countered, tired and hungry and sick of everything to do with Daniel's family but particularly sick of Peter. 'And why don't you ever have that dog on a leash?'

'Daniel's been ignoring my calls, which isn't really something I'm going to stand for, not from Two Straps, not when he's already got me into a lot of shit.' Peter caught the double doors as Edie pushed them open. 'Me and Rocky were coming to see him. Then some auld one started going psycho, making up all these lies about Rocky and her daughter—'

'Just shut up,' barked Edie, when they were out of earshot of the guards. She rounded on Peter as they turned into the parking lot where she'd left Daniel's BMW five hours earlier. 'For once in your life, just shut up! I'm sick of you, interfering with Daniel, interfering with our life! You got Daniel into a lot of shit, not the other way around. You're lucky anyone's here to collect you at all. I wouldn't have come, only Daniel begged me to. And you're lucky being a terrible pet owner is all you were arrested for!'

Edie watched Peter's face contort, making its way from shock to mockery to indignation. In the end, he wisely settled on silence. She'd had enough of him, she'd had enough of all of them.

'Where's Rocky?' he said eventually.

'Daniel rushed him to the vet. They'll be home now.' Edie pulled her car keys from her coat pocket. 'I'd say he's had his stomach pumped.'

FIFTY-THREE

· ·

Robin spent a lot of Sunday thinking about Edie. And Martha. And then, invariably, and for more time than the others combined, Cormac. She hadn't seen him since he went to help with the rodent hostage situation and she stayed with Edie the previous afternoon. When she'd gotten back out on to the road, the action had calmed down and he was gone. He hadn't found her to say goodbye.

'What exactly were you expecting?' she muttered as she folded Jack's clothes, voice laden with a kind of disdain she reserved only for herself.

She'd been so distracted yesterday, and blanking his calls for weeks before that, and all for no reason.

She'd gotten it all wrong about Eddy. Neither she nor the father of her child had any role to play in what happened to Cormac's family. How had she ever thought Eddy had the ambition, never mind the balls, to get involved in something like a tiger raid? Still, if she'd been presented with Daniel and her ex as the two possible suspects, she'd have gone with Eddy every time. Daniel just wasn't the type.

Poor Edie.

And poor Martha.

But also – because it didn't have to be a catastrophe for life to be unfair – poor her.

Ten times she must have picked up her phone, opened her messages and stared at the glowing screen. But every time she went to type, she was overcome by a memory of telling Cormac she liked him or taking his hand at the street party or pulling him closer in Edie's house until the embarrassment burned so deep in her skin, she had to fling the phone away before her whole body caught fire. She consoled herself with how Cormac had looked at Jack when they first met – like someone checking their first-class ticket at the airport only to realise the flight left yesterday – and mustered up a new-found conviction that the relationship would never have worked anyway.

Which was why when the doorbell went as the sun was starting to set and she heard her mother open it, it took Robin several seconds to accept that she was hearing the very thing she'd been too afraid to admit she'd been hoping to hear.

Soft murmurings of the elongated voice her mother usually reserved for the phone and then his deeper, good-natured inflections. *Cormac.*

She sat bolt upright from where she lay on top of the bed covers and regarded herself in the mirror.

She ran a brush through her hair and clambered to her feet, rushing to the stairs. She stopped herself from running as she saw his silhouette through the stained glass, and was just at the door when her mother was turning to call up to her.

'There you are. It's the hipster formerly known as a journalist.'

Robin peered over her mother's shoulder, suddenly self-conscious. 'So I see. Hi.'

'I'll just make myself scarce,' said Carmel, who took her time relinquishing the door. 'In the kitchen.'

Robin and Cormac stood looking at each other with polite, awkward smiles as they waited for her to disappear down the hall and the kitchen door to slowly, laboriously, creak shut.

'I'm glad you—'

But Cormac spoke at the same time: 'I just came to drop off Jack's present.'

Robin looked down at his hands, which held a square box wrapped in Paw Patrol wrapping paper. 'Oh.'

'I felt bad when he said it was his birthday yesterday and I didn't have anything to give him. I said I'd drop it off today. He made me cross my heart.' Cormac made an X on his chest. 'Literally.'

He gave her that glorious goofy smile, but only for a second. It fell so quickly she almost reached out to catch it. She didn't like the controlled expression he was sporting instead; it didn't suit him half as much as when his face was open and kind.

'It's not his birthday.'

Cormac frowned. 'But he said . . .'

Robin shook her head. 'He keeps telling people it's his birthday but it's not, not till June. I've tried explaining that what he's doing is lying but it's hard for the truth to compete when deceit keeps bringing in the presents.'

'Clever.' Cormac looked down at the latest haul. 'Sure, take it, regardless. I've almost grown out of Play-Doh.'

'Sorry.' She took the box.

'It was just an excuse to call, anyway.'

Her breath caught in her throat. 'Really?'

He shifted his weight from his right side to his left. 'I wanted to clear the air.' He pushed his hair away from his face. 'You living across from Mum and everything. I didn't want it to be awkward.'

Her face went limp again. 'Right. Of course.' He wasn't here so they could rekindle whatever they'd had. He was here so it wouldn't be awkward if they ran into each other. What had she been expecting? 'You don't have to worry about that,' she said, voice aloof, lesson learned. 'I'm moving.'

'Oh. I didn't . . . To where?'

'I got a job. It's just covering maternity leave, but it's nine months, maybe more, and the money's good. So, me and Jack are moving out. I'm going to view a flat tomorrow.' *Nearer to where you live, actually.* Not that she said that. Part of her hoped she didn't get the place for that very reason. She may have felt like a needy psychopath, but she didn't want to come across like one.

Cormac's forehead creased, his hand automatically going to his head though his hair hadn't moved since he last pushed it into position.

'It's tough to find a place at the moment,' he said eventually, awkwardly. 'Housing crisis and that.'

'Yeah,' she said, equally redundantly.

He looked at her, gave a loud, deflated exhale and smiled hopelessly, catching her entirely off guard. *Dimple, dimple, delicious dimple*. How did he always manage to do that? To make it look like he had nothing to hide when, in reality, she couldn't read him at all? But no. He was just clearing the air. Making sure difficult conversations like this didn't get any worse.

'I'm planning to turn up with three months' rent,' she added, annoyance shooting through her body. 'I know it's a bit unfair on the other people – I don't even think they're allowed to ask for that much in advance, legally – but I'm a single mother. As you know. So, I reckon I get a dispensation.'

'Robin . . .'

'I mean, there has to be *some* upside to it.'

'I'm sorry about how I reacted, to Jack. I was taken aback. I wasn't expecting a child. I mean, you didn't tell me . . .'

She hated him. She hated his bumbling words and his stupid moustache. This was good. If he kept going like this, kept talking about Jack, she would be okay.

'I froze, but it was just a surprise. That's all. Once it sunk in . . .' His eyes widened. 'I like kids.'

'That doesn't sound great . . .'

'I like *your* kid.'

Robin wrinkled her nose. She hardened her jaw. Cormac shifted awkwardly, glancing at the present now in her hands as if what? To prove his point?

So, great. He was accepting of kids. What a swell guy. What did he want from her? Holding his hand mid treasure hunt flashed before her eyes – a new memory to add to the bank of shameful moments – and her body spasmed.

'How's work?' she fired abruptly.

His head jerked up. His face reddened. 'It's fine.'

'That's good.' She shifted her weight. 'Well, I better get going. I've got to get ready for work tomorrow and . . .'

'Right,' said Cormac, but the hurt way he looked at her caused her self-hatred to soar. 'I'm sorry I didn't tell you about the job.'

Her limbs fizzed with discomfort. She squeezed her eyes shut. What was wrong with her? 'Don't . . .'

But he did anyway. 'I should have just told you I worked in the wine bar. But technically, I didn't lie. I said I went there for work. I do write theatre reviews, you know. And I did interview Pierce Brosnan, for this charity event he was involved in. I just—'

'Jesus, don't apologise!' she insisted, no longer able to control the mounting self-loathing. 'I was being an asshole. I'm not used to being rejected. I don't handle it well. Obviously. Just another symptom of my over-riding selfishness.'

Cormac's forehead creased again, his eyes darting across her face. 'I didn't reject you.'

'No,' she conceded. 'Not directly, but—'

'Robin, you rejected me.'

'I did not!'

He made a loud hooting sound, half-laugh, half-exhalation. 'You ignored my calls for three whole weeks.'

'It wasn't . . .' But she couldn't get her thoughts together fast enough to explain.

'I froze, for a few seconds, when I met Jack. But then I told you, or rather Mum told you, about my job and you couldn't get away from us fast enough. You ran into your house with Jack and then you refused to answer your phone until, as pathetic as I am, I finally got the hint and stopped calling.'

His pale skin glowed pink, just below the bones of his cheeks. His emotions always rose to the surface. Strawberries and cream. She could eat him up.

'I get it. I wasn't good enough for you.'

Robin laughed. 'Are you crazy? I don't care about your job. At least you *have* a job! I'm twenty-six and I haven't been gainfully employed for five years – unless you count selling counterfeit goods for my ex. I didn't answer your calls because . . . well, I thought he was the man Martha saw. I thought Jack's dad had been part of the tiger raid.' She paused, grimacing. 'See? How white trash does that sound? I'm the one who's not good enough.'

From behind, the kitchen door creaked and Robin turned just in time to see it closing again, a shadow disappearing behind. She put the front door on the latch so it wouldn't lock and stepped out on to the small porch beside Cormac.

She looked at him, dimple deep on his left cheek, and sighed. 'You're such a good person it's kind of embarrassing,' she said, shaking her head. 'I basically only realised how shitty all my friends – not to mention me – were when I met you. Honestly. I'm in awe of it. You're comfortable in your own skin. Do you know how rare that is? You just are the way you are and if anyone comments on it, you don't get defensive or paranoid. What do you do? You *smile*.'

He was laughing now, silently, hand to hair, mouth wide and delighted.

She raised a hand and carefully poked him in the chest. 'I know that might sound like nothing,' she said carefully, 'but that is not nothing.'

He took her finger from his chest and wrapped her whole hand in his.

She shuffled a fraction closer and they stood chest to chest, her hand in his, waiting.

And waiting.

'Aren't you going to kiss me?'

'I would,' he mumbled, glancing to the side. 'But we're standing right across from my sisters' house and if they're watching, I can guarantee camera phones will be involved.'

Robin went to tell him she didn't care, when the front door of her own house flew open. Jack was up from his nap. She rarely put him down for a daytime rest but after all the sugar yesterday he'd barely slept last night.

He looked from Robin to Cormac, who stood apart now, but his eyes lit up at the present.

Robin watched her son weigh up his options. He took a step closer to Cormac, or more specifically to the present, then threw an eye towards his mother.

'I have a secret,' he announced.

'Go on so, Jacko, we're listening.'

'It's not for you, Mammy. It's only for *boys*.' He smiled sweetly up at Cormac, and the naïve fool smiled back. Jack watched carefully until Robin had taken two steps away from them, back into the hallway. Then Cormac bent down to his level. Jack didn't yet know how to whisper. He just spoke at the same volume but closer to the person's ear.

'It's my birthday today,' he said, hand up to Cormac's cheek. 'I'm five.'

'Jack Dunne, you big liar! It is not your birthday and you are to stop telling people it is.'

Jack looked at her like he couldn't believe the betrayal. His little legs started to shake at the blind injustice. 'But Mammy, it was my birthday before, and this man wasn't there to give me a present!'

Robin rolled her eyes.

Cormac handed over the box. 'Happy nearly birthday.'

Jack took the present and sauntered past Robin triumphantly, his little hips jutting from side to side. 'Mammy! Sing!'

Robin sighed and watched as her mini egotist climbed the stairs, slowly and awkwardly because he refused to relinquish the present for a single second.

'Happy birthday to you. . .'

'. . .*Happy birthday to you.*' Robin turned as Cormac's voice joined in from behind.

She turned back to her son and they sang in unison. *'Happy birthday dear Ja-ack, happy birthday to you.'*

*** Pine Road Poker ***

Fiona:
Ladies!! My spy at the estate agents says they're about to put a house on Pine Road up for sale!

Anyone know who's moving??

[Fiona is typing]

Or what the asking price is?

FIFTY-FOUR

'What did you say these boxes were for, again?' asked Robert, standing at the bottom of the attic ladder as his wife carefully made her way up it.

'I didn't.'

'All right. What are they for, then?'

Martha's torso disappeared into the dark, damp space. She reached down, took her phone from her pocket, and turned on the torch function. 'They're for Edie and Daniel.'

'What?'

'Careful, Robert! You're shaking the ladder.'

'We're giving them our moving boxes? A week ago, we were going to call the guards on them.'

'You were going to call the guards,' she corrected.

'Because you said he was the man you saw at the tiger raid.'

Martha looked around at the attic, most of it still in the dark. There they were; stacked unevenly to the right. If she wanted to get them, she'd have to climb in, and she didn't fancy covering these trousers in dust. Ellis could do it tomorrow. Slowly, she climbed back down the stairs.

'I'll wait for Ellis,' she said, brushing down her sleeves. 'He's calling over tomorrow. Edie doesn't need them till then anyway.'

'Seriously, Martha,' said Robert, following her as far as the bathroom door as she turned on the faucet and rinsed the dusty grime from her hands, 'don't you think it's a bit strange that right when you think the husband was involved in the tiger raid, they decide to up sticks and move? Are you sure you weren't right about him?'

When Martha had left the Carmody–Rice residence the previous Saturday, she had fully intended to walk straight up to the two police officers standing in the middle of Pine Road and point a finger back in the direction she'd come. At the bottom of the garden path, however, she'd hesitated. She'd looked back at the house and through the window to see Edie sitting at the desk. She'd thought of all the things that would happen as soon as she talked to those guards. The whole event would be reopened; there would be an arrest and maybe a charge, then a year or two in limbo while they waited for a trial; then the trial, and would it only be Daniel charged? He was the only one she could identify and yet he wasn't who she wanted to see punished. She'd thought of Edie's conviction that he was good. She could imagine it. She'd made her way out on to Pine Road and thought of Edie pregnant, her biggest dream come true. She'd thought of all this and she'd felt tired. She'd felt like she did back when it was only starting, when they first moved here, when the only thing she had the strength to do was go to bed. She did not want to go back to that. She wanted to let it go.

Martha had walked towards the guards, and when she got to them, she kept going. Behind her, Bernie Watters-Reilly was making a beeline for them. Her neighbour was shouting and pointing but Martha didn't wait to hear what she was saying. She walked quickly into her own garden and met Robert on his way out.

'They're here,' he'd said, all bluster. 'They took their time about it but they're here.'

Standing in her bathroom a week later, Martha twisted the tap off and reached for the hand towel. Then she went out to her husband on the landing and told him the same thing she had told him the previous Saturday standing in their front garden.

'I was wrong.' She wrapped an arm around his waist. 'You were right and I was wrong, Robert. I didn't see him at all.' Second time around and she was still surprised by how little it cost her to swallow her pride and lie.

It helped, perhaps, that Robert didn't look vindicated. He regarded her warily, like maybe this was a test or some version of reverse psychology. He could tell, she presumed, that something wasn't right, but he couldn't penetrate the details of it. She had wrong-footed him.

'What are you doing this evening?' she asked, heading for the stairs.

He followed her down. 'I don't know. Will we watch something? We could catch up on *Tin Star*? We have the whole second season to watch.'

'I'm sorry, darling, I can't. I'm meeting a friend.'

'Are you?' he said, not exactly put out, but definitely surprised. 'That's good.' Was he remembering when all he wanted was for her to re-establish a social life? 'Who?'

'A neighbour. We're going for a walk.'

'Right. Well, I guess I could . . .' He looked around the kitchen, as if an evening activity might just present itself.

'I was going to mop the floor, actually, but I might not have enough time before I go . . .'

'Right, well . . .' He looked around the room. 'I could do that . . . I suppose . . .' he said hesitantly, so it sounded as much like a question. She smiled benevolently. Keeping her own secrets had dislodged their power balance ever so slightly.

'That would be great, darling.' She kissed him gently on the cheek and turned from the kitchen, leaving him glancing around at the mop she'd propped up by the counter and wondering how exactly one washes a floor.

This was one of the reasons Martha would be the one to stay. She could have moved the family back to Limerick and reintegrated herself into her old social circle and old life and old way of being without much difficulty. But when she weighed them up, she wasn't so sure the old her was better than the new version. Yes, her marriage had been through the mill and she no longer regarded Robert with the unquestioning approval she once had. But, equally, this no longer seemed like a bad thing. Their relationship had never been so equal. She had less faith in him, maybe, but she had more faith in herself. She was more robust, she trusted her own instincts. She respected herself.

She had called to Edie the Monday after the party and told her that she would not be contacting the police but she would also be staying put. She told Edie she forgave Daniel and she would let the matter lie, but living on the same street was too great an ask. She hadn't moved to Dublin to be reminded of what had happened every time she stepped out her front door. Edie hadn't faltered.

'We'll move,' she'd told Martha, eyes wide, chin trembling ever so slightly. 'Thank you.'

Ellis thought she should press charges, but she told him her mind was made up. He hadn't mentioned it since, though she could tell he wanted to. It was enough to know she hadn't imagined Daniel, that she had really seen what she saw. If she shared this with Robert, he would have been far more persistent than her son. He'd have phoned the police himself because in a black-and-white world, this was the right thing to do.

But Martha's world was not black and white; it was coloured entirely by her family. Seeing this particular man punished was not a worthwhile trade for the toll it would take on their lives. Sinead was getting on well at school and with her counsellor and Trish hadn't pursued the list business any further. Orla, too, was settled. So was Martha.

She was letting it go.

She pulled out her phone and sent Edie a message.

We've at least a dozen moving crates. They'll be all yours from about 2 p.m. tomorrow.

She would notice the absence of Edie, who had slipped in as an unlikely friend. But there were other people here. Pine Road would be home yet.

She glanced at her phone again. It was after seven. 'Robert?' she called down to the kitchen as she took her rain mac from the coat stand. 'I'm off!'

The kitchen door opened and her husband appeared, mop in hand. 'What time will you be back?'

'Not sure. But I doubt it'll be long.' She grabbed a hat from a cubbyhole. 'A walk-and-talk was how I put it to Carmel, but she strikes me as keener on the latter bit.'

FIFTY-FIVE

Edie watched as her husband painted. He delicately dipped the roller in its tray, careful to cover all sides equally, and, with a flick of the wrist, brought it to the hall wall without creating any discernible start lines. Deep in concentration, he covered the grubby hand prints that had accumulated in the fourteen months they'd been living here.

She could have punished him. She wasn't one for vindictive thoughts and she would surely never have had the steel for malice, but she could have, if she'd wanted to, and Daniel would have let her.

'You okay, bae?' Daniel stopped mid-stroke, and Edie realised that she had ceased boxing away photo frames and ornaments. The first open viewing was Tuesday evening and the estate agent wanted all personal possessions removed from sight. Prospective buyers wanted to picture this as their own home; photos of Daniel and Edie would only put them off. That's why the walls should be freshly white. It made the space looked bigger, and it represented a fresh start.

'Fine,' she said.

He smiled at her and went back to work; up and down, white over white.

The estate agent had been delighted when Edie phoned, especially when she made it clear they wanted a fast sale. 'Between myself, yourself and these valuable walls, we're expecting the market to take a drastic turn,' he'd said, walking from room to room, his excitement growing with each original ceiling feature. 'You sell now, and I think we might get a record price for this road.'

She had forgiven Daniel almost immediately. She did it without much difficulty. Daniel was her husband, the father of her soon-to-be child. She loved him and she knew him. She was more puzzled by herself than she ever was by him. Daniel kept saying she was well within her rights to be angry, that he would take any punishment she doled out. But the only time she felt like taking him up on this was when she thought about leaving Pine Road.

When Martha came to her with the offer, her body had flooded with relief. It was maybe twenty-four hours later, after she'd phoned the estate agent, that the injustice of having to move hit her. She had cried the whole way through packing up the bathroom. She couldn't blame her neighbour – Edie could no more have lived across the road from that family now, than they could from her – so she supposed she could only blame her husband.

'I'm not sure if these are even,' said Daniel, taking a step back and casting his critical eye over the wall. He dipped the roller again and carefully retraced the line he had just done. 'I really don't think they are.'

But she didn't want to blame her husband. Edie felt about Martha as Daniel did about her: their neighbour would have been well within her rights to go to the police and tell them exactly what she knew. But she hadn't. So, Edie wouldn't punish him either. She fought against the desire to blame him. He had, she acknowledged, been punishing himself for months.

'The walls look great, bae. They hardly look like ours any more.'

She was better now. She'd had time to accept it and weigh things up. 'Home is where the heart is,' was her moving mantra. Every time she felt the waterworks building, she brought herself back to this. Daniel and their baby – that was her heart. Wherever they were, that was her home.

She reached for the Waterford Crystal bowl and slid it down the side of the tightly packed frames.

Presuming they made as much money from the sale as the estate agent thought they would, the plan was to buy a house in a new development on the other side of the city. Daniel was selling the garage too. Maybe that was the biggest self-flagellation of all. He'd contacted an estate agent and agreed the sale before informing his father. Mr Carmody had hit the roof. He'd worked himself into such a state that Daniel's mother had sent them home before he had a heart attack. By the time they got back to their own house, he had left nine voicemails on Daniel's phone calling him everything from a 'cunt' to 'no longer my son'. A couple of the messages went into explicit detail about all the things that were wrong with Edie. These messages, at least, helped to move Daniel from extremely hurt to extremely angry, which was an easier place for him to be.

He had taken it better than Edie expected. He told her that if they were going to start again, which was what he wanted, then they should do it properly. He'd talk his mother around, he said, and the others would eventually follow. Edie wouldn't mind if that took a while.

'I'm out of storage,' she declared, taping up the box as Daniel continued to coat the wall. 'I'm going to call down to Martha and get those moving crates.'

It helped that she no longer recognised these walls as her own. Her attachment to the building was loosening. Devoid of their possessions, it wasn't their home any more, it was just another house. But she would miss Pine Road.

'Okay? Daniel?'

He nodded, continuing to draw exact lines of smooth white paint, each as wide and even as the last. Edie took her coat and favourite scarf from the small mound inside the door and reached for the bolt.

Daniel's roller paused at the end of a stroke. 'Sorry, Edie.'

'I know.'

'Tell her "thank you", okay?'

*** Pine Road Poker ***

Fiona:
It's Edie! The 'for sale' sign just went up outside Edie and Daniel's house!

Edie, hun – why the move so soon??

I'm going to miss you.

We'll always have the treasure hunt!

XXX

Ruby:
Edie, you sly dog!

Please don't tell us it was because of the neighbours. Unless of course it was Bernie. I could entirely understand if it was Bernie.

FIFTY-SIX

．．．．．．．．．．．．．．．．．．．．．．

Robin stared up at her childhood ceiling for what she presumed would be the last time. She felt the weight of Cormac's arm on her stomach and marvelled at the difference between feeling trapped and feeling anchored.

'Won't Martha be wondering where you got to?'

'I told her I was coming over here to drop off one of the moving crates.'

'Yeah, twenty minutes ago.'

The arm slipped from her stomach as Cormac turned on to his side and propped himself up on her pillows. 'And when I go back, I'll tell her I was helping you fill it.'

Robin glanced over at the plastic crate, abandoned on top of several cardboard boxes and draped now with their discarded clothes.

He bowed his head and kissed her shoulder. 'I like you.'

'I like you,' she replied. This is what they did now, over and over. Often, the messages they sent each other said nothing else. *I like you, I like you*, all day long. It was their sickening little routine and she loved it. Because Robin really did like him, and every time he said it, she liked herself more too.

Cormac lay back on the pillow, taking Robin's hand and pulling it into the cold air above the sheets. He interlaced his fingers with hers, studying the variation in shade and texture of their skin. 'Your mum will miss you when you're gone.'

Robin hooted. 'She says all she has to do now is get Johnny to bugger off and then her and Dad are changing the locks.' She bent her fingers down so they closed over his. 'She might miss Jack, I suppose, although I plan to milk her childminding offer to such an extent that she doesn't get a chance.'

Carmel, who had always warned Robin and Johnny that she didn't have her children young just so she could get her life back in time to spend it looking after grandchildren, had offered to mind Jack two days a week. He'd be in day care two other days and Eddy, who didn't have a nine-to-five to worry about, was taking him on the fifth. But if Jack was brought anywhere near anything illegal, she would deny all access. Eddy had agreed. He had nothing to use as leverage any more; there was no way he could implicate her in his dodgy dealings without implicating himself.

'Okay, come on.' Robin pushed herself up and reached towards the crate for her top.

'What are you doing?'

'My parents will be home with Jack any second. And you're driving us over to the apartment at five, right? I still have stuff to pack.'

Cormac shut his eyes in mock anguish.

'And,' Robin added, 'you're supposed to be helping your mother this afternoon, not hanging out with me.'

'But I *like* you,' he groaned.

She grinned. 'Yeah, and hopefully you'll still *like* me tonight. When I have my own apartment.'

'Do you know that place you're renting is really near my flat?'

'Is it?' Robin stuffed her head inside her sweatshirt and took her time pulling it through. 'Huh. I guess it is. I hadn't realised.' She pulled down the material and released her hair. Then she stood from the bed, in her underwear and sweatshirt, and searched for the rest of her clothes. 'Where did my jeans go?'

'You look good.'

'Without trousers on? What a surprise.'

But when she looked over at him, lying lazily across her bed, idly scratching his chest, she couldn't help laughing. 'Are you aware that when you look at me like that, you're shaking your head?'

Another two twists of the neck, then he stopped. 'Oh yeah.' His earnest, joyful smile cracked wider. 'You're a babe, Robin Dwyer. There's no denying it.'

She pushed her face into her open hands. 'How are you never embarrassed?'

'What would I have to be—'

'Robin!' The sound of the front door opening and her mother's voice followed by Jack's feet hammering up the stairs.

She reached across for one of Cormac's pale arms and yanked him from the bed. 'Up! Now! Dressed!'

· · · · · · · · ·

'There's another five or so in the attic,' said Martha, re-angling the tower of crates slightly so it stood in line with the porch wall. 'Ellis was in the middle of getting them down but he appears to have disappeared . . .'

'Oh, this is loads, Martha,' gushed Edie. 'Thank you so much. You don't realise how much stuff you've accumulated until you're moving house, do you? I mean, I don't think I'll ever be able to say I have nothing to wear again.'

She pulled nervously at that multicoloured woolly scarf she loved so much. Her left foot was tapping, not loud enough to make a sound but fast enough to catch Martha's eye.

'How is the packing going?'

'Oh, good. Great. It takes longer than I thought but, yeah, very good. It looks like we're going to get one of the first houses in this new development in Rathfarnham. A four-bed semi-detached. So bigger than our house here and a side-entrance, so we don't have to bring the bins through the house. I mean, I never realised how handy that would be until Robin pointed it out to me a while ago, so that'll be good.' She pushed a strand of hair behind her ear and yanked at the scarf again.

'That's great,' smiled Martha.

'We'll be one of the first to move in, as well, which is nice. Nobody will have time to make friends without me.' Edie's foot abruptly stopped tapping and she blushed. The two women smiled at each other until the sound of Ellis jogging across the road and up the garden path broke the silence.

'Where have you been? Why are you out of breath?'

'Sorry,' he said, stopping between the two women. 'Got distracted. Hi, Edie. How's everything going with the baby?'

The woman's face went from awkward to euphoric in the time it took to say that one word. 'Great. Really great. Thanks for asking. This week I find the smell of all meat repulsive and only seem capable of eating white bread with no crusts or cream crackers.' Her eyes widened. 'It's all very exciting.'

Ellis smiled at her, then leaned a hand on Martha's shoulder. 'Mum, Carmel Dwyer said I was to convince you to join the WhatsApp group. She said someone got thrown out this morning, so you should take her place.'

'Bernie,' supplied Edie. 'The newspaper bumped her from writing about parenting, but then they gave her a new column on neighbours. The first one was out today and it had a lot about how she'd been betrayed and abandoned.' She grimaced. 'Let's just say it was less than complimentary.'

'Anyway,' said Ellis, 'I don't know what it is, but she said you should join.'

'Oh, you should,' gushed Edie. 'It's great, Martha; it really makes you feel part of the community.' Her voice cracked slightly. 'I guess I'll be removing myself from it too . . .'

Ellis shifted towards the house. 'I'll go and get the rest of the boxes.'

When he'd disappeared into the house and up the stairs, Edie whispered: 'Are him and Robin back together?'

'Well, I don't think his hair got that damp just running across Pine Road, do you?'

Edie beamed, then she changed the subject, reaching up for her scarf again. 'I wanted to say thank you.' Edie's saucer eyes darted around Martha's face. 'We both did. I really thought you were going to hand in Daniel last week, and you absolutely could have – should have, maybe; I don't know – but you didn't. So, thank you. I love him, you know? And we're going to be a family.'

Martha smiled. 'I know.'

'I'm going to miss you,' Edie said then, abruptly, cringing. 'Is that weird? Or inappropriate? I know you'll be glad not to see me again. And Daniel, obviously.' She took a big breath. Martha could tell she was fighting not to cry. 'I really am so sorry about it all.' Edie looked around for something with which to distract herself. 'I don't even know if I'm doing the right thing . . .'

Martha reached out and placed a hand gently on her neighbour's arm. 'We do what we think is best, for ourselves and for our family.' Then she stood straighter and clapped her hands. 'Now, take the boxes and keep them as long as you like. And if you want some help carrying them up, Casanova in there will give you a hand.'

● ● ● ● ● ● ● ● ●

Edie wobbled up Pine Road, a stack of four crates in her arms. Ellen was watching from her bedroom window, a spray bottle in hand. Edie glanced in Rita Ann's front window and for the first time noticed the towering shadows inside. She felt a tinge of jealousy towards the future woman who might come to live in her house and find herself part of this street and playing poker once a month.

She would miss Pine Road, but she would take what she'd learned here and apply it to her new home. She and Daniel would be among the first batch of neighbours in their new estate. She planned to wear her Martha trousers on moving day and to call to every other occupied home and introduce herself before the sun had set.

She was going to start her own neighbourhood messaging group. She might form another one for new mums and maybe a third for whatever couple friends they made. She also had her eye on an expensive *brown* coat that she planned to buy before moving and then sort of just become the kind of sophisticated woman who wore expensive brown coats rather than furry pink ones.

When she reached her doorstep, Edie lowered the crates to the ground and turned to admire the cul-de-sac. Of course she would miss it. But the more she accepted she was moving, the more she saw it for what it was.

A curved row of twenty-one houses.

Stacks of red bricks divided by iron gates.

A collection of lives where the only automatic connection was a postcode.

A place where families expanded, imploded and renewed.

A place where people lived in company, alone and often, if they lasted long enough, both.

Pine Road was a neighbourhood. It was a street. It was just like anywhere else.